LATE
MARRIAGE
PRESS

JOHN I'VE BEEN BAD AND THEY'RE COMING AFTER ME

a novel

Pablo D'Stair

LATE
MARRIAGE
PRESS

Copyright © 2025 Pablo D'Stair

All rights reserved. No part of this book may be reproduced, stored in a retrieval system or transmitted in any form or by any means without the prior written permission of the publishers, except by a reviewer who may quote brief passages in a review to be printed in newspaper, magazine or journal.

COVER ART by Goodloe Byron
COVER DESIGN by Pablo D'Stair

First Edition
ISBN: 9798349409158

Published by Late Marriage Press

Fiction by Pablo D'Stair

October People
Confidant
kill Christian
Regard
miscellaneous language
Piano Forte
Dustjacket Flowers
Theft
Taste of Paper
Subject
Age of Crows and Starving
in vicarious tongues
the order, in which the wind
a man who killed the alphabet
Candour
the murder of linen
Carthago Delenda Est
figments of calculation
bread and salt and teeth and tongue
top state secret confidential why why why did you resign?
Vienna London Unreal
we know the death of Archimedes
how February Tolmb explained
TWO NOVELLA - September from its grave; in descending order, alphabetical
TWO NOVELLA - The Unburied Man; The People Who Use Room Five
Kaspar Traulhaine, approximate
i poisoned you
twelve ELEVEN thirteen
man standing behind
THREE NOVELLA - Leo Rache.; Transit; Michel Bolingbroke
VHS
motion in the winter
TWO NOVELLA – The Purse Snatcher Letters; bleed the ghost empty
Trevor English #1: This Letter to Norman Court
Trevor English #2: Mister Trot from Tin Street
Trevor English #3: Helen Topaz, Henry Dollar
Trevor English #4: The Akerman Motel/Apartments Per Week
Trevor English #5: This Gun from Norman Court
TWO NOVELLA - Slumber; Tartarus
Lucy Jinx
The Wank Miner
Robespierre
The Ghoul Haunted Woodland of Weir
The Disembodied Parts: a rhapsody
The Murder Ballad of J. Alfred Prufrock
Pilfer
The Blurb Writer
The Goldberg Mutilations
Animals and their Antonyms
Sing Heigh-Ho, the Carrion Crow
Prepartum
John I've Been Bad And They're Coming After Me
while Valerie was no one: two stories;
Current Perspectives in Counting To Ten: twenty-four stories
On Our Current Victimology: fourteen stories
Seven Stories About Working in a Bookstore
I'm a cigarette: five stories
The Cigarette Miscellany
People in your Neighborhood: ten stories
The Ghosts of Handsome Skin: three shorts
"atomist, reticent"; Fragments 1999-2008
"Old Woman All Skin And Bones"; Fragments 2009-2016
"Four and Twenty Blackbirds"; Fragments 2017-2025

PRAISE FOR THE WRITING OF PABLO D'STAIR

Original. Idiosyncratic. Off-kilter. Strange. The slap-back dialog, the scenes as accurate as if directed by Fritz Lang. This is D'Stair's world. Welcome to it. I envy you if this is your first time in.

COREY MESLER
(Memphis Movie)

The first thing that occurs to you when you pick up a volume of D'Stair is that it has no business being good. No credentials. None of the usual apparatus that tells you a book has appeared: publishers, agents, press releases. The industry didn't cough this one up. The second thing, once you start to turn the slippery pages, is: how the Hell can such good writing come from nowhere—Who the Hell is Pablo D'Stair, anyway? The final note, the one that makes D'Stair a little troubling, is that this writing is a voice inside your head. Nothing can prepare you for that ... Pablo D'Stair is defining the new writer. There is NO ONE else. As reckless as Kerouac's 120-foot trace paper, D'Stair's independence from all of us needs to be studied and celebrated.

TONY BURGESS
(Pontypool Changes Everything)

If our minds are hamsters on wheels, then Pablo has more hamsters than any of us ... D'Stair doesn't just write like a house afire, he writes like the whole city's burning, and these words he's putting on the page are the thing that can save us all.

STEPHEN GRAHAM JONES
(Mongrels)

[D'Stair's work] is written by someone who cares about language - you'd be surprised at the number of novels written by people who don't ... you stop yourself from skimming because you start thinking you might be missing something - [it's] too well written to skim ... again and again you're drawn in ... you get used to the rhythm and follow it because the work is obsessive ... [you find yourself] in a languid kind of suspense, bracing ...

BRET EASTON ELLIS
(American Psycho)

D'Stair is clearly a master. Like Jean Patrick Manchette reincarnated.

MATT PHILLIPS
(The Bad Kind of Lucky)

for Sebastien
for Sarah
and for Goodloe (obviously)

JOHN I'VE BEEN BAD AND
THEY'RE COMING AFTER ME

For no fact is so simple we believe it at first sight, and there is nothing that exists so great or marvelous that over time mankind does not admire it less and less.

> LUCRETIUS
> *On The Nature Of Things*

'At what precise moment' Trelkovsky asked himself 'does an individual cease to be the person he - and everyone else - believes him to be? I have to have an arm amputated, all right. I say: myself and my arm. If both of them are gone, I say: myself and my two arms. If it were my legs it would be the same thing: myself and my legs. If they had to take out my stomach, my liver, my kidneys - if that were possible - I could still say: myself and my organs. But if they cut off my head? By what right does the head, which isn't even a member like an arm or a leg, claim the title of 'myself'? Because it contains the brain? But there are larvae and worms, and probably all sorts of things, that don't possess a brain. What about creatures like those? Are there brains that exist somewhere, and say: myself and my worms?'

> ROLAND TOPOR
> *The Tenant*

*yell in vents, the intelligence
that my skeleton's between doors*

[*souvenir of what's left of that swinger*]

There used to be a band called *They Might Be Giants*. You won't know them. You couldn't. I'll explain—because though there's little point doing so, there's less doing anything else.

I worked graveyard shift at *The Calico Bash Nitely*, a motel located right at the pulse of the armpit of a town known as *Laampray*—a word with a first half some pamphlet nobody looked at or ever came to replenish boasted was of German origin, dialect called *Erzgebirgisch*, the afterthought sense of prayer tacked on in plaincake American. Name of the dialect looked like 'gibberish' misspelt in gibberish to me and the sentiment 'to dwell within prayer' was something I'd believe when I saw, down 'round those parts. A jawless fish with a sucker-mouth and rasping teeth, on the other hand? That hit the nail on the head aptly as description of both environs and denizens—look through any window, you'd see several, everyday.

During my three years of employ, I'd come across more than my fair share of curio, simple things, mostly, odds and ends left behind: pens and lighters, smutty paperbacks, loose change, coats, hats, gloves, two wallets, one purse, umpteen pairs of shoes, single socks, suspenders, panties, silk or nylon hose—sometimes small amounts of drugs, differing in variety and packaging, usually plopped offhand in the dresser drawers beside the Gideon Bibles but one time hidden in a mattress the side of which had been slit expressly for the purpose. A surprising number of people seemed to enjoy leaving copies of their homemade sex tapes in the combination VCR-DVD players built into the televisions, nothing filmed in the room, presentations brought from home, solo work to timid orgies, always cassette, never disc, and one time the action out of frame, camera either artfully or accidentally pointed at a mute television showing a repeat of *Don Cronos* while the deed went down, audio-only, in tin-can echoes of chirps and bodies clapping—then there'd once been what'd seemed like a genuine snuff film but which'd turned out to be a bit of guerrilla marketing for an independent feature I eventually tracked down a copy of and didn't think was very good. I kept everything, had a little cabinet area I called a closet in my one-room, basement apartment where the lot was stored, not a shrine, didn't date stamp the stuff, give each exhibit a little placard—an incidental hobby, nothing more, the closest I had to a life, truth be told.

Calico Bash wasn't exactly a hot spot motel nor a sought-after station of employment, so it was a breezy enough affair to pick up extra hours turning down rooms after my shift, handling little trifles of maintenance as best I could. Place never ran even at quarter-capacity and was just twelve cabins attached to a duckpin bowling alley, so it never took me long, mostly just something to do until early afternoon, the three days a week I worked midnight-to-eleven—as it typically brought me just shy of a respectable eighty hours per payday, standard wage, and since any hours beyond my scheduled thirty-three covered the week's cigarettes, I never pressed them to shell out technical overtime.

All the knick-knacks I mentioned amassing I'd lucked into being the one to discover, but there was other stuff left behind I'd have to bide my time over, queue for when I wanted to procure—mostly sundries forgotten by truckers, leftover booze, sometimes unopened, packs of condoms, the same, two bottles of prescription Viagra, bags of chips, decks of cards, but there was often bigger ticket merchandise, too, few little black-and-white televisions, portable cassette players, a saxophone. All manner of bric-a-brac was found on days I didn't work or when guests clearly cut out early and the actual housekeeper was on hand—regular procedure was items were tagged, stowed in a caged-shut cubby in the office room behind the laundry alcove. Some law said a bare minimum of ninety days had to elapse before lost or abandoned property went up for grabs—or that's what the manager claimed and everyone but me followed protocol religiously, so far as I could tell.

Of importance, there was a really swell electric typewriter I'd been forced to wait six months on while a co-worker I never directly interacted with satisfied himself the gadget wasn't antique, valuable, something he could make a quick bundle hocking down the *Guns-n-Pawn*—but the strangest and most consequential items I ever stumbled on were the manuscript, the cassette, and the letter along with them.

Cabin Seven had complained of a leak, so I'd shunted the two guests into another room then had myself a looksie, problem seemed to originate from a vent shaft which ran behind Six through Ten—in particular, Cabin Nine had water trickling from it, both directions. I never did figure out what to do about the leak, had to pass that job off to an actual handyman the manager was in-law with—but what I discovered before doing so was a package wrapped up tight in black electrical tape. First thoughts were obvious: *money, dope, blackmail photos, murder weapon*—no matter what, an absolute treasure, delectably tantalizing, the sort I quite frankly spent chunks of my life daydreaming about getting my loitering mitts around. The more I thought about it, the giddier my mood grew—after all, bugger had to've been really *hidden*, like *stashed away*, consciously, true and proper. It was a helluva time undoing any of the vent grates, for starters, then there was the fact the packet hadn't been at all within easy reach, not even arm's length, and, moreover, had been arranged flush with the side of the vent, pressed that way on purpose to make it as inconspicuous as possible—I'd never have seen it for trying if not on account of messing about with a mop to sop up the wet, some jostle or jerk I'd incidentally made causing it to tip over *splash* and afterward it'd taken using the mop handle to shove the thing enough toward Eight I could undo that grate and scoop it out.

There was an earache of getting through the tape—delicate delicate and taking all the time it took, I made incisions with a razor blade, starting around the edges to be safest, then when it seemed okay, began peeling with my fingers. Electrical tape gave way to a few layers of invisible tape which in turn revealed three Ziploc bags, each wrapped in its own layer or two of adhesive, to boot, then a grocery-store bag underneath all that. I got wondering if it was gonna be nothing but packaging all the way down, then figured it might be some kind of well-insulated bearer bond, stock certificates, a rare hockey card, sheet or two of valuable stamps—was honestly a tad brought down when I got to the outside of a plump manila folder filled with paper, three green rubber bands twined tight around it. Finally clear to cut and tear with impunity, soon I had the document out—didn't count, but it had to be several hundred pages, cheap, newsprint paper, soaked in typewriting, front and back, corrections in green ink, all over, smudges and stiff stains of coffee droplets overtop those.

The sealed envelope had been wrapped around the casing the cassette was housed inside, both taped down to the inside of the folder—a name on the envelope, also in type: NATHAN JEHOVAH. Though curiosity lacerated me, I'd decided to leave the thing sealed, and to this day I've no idea why—enormously out of character, but I recall some vagrant qualm about I'd better see what the manuscript was all about first, might be it was the sort of thing to return to a rightful owner, reward in the offing provided the goods had remained provably unmolested. It was a rather specific looking envelope too, sealed with wax not a lap of the tongue, not something I could easily dummy up with items from the drugstore despite the name on it not being in longhand—better safe than sorry, I suppose I'd supposed.

As to the manuscript, I gave the start of it a read:

> Here's what. I'm gonna do this. I've already left work, left town without telling anyone. Employer. Friends. My son. It'd be absurd to turn back. But enough's enough, isn't it? My life's ticked past middle age. I'm older than Dante'd been when Dante'd done Dante's deal, for Heaven's sake! Time to achieve something. For myself. For the world. Make a mark. Indelible. Inexplicable. Undeniable. Immortal and inimitable as the cold.

First blush, I took it to be the opening passage of a novel, but deciding to give the stack of pages a quick flit through, seemed what I had on my hands was mostly a collection of song titles, each with remarks afterward—sometimes a sentence or two, such as

> *Rat Patrol*: Lyrics crackle, guitar's off the chain, rambunctious and dirty, tres punk, oui oui. But somehow a great song wound up merely good, no culprit for how come.

or else

> *Don't Break The Heart*: A comely track. Lacking a noteworthy momentum. Placid. Currentless. Lyrically poignant but sans gravitas.

while other times a small paragraph along the lines of

> *So Long, Mockingbird*: Haunting. Lyrically inspired. Liquor razor blades so smooth going down you've already swallowed a second mouthful before you realize the ribbons the first cut your insides to. Appreciates on each listen. Portrait of an existence nondescriptly forlorn. Could be a love story gone South. Could be the loss of a teenage friendship. Could be something more private and thus experienced five times as hard. A gorgeously individual evocation of heartache all varieties.

Leafing further into the dossier, I found, toward the end, pages and pages and pages of a numbered list—no notes, song titles only and oodles of 'em. Giving my nose a proverbial flick for the bad habit of skipping ahead, I returned to the start—how many times had I gotten myself turned around with the wrong impression of this book or that film on account of I'd opened to a random page, caught some clip out of context, got building and building upon it with my own wise ideas until I figured I'd deduced the sum total, only to shoot my uninformed mouth off in the presence of exactly the wrong person?

> Here's what. I'm gonna be the chap to sort it out, for all day. Rank, definitively, the music of *They Might Be Giants*. Not in some namby-pamby, school yard prattle, take half-an-hour to come up with some

halfcocked order anyone could shrug off. This isn't humble opinion, personal postulant. This is Science, Philosophy, like they both were the same back at the start of it. Here's what. Everything. All the music. Put exactly where it fits. Meticulous. Sacrosanct. Pangea reassembled. I'll rank the albums as single entities, first. All of *Lincoln* against all of *Nanobots* against all of *My Murdered Remains* against all of so forth against all of so on. Rank the songs within each album, next. Top this off by compiling a no holds barred Master List. Rating the songs against each other. Every last one. A real knockdown, drag out affair, a merciless melee!

Noticed a signature on the back of the second sheet, end of the fourth page, technically, blue ink rather than green, not particularly legible—squinted at a squiggle with the appearance of a child's haphazard illustration of the seashore. This detail gave a different tint to the content of the first pages, drove home their mystique: honest, direct address, material which'd been drafted specifically to be found, which struck me quite eerie and was likely some kind of joke—or better say some manner of oddball art project, message in a bottle, note tied to a helium balloon … something about it gave me the creeps, anyway.

> I've given this thought. No problem there. Here is the culmination of decades of passion. Here is a life of cogitation bearing fruit. Otherwise would I do a thing like this? Scamper off during my lunch break without a word? Terrify my loved ones? Endure Lord only knows what repercussions, personally and professionally? In no sense! I'm not a maniac. There just sometimes comes a time and for me, for this, that time has come.

Third sheet began with the heading FULL LENGTH STUDIO ALBUMS and I got the idea how, in between the author's editorials on whichever tracks, he'd set down certain longer bits, some which I took for general explanations of the rubric being utilized

> But ear-worming isn't where it's at, full stop. Catchy ditties, as often as not, are unmasked to be of lesser lasting value than their toe-tapping promises. *Perfect* means you not only could listen to the buggers over

'n over 'n over but, frankly, the power of Christ'd compel ya! Certain songs become more than part of your soundtrack for some few days, a week. They're lifelong. Blood borne. Pathogenic. Lyrics muttered as nepenthe while rickety trains chugga-chug ya to and from the dead-end clock you punch and make it seem worthwhile, rise in personal prominence to the pitch full-blown fantasies are entertained. You're back in time. Had written 'em yourself. Performing not for fame nor fortune, no no no, just booking your group for the Talent Show in hopes the teacher you'd crushed out on since Freshman Year'd crush back, even if ever only under their breath.

while others came off as explication of certain esoteric rationale which, while textured with the same personal in-reference suggesting individual experience as the general method-behind-the-madness passages, were also nothing narrative

> Take as another exhibit: the scrumptious cover of bubblegum era hit *Maybe I Know*. Wowee our Johns did right by it! Platonic Ideal of transmuting someone else's material into their own. No no, doesn't beat *New York City*, doesn't beat *We've Got A World That Swings*, don't be dumb, and only maybe matches *Bills Bills Bills* maybe trumps it maybe falls a tap short. Odd thing's how it isn't a blow to discover the tune isn't genuine *Giants*, cause man alive, you'll need to belt a stiff finger of scotch you first learn the aforementioned trio originated elsewhere!

Sometime around half-past-four, fatigue always started messing with my focus, my habit being to glug one more swig from the flask of *Bulleit* I kept handy, chain three more cigs, then mill outside doing physical gestures which weren't any identifiable exercise, nor anything which'd wake me up, but this night, I just sat there with a gummy head more than any discernable feeling of illness, wondering if I was coming down with something—figured I'd probably got fungus in my lungs from gophering in the chilly damp vent, couldn't even concentrate enough to inspect the manuscript, which kinked me in a sour head ... all the world around me felt a drag. For as much as I claimed to love the anonymous mottle of life overnight, *love* didn't mean I especially enjoyed it—by the time the first bit of morning seeped through the soot glass, I was ready for sleep despite having only dragged myself awake not seven hours previous. I wanted to be back home, where nighttime was fine, any time was, even forever—home was where time existed in the form of blue digits displayed on the same microwave that burnt holes straight through anything not set carefully at the edge of its rotating glass dish and rattled like a dyspeptic locomotive when it beeped, the hour always something it felt I was taking someone's ill-advised word on. Lush in the permanent, artificial-lit buzz of my underground habitat, I never got sleepy, or always was, it just didn't matter—junkyard lamp operated by wall-switch, three bulbs which'd become two, become one, a t-shirt draped overtop giving everything a diffuse, chlorinated look as though soaked in a jar of lukewarm limeade, one minute couldn't be differentiated naturally from its predecessor, thus insomnia's curse was taken off, felt like sleep slept too intently to be restful, a dream too lived to've been dreamt, that's all.

 I grumbled through the two people I had to deal with in the last half-hour, first a check-out then a check-in—the former could've just toddled off but needed receipts and directions, of which I only tendered one, the latter I could've made wait until after eleven, except he'd stayed many times previous plus was generally savvy enough to've asked what in Hell I was playing at were I to've tried being a stickler—then endured some how-de-do with the housekeeper, who also bussed tables at the duckpin lanes, when she came in for the keys we kept in a locked cabinet beneath the computer ... didn't mention how I wasn't gonna bother working extra to spruce up the departure's room and she didn't remark how I hadn't.

 Over an indulgent breakfast of filling station pizza and coffee, I nestled into an outdoor table around the corner from the breeze, giving another inspection to the cassette box—it occurred to me the recording couldn't be a recital of the manuscript's content, sixty-minute run time, either total or per side, two hours max, either way, and I doubted thirty or forty of these cluttered pages could fit into that, even if read at breakneck. Did a guesstimate of how many words to a page, this many per line, approximately blah lines per, carry the seven, times however many—nope, reading the entire volume'd take forever.

Opened it to give the theory a test:

> ... when I show up, home again, what will I have to say for myself and why should I need to explain? What're the odds I'll get canned from my cardboard gig? Accumulated sick-time'll retroactively cover the hooky or I'll just find another analogous dead end. Except I want to explain. Why shouldn't I? No one's in a lurch any moreso than if I'd become bedridden, comatose. People get kidnapped. Every day. From my family's perspective, why not just look at it that way? Plus: it's what happened. Shanghaied. By Art. Idea. My soul drawn by need, not whimsy. Once released, why shouldn't I say where I'd been, cockcrow the adventure of what I'd accomplished! Integrity. Isn't what I'm doing truthful to the tooth? Don't I believe seeing the world this way is something to instill? Art can reach out. Bag over your head. Bind you to some radiator. Life must contain sudden extravagance! Thoughtlessness one's well cognizant of! Sacrifice worth its weight in gold! Some things utterly need to happen, not be fit in, false starts, snips, snaps, crackles, coughs. Obligation shouldn't run roughshod over yearning. Not forever. Aren't I where I'd hope my son would be, were he me? Imagine him my age but where I'd typically be ... I could sick-up in contemplation of that!

Phony experiment, as I couldn't speak aloud because of chewing, swallowing, though was clever enough to think in approximately my normal talk-rhythm, hedged the result on the side of 'I'd get at least X-many-lines-more per minute were I familiar with the content' then factored in how a writer probably reads faster than me—but even if I'd gotten quadruple where I had, we were talking ages more than two hours to spit out the whole nine.

If not for the pizza immediately requiring a bowel movement, I'd have read on, but physical and mental wellbeing took priority—drove to my apartment in the self-inflicted anguish nourishment tended to result in, totally forgetting a stop I should've made, lied flagrantly how I'd pop back out once my predicament'd resolved, and by the time the near thing of getting inside, to my toilet, suffering the indescribable throes of three-slices-three-bucks had been survived, I wasn't in much mood for the written word. Smoking a cigarette I knew'd be interrupted by false alarms rousting me back to the potty, I popped the cassette in my player and a voice smooth as gravel filled the space around me while I verified four green sticks in a square meaning *Zero* showed on my answering machine display and spent a moment regarding a Post-It note I'd set on the wall near the phone—*Congratulations on Three Weeks since your last message!!!* with celebratory illustrations alongside it, *Three Weeks* written in brown magic marker beneath tally marks in orange I'd kept beside the capitalized word DAYS for four sets of five.

Took a swig from my flask before I set to dutifully refilling it and one more halfway through the twelve seconds that took, remarking to myself how sometimes I really could keep to a habit, exhibited the discipline of a Shaolin monk—had been so darned proud of myself when I'd bought a carton of cigarettes, for instance, the money it'd saved me seeming to promise a fortune over time ... but no such luck ... the empty carton lay there, potato chip bag atop it, and each day I'd reach my hand inside, vain hope that a pack'd been overlooked or else snuck in by an enemy as a zany prank to make me slowly come unglued. Finished off the chips, exquisitely stale, and regretted scarfing them so unmannerly even while I had a greasy few handfuls left, regretted it harder as I took the final swallow, cleaned fingers on the hips of my pants, knowing I could've used the crumby bits in a peanut butter sandwich, stiff bread, discount grade paste, enjoyed a meal with crunch that would've been borderline chewy—my mouth watered for the future I'd squandered.

Cut the cassette off when I realized I'd not listened to a word, then began a more professional inspection of the case it'd come in for secrets and the like but found nothing of interest—even the blank decal labels all accounted for. Spent a pointless few minutes trying to work out something funny I could spell with them on the outside of my door—my name followed by DDS or *Esq.*, *No Solicitors*? The limits of my imagination deserved another quick tipple of bourbon—a toast, that was all, to the nit of my wit! ... plus, what could one more hurt when I'd already had enough the day was lost to me and a lost day amounted to so little calling it *lost* seemed to be spending a dollar on eighty-four cents.

While I sighed another cig I'd not quite meant to start, I flopped to my desk chair and tried to get my head wrapped around the document: the bulk of the green-inked corrections were no more than adjective choice—*fiercely* became *teeteringly*, *brusque* became *arrogant*, despite *brusque* seeming better, and the statement 'Never worked phones you'd humped a till, pushed papers, jerked soda, moved a mop around' had tacked to it 'some part of any soul can taste the croup-cough of drudgery at minimum wage' which was underlined thrice. Must've been the author'd pounded the text down relatively without thought—maybe not Kerouac, pages at-a-time, but not *tack tack tack* read it back *tick tick tick*, '… hmn … lemme see, here …' scribble scribble *clackity-clack* in real time. Certainly nothing transcribed from a handwritten source, either, every handful of pages, bloke'd probably paused to read it aloud, pacing their cabin, annoyed every time the same words were used too many times in close proximity, learning the traps of their unconscious predilections causing down-and-out heartache—*akin to akin to akin to, rather as though rather as though, disquieting disquieting, ineffable ineffable, seemingly seemingly, a knack for a knack for, finger on finger on finger on*. Recognized the noia in the little dots, underlines, and *X*s along the margins, meant to guarantee nowhere a replacement was needed could be clumsily brushed past—my wife'd been the same way when she'd been my wife and I'd begun to feel inferior for it, seen as less-than, quite demonstrably. When she'd have me read early drafts of whichever article, screenplay, short story, I'd never notice these *missteps*, as she called them, nor would've mentioned them even if I had—said to her, on occasion, how it didn't matter, nobody noticed those sorta quirks, and sometimes they even seemed nice, natural, like talking, plus what did she care about people, anyway? 'What do you mean *people*?' I mumbled her voice in my memory ' … you're the only one bringing them up, ever— why're *you* so concerned with people, maybe I oughta ask.' 'I dunno …' I sighed as I'd sighed so often before, sinking from it into a deeper recline and my waterlogged moot points. Frankly, after she'd explained to me, I could well understand what she'd meant by 'the flow of the sentence, the cadence' and how different a picture so slight a blip paints, what magic might be evoked with variety which lack-of-variety lacked—I was simply an uncurious cat, all part of my charm, would let my own mind handle everything, stimuli response, I'd supposed. 'Who even remembers what words they read, when you really think about it? Memory'll substitute one thing for another—even one's own memory of what they write'll be overwrote, over time ... I mean ... don't you agree with that? How can you not ..?'

Yes yes ... I sat dribble-conversing with myself, relitigating the semantical grouses of yesteryear ... always much easier to prevail when I was the only one talking and the split had years ago been made official ... but nothing went without saying ... and though what was worth saying might not be worth saying twice, why let a thing like that stop me ... funny how her points seemed sounder than mine to me, though they'd technically become my points, by this point ... I wasn't quoting her, after all ... didn't know what it meant to feel smarter than myself ... except it didn't seem something to feel ashamed of ...

Put on a movie and slouched, tipsily enthralled the way one only could be in my precise condition—realized I'd nodded off and meantime the flick had finished, rewound, started over, though if not so familiar with it, I'd never have known. Wondered if anyone'd ever drifted off, nodded awake just as the film got to the moment they'd drifted, then watched a tad further, nodded off, popped awake, film picking up on the image and sound their attention had broken from—did some calculations, or attempted to ... if a film was ninety minutes ... and if you fell asleep every five ... and the film cycled through ... and you woke up, watched, then drifted off again, five minutes later ... repeat repeat ... repeat ... how much time could you lose to that one movie ... in a room like mine, no windows, no hint of outside, there was simply no telling.

[*home and friends and new york times and lawn*]

Found the manuscript Tuesday, didn't give it a second thought until stopping into *Video Grog* on my way home from *The Calico* for a typical Thursday browse and to rent a couple flicks for the long four days off I'd have to weather—shared a cigarette and shot the breeze with a clerk called Simon, right then getting off shift, and it was Oldtime Dougie working the place, proper, his gut leaked all down the counter while he sorted out another jigsaw, this time a chintzy reimagining of one of the Sistine's lesser-known panels. Heard him out about his typical gripes, business on the brink of collapse, same as it'd been at least bi-weekly since I'd first started haunting the joint—worst mistake of his professional life continued to be having given away those free memberships for a few months, eight years back, though I jibed him how the legitimate worst mistake was letting his DVD section become so sprawling, not to mention most items on offer were Blu-Ray or Ultra 4K and all manner of designations I, frankly, found distasteful. He guffawed in that air-horn way of his, told me it was only on account of my patronage there even still were VHS, and that what he dreaded was the fateful day I finally realized digging fossils for cheap at *Mappy Land Thrift* would save me a ransom, in the long run—'Other than you and some dinky chick who rents for her mom on the Memory Ward, once a month, I couldn't give those clunky old relics away!'

'You could always let me buy these,' I winked, wave of a hand to indicate the last shelf-unit housing several hundred VHS display boxes which used to span the entire left-hand wall of the shop, presently stacked so only the tops faced outward, twelve high, ten across—black or white block-letter titles on a glorious mosaic of out-of-date background colors.

'Why would I sell to you when I can rent?' he said in a tone like talking about me behind my back. 'I'm a businessman, after all, and you're a rare breed of obsolete sucker—a rube preserved in amber!'

'I could point out …' I whispered back in mock-up flirtation '… I've rented more than a couple tapes enough times I ought to've owned them outright, several times over.'

'Which is why I love you, Lemon! You're a dues paying member of the under-educated class, a walkin' talkin' Dylan lyric.'

Grinned because I knew exactly which one he meant while he told me to help myself to a pink lemonade, gratis, per usual, then decided to poke around the unalphabetized bins of used CDs awhile, see was there any *They Might Be Giants*—came across two discs, first one called *Flood*, kinda an eyesore, faded antiseptic green, nothing grabbing about the design, just some mutt in a rowboat and didn't like the insignia design to the title, the second called *Apollo 18*, ugly bugger with a picture of some tangled up squid around a bored looking whale, too black, too white, too orange, and derivative, beside … buck-fifty a pop, though, and with their original inserts still present and accounted for, I figured no reason not to splurge. Got up front where Oldtime gave my selections a more than cursory inspection, probably because he'd never known me to purchase music, curious what made me tick in that department—mentioned how he thought maybe he still had a VHS of some of the groups' music videos around, not to rent, this time, because why waste valuable shelf space, but were I interested in that kind of material he'd permit me to buy. Settled on a five-spot for the videos plus both albums while it took him ten minutes to unearth the tape—no original box, store packaging, so clearly he'd rented it out, once upon a time, which meant he likely had a lot of other unshelved inventory, too, though I left off saying so.

'I'd never've taken you for being into this stuff,' he told me in a tone of voice peculiar for its lack of judgement, considering the verbal content.

'I've never even heard of 'em.'

'Why the sudden spree?'

'Some girl at the motel mentioned 'em yesterday,' I decided to lie.

'Girl, the motel, eh?' That seemed to intrigue him to the tune of a few pregnant nods, after which he pivoted to telling me he hadn't much listened to the junk in ages and couldn't think of a single solitary girl he'd ever known who'd been interested alongside him. 'Not the sort of girl you go hunt out what they recommend, anyway.'

'You're a fan?'

Wobbled his hand, noncommittal—been too many moons to properly say, but supposed, for a while, it'd've been fair to've called him that, junior high, high school, spot after. 'The music really started to fall off after an album called *Factory Showroom*, if memory serves. Overproduced to the point of embarrassment, pale imitation of itself.'

I didn't care anywhere near enough to press for further insights, just rented a found footage flick, also called *Apollo 18*, along with *Eye of the Beholder* for the fifteenth time, and *I, Madman* for at least the eighth—same as always, made sure it was honestly cool with Dougie about my not paying for the pink lemonade, since he must've given me thousands of dollar's worth of the swill by now, to which he snorted 'I get it for free, some reason, and can't sell it for even that much!' before giving me the power handshake as I split.

I did swing by *Mappy Land*, but only to feel myself the savvy shopper, playact some price comparison, a moot gesture, through and through, as I'd never abandon the *Grog*, first of all, and second, *Mappy Land* never had any selection—it was almost magical how their inventory consisted of either relatively modern stuff, practically the last batch of flicks to get VHS release, or else *Dorf on Golf*, select episodes of *The New Red Green*, and *Video Game Tips 'N Tricks* vids I earnestly did want for my collection but worried having would get me in mind to track down an old *Sega Master System* which'd mean money I didn't have plus time I didn't want to admit I had plenty.

Tried to listen to *Flood* once I was back to homebase, had it on while I puttered about undressing, slipped into lounge pants, baggier tee—real quick cottoned how this jazz didn't shift me, cartoon coolkid vibes with hipster cologne oozing out every pore, the sort of nerdy tinkersmithing that tried way too hard to put on like it wasn't tryin' to be clever just, aw shucks, couldn't help being born that way. I wasn't fooled and couldn't stand the posturing of that kinda rot—have a sound, by all means, be weird and wild as you feel, *The Cramps, Talking Heads, Daddy Dewdrop, Zager and Evans*, just be at least the least little bit genuine about it, please and thanks! In for a penny in for a pound, though, so after enduring a tedious offering called 'Your Racist Friend' I switched to headphones, settled into the comfy chair I used as a bedroom, feet up on the short bookshelf built into the wall, always empty except for them, lit a ciggie, and took out the album insert—following along with the words made the task of enduring the nineteen tracks less obnoxious and I was honestly intrigued how, in the only song I actually enjoyed, there was an entire verse printed in the booklet which wasn't sung, best lyric out of the bunch, too, by a length! Thinking it genuinely nifty if the band'd done this on purpose, promised I'd give their *Apollo 18* its fair day in court, right after a shower, a sausage biscuit or two, and a pull from the stale two-liter of *Jolt Cola* I kept forgetting I owned—regretted it, awfully though, because Christ, what a rotten piece of work that turned out to be! Suffered through enough to kinda Stockholmily admit I enjoyed a ditty called 'Narrow Your Eyes' and how 'See The Constellation' woulda been passable if not for going on so much longer than required—but by the time things wound round to an interminable spooling of ten-second long minisongs, collectively entitled 'Fingertips,' I called it a day. *Clunk clunk* tossed the jewel cases onto the desk, swiveled around, and decided to scrub the taste of pretentiousness off of my teeth by watching the found footage *Apollo 18*—flick was a metric ton better than I'd figured it was gonna be, turned into one of my favorites of the subgenre, actually, up there with *The Last Exorcism* or *Skew*, though a far cry, still, from *The McPherson Tape* or *388 Arletta*.

Napped instead of exercising for the tenth time in a week, woke to realize there'd been a message blinking on my machine I'd somehow overlooked—my kid Viggo, requesting a callback, nothing life-or-death, no worries if I wasn't free, just he missed me a little and there'd not be another safe chance to gab until all the way after next weekend due to whichever details of his teenaged life. Gave me instructions for when the coast'd be clear, his mother still harboring no Earthly idea we'd reconnected and kept in touch as often as possible—swell kid, knew it'd be long distance, so read off the number from some prepaid card he'd procured in case I was behind half-a-yard in my finances. Decided to dial him, regular, and to seem airier still, like things were coming up roses on my end, straight on the line asked him had he ever heard of a rock 'n roll group called *They Might Be Giants*—didn't ring any bells, named a few songs, rang even fewer.

'What do they sound like?'

'I've no idea,' I decided to say, no point lumping any influence on the lad.

'You haven't listened to them?'

'I'm about to, figured if you do the same we can maybe compare notes—but it was pure lark, picking their albums up.'

Said he'd check it out, maybe, at which point I changed the subject to what was new and exciting with him, had he ever asked out this or that girl, how'd the fight he'd gotten into turned out, how much hot water had it won him with the school superintendent or whoever, what did he want for his birthday—to my surprise, he laid out a whole spread regarding that last item, explained there was nothing for me to get for him, quite the contrary, a top secret treat'd been planned for me, despite he being the one turning seventeen. Seemed there was a film festival going on in some town called *Mill Creek*, totally up our alley, a showcase of overlooked horror thrillers, gems and trash alike, celluloid fallen into the public domain when it could even be found, prints most folks'd consider scrapple, new indie shoestring productions by complete unknowns getting their brief glimpse of the sun in place of their fifteen minutes fame, plus guest speakers probably not even I'd ever heard of—which sounded like paradise, considering one of the things I adored about watching bargain bin, five-flicks-to-a-disc faff was never having to know the identities of actors, directors, Abel Ferrara notwithstanding.

'All you need is to show your sorry old ass up! Most exciting thing is… well, I dunno if I want it to be a reveal when we get there or to have you try a guess, here and now.'

'The auteur behind *Doorbell Camera*'s gonna be in attendance and we'll finally have all our deepest questions about that background sandwich answered?' I immediately offered, using our pet-name for *Unknown Visitor*, a film most considered dreck but which happened to be a touchstone of ours.

'I wish! Unfortunately, there also isn't gonna be a screening of whatever that movie is about the chick trapped under the ice while the killer waits above—you know, the one you can never remember the title of and which I still doubt exists outside of your bug-addled brain—but you should take another guess, anyway.'

'Cast and Crew screening of *Roland*?'

'Nope.'

'A Director's Cut of *The Apple*? Alternate ending to *Death Bed: The Bed That Eats*?''

Now I was making him feel bad! 'What a crap festival I've booked us at.'

'Well Vig, nothing's ever as wonderful as what's in our heads—kind of the reason to have one.'

He concurred, but then told me since I'd twisted his arm, fine, he'd go ahead and blab: 'There's gonna be a whole theatre dedicated to playing *Hidalgo,* dad! Just over and over and over—gonna do it all themed up like a stupid desert and everything!'

I burst a cackle of laughter, playing right along with our well-worn in-joke about how my having showed him the film when he was little proved I didn't always have the perfect taste I pretended, then pivoted to mirthfully wanting him to tell me, once and for all, what he'd so hated about the damn thing. 'First of all, kiddo, I never actually *recommended* it—you were fucking seven-years-old and I was trying to screen some family friendly fare, for a change—but more importantly, it's a perfectly fine film!'

'Oh I know, trust me—it's your personal favorite, a stone masterpiece!'

'*Hate* is such a lunatic word for so milquetoast a flick, Viggy—can't you be merely indifferent to it, like the rest of humanity-writ-large?'

'Self-respect keeps me from stooping so low—and I know you're about to be disappointed, but that's not the *actual* surprise ...' I rolled my eyes and sighed all exaggerated how it'd take a Hell of a lot to get me out of the doldrums I'd plummeted into the briars of for having the *Hidalgo* rug pulled out from under me, to which he gave a dismissive *tsk* then explained '... I shit you not, dad—both Steven Traxler and Alan Blanchard are hosting a private screening of *Slithis*! And remember that band *Slithis Survival Kit*? Bastards're actually playing live! Fifty guests, invite only! There was a lottery then a bidding war amongst scalpers—but we're in like Flint!'

This about blew my tiny, provincial mind and I warned him that '... if this turns out to be a crank-yank, you'll be summarily disowned and, what's more, your body'll never be discovered, even by barnacles!'

He told me it'd be amazing if I could find him a white hat so he could attend the shindig in character as Wayne Connors, but, if not, he'd just grab something Army surplus, show up dressed as Bunky, then rattled off a list of what all else was screening: '*Terror Point, Track of the Moon Beast, Spiker, The Clones of Bruce Lee*—three perfect days of the sort of flotsam the hep world casts aside!'

Boundlessly proud of him for seeing it that way, told the boy how other people and their mangy opinions were worthless—if I ever taught him anything, let it be that. 'You see something, hear something, you dig it, you don't—that's all there is, fella. Beware fandoms and factoid spitters of all stripes—they're the future, brother, and it's murder.'

My heart positively swelled when, like a beloved mantra, he quoted my oft-espoused sentiment: 'Every opinion that can be had about something will be had about it—and if something's encountered an infinite number of times by an infinite number of people, every opinion that can be had will be had, infinity each'—was so moved, in fact, I unconsciously knocked back a swig from my flask, then played it off by claiming it was the stale *Jolt*, coughing as though from a bad swallow while he laughed at me about it.

We riffed awhile longer about our palpable excitement and I tried to finagle out of him how many pretty pennies this extravaganza had set him back, promised I'd front him the amount, or at least part of it, though knew full well this'd be nigh impossible—he insisted I wasn't to give it a second thought, his view being that '… if years ago a brick safe had fallen and hit you on the head when you were walking down the street, I'd be going to the Fest without your help, regardless, so your presence is simply bonus, like bag fries.'

'I'll do my best about finding the white hat, anyway,' I beamed, glad to avoid any direct broaching of whether his mother knew about this caper or how he'd worked it to be away from home multiple overnights on his lonesome, figuring such show of trust in his ingenuity was best left tacit, subtextual—he reiterated I wasn't to sweat it, then told me he had to take off.

'Big date? Big fight?'

'One of those things I misspend my youth on, yeah—I'll check out the band you mentioned, too.'

'I expect your full report, in triplicate,' I sternly informed him, hung up, then, in swell spirits like only my kid could leave me, checked out the music videos—quite enjoyed the honest-to-God screw it, roughhewn, pals with a camera making it up on the fly kinda energy to the photography of the first, though the accompanying ditty was an almost instantly forgettable trifle called 'Ana Ng' … and it was all quickly, sharply, downhill from there. Supposed I understood what Dougie'd been driving at when he'd mentioned the group's output becoming repetitive—in short order, the vids seemed to be not even riffing on each other but slavishly recycling the same lackluster ideas and images, a slog to soldier through even the two, three minutes of each, zero I had a hankering to revisit let alone write home about! Final two offerings were shorts from the cartoon *Tiny Toon Adventures* which I must've somehow missed despite being a big fan of the program, back in the day ... or maybe I'd seen 'em ... the images had a familiar whiff ... could probably show me all kinds of things I'd watched as a kid and they'd be news to me. It was no skin off my teeth, of course, and hadn't cost me but twenty dimes plus two nickels tax—bet I could even've wrangled a refund had I pled my case ... except, why bother? Nice little diversion and I'd place the artifacts in with the manuscript, the cassette—a fine set of props for an exhibit they'd make, a neat little story to tell ... except, again, why bother ... not to mention, to whom?

Viggo's enthusiasm still coursing me, figured I'd better listen to the damn albums at least a few more times, be able to come across as erudite if the punk brought them up, tried to get me with a *Gotcha!,* not that we'd probably wind up having listened to the same selections, he having access to all the world via computer screen— trying to raise a proper analog citizen could only go so far, seeing the long distance we kept, and I was always on eggshells not to lambast new technologies or ways of interfacing with and responding to Art I'd no way of knowing whether he found worthwhile. As a matter of fact, it'd be wisest to prepare two sets of opinions: my *honest* one plus a *positive* one, in case the twerp fancied the bilge—I'd not play a trick on him, per se, wouldn't baldly lie how I was kooky for the music just because he happened to be, would simply tilt my part of the conversation more along the lines of I'd need to give matters further audit, emphasize the few tracks I'd found passable, lay off talking about the others, give him the ol' 'Well if you're digging it, boyo, I gotta spend more time, get myself thinking straight—what songs did you listen to?' Subsequent time we gabbed, I'd behave as though still on the fence, but admit I much preferred his recommendations to what I'd gotten an earful of, previous—claim, in fact, how I'd grown more appreciative of certain stuff I'd initially poo-pooed and then, over time, incrementally, attest to being a fan in equal measure to him, no suspicion raised.

Except '... Oh goddamnit, nope nope nope ...' I dug *Flood* even less on a repeat—at best could say I'd added 'Letter Box' to my 'it's perfectly fine, so far as *that* goes' list, but what might possess a man to listen to the track on the regular was Biblically beyond my comprehension! A song titled after the band was more-or-less emblematic of their weirdness-for-weirdness-sake antics, two dudes making it up as they went but without bothering to make what they made cohere to anything save their own giddiness at being a kinky little unit—brought to mind thoughts of people putting on airs in high school, of that pretty girl who'd never date you back then changing her mind, thirty years and a spine surgery or rehab stint later, or of the quiet kid you'd regretted picking on with the others who'd done well for himself but, big picture, no better than anyone else and less than you'd secretly hoped. As for *Apollo 18*, enjoyed 'See The Constellation' only a touch less, and still not enough to write off completely, kind of got along with a song called 'Mammal' in a cutie-pie, nostalgia for *Sesame Street* kinda way, but hotly despised 'The Statue Got Me High' and loathed the video that went with it—most intolerable of all, though, was a tune called 'Dinner Bell' which I knew'd be stuck in my head and felt so tricked by I wanted to scream … not that there was anything to get bent out of shape about … to each their own … sleeping dogs, bygones bygone … the stuff merely irked me, was all … if Viggo liked it, maybe I'd find a way to make our first major disagreement in life into a kind of bonding experience …

Nabbed up the manuscript to give a looksie at what the mad-hatter'd written about 'Statue'—rather elated to discover he'd ranked it dead last, so far as that specific album.

> Here's a little something I shall never understand, someone help me out: people enjoy this song, even consider it an unassailable offering. But follow your nose, simply inspect and you'll discover something-near-to-odious in how commonplace and fences from inspired the piece is. It serves no function and functions on no level. I'd swear it was buncoed onto the album by some quick-change artist except such people have standards about that which they pawn off. Perhaps blackmail was involved. Nothing lyrical of the muttiest pedigree. Not only

tuneless but grating. Even Linnel's voice seems stripped of its chipped-cabinet calibre and its crayon-smeared-on-lacquered-countertop timbre.

Guy had the three I felt were okay down relatively high in the rankings, so I was torn—out of curiosity leafed to see where *Flood* and *Apollo 18* had placed in with the albums, overall ... fifth and seventh, out of twenty-plus offerings ... apparently something called *State Songs* was the crème of the crop, a pronouncement which our mystery critic admitted was controversial and had much to say about, including:

> '... 'If it's not both Johns, it's not the *Giants*' is what some feckless carbuncle out there might banshee my way. Bah! Some people might anything! Let the big big whoredom get in a crybaby twist. I'm hardly interested in nitpicking with any nitwit who tries. By all means like things. Love them. With my blessing, go forth and multiply! Leave groupthink out of it, though. Boast some independence and a touch of dignity. Sheesh ...

Such proclamation didn't pique my interest so much I'd go out of my way to acquire the album, but enough I spent another few minutes perusing passages, and thus discovered how the album placed dead-last was also a solo project, but from the opposite band member, working with an outfit called *Monopuff*—its designation something the author came across genuinely distraught over.

> Something has to be first. In this case such thing has to be last. Simple truth. The sight of it, however ... Christ! So blunt. The Ka-splat of a bludgeon! A snubnose's Ka-blam! Something private down in me quavers, the waving cilia tracing my tummy stir a citrus reflux of disquiet, evidence I've not girded myself for what's to come. How could I not've foreseen this eventuality? Something like it was bound to happen! The album containing one of my personal favorite tracks ranked last? There's logic in it, but not mathematic—or the other way round. Not that it's a pejorative placement. Every album'll house something top shelf. Such is the wizardry of that pesky duo of Johns, their dirty rotten shell-game. At the bottom of the Studio Album list,

a hair's breadth separates this from that, maybe even moreso than toward the top. Yet still! The titular track of this album, in particular, is likely to wind up in the Top Twenty-Five when it comes to the free-for-all of the Master List. But I suppose Dylan's 'Brownsville Girl' lives on *Knocked Out Loaded*, for Pete's sake.

Made me wonder if whoever'd wrote this malarky was legitimately cracked, had squirreled the document away out of abject paranoia he'd be brought up on charges in The World Court—combined with the introductory pages, the compendium reeked of manifesto more and more, prompted the words 'mental health' to be uttered in the way such term is chosen when anything but mental health is meant.

[*nametags of pseudonyms*]

The day I was set to return to work, it was one of those things which if not for—whatever the impetus, suddenly had a peckish to take the electric typewriter I'd inherited from *Calico Bash* out for a spin, as 'til then all I'd done was stash the clunker in my closet collection, no clue if it even functioned. Best I can figure is the manuscript must've lodged something in my brain about typewritten pages, maybe the desire to open the Nathan Jehovah envelope played a part, too—that was some high-quality sheet of stationary, lemme tell ya, but I reckoned I'd be able to track down the same brand were I compelled, and as for the wax, no problem, wasn't as though there was the crest from some arcane cabal stamped in it, so I'd spring for a birthday candle the approximate color and do it up good enough ... provided I found typeface near to the fairly generic font in evidence, it stood a fair bet I'd be able to sate my curiosity with no risk of queering the deal were the documents ever returned to their rightful owner or intended recipient.

What happened went precisely like this: pleasant hum and almost saintly scent of warming ink spread like margarine through my room as I spooled in a junk-mail flyer, its fluorescent yellow-blank back all set to be inked—*clackity-click-clack* nothing. Hit a few more keys *snicker-snack snicker-snack* all mechanisms clearly functional, but still no letters appeared—poked around, sorted out how to open the top panel *pop pop* set it down, had a looksie at the guts, at a glance all systems seemed go *spit-spit-spit* pecked this key or that, finally spotted the culprit, toggled a little switch then *tackity-tackity* and hot diggity-dog, we were off to the races!

Bulky apparatus repositioned on the desktop, now I had trouble sorting the hood back on, didn't seem to intuitively snap to place, no obvious outcroppings or grooves suggesting a method, so I turned the mold over and, blow me down, found a blue sticker on which was handwritten *Property of Rasputin Evangeline*—I couldn't make up such a fluke, gun to my head, was gobsmacked at the fact someone'd put a label like this on their obsolete typewriter, not to mention someplace no one'd ever be likely to find it.

Next order of business was fairly obvious, Caps Lock, typed out NATHAN JEHOVAH—held the envelope next to the name, noted the unmistakable smudge to the V, then tested out copying a fair chunk of text for a fuller comparative specimen.

> Once in a while, the final doesn't improve upon the germ. Such're the breaks. Doesn't mean the superior impetus wasn't a glorious accident. All liking The Demo more than The Official reflects is quirk in whichever listener. I'm daffy for plain clothes rehearsals and ho-hum about full stage productions, slaphappy for typographical errors. But those're idiosyncratic preferences which don't change the fact that the way larval music sounds when recorded into a cassette player in the living room with only one microphone isn't the choice of the artist, or rather is that moment's choice, far far from their definitive word.

More than ample example for even an untrained eye to pick out particulars proving the writing identical and, with that sorted, I awarded myself a smoke-break to reassess the situation, attempting to explain to the satisfaction of any onlooker, concisely, what it was I hoped to achieve, exactly, and to what end I felt it important enough to expend the energy—when this didn't seem strictly necessary, reminded any invisible auditors that having a mystery on one's plate was a gift, in itself, didn't matter what the solution turned out to be: What was I supposed to do, dogmatically refuse to solve a puzzle until it proved impactful to my life, specifically ... nonsense!

By the time I was en route to my overnight, any antsiness or feeling of surveillance had passed and the next obstacle to surmount was my own memory bank—when had I obtained the machine, exactly

JOHN I'VE BEEN BAD
AND THEY'RE COMING AFTER ME / 27

... inside the year? Felt a right simp for how I couldn't readily recall, but my days didn't exactly take pains to dress differently—it'd been winter, though, which meant nearly a full year back, yes. Only one person by the rather distinct designation *Rasputin Evangeline* had ever registered at *The Calico*, decades prior, so that proved a kinky ripple—tried all sorts of games with the computer records, but the flat fact was, other than the one, no *Rasputins, Evangelines, Rapustins, Evengalanes, Ras Evenages, Rasps, Putins* or anything coming close had bunked down. Therefore gave a squint through the physical Guest Register, going back to its start, which was more than back-in-time enough, as well as riffling out cabinets' worth of room receipts—not a sausage. Even did my best to narrow it down by how, logically, Rasputin had to've been a fella who'd stayed in Cabin Eight or Nine, threw in Seven, added Six and Ten, still came up dunce, then went through the same shimmy-shake with the moniker *Nathan Jehovah*—snake eyes, all around.

Curiouser and curiouser, I chain-smoked in the greasy chill underneath the soupy pea-green of the sign buzzing *Motel Office* and attempted to shiver myself to some clever deduction—most apparent was the author'd used a wrong name at check-in, second to that, a guy actually called Rasputin Evangeline had got someone else to take out the room, then stayed there in their place, and a few variants on such scenario went Rasputin Evangeline was a made-up handle, out-and-out, or else the Rasputin who'd booked the joint, ages ago, had returned but not wanted it known that he had. Might've been lots of things, the more I put my mind to sleuthing—such an outlandishly obvious trail of events but with such bewildering elements impossible to reconcile was intolerable, really! Someone with the same name as a guest from a half-lifetime prior *had* taken the room and typed up a ridiculous compendium, hidden it as though in a B-movie, left their typewriter behind, never came back for it in the course of practically an entire year, and meanwhile I'd happened to've waited out six months, taken said typewriter home, and also been the person who'd discover the stashed document, entirely on freak chance, plus found the poppycock written interesting enough

I'd explored the matter, whereupon I'd decided to test out the typewriter, only to verify it most certainly belonged to the manuscript's author, beyond a shadow of a doubt—I mean come on, already!

Sometime around three in the morning, I took a third swig of *Bulleit* from my flask, swallowed harsh, coughed, thumped my chest—brainwave! I'd proceed from the sound assumption that the author'd composed the whole shebang right there at *The Calico*, which meant they'd dwelt on site for a fine solid jaunt—the content was lunatic substantive, couldn't've been dashed off in a single day even with the help of serious amphetamine, then add into the bargain how it seemed an honest, thought-through appraisal of all kinds of those songs, and it was a cinch to say attentiveness had been required, rest periods taken between bouts of drafting. 'Then let's consider it likely they'd checked out on a day I hadn't worked …' I subvocalized, roaming the parking lot, another smoke after another swig '… since the typewriter'd already been tagged and locked tight in the office when I'd first laid eyes on it …'

Points to me, because only one name fit the bill: bloke called *Sullivan Shallcross* had rented Cabin Eight for twelve days, right around when probability indicated he should've, added benefits to my case being the room'd been paid out in cash, extra deposit required since the tenant wasn't a licensed truck driver and no identification'd been provided—interesting too, was how said deposit hadn't been redeemed, meaning Mister Shallcross had likely departed before the technical end of his stay and obviously'd never returned, even despite a few hundred smackers worth of he ought to've. Cash on the barrelhead, crazy concealment, signs of having to beat feet before he'd expected to—a costly endeavor for an underground music aficionado, I daresaid! All in service of what—his manifesto on some geek band who one time had songs in an old cartoon? Minute-by-minute, the mystery deepened into an itch impossible not to scratch, a veritable scab impossible not to pick at, in fact—'Sullivan Shallcross, who are you?' I put to the empty around me '… or rather: are you honestly Rasputin Evangeline or actually Sullivan Shallcross? Registered under a phony name but used your real on the typewriter—real to register, incognito mode years ago?'

Couldn't get shut of how much it seemed to me the actual identity was Rasputin E. and S. Shallcross the alias—label on the typewriter had to be a clue, detective fiction and movies-of-the-week insisted that's the whole reason such a detail'd be present, and writers don't just take such routes to make it easy on themselves, centuries of observation prove out that's simply the way of the world, honest rendition always unfairly coming across a hackneyed trope crutched onto for ease. Truth was: the confluence of what it'd taken to get all the pieces in play positively begged for every last crumb to be turned over, tasted, seen for all it might possibly be at whichever longshot—a trail had been left which might only be ferreted by someone on the proper wavelength ... or something along those lines. The alternative was to subscribe to a worldview purporting we're random mechanisms doing seemingly specific things for no reason except we've been wound up to—which was fine and dandy, I supposed, but seeing things that way simply led to accepting my own snooping as *tick-tock-tick-tock*. Regardless of semantics, all I'd earned was a dead end—Rasputin Evangeline, Sullivan Shallcross, what did I care when I lacked the foggiest concerning how I'd ever find either?

Never a dab hand with computers, attempts to utilize the Internet from the front-desk were losing propositions—typing people into a search engine spat out multitudes of options all amounting to endless twaddle clearly nothing to do with either, photographs appeared which, when I'd click to research them further, led to those same images on webpages containing no hint of the names, not to mention the visual versions of Evangeline and Shallcross I encountered ranged from teenaged lads on lacrosse teams, present day, to daguerreotypes accompanying obituaries for elderly gents who'd been tucked snug underground since they'd died of being bombardiers circa Nineteen Forty. Next came mountains of anime, articles from specialized journals, many in languages I'd little use for, more I didn't exactly know how to identify, dead links, re-routes to pornographic forums where a certain Sullivan Evangeline had penned all sorts of eye-opening yarns concerning babysitters and neighbor's mom's obedient dalmatians, available for download or as on-demand paperback, transactions rendered in Pounds Sterling—I went so far as to spring a debit card dollar for a trial session of an allegedly reputable People Finder service, but such expenditure yielded a whole boatload of zilch then took almost an hour to find a way to cancel so I wouldn't get hit with a recurring charge ... it was a good job I had so much nothing going for me, as otherwise who'd have time or the patience for such wacky hijinks?

Dealt with a check-in then took a drink and really had a private word with myself about cooling my jets—this was hardly the sort of discovery to lose one's perspective over, just a folly with zero sign it'd end in even the mildest profit, best case. But there had to be something to it—and if not, I'd vastly prefer getting to the bottom of it pronto, rather than letting it drag on, cluttering up the rest of my vast interior life. So next shift, dead waste of night, I entered Cabin Eight, pulled the grate out of the wall, strategically positioned flashlights to be certain the entire tunnel was illuminated, popped my head into the stale cavity, inspecting first left then right—soot and cobweb and nothing. My thinking'd been how there might've once been a piece of paper taped to the package I'd found, a label affixed which'd come loose due to the damp, or some kinda stroke-of-luck evidence that'd solve everything—bugged me something fierce when there wasn't. Had a few smokes in the room while I gesticulated and put questions to myself in the various mirrors, one above the bathroom sink, another across from the bed, half-obscured by the television set—in short order decided I'd spare no expense, not allow a glitch of light or dinginess to've tricked my eyes, always a firm adherent to the dictum that a game's not worth playing unless played to the hilt. So doing as the caveman'd done, spent some time fashioning myself a clever tool out of a mop, wrapping a few towels around each end, securing them to place with packing tape, the result a make-shift Q-tip the bulbs of which I finagled into the shaft where they could stuff full the confines—if the mop-handle hadn't been collapsible, I'd've had to've split it in two and no doubt would've. I unscrewed a leg from one of the wooden office chairs, used the tape to further affix it as an extender to the gadget so that, for certain, I'd be capable of pushing all the way from the vent in Cabin Eight to the ones in rooms adjacent—a preposterous amount of effort went into the endeavor, trial and error, so on, but I managed to scrub the bugger all the way down to Seven and Nine then, when in said Cabins, prodded it all the way back, for checks and balances, went so far as to disassemble and reassemble the gizmo until I'd checked every cabin I had present access to, on the off chance Rasputin'd taken out more than one room, had a cohort who'd dwelt in another, or else snuck into a vacant cabin to better stash some related paraphernalia ... I'd put nothing past the shifty sot!

By morning, I was admittedly taking the whole business dreadfully personal—a sourness coated my mouth, seemingly all the way into my overwarm belly, as I consumed twice as much gas station breakfast as I already couldn't afford then chain-smoked outside my building in the drizzle, trying to keep my mouth from betraying how many of my calculations were whispered aloud. The author had to've desired the manuscript be found—otherwise, why hide it? Common sense dictated how if it was something to scuttle, he ought to've set it aflame, chucked it down the nearest dumpster, dusted his hands on his thighs, and been done—instead, clear layers of what I'd term *duplicity* made the hiding place all the more fashionably secure ... which meant it'd be less accessible to those not meant to retrieve the contents, by design ... therefore, the word I was looking for wasn't *hidden* ... the package'd been *left* for someone ... and with precise purpose in mind. Nathan Jehovah seemed the obvious answer, except: why hadn't such man ever materialized? Furthermore: if Rasputin's goal was for Jehovah to be custodian of his life's passion, why not secure the materials in a Post Office box, a storage unit, or even a vent shaft someplace more auspicious than *The Calico*—did the fact that he hadn't done suggest Nathan was specifically *not* the intended audience, an envelope marked as pertaining to him left for an as yet unknown entity ... or did it mean Nathan was supposed to *find* the volume, not merely be proffered a prize ...

was there something meaningful in that act of discovery, a treasure hunt without which some affair became defunct of vitality?

I spent increasing amounts of time poking through the writing, would almost go so far as to say *pouring* through, with hope some marginalia might contain a solid hint—nothing in green ink seemed anything but edits, further elaborations on such-or-such finer point about whichever tune, but I took one of the legal pads from work and began transcribing the handwritten content, entering my own trivial scrawls, circling things I'd compile into lists then cross out, all of it utterly meaningless! Even trotted out the playground game of seeing if the first word of first section followed by the second word of second, third word of third, so on so forth, added up to a clear statement, when combined—it'd worked for Ewan McGregor, after all, and that'd been a matter of geopolitical gravity ... but a few different version of this gambit yielded no more than the gobbledygook anyone reasonable would've not wasted time not expecting.

Thought I'd made a breakthrough when it occurred to me how belabored a point had been made about dubbing that *States Songs* album Number One—cross-referenced the names Rasputin Evangeline and Nathan Jehovah with the sixteen states tunes'd been rendered about, special attention paid to Louisiana as, per the notations, that track wasn't included in the official release, only as a single, a fact which, to Rasputin, had indicated how it was a double exception, included in the official album list and dubbed the best of the bunch, to boot, a lengthy, bracketed paragraph proclaiming with flourish how to do otherwise would've been patently absurd ... if there was anything to find, though, I couldn't ferret out what.

Next: inspected the two blank sheets at the end of the volume like I was Prime Time television—held them up to various light sources to investigate whether there were indentations I could scrub to life with the shushing back-and-forth of a Number Two pencil, watermarks, any sign of invisible ink. That thought about made my heart sink to my shoe bottom, as—holy bones!—what if there'd been something important on the packaging the bastard'd been wrapped in, a blacklight waved over it and presto! Wondered where I might find such a device—one of the shops for teenagers in the mall, a forty-five minute's drive from me, or could the odd lights used for aquariums produce the same effect?

In addition to every query I had being moot-and-a-half, it struck me I was barking up the wrong tree, entirely—after almost an hour of earnestly fretting, like a rolled up magazine to the back of the noggin' it struck me how there wasn't gonna be any address, simply because if the package'd been intended for someone specific they wouldn't need to track themselves down, so, for the love of God, why would they need to perform a magic trick or consult a forensic laboratory, and if it'd been left for a stranger, such as myself, what gives with any hokum at all?

Mood sunk until I figured a touch more than a mild drunk was not only in order but well deserved, settled in to watch cassettes of *Diagnosis Murder* I'd recorded almost three decades prior, local commercials and everything, figuring the ingenuity of ol' Doctor Sloan might get me in the inventive frame of mind necessary to win the day—when it didn't and I couldn't even guess the result of an episode I knew I'd seen more than once, on top, I felt stupid the way I had back in grade school, missing something obvious the exercises on some Ditto made me feel a flunk for having to only guess at. 'You're looking for a person ...' I kindly-female-teacher voiced to my room in the scribble scrabble of television flicker '... you're looking for a *writer* ...' nodded, earnest, like at Social Studies '... for a *music* lover ...' nodded more—but nod though I might, no avenue forward presented any more than unstudied Spanish vocabulary ever could've. Snarked dismissive how there was also the matter of 'What're you gonna do if you *find* this author?' Funny such question taking so long to've occurred and how I'd never once considered how they'd likely be annoyed, bark at me that they hadn't taken the trouble to stow their life's work in a motel wall only for some clown-college dropout to trot it back to them, tail wagging— Lord have mercy! In reflection of this, I pouted my lower lip, hangdog, all apologies, earnestly whined 'Aw gee—I know you hid this and all, but maybe if you told me who you wanted to find it I could go give it to 'em ...' only such patent illogic made my fixation creak tighter and tighter '... okay ...' I now paced, swigged, smoked '... okay ...' limply shadowboxed, sat, stood, sniffled '... okay ...' tried to reckon what sorta scenario would *require* hiding a manuscript ' ... you're in a *hurry* ... enough you don't do anything *normal* ... no time to ship it to an old friend, leave it for a mailman marked Hold For Pick Up, so on ... but not so rushed you can't wrap it all up and hide it ...' but that wasn't any scenario, ever, so I clapped at myself, snapped fingers, shushed smoke around, and turned my back as though it'd outwit my doubts '... Lookit: if you had to split because someone was *coming for you* ... and they knew you'd been in a *motel* ... and all the while it was the *manuscript* they wanted ...' but got deflated at so easily subverting my clever little thesis with '... well ... when they didn't find it on you, your motel's the first place they'd go next ...' and *The Calico* wasn't exactly tough to search, even all the way through. Scuffed the carpet, dejected—until another stalwart jab of *Bulleit* found me a foothold! 'Makes sense to assume that if the author'd needed to lickity-split outta town, it'd been on account of he'd wanted to make sure no one'd know he'd ever been in this or that specific motel ...'

Yessir, if it were a film, I could see it all—dude'd checked in under an alias, paid in cash, got wind whichever pursuer had wind of him, hasty escape, kept off the grid awhile, made a point of showing up twenty-thousand leagues from where he'd actually been, at which time he'd started using credit cards, having his picture took on shop cameras, making it seem that's the general location he'd holed up in a long while. 'To what end?' I didn't want to ask and so decided to detour from with a petulant snort of 'They'd have to tell me!' If my cobbled up narrative were even in the ballpark of the truth, it served to reason how whoever the package was intended for had been hipped to it or that the author had reason to believe they'd find it eventually, all on their own—which was so a fair point, I was disgusted with myself for making it, tried to think up something less fundamentally sound, the sensation of lost momentum causing me to sulk into my chair like soiled laundry, distressed by how morbid

I was letting my thoughts dip and that I was growing convinced of some pretty wild leaps, embarrassed to admit my digressions and world-building made more sense to me than any tangible fact at hand ... which was to be expected ... things you care for get harder and harder to let go of ... whether I liked it or not '... so facts be damned ...' I murmured acidic, fully aware who I pictured the seethed words being seethed at.

Tore from my chair with the curt decision to yank open my curio closet, from out of which I took the Jehovah letter, brandishing it around like a cudgel—if there was something, it was gonna be right inside the envelope, so what was I pissing about like some mutt for, running myself in circles without having exhausted the obvious? But holding the flimsy little missive I suddenly felt too pathetic to go through with breaching it, acutely aware of what I'd look like were somebody watching—a joker driven to desperation by his own puddle-brain, a hand-to-mouth dweeb going all to pieces about a puzzle so obviously meaningless it was tantamount to self-committal to demand the goddamned answer key! 'Have some self-respect ...' I demanded '... allow for belief in your own intellect, fer Chrissake!' Annunciating the syllables compact, I told anyone even remotely concerned 'I am putting the letter back,' then stood there resolute a whole minute to prove it—there was no hurry to reach the conclusion of anything ... and not only did I truly not care, I surefire wasn't gonna three-quarters drunk myself out of the pleasure of outsmarting whatever this turned out to be.

[*heard over the radio on w.e.e.i.*]

It was a near thing on the last shift of my workweek which prompted me to make photocopies of the manuscript—or was the appearance of a close call, anyway. I'd stepped back inside from a cigarette, head bipping and bopping with some vague interest in a new line of exploration, then stopped short and felt myself tense in the abrupt way I'd imagine only gunpoint is supposed to result in, heartrate tilting a surprise incline which caused a fritz of lightheadedness—the document was gone. Nothing on the desk where I'd've sworn I'd last seen it except the remnants of a meal I'd cobbled up out of scraps purloined from materials various other staff members kept in the filing cabinet drawers assigned to them as lockers—a slice of wheat bread, untoasted, two miniature *York Peppermint Patties*, plus a pack of Saltine crackers acquired from the shared breakroom, topped off with an unsugared cup of the coffee we supply to guests, purple flavored *Now-and-Later* for dessert, several of which I yo-inked every shift because there was an economy-size sack of 'em I didn't figure anyone'd ever inventory. Lifted the clipboard, the keyboard, patted the various papers affixed to the face of the inside counter, looked on the carpet beneath the desk, the tile by the customer chairs in front, even rolled up the floppy mat there, and shook out every magazine—felt myself become clammy while I literally stood slack jawed, roughing my hair, making pipsqueak coughs of umbrage.

Stepped back outside into a fresh smoke, trying to reckon up from down—scrutinized the sloppy wet pavement, worried I'd absentmindedly brought the writing along last trip, it'd dropped unbeknownst, the poor-quality pages soaked through in an instant, spongy pulp of slaw washed away while I'd inhaled, exhaled, lost in my Lala Land. A false wave of relief coursed me when, like a prayer small enough it might be answered by mistake, I sighed, rolled my eyes, and said 'The car, idiot' with a butted palm to the brow for good luck—and despite I knew right well I'd been reading it just earlier, in the Office, did the entire production of opening the door, padding around, gutting the glovebox, popping the trunk.

Pouted a swig and another ciggie until I needed a piss, was grumbling the choicest fuck-words on file as I shouldered into the washroom like a bruiser—and there it was, lazing on the shelf, across from the toilet! Laughed aloud, memory flooding in of that's right where I'd left it—had even joked about letting something so innocent brush against the three porno mags which'd been present since the middle nineteen-eighties, judging by torn leotards and hair height. Took another swig of *Bulleit* while I flushed in celebration, giddily expounding as though to a Late Show audience after delighting them with a raucous anecdote '… I'd merely been pudding headed, no prank to decipher, at all! But lordy lord, why was I mucking the original of so unique an item around like some jerkwad? Nevermind losing it—how about spilling my coffee or what if a gust of wind got the best of me in a brief moment where my wool-gathering guard was left down!?' Yessir, the make-believe Letterman agreed, sincerely hoped I'd ratcheted things up in the sensibility department to keep everything from ending in tears, called a commercial break but asked if I could stick around.

On the drive home, swung by a strip mall Copy Shop, made three Xeroxes of the entire shebang—cost me a pretty penny on top of an arm and a leg, but once I'd started down the path I'd felt committed, justified the expenditure by promising to make one iteration a surprise gift to Viggo, really tart up the tale surrounding its discovery, paint myself as a Cosmopolitan figure of terrific intrigue. He'd love such a trinket, no matter his opinion of the music at its heart—or it'd wind up lost under the junk on his floor, never to be thought of again … if he still junked his floor … realized I'd no idea what his present lifestyle consisted of … point was: it was a thought, so it counted.

JOHN I'VE BEEN BAD AND THEY'RE COMING AFTER ME / 39

My intention'd been to put the lad's copy in the post, straight away, but glazed on by the place I coulda done so without noticing, didn't feel much like turning around, and it'd be closed by the time I next ventured out—not that there was any particular rush, plus now that I had occasion to meditate on the matter, I doubted the wisdom in mailing any package. No doubt his mother screened the mail, in a general way, and a plump parcel with my return address wasn't about to get the rubber stamp—my better angels whispered how surely she'd not gone so far off the deep end she'd literally deprive the kid a dispatch from his father nor commit a federal offense by opening one in his absence, though his age made the latter somewhat a grey area, I supposed. Regardless: I could roll out a fake name, some in-reference like *Tony Trelos* which'd clue Viggo in how it was from me, thus he should keep cool, not blow the gaff—maybe find a unique box, some old brown paper to wrap it in, a real artifact-looking *objet d'art* ... or better still, could doll it up as though it'd been sent from a scholarship program ... except that might make his mom open it, even more ... 'Well, anyway ... I could do something along those lines ...' I sighed aloud. Verdict was: best bet was to hand it off at the Film Fest, as all the excitement of everything else going down would make it seem more spectacular and tethered to time we'd honestly shared.

Before calling it a day, tossed two of the trio of copies in the cabinet, alongside the original, then during my next *Calico* shift hole-punched the one I'd kept out in order to fasten it into a flippable booklet with some brass colored do-dads plundered from the supply cubby—and now that I could afford to be more cavalier, the bugger became my sidekick, leafed through it on the can, brought it with me out for smokes and when I'd close myself in whichever cabin to take a load off. Started out, I'd turn to this page or that, willy-nilly, but eventually figured why not go through it in chronological order, as made most sense—grinned when I realized I'd behaved in this exact same fashion with regard to reading a mass market paperback *Doctor Who: Fourth Doctor Guidebook* when I'd been a touch younger than Viggo, flitting about in the volume like a flea to begin with, getting strict, waffling back to such behavior even after committing to a front-to-back approach.

When one of the remarks about a song piqued my interest, I'd pull up a website called *WatchYourself* in order to give the tune a listen, as not only was the full audio of pretty much every offering the band'd ever recorded posted, but random folks the world around uploaded all variety of clips concerning the group—talk-show appearances, radio interviews, music videos, low-fi bootlegs of record store appearances. Humorously enough, there existed a plethora of Personal Ranking vids—these ranged from short presentations like *Top Ten TMBG*, *The John's Albums: Best-to-Worst* to what I supposed were more esoteric gags for 'true fans,' such as *Linnell Sings About Car Crashes and Hospital Beds* or *Five Examples of Flans Rocking Harder Than Jack White*.

I'd blithely compare various public rankings to the 'definitive,' utilizing the quick-reference lists at the back of the manuscript, intrigued how, though some videos came near the 'proper order' of a particular album, no presenter ever matched up flush, spoke with the same bombast, or hocked up as robust a flavor of dictatorial authority as Rasputin Evangeline—most stammered through their unrehearsed, to-camera spiels, repeating like nervous ticks how 'Once again, this is only one man's opinion' and every last uploader seemed interested in having 'a discussion in the comments,' ponderous chains where lonesome re-tellings of first listens or first dates at live shows and motely links to fan art were burped up in a treacle of Kumbaya.

I continued to be disenchanted with the music, though confessed a preference for seeing it performed live—dug some of the early Demos, too, though only on account of their grimy aesthetic reminded me of myself, brought on a pleasantly contemplative headspace wherein my mind wandered around postulating how maybe I coulda done something else in life, made an accomplishment in some arena if I'd put elbow grease into my youth ... though admittedly, I'd probably be fond of the early, amateur renderings of any million failed bozos who'd amounted to less than myself, in the long run, forever enchanted by the groove of unwashed wannabes, whatever the media. For a fact, even while poking through *The Giants* oeuvre, I'd come across other bands whose output I preferred by country miles in terms of emotional heft, cleverness, or lo-fi crackle—*The Detroit Cobras, The Sad Little Stars, The Thrills, The Kills, Guided By Voices, Left By Snakes, Hundred-Hundred, Debtor's Island.*

Listened through a song off what Rasputin'd ranked the worst Full Length Studio Album, that solo project from Flansburg called *Monopuff*—Evangeline's noted lament had stuck with me, the anguish over placing the disc with one of his personal faves on it dead last, the cold-comfort of awarding it 'best of that batch' doing little to balm his spiritual bruise. Most I could go was to consider the song spiffy in a glossy-cardboard way, neat like a cereal box sometimes might be, though I shruggingly supposed I considered it my favorite out of what I'd heard of the boys to date, as well—such dubious honor notwithstanding, Rasputin's whooping enthusiasm for it lowered him in my estimation, caused his bulbous manifesto to seem all the more over-the-top, because set in relief of videos of folks, young and old, rating the music in reasonable, unrehearsed, off-hand, and, most importantly, non-dogmatic manners, his Zarathustrian pomposity took on dayroom-in-the-sanitarium shades. *They Might Be Giants* seemed singularly dear to all who'd heard them, but no more than any other band, fisticuffs or territoriality need not apply—normal, reasonable people, after all, either tacitly or explicitly admitted to the subjectiveness of their opinions, and for all the saccharine-sweet hoo-rahing on display there were enough Socratic back-and-forths about contentious points to set things on balance, each and every one handled with prim courtesy.

Yet still ... there was something refreshing in the text I'd unearthed which made me instinctively not want to judge its author too harshly—his screed was a yawp of 'I was here!' exuded the gusto of posterity, and all his zesty hem-hawing and slipshod editing coalesced into my creeping suspicion that other folks ranking the music weren't legitimately *invested* in the concept of doing so, were just doing so kinda to do so ... which made me feel glum for the state of the world ... found myself pacing the parking lot, smoking while speaking my two-cents under my breath '... I suppose what they do is all in service of feeling human, connected, some sorta neo-organic interaction for our increasingly mechanized ethos ... or something ... meek confessions of the desperation inherent in the sprawling technological void ... *Put yourself out there, but always deprecate, never make waves* seems the go-to philosophy of nowadays ... or else make so many waves they boom out gratuitous, beg to be labeled *satire* or *the point to wriggle out of or double down into* ... all our voices have become is the flimsy commerce of a repetitive ghost town ...'

Came across *Monopuff*'s second album, *It's Fun To Steal,* free to listen, in its entirety—a solid half of the material I could do without, didn't even make it all the way through certain tracks, though didn't cut bait before giving each its fair shake, made survey enough to get the gists, by no means pretending the stuff'd take a magical turn for the better after thirty insipid seconds'd snuck by. Only *irredeemable* turkey was an offering called 'Pretty Fly,' which I was so repelled by on every level from sub-atomic to spiritual I had to reference the compendium, chuffed to learn I was 'of the right mind,' the beast having been dubbed Worst on the album, by a length and without quarter—meanwhile, the tune Rasputin'd ranked first was fairly pedestrian, entitled 'Poison Flowers' ... not bad, but smacked more of *The Giants* than the rest of what *Monopuff* had on tap, wouldn't be surprised to hear it on one of the group's joint efforts. My top-spot woulda gone to 'Dashiki Lover,' hands down—even chuckled aloud how Flansburg should be in charge and vowed I'd stump for office with that as my platform, by gum! Guy seemed a total class act under whose stewardship *Monopuff* radiated a structured yet freewheeling cool I could get behind even without being a fan—the collective didn't seem to give a whore's hoot what anyone thought of 'em and, of greater value, didn't care whether or not anyone knew it. For my money, they trumped *They Might Be Giants*, a cinch—meaning I held the group in knee-high esteem, at most. Rasputin obviously felt otherwise, having set a Linnell solo outing tippy-top, his compatriot's venture rock bottom, and in the overview of *It's Fun To Steal*—itself perched at a respectable Nine out the Full-Length Studio series—explored that very point rather pedantically.

Time seemed to be moving with insouciance—at X moment loafed, at others content to crawl, then all at once acted as though it'd realized its sorry lack of professionalism, counted on its fingers approximately how many songs I'd listened to, guesstimated the length of each on average, and decided 'Fine, it's round about this o'clock, have it your own way!' When it wound round to I was ready to pack in for the night and putter about in my typical end-of-shift style, I came under the soggy and smoke-stale sensation of having been awake for a day during which a week had elapsed, the approach of a perpetually drizzle-grey dawn not helping—nor did being startled by the arrival of a guest, especially an ugly young Turk who did that unforgivable thing of shaking out his coat's sodden sleeves *spatter spatter* to the walls at both sides while I awkwardly joked about having forgotten there even were such things as customers.

'During the day, we get very few people, but at night this place is like Mars,' I affably quoted the McGregor version of *Nightwatch*, but quickly found out I was dealing with a thug in no mood for making adult-aged friends.

'How bout you shut the fuck up and do the job they pay you for, or's that illegal? Shit guy, would it be alright if I took a room or do I gotta sponsor the Special Olympics, first?'

Utterly flummoxed, I went through the motions of yeah, sure, of course, fill this out and sign this and it's that much and did he have a preference concerning cabins ...

'The fuck do you mean *cabins*—what're you, Long John fucking Lumberjack?'

Figured he'd meant Paul Bunyan, but knew that didn't warrant verification, so altered the question to 'Do you have a room preference?'

'The fuck're you asking—my *preference*?' he ran a wrist under his nose, revealing knuckles bloodied by fresh tattoos across them.

Explained the term, in context. 'We have twelve rooms, three presently occupied—'

'Give me room fucking *eight*—that okay with you, Professor Potts?'

No idea what to make of that bit of name-calling—a teacher he still nursed a grudge with or a character in the only book anyone'd ever read aloud to him?—I simply meeped and fetched him the key.

He exited with 'Some free advice: you need to watch your dick, guy,' followed by *ringaling* of the door opening, the clatter of it closed—waited to hear a car engine, see headlights, but nope, the guy must've wandered in on foot from someplace ... which made sense, considering his waterlogged state ... thought of the Interstate on-ramp, five or six miles distant ... of signs warning *Hitchhikers May Be Escapees, Show Caution* ... wondered were those only from movies ...

Being accosted so gruffly had my forebrain crawling and it was exactly then, drenched in unease, that I moved to close out the computer tabs I'd opened, and had I not been so jittery, probably never would've glimpsed the thumbnail for a video, off to the side, fifth down the Recommendations the service spit up in a side-bar, ostensibly based on my recent viewing habits—didn't seem connected to *The Giants*, but regardless, the sight of the tiny box froze me, a sensation strange which for being strange turned it stranger still, a distinct-yet-inarticulate feeling I'd fully experienced before I'd for one second considered why there might be a feeling to have and a feeling which, once I'd realized why there might've been one, I began to wonder why I had.

Cued the video up proper, image enlarged, and waited out a touch of buffering for playback—the still was a screen-capture of a local-to-somewhere News report, arial view of a crumby drainage canal beneath an overpass in some rink-a-dink town which'd seen better days, one very like *Laampray*, so much so my first thought was 'I wonder if it is.' Yellow lettering at screen bottom declared *Body Of Dead Man Still Unidentified* and the title given to the vid was '*What's Gonna Happen To Chess Piece Face' Part* ... until I clicked to open the About box and the remainder of the title revealed itself ... *3: They Know But Ain't Tellin*. Blinked for a minute, then read how this was a spot of amateur True Crime reporting by a dude who went by the moniker *HotelDetective1981* ... which clicked my gears turning ... flapped through the manuscript until I landed on the listings for the band's self-titled, debut album—which Evangeline had instructed any reader to NEVER FUCKING CALL THE PINK ALBUM in all capital letters, three times underlined, closed in a many-times-traced-over box, the directive further emphasized by three soaking green exclamation points. TRACK TEN *(She Was A) Hotel Detective*. TRACK FIFTEEN *Chess Piece Face*. Blinked some more, scoffed a swig from my flask, and smacked a palm hard to the desk with a somewhat creeped out 'What in the name of the great good lord!?' then listened to both songs—first was abysmal, an embarrassing stinker on all levels, sounded little more than a buncha grade-school dorks playing dress-up, really convinced they had something out of this world when what it amounted to was the aural approximation of a Mad Libs illustration, all the style of the free comic included with an off-brand toy ... but the second was uncanny in its eeriness ... I agreed wholeheartedly with a phrase in Rasputin's appraisal:

> The soundtrack of a dream you have when you're six years old with a slight fever and keep waking up during hours you'd never been conscious for and need to relearn the air.

This was the music which played over a cut-rate title sequence the 'journalist' had put together for his 'micro-docu-series' and which, after an excruciatingly overlong fade-to-black, clunkily cut to the man himself, facing his monitor camera, the audio glitchy, captured direct from the computer mic, room behind him poorly lit, clapboard—nasal voiced, nebbish, the guy looked like Chef Boyardee pasta which'd been left soaking in the sink overnight, all its orange rinsed off, now surrounding it in an electron-cloud aura, and started yakking away about 'Welcome back, seekers,' thanking his theoretical new followers, providing a convoluted 'story thus far,' editing all off-puttingly out-of-joint, anytime there was a pause even a half-second in duration some program'd automatically spliced out the silence. Noted the video was five months old, had been viewed a whooping twenty-four times, which may or may not've included my own click, liked once, disliked five times, and that public comments weren't enabled—followed a link to the creator's personal blog where 'a few other investigations can be found, for those interested,' the ones going furthest back text-only, white prose on black background with sundry public domain images pasted in for mood, these giving way to Audio Downloads and, eventually, everything from the most recent three years had graduated to 'video reportage.' The *Part Three* I'd stumbled on was the latest morsel on offer and, from what I could tell, the absence of something fresher constituted the longest gap between material since kick-off—reckoned the journo'd closed up shop or else finally caught on to the Law of Diminishing Returns ... or maybe got himself laid, won a sweepstakes ...

Hotel's interest in this particular piece of the macabre had been piqued 'for reasons three-fold,' according to the teaser text accompanying *Part One* of his opus: *First, a genuine murder, smack-dab in my backyard; Second, the victim not native to the area, identity unknown, fingerprints, dental records spitting out goose eggs; Third, the only clue investigators had to go on was a small tattoo on the cadaver's shoulder, an illustration of 'what looked like a man with a chess piece for a face'*—that phrasing a direct quote lifted from a legitimate newspaper article, accompanied by a police rendering of the icon in question, which appeared in the video under the superimposed words 'If anyone has information, please call,' no contact number in evidence. Doodle looked exactly as described: cartoonish little body with what I thought was known as a Rook from the neck up—'Chess Piece Head' might be more accurate, as there were no facial features to speak of, but I got where a superfan'd be coming from, any stretch to work their heroes into whichever available caper. And Hotel was a fan—boy howdy, wasn't he just!—a 'lifelong devotee of John Flansburg and John Linnell,' who were, he explained to 'those woefully underinformed' in a parenthetical included with the text accompaniment to the video, the founding members of *They Might Be Giants,* only referred to in his reportage, verbal or written, by proper names, first and sur, any mention of the band as an entity seeming an unconscious slip of the tongue.

Quite a tedious bloke, Yeoman's work had been done to convince viewers he was an authentic main character in an ongoing, serialized drama—never fear, he'd promptly 'shared what he knew about the connection' alongside his 'own personal theories' with 'those in charge of the investigation' the result, however, turned out to've been 'nothing but a fat disappointment in the form of a condescending thank you followed by the stiff brush-off' as 'the detectives in charge seem pigheadedly unwilling to share and share alike' even though, according to *Part Three,* Hotel felt it outrageous how he'd not been credited for 'giving them their big break' seeing as 'the case must've been closed by now' or else why had 'the hep press seemed to suddenly have lost all interest in it?'

Some quickly looked up articles revealed the crime in question to be grisly stuff: poor sucker had been found dumped after being stabbed umpteen times in all manner of body parts—no defensive wounds, but signs he might've been tortured before getting his throat slit up a treat, after which the carcass'd lain in the spongy underbrush along the drainage canal several days, cloaked with rearranged debris, and had at by wildlife and vermin to such extent a full determination of wounds or time-of-death was nearly impossible, per the *Yapikir County* Coroner.

Next funny thing was: Hotel Detective seemed to've been on the button—a very short time after his *Part Three* had posted, the crime, indeed, seemed to've been solved ... or the body'd been identified, at least, the tattoo what'd finally done the trick. No mention of any connection to *They Might Be Giants,* of course '... but those murky goombahs likely know which palms to grease and who to take for a drive down by the docks to keep their names outta John Law's mouth, *capice*?' I toasted a double tilt, chuckling almost enough it spritzed from my nose.

The murdered remains belonged to a chap called Benjamin Visa—

his ink obtained ages ago, when he'd been yet a teen, positive identification by way of an ex-wife who'd reported him missing, survived by a seventeen-year-old son, unnamed ... an Officer Picador'd asked for the family's privacy to be respected during their trying time ... no comment on motive ...

I stared in a kind of numb daze, watched all three of Hotel Detective's clips, again, re-read the article about the body being identified—satisfied but also far from.

[it's just a query and you mustn't let it in]

Despite a baseline excitement over how each new quirk proved it so, I maintained my aloof skepticism all the way until no one could: this was definitely my guy, Rasputin Evangeline and Benjamin Visa one and the same person, author, corpse—ventured all the way to a public library I'd only learned the town had to sate my curiosity, such satiety only stoking it all the more intensely as I spent the better part of a day sat amongst folks who looked just shy of literate enough to spell it but were doing their remedial best.

From a variety of reputable sources, I pieced together what seemed a rather definitive timeline of Visa's disappearance and death—in pencil in a green spiral notebook, increasingly nervous each time I jotted down a more refined version, explained the chain-of-events to myself, bullet-point by bullet-point, and by closing time had twenty crammed pages, each a new beginning-to-end iteration of the man's final days. Wanted to get rid of them as I went, but never felt certain I had the whole run committed to memory, though also never backtracked to review a previous sequencing once a new one got started—there was simply an unbidden, queasy hesitancy in crumbling, tearing, even scribbling over what I referred to as The Master Copy. In my mind's eye gathered future inquisitors for whom every last spec was to be preserved, as though I'd be called upon to explain the affair in official capacity, the only one who'd be capable—it'd become my pet, that's the simplest way to term it ... wasn't at all sure how that made me feel, but it sure didn't make me feel bad.

In summary, it'd played out as follows: Out of the clear blue sky, one squarely middle-class and buttoned-down day, our Mister Benjamin Visa, age forty-four, same as myself, up and decided to do a cut-and-run on his family—married eighteen years, divorced four, kid in the picture since he'd been twenty-seven. No word of explanation had been proffered to superiors when, middle of a mid-week workday, he'd exited his place of employment, some kinda nondescript firm where he'd held a faux-senior position attained only eight months prior after more than a decade on staff—car left behind in the employee garage, he'd trotted by foot then by city bus the fair distance to a train station whereupon, in cash, he'd procured a cross-country ticket for a berth which'd departed the very same hour of purchase.

I reckoned he'd been ferreting away small amounts of dough over a period of time which'd wound up enough to cover travel, his room and deposit at *The Calico*, plus food enough to survive and whichever method of further transit had wound him up in Hotel Detective's backyard ... though he may've hitchhiked that leg of his journey, there was no way to verify *everything*. My reasoning went: he'd been reported missing the very night he'd ducked out, misadventure or foul play suspected immediately instead of any assumption he'd pulled a runner on familial obligations in order to shack up with some franchise broad he'd cultivated a secret life with or else have a whirlwind with some new lady love—this on the strength of there existing no evidence he'd made withdrawals from any of several bank accounts, some jointly held with the ex-wife, and that his credit cards hadn't been active for the bulk of what time he'd remained unaccounted for.

Regardless, the now-deadbeat-dad had remained aboard the locomotive nowhere near the length of the country, instead debarking in *Laampray,* a mere state or two from his hometown, whereupon he made the short stroll to *The Calico*—several times a night I could hear whistles from the station I'd never laid eyes on, could hear the clatter and dings of the crossing, as well. His room was booked for a total of twelve days with instructions tendered how he wasn't to be disturbed, no ifs ands or buts—not to worry about turning down the sheets, refreshing the towels, if he required any such business he'd ring the desk direct. Check-in had occurred on a night I hadn't been on duty and I figured he'd also scampered on one of the nights I'd been home, which in that particular batch of days made it most likely he'd scuttled on the eighth day of his stay—this based on when I'd first seen the typewriter ... though it might've been the ninth day, I didn't forcefully drill down on the calendar math, as such seemed fairly moot. Fun fact was: he must've let staff know he was scooting when he skedaddled, as my days back at work would've constituted the tenth, eleventh, and twelfth of his brokered stint, at the very least, but the typewriter being available the second shift of my return, which is how I was now certain it'd played out, indicated the room had been vacated and freshened during dayshift. Further review of motel receipts illustrated how, yessir, Cabin Eight had been rented again during what would've yet been the not-quite-fortnight Visa'd booked—ergo: the squirrel hadn't requested to be refunded for the excess days nor had he collected the deposit due him at departure. The reason why any of that was had died with him, I supposed—but I had it all down in graphite, conclusive, between blue lines, wide rule.

 The town of *Yapikir,* where his remains'd been discovered, was a solid hundred miles North of *Laampray*—nothing in any reporting I could find suggested he'd taken out any lodgings there, no publicly divulged information intimated that investigation had turned up anyone he'd stayed with who might've shed light on his state of mind or situation, and it seemed scant few local individuals recollected having encountered him while he drew breath, though enough were anonymously on record it was clear he'd roamed those environs at least three weeks prior to being slain.

 The grimy canal was determined to be a tertiary crime scene—no doubt about that—zero indication where he'd actually been dispatched, murder weapon identified as a 'generic, serrated blade, one which could be found on sale at any grocery store, and several *Dollar Generals'*—a quote I'd excitedly jotted down because it tickled me, quite a bit, the sort of miscellaneous detail I could only speculate a rather bored journalist would insert into a narrative running on fumes.

What was most halting in all I discovered were several oddities I had to take with a grain of salt due to their pedigree: the story had been written up, at length, on a rather salacious stranger-than-fiction website known as *Murther Most Foul*, sort of enterprise I'd obviously never heard of but which smacked of being the sort of kooky destination at least bunches of people more plugged in than me adored, a polished enough veneer, going strong fifteen years, subscription tiers for memberships and all, regularly updated, many times daily, vibrant discussion communities, masthead comprised of mostly former newspaper reporters hailing from hither and yon, clips of various of its authors being featured as talking heads during news segments or documentaries, two or three of them also quasi-accomplished screenwriters, and I'd even seen a made-for-TV flick based on one of the sites most lauded offerings. However, there was a portion of the place dedicated to 'Supernatural Encounters and the Unexplainable' which dealt in subjects up-to-and-including amorous affairs with the ghosts of dead relatives, UFO investigations, and exhaustive featurettes detailing Conspiracies Uncovered, one which seemed to've been novelized in a rather rink-a-dink edition, its central claim being a well-known product recall was attached to an unreported string of mass poisonings orchestrated for corporate blackmail, a narrative eerily reminiscent of an episode of *Law and Order: Criminal Intent*—regardless, the absence of bona fide documentation concerning certain key elements in Benjamin's demise made the joint all but the only game in town for inquiring minds like mine.

According to *Murther*: Visa's killer, a young fellow, no stranger to the law for about as long as he'd been kicking around, had been apprehended—when his photograph first appeared on screen in front of me, I tensed, my breath catching, could've sworn it was the very lout who'd so gruffly barked at me he'd wanted Cabin Eight, the previous week. This jolt was so rattling to my nerves, in fact, I'd had to take a drink to get my head ungummy, verify that guest was no longer on premises, and only after a nicotine calm-down followed by a fourth fifth and sixth long inspection of the creep's photo did I feel definitively secure the jagoff I'd been spooked by was a whole other entity—Visa's murderer sported identifying marks I'd have noted, a dent in his nose-bridge like someone'd cut out a wedge with an apple peeler, large mole over left-side eyebrow I'd at first taken for a smudge on the scanned bit of newspaper the article included. No name was given, but whoever he was presently resided behind maximum security bars for a natural lifespan plus a month or two afterward, which made sense, considering the scale of the crime— what didn't have a scrap of reason behind it, however, was another write-up I found on a different website, called *He Am Dead*, this one specializing in lurid retellings of 'true world macabre occurrences with otherworldly or unexplained elements at their heart.' According to a novella-length piece entitled *The Final Freedom of The Doc Cunningham Killer*, Visa's executioner had, in fact, been in lock-up for three years prior to the murder, set to remain incarcerated another eleven, but had gone inexplicably absent from his cell, one morning and *No available, internal investigation from the prison has turned up any sign of how Doc might have fled, let alone traversed, unmolested, across multiple states in the period he'd remained absentee*—re-apprehended without incident in a bookstore *idly leafing through magazines while waiting for a job application he'd filled out to be reviewed by the manager-on-duty* the villain had confessed to Visa's murder *his handiwork proved forensically, though he'd refused to divulge what had driven him to commit so heinous an act or to provide a single detail concerning where, precisely, the actual butchering had gone down.*

These stories got me thinking about Hotel Detective's lack of follow-up—for Heaven's sake, such a fantastical string of events seemed right up that poor loser's alley! I couldn't rightly believe he'd not posted a Part Four to his precious documentary, especially after so garishly positing himself in the role of 'lone hero plumbing valiantly for the truth'—revisited his site, poured over every last entry, clicked on his profile, and some further clumsy navigations eventually awarded me his proper name, which when added to his hometown earned me the splash of cold water that he'd died in an automobile accident only a week after Part Three had posted. Not a matter of drink driving, what'd been theorized—and by the same Officer Picador who Hotel'd claimed hadn't been cooperative, no less!—was that the fatigue of long work hours at an auto-auction, or else successfully swerving to avoid an animal, had led to his careening, crashing through a barrier, plummeting down a gulch, and ejecting via the windshield to slowly drown in the bed of a muddy pond, limbs too shattered to keep his head above surface.

    Spent awhile trying to pin down tight the exact ordination of matters—seemed to me: Visa left home, checked in at *The Calico*, wrote and secured his manuscript, left after eight days, bummed around in Hotel's neck of the woods awhile, got dead, after which Hotel became interested due to the tattoo, started up his blogging which went on about two months, reached out to the cops shortly after uploading the video I'd first encountered, and a week after that was dead, as well. Nothing I could locate online provided a precise date for when the so-called Doc Cunningham Killer had prestidigitated from his cell—and it dawned on me that no specific penitentiary was mentioned either, nor was it made clear whereabout the bookstore his arrest had taken place in might be found, so it remained vaguely possible that rascal had been apprehended following Hotel's accident. Not being able to tie all three events together seamlessly grated on me—kept hoping to uncover a different report with a discrepancy in chronology which'd show Visa'd left, killer'd escaped, Visa'd died, Hotel'd wrote his piece, had his accident, killer'd been caught, but the matter of Benjamin's murder was well forgotten by now, no contemporary insights given with hindsight's benefit. Not to mention how, so far as I could determine, The Doc Cunningham Killer was no more than a work of hack fiction—other than the one piece on the one site, there existed nothing written about such a fiend, while even make-believe murderers from television programs canceled after single seasons had entire fan-sites maintained for them, replete with fully fleshed out biographies!

So far as it seemed, literally nobody apart from myself had any idea Benjamin Visa'd ever stayed at *The Calico Bash Nitely*—the motel wasn't included in any official news report and neither cops nor private dicks had ever nosed round enough I'd heard tell of it, plus nowhere in my information was there any mention of the alias *Sullivan Shallcross*.

My growing suspicion went that Visa'd taken pains to make certain his presence in Cabin Eight—in *Laampray*, full stop—could never be known—why in Christ's that might've been and for what reason, exactly, he'd stashed the original of his *They Might Be Giants* opus in a wall there, I'd still no idea, but it seemed undeniable he'd gone out of his way to make that document difficult to find, even on top of the precautions taken to see to it his presence in the room would never come out. A man had plum run away from home to write about a band he liked and, afterward, had roamed around, apparently aimless, in a random burg with no more than the money in his pockets, only to be horrifically carved up, no evidence why or where, by a magically escaped convict—all just on wacky coincidence? *Coincidence* was a notion I'd never put much stock in and too many were piling up to justify use of the word with a straight face—the 'coincidences' couldn't all be due to nothing, and if they were due to each other it meant at least some of them were true, yet no cogent theory existed to reconcile any, despite how I cudgeled myself.

'He'd been on the run ... the entire time ... from the moment he fled work ... or even from before that ... concerning what he'd written ... or what he was *about to write* ...' I mumbled it through, deciding there was no other way to explain things ... so was there *honestly* a secret hidden in the manuscript, as I'd suspected previous? It legitimately seemed possible, so despite I'd already exhausted my wits with rudimentary code-breaking, I gave that another fruitless spin—perhaps something to do with the order he'd ranked the albums, a pattern disguised in their dates-of-release or which tunes hit where on the Pop Charts ... did the green text have value ... or did just the words the green text replaced ... was it something as crafty and universally impenetrable as a substitution gimmick, if you didn't know which pages of which novel to use you'd never determine which letter of manuscript corresponded to which letter of index or else how many words to eliminate between others to land on the true message revealed?

It might very well have turned out Benjamin Visa'd died as some workaday Hitchcockian everyman, caught up in an intrigue of great import, in way over his head, navigating a volatile situation which'd necessitated ludicrous methods to vouchsafe a record of whichever mortal discovery he'd blundered his way upon on the off chance his number was punched by those who lurked in the shadows, that he'd fled his family seemingly without word or scruple for their own protection, to ensure they'd not even know there was anything to know in case they were questioned—the fact it'd been the same Officer Picador who'd stated the family'd requested privacy being quoted in conjunction with the investigation of Hotel's accident gave credence to the idea Visa may've felt nobody ought be trusted, from close friends to law enforcement to the President of these here United States!

Yes ... this made sense to me as much as it didn't ... and throw in how with enough spit-balling hypotheses anything'd link to whichever thing else and I was out to sea, oh boy! The arguments against circumstances so labyrinthian outweighed any support, I supposed, and even if an investigative mind megawatts cleverer than mine'd found what Visa'd written, its superficial contents served as yet another layer of electrical tape or Ziploc bag—so what good were they to any unassociated party? There was no clear method by which to connect the writing to the person who'd written it except the one I'd insanely landed on—and who in their right head would've done all I had, by half?

Questions such as these did me no good, of course, as I was either gonna press on or let the mystery go to the grave with me—I mean, I loved *Sherlock Holmes and The Dancing Men* as much as the next guy, in junior high had certainly pretended that was all there was to decoding, but if something covert was concealed in this stack of newsprint, getting to the bottom of it would be next-level wind-talking. First matter of business would be to actually read the entire document, meticulously—doubtful any oddity would leap out, as secret codices with carefully constructed ciphers would be designed to appear anything but conspicuous, not to mention that my being a dilettante so far as a subject matter about which erudition might be required kneecapped me, utterly. My instinct told me the presence of the end-page lists, presented in simple, numbered format, without commentary, held the key, though my instinct easily could've been laziness—I wasn't champing at the bit to plod through three-hundred-plus pages of esoteric propaganda on music I didn't give a fart in a stiff breeze about, after all!

There was also the cassette—buried in the middle of Visa's sore throat monologues might be a distinct and unambiguous statement of instruction, how to unravel the kit-and-caboodle! It was no *guarantee* the poor bastard'd stumbled on anything Top Secret, after all, and with hogwash such as that set aside for a moment, it made sense there might've actually existed another party who'd simply been informed of where to pick up the concealed materials—might've been important for them to wait X amount of time, in the event of something dreadful happening or else to ascertain that no one was surveilling them who might connect their trip to Visa, *Laampray*, *The Calico*, *The Giants*, or whatever else. Or perhaps a message had been dispatched, but the intended recipient never received it—shunted to their Spam folder or they'd suffered some health emergency, in no shape to do diddle about squat, regardless of desire. For that matter: why not suppose that brute who'd gotten me so shook up had been emissary to the party informed—or had clobbered the rightful heir then been sent to retrieve everything on behalf of whoever it was whatever it was was hidden from!

By the time a week of this three-ring circus had rattled about my every waking moment, I had some rather stern words with myself about how the last thing I suddenly was gonna be was Bulldog Drummond or the Inch-High Private Eye—plus, what did any of this rot have to do with me, was it seriously interconnected, or was I taking wild liberties, filling in blanks, dot-to-dotting dots not a jot to do the one with the other? Other than something marginally interesting to think about, what good would poking away do me—I couldn't even excuse it by saying it'd make a crackerjack story to tell on account of who the Hell did I have to tell stories to!? For that matter, I became antsy when it occurred to me I'd been of a mind to share the intrigue with Viggo—for sure, we could bond over it, but I couldn't shake it being bad juju to broach, wished I'd never asked him had he heard of *They Might Be Giants*, even, wished I hadn't bought *Flood*, *Apollo 18*, the VHS of music vids off Dougie! Felt I oughta get rid of such falderal ... but talked myself down ... if only for even more paranoid reasons ... because wouldn't it be weird if someone came asking me about such innocuous items and I suddenly didn't have possession of them anymore, no logical explanation how come? If such person knew about the manuscript plus knew I'd bought some music I'd tossed overboard, they'd put one to one and two would be all there was to it ... not that anyone *would* come looking for me ... it was me looking for people nothing to do with me which had me in mind doing that was something people did when people typically did anything else, instead!

It'd be another kettle of fish had Visa's killer never been apprehended—some demented rascal still at large with me holding the hot potato of a dead man's secondhand typewriter might raise eyebrows, under the wrong circumstances ... I'd wiped it clear of fingerprints, disposed of the original wrapping the manuscript had come in, made certain no 'physical evidence' 'connected me' to 'anything' ... but same time: 'So what if it did?' ... typewriter had been left behind at *The Calico* ... I'd waited six months before being allowed to have it ... plenty of other people had touched the contraption ...

Truth was there existed no puzzle to solve and zero Third Act twists to bulwark myself against—which left me with mere, banal responsibility. Benjamin's manuscript belonged to his family—people who'd literally no inkling why the man had so curtly vanished. His death was a macabre, inexplicable occurrence—even if it wasn't to do with why he'd left home, it remained undeniable the family had the right to know more about his final days on Earth than I did! Simply being cognizant which town he'd cockroached off to and what he'd busied himself with while dwelling there might provide a peace of mind I'd no call to impinge on—might, in the context of their lives, mean everything while, in the context of mine, meant so many things it summed out to none.

Trouble was, I didn't want to part with my find, more than ever—certainly could invent noirish rationale suggesting it might be savvier not to hand over anything original on account of how Benjamin's leaving home might indicate the ex-wife, or someone else near to the fam, was intimately connected with his homicide, therefore the manuscript and cassette being tendered to any of them'd ruin the chance for 'justice from beyond the grave' ... but what tangled me up was far more basic and self-centered than that: I'd become invested, done all sorts of legwork, was the only person who knew what I knew, and thus figured I was owed at least a keepsake! What difference could it make if I held on to the original, when all was said and done, especially when I'd give at least one of the copies to the family, even both, and the cassette could be dubbed without any bother—no one had any way of knowing what I'd found, exactly, nor did I much reckon I'd be asked. The idea more and more got hold of me to play it safe instead of sorry—imagination or not, I was seeing things, unexpected visitors, uninvited guests, so forking over what I'd claim was all I'd ever had, and which no one would have cause to doubt, killed all birds: family legitimately got information plus artifact of what Benjamin'd been up to, and if there was something murky yet requiring knowledge of where the original'd gone, I'd be removed from suspicion, any interested party left to figure Benjamin'd lugged it with him to *Yapikir* or whatever thing else.

Decided to stash the genuine materials in my letter slot at the Post Office, as there was nothing more secure than a federally protected institution—it felt the most grown-up decision I'd made in a very long time.

[*flow from your crocodile eyes*]

I firmed up my resolve to deliver duplicate materials in person—no compelling reason to go that route, as even my paranoia didn't support it as the more cautious method, but since the whole purpose of the excursion was to explain where and how the stuff'd been discovered it seemed the most sincere approach. Even still, I wasn't sure how fully forthcoming I oughta be—no point doing it at all if I didn't name the town, certainly, but perhaps it'd be most judicious to claim I'd discovered the manuscript underneath a dumpster, behind the lighting fixture of an eatery restroom, or whichever curious place else. Couldn't go too far with false information, however, as were I to purport I'd merely been passing through *Laampray* or if I left a wrong name and some dummy contact with the family alongside an altogether bogus narrative concerning where the writing'd been lit upon, things could wind up looking grim for me—supposing I did so, then some inquisitive soul took it upon themselves to give a detailed peek into the affair and suddenly I'm there in town, working at *The Calico*? Everything I'd laid out would take the tinge of misdirecting cartwheels—no no it wouldn't jibe, would prompt further inquiries of precisely the variety which might crop up were I to've sent a package anonymous from a Post Office in another town. As it stood, not only was I being responsible, I'd be painted in a polite, innocent light—near to how I'd found the materials and close enough to when was all anyone could ask for. As to how I'd figured out who to return the paraphernalia to, a couple of doctored in details would do the trick—story'd go something along the lines of there'd been a label on the cassette, Benjamin's proper name right there in black-and-white, such object in evidence, and also went right ahead with typing BENJAMIN VISA onto a label I affixed to a manilla envelope, three green rubber bands tight around, just like the actual had sported. Only thing I held back bringing along was the Nathan Jehovah letter—not for any special reason, just on account of I'd honestly forgotten about the bugger having been slipped between the original manuscript's pages before locking the items up. If push came to shove, I'd hedge whichever conversation a bit, present myself as tacit by nature, apologize for how I didn't have real answers—the more my being there came across as a spur of the moment, conventional desire to explain what I knew, the more I'd be able to and then never have to, again.

It was a substantial trek from *Laampray* to Benjamin's family—left during my next stint off work and travel took the better part of a day due to road construction followed by a big rig being stalled across a two-lane road in the middle of nowhere, hills on both sides so that no car could slip around, either direction. Gave me a bunch of time to listen to the cassette.

> '… this isn't a game of pat-a-cake. It's exacting. For example? The Dial-a-Song stuff from the early days? Probably a thousand of those! They'd garble the entire enterprise. On the other hand: the Demo versions of so many things are without doubt monumental. Deserving of consideration. Gems, in fact. Sublime. But pitting Studio stuff against Demos, exquisite as said Demos may be? It's a bridge too far. De facto crackpotism. Anathema to our purpose …'

It was all a lot of freewheeling yammer, a meander of notes made in between sessions of composition, was my guess—once I'd let the tape cycled through twice, I felt secure there was no cipher to uncover, simply let the thing play, tuning it out mostly, though I did become oddly attentive the more loops it wound round, certain phrases stuck out and the way Benjamin spoke was kinda fun, like when an actor gives a line and you find yourself imitating it without explanation all during your daily life.

'… even the most impactful Demo remains yet a germ. Per the artist. A sketch. An idea. For my money, the scratchy ol' cassette tape iteration of *Birdhouse In Your Soul* is preferable to the official rendering. I adore both, of course, and well apprehend it's one of the band's most beloved offerings, as known from the album. Throngs would flat out name it the *Giants'* masterpiece. Nope. Sorry. Not only not their best track, full stop, but that Demo's three trillion tons better than the Studio release. Lyrically, there's no comparison. Not to mention the hollow hush of its sound. I'm even more stark raving passionate when it comes to *Rocket Ship* versus *Spiraling Shape*, *Snapping Turtles* versus *Bangs* …'

There was something tantalizing to it all, a quality which made me almost wish I had a horse in the race, was a fan with a counter-opinion, an antagonist—that I had any idea at all what this looney-toon was on about or why the fervor on display existed!

'… however: to judge the one against the other isn't merely suborning blasphemy, it simply doesn't cut muster. Demo. Studio. The artists never released those Demo tunes in what any consensus would call a proper way. Not any moreso than how now-and-again a writer shows around their journal, an early draft, gabs about an idea they haven't worked out an honest jot of. Likewise with film. Raw footage, ambient audio is terrific. But only the final edit can be loved or hated. See—that's the heart of it, the clear difference. You can love a rough take, might lust after an early draft—can you hate it, though? Impossible. Ignorant. Of Art. Of everything.'

Arrived in the town of *Sarnath* late, stayed the night at a motel far classier than *The Calico*, which made me chuckle considering it was as dirt cheap a dive as they come—obviously shunned by the locals, chain hotels across the boulevard gulping any and all tourist or conventioneer trade, parking lots jammed to bursting. Planned to visit the family late morning, early afternoon—would remain in town overnight, too, check out the subsequent day, waste awhile taking in a movie, before the drive home. 'Don't want to disrupt my typical sleep patterns' is how I put it to myself to sound medical, curbing the guilt of how wasteful I felt I was being with my limited finances.

When I first made approach to the address I'd verified, I trilled with anxiety, drove a few passes up and down the quaint residential block, hands sweating into the wheel through the pencil scribbled directions from a website I'd jotted on torn loose-leaf before leaving work—everything I was doing suddenly felt a very preposterous, monumentally wrong-headed venture. How could this whole song and dance be anything but incredibly awkward ... though I might be able to use discomfort to my advantage, in and out in a blink, maybe all business conducted on the doorstep ... option remained available to leave the boodle in the mailbox, without explanation ... or I could easily abort, temporarily, find a library, type something up to include ... what was I expecting, a heart-to-heart, rent garments, weeping, invited for tea, 'Here's a scrapbook of our happy days with Ben, may the Lord bless and keep you for giving us closure, do stay in touch'?

Took a bracing swig of *Bulleit*, burnt a cigarette to cover that, dinner mint which'd been rattling in the cup holder to thin the both out, and was already opening the screen door to knock when I realized I'd left the goddamned envelope containing everything on the driver's seat!

A woman opened up, slim as though shoulderless, clothed like a springtime coatrack, hair a boyish cut which enunciated her femininity to the point of a scold—eyes indicated an instant disliking to me, similar to what I witnessed in most interactions with shop clerks and waitstaff, but her wanting to know if she could help me was expressed placidly enough.

As wilting and foppish as I could manage, wishing I'd combed my hair at least, I introduced myself in the form of an apology—she didn't know me and I was quite sorry for showing up, in the flesh and so importunately, but assured her I'd done so because it felt less intrusive, odd as it may sound to say, and that I required only a moment of her time, had nothing to sell, just a little bit of information concerning her husband to impart.

'My husband?' The question sounded different than it should've.

'Benjamin.'

'You knew *Benjamin,*' she nodded in a way that betrayed something I'd have termed sarcasm but been unsure of myself for doing, strange emphasis to it all around, a frame of reference foreign to me but one which I intuited more than justified the tone.

'No, I hadn't known him ...' I apologized again, took a long breath '... maybe I ought just to've sent a letter.'

'It's alright.' Her face softened and she motioned me to please step inside, begging my pardon but I'd have to excuse her a moment as she'd been about to place a telephone call which couldn't be put off, would keep her only a moment.

I took a seat in a living room which intimidated me horribly despite it'd be called just-shy-of-well-appointed by someone not as lowly, then stood and did the corny thing of ambling around slow, hands clasped gently behind me, idly examining the décor and all—it felt like a cartoon or else I did while in it. The modest row house was a mansion, so far as I was concerned, and there was a smack of phoniness to the personal value exuding from the furnishings, the wall color, the framed pictures, which books remained laid out and which were shelved—that or a classiness beyond my reach or comprehension. I was perked up by a series of posters, one large, the others flier sized, all advertising a band called *Benny and the Roids*—not only did I recall the grainy old educational film it'd taken its moniker from, but the album the promotional materials proclaimed themselves in support of was titled *Zorak Is Many Things*, a line of dialogue I'd often quoted to Viggo and even more often muttered to myself in non-sequitur conversations, using the evil mantis's voice every time. The larger poster, which proudly declared *Tonite At The Foghorn!* listed the band members by name, their visages presented in mock-up of mugshots—lead Singer was *Terrance Visa* and smart money said that was the son, so there was some bonus information I'd had no ready strategy to work out of the wife except some ham-fisted 'The manuscript was addressed to his child *Anthony* ...' a slip she'd hopefully've corrected and which I could've bashfully followed up with an affable '... oh gosh—yes, *Terrance*, sorry—*my* kid is Anthony, just one of those blips!' None of the materials I was presenting would bear out such claim, of course ... which I realized in conjunction with an increasing comprehension of how grab-ass I was at this sort of subterfuge.

I was examining a photo of Benjamin's widow, posed very lovey-dovey with a man, when she entered, cup of coffee in hand—she'd left it black, but could go for milk or sugar. 'Black's fine—that's what coffee's meant to be, hot water poured through dirt shouldn't put on airs, eh?' I toasted, grinned, sipped, lifting the picture like I was gonna offer remark about how happy she and Benjamin had seemed when she pre-empted this by telling me 'That's my husband, Reggie,' adding how he was presently at work—I nodded, happy to've been spared an unforced *faux-pas*, and used the moment as natural segue into reiterating that I'd never met Benjamin and promising I'd certainly not meant to come off as snooping around. When motioned to the sofa, I sat, sipped my coffee twice, set it on the pig-shaped coaster done up like unrefined wood, though clearly composed of a kind of plasticine, then graciously thanked her for allowing me an audience—her warmth was somewhat unexpected considering the impression I'd gotten at the front door, made me feel unfooted about broaching anything macabre ... what the bloody Christ was I playing at, sitting in the home of a complete stranger's widow, however remarried she might be, about to lay out for her how I'd chanced upon her croaked former-hubby's freakazoid fanzine stashed in a motel wall ... plus, I still wasn't for sure I was gonna tell her that much, far more inclined to go with some theater of the pretend, though nervous how in the clutch I'd learn any line I'd rehearsed was conspicuously absent from my repertoire.

Smalltalk shrinking fast, before I knew it, and unable to think of a seamless preamble, I blathered her the following: 'I know how hinky this is gonna sound—forgive me in advance if it comes off insensitive or spills out all a jumble, I'm hopelessly pedantic and've never engaged in this kind of thing before. I work at a motel in a town called *Laampray*—real pimple of a place, hundreds of miles away, like what dirt would call dirt shaped into claptrap houses and a corner store where even the shelves expired last week, nevermind the stuff on 'em, you know? Sometimes guests leave stuff behind in their rooms and I have a kinda hobby of collecting it whenever something seems noteworthy—we hold onto it a long while, first, in case an owner comes back, but then it's up for grabs, like how Pawn Shops operate, only no money changes hands. Quite awhile back, I was finally able to claim this old electric typewriter no one'd come round for, and with it was an unmarked envelope which, when I opened it up, had a photocopy of a manuscript written by your husband Benjamin inside—I brought it along but, sorry, left it out in the car—and I just kinda gave it a cursory peek then set it aside awhile, didn't think a second thought, time marched on. Quite recently, I was changing apartments, packing up, getting rid of junk, and so happened to give that document another gander—decided I'd check out the author, see was it ever published, heck, maybe wondered did I have a valuable collectible on my hands, a lucky commodity, I dunno. Searching up the name, I learned about your loss—I'm sincerely sorry, by the way—and was kinda knocked out numb by, you know, the circumstances ... of your husband's ... *decamping* ... and it struck me a little bit weird how, since he'd been missing for awhile before they ... discovered what'd happened ... how no cops or anyone had ever stopped by my motel. Not in a weird way—though I know it sounds weirder, prefacing it like that—but the place I work is more or less a fleabag's snot-rag and a lotta times, well, the guests who stay there want it like no one'd ever know they had—which sounds so much worse than I mean, I'm not suggesting we trade in hourly rates or subsidize ourselves with prozzies, nothing like that! It's mostly truckers playing funny with their records to get comped or just sometimes its pretty clear someone isn't choosing us for a standard vacation when there's literally a *Days Inn* and a *Sleep Inn* and even an *Extended Stay* two miles up the way, into town proper ...'

I watched myself losing my thread and the fact I was making things up as I went was either alarmingly obvious or coming off as a purposeful stalling technique—felt certain I'd begin erupting flop-sweat any second. But the woman simply listened cordially, entirely nonplussed, as though deeply appreciative of all I was relating her yet betraying no hint of curiosity about what I might be driving at—figured maybe none of what I was explaining was news to her and told her as much, apologized, again, then found myself unable to keep from prattling out further improvs which, though they felt clever in the moment, I'd no doubt cringe over as soon as I could scream and bang my palms into my fuckwit steering panel. Unprompted, went on quite at length how, alongside my desire to return the manuscript to the departed's family, I hadn't been able to glean whether the case of her husband's death had ever been officially resolved and, therefore, figured an off chance existed that his whereabouts during the week or so he'd holed up in *Laampray* might mean something to someone, be a missing link, allow her some closure … felt I was flicking little telltale grins throughout this, as though Tourettic in my left cheek, despite it wasn't a godawful adlib, all things considered, and did accomplish a showcase of my clean lack of any in-depth knowledge or agenda.

She smiled sweetly as a gentle knock sounded on the front door, stood, motioned how I ought please remain seated, and said 'Benjamin is my *ex-husband,*' before turning the corner to see about who it was calling.

I sipped my coffee, eyes narrowed, feeling chastised—more than chastised, in fact, frankly took a fair bit of umbrage with her tone … reminded me exactly of how my own ex would say the same thing about me to whoever wasn't even asking, plus, it was a rather discordant prang, utterly out of harmony with her every gesture else, and struck me as very undeserved. I was in the furrow-browed midst of some quick calculations concerning which remark of mine had soured the air, when in stepped a uniformed police officer, the woman drifting just behind—he was postured almost like having a hand rested on his sidearm, except both hands were nowhere near to that, asked me my name like he didn't already know it from having been told, one minute prior, and a quick two-plus-two told me four was the phone call she'd made when I'd first arrived and how, from that point to this, she'd been nothing but playing nice out of fear of direct confrontation, awaiting her back-up. Cop asked me what business, precisely, I had with Mrs. Strauss and I blinked once before comprehending *Strauss* was the woman's new husband's surname, or else the return to her maiden, then stammered how I'd not meant any offense, had offered to leave, straight away, and would certainly do so, there and then, but had been invited inside—correctly, he pointed out that I'd not answered his question, moving a step forward, no substantive change to his posture but an unmistakable alteration to his presence indicating I'd gotten two clicks of the dial nearer to him acting on me physically or drawing the gun.

'As I'd told Mrs. Strauss …' I began, hands up, peaceable, easing myself to my feet '… I work at a motel and found something that'd belonged to her late husband, came by to deliver it and, yes, to make certain his whereabouts had been known—because he'd been registered under an alias during the period of time he'd gone missing and I'd no way of knowing whether such information'd be an aid to the case.'

In that moment, I honestly believed this was just what'd happened and why I was there, unconsciously made what I knew'd come off a flippant gesture, sharp shrug, turning my palms up and leaving them in the air between us, tight as a jab—patronizing, borderline angry, the officer told me that while my civic concern was certainly appreciated, that case was closed, so unlicensed, amateur intrusions such as mine carried no currency. Nodded my understanding and promised I'd go about minding my own business, unless I was somehow being charged with something, then stammered once more how Mrs. Strauss, herself, had welcomed me inside—meanwhile the woman had touched the officer's shoulder, almost maternal, almost lover-like, and, to my surprise, spoke in my defense.

'He's perfectly correct. His intentions were related explicitly at the door. Didn't barge his way in under a false pretense. Behaved like a perfect gentleman.'

This affidavit seemed to both ease and disgruntle the officer, who straightened his posture, took a grudging step back, and clasped his hands lightly behind him, eyes remaining trained professionally on me, unblinking, while she cleared her throat, made theatrical fold of her hands in genial place of the slap to my face which'd been simmering since I'd arrived, and told me in lullaby tones: 'I want you to listen, Mister Limoncello—in witness of Officer Picador and in terms entirely unambiguous, I hereby inform you that I've no interest in further communication with you, nor will I tolerate any association with what you, or any other ghoul, thinks about or has to say concerning my late ex-husband or this stupid band he'd glommed on to. I respect that you will take these words to heart in the spirit they are offered and that, if you are in touch with any of Benjamin's former *compatriots*, will explicitly let them know they are—they *remain*—unwelcome in this household or anywhere near my family.'

I felt it important to get across a reminder that I didn't know her ex-husband or have a soul in common with the man, but, at a loss how to accomplish such task without incident, did nothing but noisily part my dried lips—by the time I'd loosened my tongue enough to speak even 'Yes, of course' the officer had given me a paly slap to the bicep and instructed me to follow him off the premises. We proceeded in silence all down the driveway, my disquiet at his keeping pace tying queasy knots up my throat—he allowed me to get a little lead on him, but as soon as I was to my car, called out I was to hold my horses, closed the distance between us, leaned against my driver's side back door, arms folded, and spit a good distance off to one side.

'Here's what you need to understand, on a fundamental level, so you'd better listen up, I'm only saying it once and out of the courtesy my present-moment on-duty status requires of me: Mrs. Strauss is off limits and has been through more than enough without this bullshit mumbo jumbo or whatever you all want to call it.'

I swallowed instead of wondering why he'd stated the matter in so plural a way as he pressed on with how he didn't care about 'crimes being of public record' nor did he give a good goddamn about 'journalistic rights' as, frankly, he didn't much reckon 'duck-fucking basement-soup bloggers getting hard-ons about their half-dozen followers' ought be counted amongst the members of the Fourth Estate.

I nodded, rabbit quick, more because I felt his remarks clarified the oddity of being lumped in with whichever accosting persons unknown than because I followed why I was getting a lecture.

'I'm giving you the benefit of the doubt how snooping to do a little write-up was all you were up to, back there.'

He let this statement hang for me to pick up on the implication that he in no way believed whatever line I'd laid on the widow had been anything but a put-on to get my foot in the door—which was fair, seeing as she'd no doubt briefed him with summary before he'd entered the living room and I didn't have any document on me, nor was I about to make a show of retrieving it from the car like a smarty-pants, though there it was, plain to see, passenger seat under a bag of gummy *Smurfs*.

Voice hushed, but more frightening for it, he stepped in closer, smiled, and, somehow purring a hiss, explained that if I was '... the kind of someone Mrs. Strauss has every right to take you for ... well, let me just say that if you and I ever have occasion to interact again that's gonna be a dead horse of a different color than today, *farshtey*?'

Yes, sir, I grokked him, hadn't meant a peep of offense, wasn't a blogger, didn't even own a computer—all this'd been was I had a few days off work, thought I'd do my good deed. 'I take it I'm free to fuck off?'

'Identification,' he beckoned with a hand gesture and a roll of his eyes like I was being an idiot for thinking there weren't some formalities to tend to.

Fished my shabby excuse for a wallet out, fumbled my driver's license over to him.

'This your right address?' he raised an eyebrow.

Blinked, shook my head, mumbled something about sorry, then thankfully found my change-of-address card, obtained almost a year ago, this earning another look of suspicion.

'You live in *Laampray*?'

'Yep.'

'Say you work *where*?'

Told him about *The Calico*, all of it written down, pad closed with a slap, and as he tucked it to his breast pocket, he like an old buddy told me 'Lookit—dead man, he's nothing to do with her. Ex-husband even back then, get it?'

Told him I certainly did.

'You struck me as someone who would,' was his curtain line, glowered in unison with his waving me toward my departure.

[*fills my johnny cup with gloom*]

The *Foghorn* was a pub sat behind another pub, a half-muttered afterthought squeezed into the blunted curve-end of a cul-du-sac at the mouth of which stood the first establishment's dumpsters and three newspaper machines with their fronts busted in—one brown lightbulb above what turned out to be a disused Vend-O-Matic was the only illumination vaguely proving a door to the joint existed, a pack of off-brand *Fig Newtons* inside, three rungs back, accompanied by a baggie of *Grandma's* peanut-butter cookies left to the weeds for lord knew how long. In the runny nose drizzle and dark, I was able to make out that the brown-brick facade was plastered in photocopies of *Benny and the Roids* gig posters, various colors, several variants, all Sharpie and Bic pen illustrations clearly traced over multiple times by uncertain hand. Entrance opened directly into a coatroom, cigarette machine and tabletop *Arkanoid* console both out-of-order, a beaded curtain missing enough strands that an empty booth covered high with emptied cardboard boxes stood visible, chatter of half-dozen or so patrons and a song I'd no idea what on the jukebox providing appropriate soundtrack—I kept my coat, unbuttoning it as I approached the only employee on duty, taking pains not to seem a tourist, air to my slouch of 'Yep, I'm here on purpose' so the less attention paid me the better.

I'd phoned ahead with nothing more than a loose hope some roundabout chitchat might land me on an excuse to be informed of a method by which I could get in touch with Terrance, chuffed to discover his band was doing a set that very night—as a suspiciously underpriced double of *Bulleit* put me at ease, I watched the trio of musicians fiddle with amplifiers and tap mics which it seemed weren't plugged in yet or were but not to electricity. Girl tending bar told me, yes, she was who I'd spoken to earlier, hipped me she'd hipped Terrance I was coming—explained that was him, there, busy setting up with the rest, without bothering to single out which him he was, precisely, then had to answer the house phone so didn't register me giving her a thumbs-up of appreciation ... which I was glad for ... felt like a codger and more than a little bit the sorta perv people read warnings about.

Soon had to take a leak and was surprised at the spaciousness of the Men's Room as well as its number of lightbulbs, not to mention how all of 'em were red, two rows and a long, brighter-red-but-not-pink neon stripe circling the rectangular space—also didn't quite understand why the two urinals had mirrors mounted to the walls above 'em, in which I could see clean to the tall mirrors at the sinks, the one I stared at myself in while voiding accented in various graffito, green marker like the math geniuses use except this particular Will Hunting seemed more interested in proclaiming *Timothy Dalton can fuck off,* in three-dimensional block-letters casting three-dimensional block-letter shadows, than linear algebra or graph theory. I'd squinted hard upon approach to be certain I wasn't fooling myself about what was written, figured it probably pertained to something too-cool-for-me like a band name or album title, and soon the words blurred in hip cinematic focus-change as I trained a gaze intently on the fellow taking his time with soaping hands and rinsing, making a real surgeon of himself, mitts held aloft, waggle waggle, to air dry before finally tugging some red paper towels I figured were really rough brown from the mounted dispenser, one set used, crumpled, tossed down the hole in the counter, another set, another—he wore a three-quarter length trench which looked fashionably textured, houndstooth perhaps, as well as fitted trousers, polka dotted, cuffs tucked into Chelsea boots with buttons up one side instead of a zipper. Could've sworn it was the thug from *The Calico,* but at the same time couldn't think why it was I'd swear anything of the sort—did this suave sunuvagun, combing his hair slick into pomaded rows, and the blaggart who I still felt assaulted by look remotely the same? Couldn't honestly say for sure ... but when this dude was still around, sat to a booth with two girls, one decked out in goth apparel, the other dressed like she'd just gotten off the bus from eleventh grade, it eased my mind—not the guy, no cut on the nose ... except I caught myself ... waitaminute ... and realized, no, that was a picture of The Doc Cunningham Killer I was thinking of. Did this one have tats on his knuckles, would've been the better question—tried to keep from being too obvious in looking over as though only around, got the feeling he'd caught me inspecting him in the John and had already clocked my attempted sly glances from the bar perch, uncomfortable how it was probably me he was whispering about to the girls to produce the giggles I couldn't hear but saw the wavelength of in ripples of powdered white cleavage.

The photos on that poster at Mrs. Strauss' place weren't of any of the three fellas on hand, so traded glances a few tentative times with a scrawny lad who I'd assumed was Terrance Visa, but Terrance turned out to be the portlier chap that the one I'd been eyeballing soon tapped on the shoulder, thumbing my way, Terrance-proper briefly grinning, welcoming wide, with a hand gesture of give him a couple of minutes, yet—my mind blanked for a moment as to whether I knew what his father had looked like, lack of recall leading to recalling I didn't, which felt peculiar enough it called for another drink ... I knew the man's Rook tattoo, that was it ... but such seemed distinctly incorrect ... there was a picture in my head of the guy, several, animated ones, the Technicolor film grain of his Rotoscoped body at the crime scene and in various places before and after, all from umpteen camera angles. Took the double shot all in my mouth, held it, let it warm to velvet, swallowed slow and measured, told myself I needed to stop spending long hours in the kingdom of imagination, then reminded myself, no, I didn't, quite frankly—this forthcoming encounter with Terrance marked an end to my association with anything real, so far as this caper, thus I might as well pen a fan-fiction of all I thought'd gone down, screenplay on spec, load the cast heavy with fan-favorite character actors, Stephen McHattie,

Clu Gulagher, Brad Dourif, Bruce Greenwood, Jack Klugman. Chuckled at my fatuous head—wanted to ask the woman serving me drinks as though I wasn't quite there 'Where in Hell am I and why the devil is that, again?' Like on cue, she turned to approach—closer inspection got me thinking this dive was where she'd wound up the morning it'd finally dawned on her people hadn't been foolin' about amateur porn getting you nowhere fast—and I re-introduced myself, this time with a rakish handshake on offer, which she teeny-bopped up and down on her heels in acceptance of, wondering was I a fan of *The Roids* and how had I heard of them, which cassettes of theirs did I own copies of, 'cause maybe we could trade. I took the honest tack with her of admitting I was new to the music, except peppered in the harmless deception they'd been recommended by a pal I'd been supposed to meet, but he'd canceled last minute so I'd popped in alone—a statement which I could tell simultaneously puzzled and pleased her. Asked was she a big fan and learned all about her being into them since high school, apparently, which, less apparently, had only ended for her three years ago despite every line in her face suggesting she'd already seen the best parts of her middle thirties shrink in the rearview—followed her finger as it pointed to the empty drum set while she explained like a peacock how she'd lent it to them, a kind gesture which'd really turned her life around, it seemed, a factoid I managed a 'Fair enough' to, raising a little toast, noticing she'd already set me down another double.

Blink and Terrance was patting my back, balancing plop on the stool beside me, relating effusively how thankful he was I'd come by, his being seventeen every bit as apparent as my forty-four, felt miles out of place, the hip teacher who'd agreed to come see a movie despite it probably painted them wrong—I was an adult and this kid was a kid, anyway, the way he looked at me was as though I honestly not only had something for him but that I would've had something, generally, even if not for finding a package in a motel's ventilation shaft.

Took a moment, right off the bat, to clarify, without ambiguity, that I hadn't known his father, in any capacity, then tested the waters a bit to sound out whether this little adventure was gonna wind me up with a boot in the groin—narrated how I'd dropped in to see his mother, a revelation to which he immediately scoffed, told me I shouldn't have bothered, hurling some epithet I'd never heard before the woman's way, then dove straight into wanting to know all about whatever I'd mentioned to the bargirl about his dad.

'Do you know a band called *They Might Be Giants*?' I decided to begin, his palm immediately slapping the counter while his voice produced a cracked yawp, after which he immediately quieted down, leaned my way, and whispered with almost flirtatiously conspiratorial throatiness 'Holy fuck, brother, is this about *that*?' Seeing no harm, I admitted my ignorance so far as what 'that' was, but told him 'I think so, at least a little bit, yeah.'

Seems 'that' meant a sudden bent into leftfield his old man had taken shortly before disappearing—I was to understand how he'd known his pop to be a fan of *The Giants* ever since he possessed memory of, the music often soundtrack for driving to school and doctors' offices ... but this 'thing toward the end' was different. 'He went to a concert of theirs, like he used to but hadn't done since forever, and when he got back it was *bang!* all he'd wanted to do was yap about the group, tracked down physical copies of literally every album, single, rarity, and burned discs of as much obscure bootleg stuff from the early days as he could find, insisted I listen to every damned crumb of it ... though I never honestly did, except for a little.' He shrugged how the idea, so far as he could tell, had been to belatedly bond over a mutual enjoyment. 'It was kinda as though he wanted to provide us a safe, sturdy scaffolding to build on, we could chat all nonchalant without having to dredge the past, I think, no need to interview each other about current events or whatever, a downhome parental ploy to keep the avenues of communication open in case I wanted to pivot to something pressing on my mind.'

Kid abruptly pointed at my drink—magically refilled—with a timid look of would-I-mind, downing it before I'd properly worked out whether my obligation was to give permission or deny it, considering I hadn't ordered the fucking shot to begin with.

'Kept telling me stuff about how he'd rank the albums, we played little games of This Tune versus That while we drove around or ate burgers, was always hinting at me how he had some bigtime endeavor on deck, meaningful, his purpose in life revealed—I thought it was corny but kinda neat, too, all real fun and Infomercial, diggit?'

While this sank in, despite I could tell the lad was champing at the bit for whatever details I had on tap, I inquired after his living situation: he was only seventeen, still in school, but didn't live with his mom—was I getting it right?

Scoffed again and explained he couldn't 'do the impossible'—surprised I hadn't guessed that from having met her for even ten seconds. 'Not officially emancipated or nothing' he pretty much crashed with various friends or kindly adults he got to know through *The Roids*—since he kept up his grades and even went to the dentist on the regular as he was supposed to, no bother ever came to mommy dearest, and the arrangement kept him pleased as Punch.

Wondered did he know of the framed posters his mother had around the parlor—wondered had he framed them, sometime more pleasant in life, had his father ... wondered, even if so, did he know she'd left them up on display despite flushing all images of Benjamin from the mantle. 'Mom isn't a *Giants* fan, herself?'

'She doesn't know *The Giants* from the growingly pliable hole in her ass,' he sneered, informing me the group was a lifelong love-affair of his father's, parenthetically adding how he'd gotten the sneaking suspicion the man had only *really* listened to them during his youth, though, 'up through an album called *Long Tall Weekend*'—furthered how the impression he'd come under was the later albums, along with a bulk of the rarities and what-have-you, had only been explored during the year or so they'd made the band their thing. 'Don't quote me about it, I could be way wrong—I mean, it was pretty clear he was terrifically fond of some old *Dial-A-Song* stuff, for example, always brought to mind the same anecdotes of experiences out of his misspent adolescence, I could regale those to ya verbatim.' This verifiable passion notwithstanding, during some debates it'd sounded to the lad like his dad's enthusiasm for certain material was quite fresh. 'Not to mention how there were odd times he was all mile-a-minute about what I knew were more current releases which I'd never seen him own or listen to, going on and on about 'em the same as though he'd been developing detailed thoughts about each and every track for decades.' Kid kind of joked how it'd all struck him as an 'atypical mid-life crisis'—reminded him of the way his mother talked about her born-again brother-in-law, except she did so viciously while he found his father's fervent devotion to 'some niche rocknrollas' quite charming, a breath of fresh air for all of its peculiarity. Seemed slap-happy to be speaking about his dad, frankly, poured words like a broken faucet—woulda gone on and on, forget I'd told him there was a specific reason I'd shown up, had I not wended things round to it, finally.

Explained succinctly about Benjamin staying at *The Calico* during the first stretch of his disappearance, retold the story about the typewriter, and then shot off yet another fictionalized version of discovering only a photocopy of the manuscript.

'You have it?' he almost spit out some alcohol-laden version of *Fanta Grape* he'd meanwhile been served.

I nodded, probing for clarity as to whether he'd been aware his father was actively composing the compendium—like did he know that was why the man had taken off, been given forewarning, expected him back.

No no no, he hadn't meant that—was just excited in a general way. 'I never could prise a straight answer out of the coot about his final rankings, but that was the thing he was always on about, *The Definitive* and all sorts of blither-blather—are those in there?'

'Everything, including the kitchen sink and the baby tossed out with the bathwater, is in there, so far as I can make out.' Outlined, first, the scope of the document, how there was a little introduction which insisted 'herein lay The Absolute Truth, nothing subjective about it,' an ordination no living soul would be capable of arguing against et cetera so on—then let him in on my limited exposure to and knowledge of the band's output, finishing off with 'Your dad's little opus seems *thorough*, though—let's put it like that.'

'Yeah yeah yeah …' he nodded, enthralled, said his pop had always told him he was gonna do that, one day '… whatever it meant!'

Out of curiosity: he'd said the two of them spoke about the music a great deal—were they actually *always* in perfect agreement concerning which was the better song, the worse album?

'Not really …' he scrunched his face, seemed deep in a specific contemplation for a beat, then pointed out how '… I honestly don't think it'd gotten that far along when we were shooting the shit—always seemed to me he was only spit-balling, getting his own opinions in cohesive order, coming up with how to differentiate *what* from *what-else*, not necessarily telling me anything conclusive, think I was a sounding board or a test subject. Guy never could recall where he'd ranked *The Spine* or *Book*, for example, and told me certain albums like *Lincoln* were still duking it out for position, all a delicate, very particular thing, or so he explained. At the time, I figured he tarted it all up in order to keep me engaged, make it fun—I mean who really cares, right?'

Retreaded some ground about if he'd had any indication where his dad had vanished to, had *Laampray* been a town they'd once lived in, ever visited, mentioned in passing—not only no, but turned out the kid'd had no idea his father had been 'like Missing Person level missing' until the reports of his death, intimated a bit more about his motley homelife, how maybe one time or two when he couldn't get through to his old man on the phone he'd deigned to ask 'Mrs. Strauss' if she'd heard anything, but the woman'd always seemed exasperated, rattled off this or that company line about the deadbeat was either busy with work, out of work, or on a muff-diving excursion, not that he'd put questions to her with much frequency.

Thoughts of Viggo superimposed overtop all I was being related—wondered if desperation lurked in any of our shared references, how many communal enthusiasms were merely the only way he reckoned he had any hope of getting a word in edgewise with me, of maintaining what he probably considered a fraying and tentative connection, at best. If I disappeared, died, would he light up like Hellfire, hang on every word of whichever bizarre yarn he'd be spun about me by some random stranger, same as this poor young man ... if so, ought he to?

Took a drink when it suddenly seemed to me that while visiting the ex-wife had been legitimate, foisting myself on a child, whatever his circumstances, was more than a toe strayed over some moral dividing line—Terrance had little choice but to be awash in a kind of mourning and my swashbuckling in with tales of skullduggery couldn't be helping ... might well be illegal, for all I knew! I was drinking alcohol with him and, whether he knew it or not, my purpose in meeting had been to obtain information rather than to supply therapeutic insights—the word 'plying' would be deemed dictionary appropriate by even the measliest attorney. I tried my best not to order more *Bulleit*, but it was little matter—as I'd clearly been labeled a friend, the girl in charge of the bottles abracadabraed me full any time I'd empty.

'You do have the manuscript with you, right?'

Rolled my hand how, yes, of course I did. 'Sorry, didn't mean to sit here cross-examining you.' Felt odd how little curiosity he exhibited about my appearing from outta the thin blue sky, considering all I'd told him ... and was also busy doing math ... figuring the barkeep must've been a senior when he'd been a freshman ... had they known each other in high school ... or maybe he'd started *Benny and the Roids* while in junior high and she'd only first learned of it, later...

Needed another trip to the head and made some remark I hoped came across as a joke rather than an invitation for him to come along, doing my best to seem I had sea legs beneath me as I crossed the room, noting how the slick fellow, the goth, and the jailbait were absent—red light over me furthered a sense of disorientation ... far too drunk ... might be good to vomit preventatively ... only thing keeping me from it was the worry how, once I got going, I'd not be able to stop ... soaped my hands at the mirror ... did an impersonation of that thug playing doctor ... except reminded myself he hadn't been that thug ... glared at my saggy-baggy reflection, scolding finger like what was my endgame here—why was I playing at having the goods to deliver, explanation-wise ... this was supposed to've been 'Here's something belonged to your father, go have yerself a fine life' rather than the evening it was morphing into ... vowed I'd get back out there, make the rest short and to the point ... which point, I didn't know ... but apprehended I'd now spent more in-the-flesh facetime with this delinquent than I had my own son during the past two years ... none of which should be anywhere near the vicinity of 'a fair depiction of my reality' ...

Despite this fine peptalk-cum-dressing-down, no sooner had I swooped back to the counter and hupped to my stool then I found myself asking, in tones of late-night-picture-show 'How much do you know about your father's death?' I'd simply had to inquire, it seemed—and right on the heels of doing so, let him know I was parked in the lot of the adjacent pub, *Giants* manuscript secure in the back pouch of the passenger seat. Unphased, he eyed my refilled shot glass, took just a sip, then told me he'd been told the guy who'd offed his dad had been arrested in Florida and then the rest of a story nothing like the one I knew—according to Terrance, the perpetrator'd been some junky nobody, confessed to how he'd lured Benjamin to a remote location by way of some convoluted business involving a confederate, said confederate identified as a kinda scraggly runaway girl who'd apparently overdosed shortly after, and the admitted killer'd been trussed up, but good, down for all sorts of scumbaggery, violence, and larceny, on top of Murder One.

Was this a marginally sanitized version of events given to him by his mother—or had I truly been chasing bogeys, before, what I'd read nothing more than internet fiction which those in the know would never mistake for hep reportage? 'You never heard, before today, how your dad'd wound up in my town awhile, right?' I pressed, again. He blinked, seemed to understand something, though I don't think he did, then admitted with a kind of bashful shame how he'd given up following any news updates, dropped off keeping in touch with the detectives, just knew how the actual killing had gone down in a whole other state than the dumping, and that, so far as he remembered being told, the 'murderer dude' had driven for two days with his father's rotting body in the trunk—so not the *sanitized* version, even marginally! I told the kid 'Jesus' and he agreed ... then couldn't stop myself prodding for where the killing had taken place, according to what he'd been told.

'Some town in Vermont ...' he shrugged, adding how the only thing weird about it was that one of his dad's old best friends had a house there '... but I've no idea had that been where he'd crashed or for how long.'

Some puffing on the microphones and a half-dozen clangy strums of electric guitar stole his attention and it struck me I'd been pumping him for intelligence an obscenely long while. 'I'll get you your dad's book,' I said, winked paly, standing like obviously I was keeping him from something far more vital.

'You can give it to me after the show—we can chat some more, if you want.'

Half-lied how I had to get back home, had a job, heading out that very night.

Pouted his lip, but told me 'Cool.'

'I'll leave it with our gal Friday,' I bowed toward the bargirl, as it seemed the band's set for an audience of two was raring to begin.

Told me 'Cool cool,'

Almost turned to go, but the last thing I couldn't resist finding out was 'What's the name of your dad's friend in Vermont?'

'*Nathan Jehovah* ...' he told me, no hesitation, finger-gun, grin '... practically an *uncle*—dad always called him a brother, that kinda thing.'

[*and which the pony is a phony was a lie*]

After a night I'll describe as nondescript for having no memory of, I woke on one of the twin beds in my motel room to the ruckus of housekeeping wanting in, responding to my bleary apologies with a brusque reminder I should've checked out a full hour previous—showered at a rush, handed in my key, received assurance there'd be no punitive charge for my oversleep, then was in my purring car, trying to decide if it'd be safer to leave it in the lot or to find a shopping mall, a gym, somewhere towing seemed unlikely. Once on foot, air warmer than courtesy dictated it ought to've been considering the season, it took the better part of two hours to find an area of town where I didn't feel myself a spiritual sore thumb—existing away from my postage stamp in *Laampray* for even a short while was more existentially taxing than I'd ever dared guess, matinees at the Bijou Theatre amongst the dry-cleaned and purpose-laden just weren't gonna allow me to sink into myself the way I needed to, the drugstores of *Sarnath* cleaner and better equipped than the hospitals in my neck of the woods, and the supermarket I ducked in to relieve myself reminded me of my poor decision making, the low-low prices reinforcing how the gas station diet I subsisted on set me back more than double what it had to and for items likely teetering on expiration. Eventually found a second run cinema, real dump, scent of three day old mop water tight to the lobby, no one working concessions or ticket window—let myself into the third of the three auditoriums without having bothered with what was *Now Showing*, enjoyed the suspense of wondering whether the projectionist was even required to start up the picture, considering there were no recorded patrons ... plus how would I explain myself were I caught out? Soon enough, the auditorium lights dimmed proper, *Coming Attractions* cuddling me in their Linus blanket while I decided to push my luck by lighting a cigarette, such courage further rewarded with a tipple from my half-empty flask—turned out to be a fine enough thriller, something I'd never heard of and starring a person whose performance was fancy enough I could convince myself it was a gem, got quite invested as some well-worn tropes snoozed by and found credits rolling too soon for my liking. Hadn't given any of my current thoughts a moment of proper reflection, so intended to theatre hop to try again, but suddenly the lobby was all a bustle of teenagers—I felt awkward enough even being seen, last thing I wanted was to be chastised and made an in-joke, gawked at while ejected into the late afternoon.

This jostle of nerves screwed me back into my right head—loitered in the lot until I'd resigned myself to the fact no mumbled utterance would summon my car to me presto, started the long slog back toward it, counting on my fingers whether it was that night or the next I'd be expected at work, rather stunned at the result of the arithmetic proving I hadn't planned the trip incorrectly, still had tomorrow, though should've made different decisions considering how late it'd be when I got in. Did my darndest to think up any other task I might accomplish in *Sarnath* but came up dunce, sighed several times in-a-row outside my car, few more times in it, and was back on the road for miles and miles before it struck me my little diversion was truly all over and done—overcast enough it seemed night had fallen, I tilted the volume dial to hear the cassette which'd been hissing next to silent.

> '... we aren't about to count the Children's Albums amongst other Studio Albums. No slight in this decision. The kid's stuff's *Giants* proper, surefire! Just isn't appropriate to have 'em vie for position against the grown-ups. *Here Comes Science* squaring off with *Apollo 18? Why?* versus *Factory Showroom? No!* throwing down with *Book*? What a crock! Equity not equality. Name of the game. As for odds-n-ends? One-offs composed for movies, television, inclusion in

such-or-such third-party project? Those're good, great stuff, some of the best, and uncannily so! I mean, try telling someone 'Tippicanoe And Tyler Too' isn't top shelf, see how far it gets you. Still: what to do about these orphans? Treat the vagabond lot like a single separate album? But we couldn't well weigh it against other albums, proper, nor against legit Compilations. Wouldn't be fair. No sense of ordination, of what's left on versus what's cut off. Those songs? Band chose to leave 'em rootless. Rootless they'd be left ...'

Ghouls ... the term had stuck in my head and still pulsed there '... ghouls ...' I mixed into the voice from the speakers, adjusted it down to hold my own attention—the way Mrs. Strauss had so individualistically bitched the word, a term-of-art rather than a general put down '... bullshit mumbo jumbo ...' I added, slowing to get a cigarette stoked. Those two phrases seemed to be referencing storylines more involved than bloggers like Hotel or even proper journalists pestering her about the death of her ex—even with the oddities present in either version of Benjamin's murder, the escapee or the cross-country junkie, I doubted reporters were constantly pounding on the poor widow's door, not months later, certainly, when there were other crimes to be profiteered and this one hadn't exactly penetrated the zeitgeist. 'Junkie coulda been the escapee ...' I supposed as though to a documentarian, recollections of what Terrance had said gaining more clarity as my hangover downgraded to lingering headache and a sting to heavy-lidded eyes '... only real contradiction is how the kid said it was known where the killing took place ... mighta got that direct from detectives or else the website piece'd been written before that morsel'd become public ...' not that I'd go back and clarify, didn't affect my thesis one way or another ... *ghouls ... mumbo jumbo ...* Who and how often could people have been stopping by, poking in pesky noses, that the goddamn police were on standby ... and who was Mrs. Strauss, anyway—the Queen of Sheeba? ... sure, Officer Picador might've been a close family friend, might even've been a backdoor lover to go by the smack of soft familiarity I'd sensed ... but it was more than a soupçon peculiar how my encounter with the man had played out, regardless. 'No sooner do I knock and give a drib drab Hello than she's gone ahead and dialed up reinforcements ...' not for a blogger and neither for something dated back half-a-year, she hadn't ... so served to reason some 'ghoul' must've recently accosted her ... and whoever such creature was must've spouted 'mumbo jumbo' fitting the description of 'bullshit' concerning Benjamin's *They Might Be Giants* obsession '... because she had said *that band ... that stupid band ...*' couldn't quite put my finger on what else'd been said ... something with an implication that sat heavy ... couldn't even bring to mind whether it was the Officer who'd said it or Strauss ... I was foggy ... turned up the radio just to distract myself.

> '... for that matter, were I to count all the Dial-a-Song selections, the Demo versions—well!—wouldn't I be bound to count every last Live Performance of any and all songs those crazy cats'd ever played? What a fiasco. Forced to consider their list forever unfinished. An impromptu whim while on stage might yield a whole new verse, for that matter, like how it's only live they ever sang that one verse! How would we ever know for sure there doesn't lurk some cache of private recordings, a trove of alternate takes the Johns have shoved in old shoeboxes, left forgotten under the sofas of their summer homes?'

Turned it back down like a spasm at a sizzle-snap of remembrance—the kid had fucking said *Nathan Jehovah*! 'That was weird, eh? Because of the letter and all ... yeah ...' I subvocalized '... yeah ...' Such detail added texture to the difficult-to-quantify quality in the disconnect between mother and child, suggested the proper material to caulk up all holes in an otherwise patchwork narrative, hinted at a subterranean story thread—Terrance knew enough to provide a pointer, but from so clear a remove it seemed he'd been fed a tailored version of events, while meanwhile it sure presented as though the mom and the officer had erred on the side of acting immediately, as though I was in direct cahoots with someone. 'Someone who'd been warned away, previous ... but who would've felt within their rights to've made multiple overtures ... trespassed on enough occasions police would've become involved ... made inquiries about

Benjamin's writing ... mumbo jumbo ghoulish enough to keep pestering the bereaved about ...'

Nathan Jehovah—if Terrance knew even vaguely about his dad's intention to write up his Official Rankings it served to reason Benjamin's best friend, practically a brother, knew all about it, as well. 'Might be Nathan was marked excommunicado ... I'd been mistaken for a crony ...' Felt a mighty fine gumshoe for getting that business smoothed out, though woulda felt a whole ton better if I could tell myself what I intended to do with the information ... if it turned out 'the information' was information and not just 'a thought' ... and would feel better still if I could come up with an excuse for why I was thinking about it, at all—banged the steering wheel, belted out an obscenity in the hopes that'd be the end of it, another, slapped the wheel, again. 'What, precisely, is the mystery here?' I demanded of the road around me, new cigarette bippity-bop between my lips—ticked off on my fingers *The Story Thus Far*: acquired typewriter, unearthed the manuscript, manuscript had connection with typewriter, author unknown, author found out, manuscript returned ... eyes flicked to the radio and then rolled as it struck me I'd totally forgotten to leave the copied cassette with Terrance, though I supposed it was hardly relevant. Repeated the sequence of events, aloud—there was nothing the scantest bit out of order to set in, I was merely nitpicking events either well *a priori* to my dubious 'involvement' or else related only tangentially to what I'd encountered in my 'investigation.' There existed zippo to 'solve' other than, at a stretch, the purpose behind Benjamin holing up to write anything in the first place and why he'd hidden it—but only the dead would know that! If I tried to lace things up so that, say, Hotel Detective's car accident had been arranged by Officer Picador on purpose because the twerp had bothered Mrs. Strauss once too often—the asshole had all but threatened violence and death on me, after all!—or that Benjamin's murder was component to a conspiracy Picador and Strauss were connected to and that the whole shebang centered around a crackpot manifesto concerning musical preferences— Christ on his throne!—even I had to admit I was playing Parcheesi without the back of the box to explain what the damn game was about.

It'd been a good run, but I ought *really* fold up the tent ... except: what else did I have going in my life? ... plus: this was *legitimately* interesting ... not to mention: it wasn't as though it was *de facto* 'more responsible' not to indulge my curiosity ... especially miles away from anyone involved in anything ... ticked the volume up ... drove ...

> '... not that I'm suggesting instrumental tracks are poor, writ large. Don't go getting that bastard impression. Linnell, especially, has some sorta wacko-ward knack for wordless composition. Swoon! I'd be hard pressed to honestly say he oughta lay words overtop a tune when he doesn't deign to. No doubt he could. Abstract phrase-turns stored always up his sleeve. But his lyricless offerings were bonkers prestidigitation, in their own right. We must simply always rank instrumental tracks last on a given album. Aren't what one listens to the *Giants* for. Darling though most all of 'em are. Let's not speak falsely ...'

Laampray met me like a soggy boot that was still better than barefoot—startling how leaving for a quick minute put in relief where I was. The streets of *Sarnath* versus *Laampray*—cripes! This town could fit into the seasonal Halloween shop on the upper floor of one of that town's three shopping malls—one member of the parttime staff likely possessed more poise and erudition than the town council I wasn't for sure we even had. For heaven's sake, I couldn't say for certain there was water in the water-tower bearing the faded paint of our high school mascot and doubted very much that, if there was water, that said water'd be potable or contain fluoride—I very much doubted all of those things, in fact! Yet there'd been a time when I'd come here, not on purpose but not not, for a reason if less than an objective—my life had, at one point, made starting the life I was in seem soundly the next step.

Parked like a grudge not quite ambitious enough to be a curse, avoided the dog droppings it felt I'd avoided several dozen times previous despite their still seeming plump and fresh, entered the main building, vaguely wondering for the thousandth time what the apartments up the elevator resembled, before heading to the stairwell and *thud thud thud* down it, to the left, the scent of the musty laundry room and gasoline emanating from what I called 'a pile of lawnmowers' in a storage area playing touchy feely with me as I sighed to my door—my key fit the lock and the latch turned too smoothly ... already unlocked ... the knob too, when I gave it a tentative turn ... let out a squinted prayer this was indicative of nothing more than a visit from Maintenance, but it being four in the morning and the fact Maintenance had never once come when I'd called them, even about active toilet overflow, made such eventuality seem lotto levels of unlikely.

But here was a moment I'd always kinda daydreamed: my room had been tossed, a textbook ransack—Mother of God, whoever the intruder or intruders had been, he, she, or they'd slit open the cushion of the futon and dug out its innards, had likewise savaged the chair I slept in then toppled it over, seemed to've rolled it firmly into the corner, maybe giving it shakes to see would something fall out, cabinets all hung open, microwave door, dishwasher, everything had been slapped from the bathroom sink, the toilet tank unlidded, lid in shards all over the shower floor, desk drawers on the carpet, overturned, electric typewriter's top removed, flung a good distance toward the bathroom door, my radio's cassette door popped, CD port torn off entirely, television turned around, tipped over, VCR upside down with my VHS collection spread over the floor, every last of 'em unboxed, books a disheveled pile, the sundry curio in my closet a mess barring the door from closing proper, even the corners of the carpet had been cut into and tugged up.

For a moment, it amused me how my entire life didn't even truly make this single-room squat of mine too messy when pulled literally inside out, then it almost flattered me to understand someone thought I'd have been sneaky enough to've hidden something underneath carpet—I wouldn't have and, furthermore, knew myself well enough to assert that, even had it occurred to me how it might be *theoretically possible* to do so, I'd have lazily convinced myself it couldn't be done *in reality*. Then a bolt of jarring panic had my ears ringing—I turned around and around and considered that the crooks who'd done the damage might yet be present, literally giggled when it dawned on me I could see the entire room, nobody home ... not that someone couldn't've been waiting outside, spied my return, be that very moment moving in stealth down the corridor, aiming to catch me with my pants down. Moved the overturned sleeping chair against the door, television up against that, futon next, all which made the entrance impossible to penetrate, a tight line of garbage furnishings extending flush from its flat to a tense lean against the opposite wall.

I suppose my mind jumping directly to thoughts of the original copy of the manuscript made sense, seeing as I'd only so recently taken pains to secure it off site, despite it being true this invasion could've been no more than a workaday burglary or even a case of someone'd got the wrong address, all the trashing things and fury on account of being informed drugs were meant to be stashed someplace, the wrecking crew sent to retrieve 'em going ape out of vexation and impending withdrawal—because who in the name of the great good Lord would've taken it on themselves to've caused all this mayhem for Benjamin's manuscript and how would they've had any clue my basement flop was someplace it'd be? I'd been away from home not even three days and, other than to my son—even then extremely vaguely—I'd never mentioned *They Might Be Giants* and, until Mrs. Strauss, hadn't once breathed a word of the cursed volume to a living soul—racked my brains to find an inaccuracy in this, but no, nope, nobody at all coulda had such a thing in mind. Even visiting Hotel Detective's blog and looking into the circumstances of Benjamin's murder had been practically ages ago, plus how the devil would any of that be traceable or trace to me, specifically—and why in the world, beside?

I'd spoken to Strauss, Officer Picador, Terrance—nobody else. Terrance being involved was a non-starter—unless he'd been coyly lulling me into a false sense of security so that I'd specifically not suspect him of anything ... but such theory exhausted me even to postulate. I'd already entertained the dark thought Picador may've cleverly done in Hotel, massaged the accident scene to make it seem no foul play was involved, so my mind went to him—but was I truly suggesting an officer of the genuine Law had driven out to my home and done this, right on the heels of our chatting, or that he was in cahoots with some thuggish personality who'd have acted on his behalf on the double-quick? That was going a bit far, even in the realms of lunacy I was willing to dip my toe, by this point! So maybe Strauss had looked me up ... sent someone ...

Needing to stop everything, I took a seat on the floor, leaned against the shut bathroom door, attempting to get my heart to stop racing—nobody knew there *was* an original manuscript and, if they assumed so on account of the copies were copies of an original at some point, there remained no call to suspect it'd be anything to do with me. Would've made more sense for them to've smashed up *The Calico Bash*—going by my story, which there'd be zero call to disbelieve, it'd seem all I'd ever possessed was a duplicate ... *ergo* if an original'd existed but been hidden, it'd more likely've been arranged by the author, maybe in the room where he'd cobbled the damned treatise up ... only no one would know which room that'd been! There was a wrong name on all the records and even a cop wouldn't have time or jurisdiction to do the same kind of digging I'd done, on that front—without a general timeframe and knowledge of which cabin the book'd been discovered in, my search couldn't be replicated ... which helped calm me ... and some *Bulleit* batted clean-up ... a cigarette working as water-wings ... '... okay ... good ... this is good ... keep going ...'

Why would a party sinister enough to commit a felony conclude it worth the risk of doing so on no more than the supposition I'd have gone out of my way to deliver a facsimile—not to mention: what was the bloody difference? The Xerox was exactly the same as the original, no page elided, no line of text redacted—neither Officer Picador nor Mrs. Strauss had even asked to set eyes on it when I'd have put it in their hands, no contest.

'The bartender I'd left it with? Someone the kid had spoken to ...'

swig, pace, flick, poof, pace, inhale, exhale, pace, swig. '... doesn't make sense ... doesn't make sense ... good ... good ...'

Clearly I was up my own ass, mind on tilt due to fatigue and shock—made as much sense as anything to reckon there was an inky third party I'd never seen nor interacted with behind everything, *They Might Be Giants* compendium not even entering into the affair.

As it struck me more and more that my private dwelling had honest to God been violated, my personal belongings left in shambles and largely in need of replacement, both fear and anger began coursing through me, displacing the need to link fancy unto fancy—I trembled with nervosa, jittering as though I'd been caught doing something wrong, no way out of a deserved consequence. Hit the wall hard enough I regretted it, the pain an unfortunate reset button: I did have the precious manuscript—so what was the matter with outright asking me for it, were the fucker really at the heart of this matter? Where were the goons who oughta be strongarming me—why wasn't some hood trying to force their shoulder through the door, that very moment, and why hadn't my head been bagged in the parking lot, a gun jammed in my ribs while I'd squirmed in some dubious backseat? This nonsense, as it presently stood, just sucked, was pointless and unfair—I couldn't afford to replace my chair or my futon, that was my only television and VCR! I gnashed my teeth, stood, did some approximate karate moves around, then sawed the air in impotent indecision ... do I report this ... now, come morning ... do I stay the night, spring for a motel, see if someone at *The Calico* was sympathetic enough they'd allow me to lay my personal blanket on the floor of a vacancy as a former co-worker had done for almost a month while between apartments and marriages?

The destruction of my entire homeostatic environment probably didn't carry a price tag enough to warrant charges being pressed—even with the breaking-and-entering thrown into the mix, it'd be a smack to the backside for whichever scamps were behind it. The door hadn't been broken, carpet could be stapled or superglued down, therefore the building management didn't seem likely to go to bat for me—in all likelihood, I'd be the prime suspect, some down-and-outer angling to drain a few bucks from a Victim's Compensation fund or else screw his landlord out of something for not better securing the premises ... or a flatfoot'd conclude I actually was mired in the drug biz, a skeevy pornographer, knee deep in some illicit thing else. Look at this dump, this mole hole—who'd have bulldozed it if not looking for something not on the up-and-up?

On and on I went, thoughts a jumble, peace of mind tattered, but started getting my belongings back in order, stacked to the wall, put to the shelves, drawers into desk, so forth—had gotten myself reasonably consoled, decided there was no percentage in raising an official stink, certain this had to've been an oddly timed, completely random if altogether non-innocent act, considering the neighborhood I resided in and a handful of factors else. It didn't necessarily count as *coincidence*, rather seemed I was force-feeding a narrative because of the likely-all-in-my-mind intrigue I'd been letting myself get too caught up in—I'd simply been away for a day or two, my place burglarized, woulda happened while I was at work, orchestrated by a crook who'd kept vague tabs on my general patterns and who'd figured that's where I'd been when my car hadn't been present ... take away all the silliness I was, of my own volition, foisting into my life and this would be just another in a long line of crumby, but entirely run-of-the-mill, happenings.

Except something still felt off ... I paced, giving intense inspection to every surface, including the ceiling, my eyes coming to settle on the radio ... I blinked at it, unfocused, refocused, unfocused, refocused ... decided maybe I'd put on one of the damned *Giants* albums, just for a kind of lighthearted coda to this exploit I was sure sour on, now ... blinked ... unfocused ... refocused ... absently scratched at the side of my face ... until I realized it was hurting me to ... stared at the absence of the CD door ... *Ping!*

Flood, Apollo 18, the music videos—I looked everywhere to verify it absolutely and, yes ma'am, the discs, their jewel cases, were gone, the VHS absent as well, video store box left empty—then *blamo!* yanked open the curio closet and dug, found the second copy of the manuscript conspicuously absent, tore around the room to be certain it wasn't anywhere amongst the shipwreck. *They Might Be Giants* were the only thing missing, which, no, could positively not've been a coincidence—which meant neither could anything else.

[*neck deep in the quick, quick*]

My mailbox hadn't been jimmied—little victories, I supposed, and it made me feel quite prescient, into the bargain. Spoke to a bored old woman clerking the desk who seemed not to buy my angle about asking after security and consequences for tampering with Post Office property on account of a book I was working on, the conversation nevertheless satisfying me how there'd be all manner of Hell to pay for anyone who so much as attempted a deed as dark as letter theft—inquired whether the Post Office had safe deposit boxes and what would those run someone back per month, but she informed me how banks have those but they weren't a bank, no idea the price-tag, then I wondered if I mailed something marked Hold For Pick Up how long it'd be kept, what was required of someone to retrieve it.

'The United States Postal Service isn't a poor man's storage shed—and sir, what is it you're *really* looking for?'

'Nevermind.'

Slugged into *Video Grog* only to have Oldtime Dougie ask me if everything was alright in a way which was particularly off putting—I maintained my cool, responded as though it'd been just a casual 'How they hangin' despite noting the tone, but when he doubled down, I couldn't play at ignoring the implication without it being clear I wasn't playing. 'Why do you ask?'

'You look drawn.'

'Do I?'

'More than usual, yeah.'

'Geez …' Went with telling him I hadn't been sleeping, family issues, and there was something screwy going on with my bowels, only to learn the hard way how, unfortunately, he'd once had something of a digestive tract fiasco, so demanded particulars. 'Didn't know you're a doctor, Doug,' I tried to banter but snarked, instead.

'Just trying to help,' he understandably bristled. I apologized, listed off some symptoms for him to ponder—he'd had some but not others, so must not've been the same thing I was going through, count my lucky stars. 'How'd you like *The Giants*, by the way?'

'What do you mean?'

Adjusted his gut a half tick. 'Seriously—are you okay?'

Sighed how I hadn't meant to snap at him, was just crabby, a lot on my mind, was okay, really and 'Yeah—*The Giants*? Didn't much dig 'em, quite frankly.'

'Oh no?'

'Naw.' Different strokes, he'd heard—though floated how I might enjoy their newer stuff. 'Thought you hadn't listened to it.'

'I haven't, but the fact still remains.'

'You're quite the philosopher, Dougie.'

He told me to help myself to a pink lemonade.

My second shift back to work, I grew intent on coming up with some clever experiment to determine if the vent in Cabin Eight had recently been fiddled with, resolved to spend as much time as was required poking around, right away met with unexpected peculiarities—could swear it was a different television set on a different bureau, neither one positioned exactly as last I'd been there, definitely a new cut-rate painting on the wall, one of the many starving-artist offerings kept in the storage area behind the laundry, this particular masterpiece, for reasons unknown, literally nailed into place. I'd have to find an unobtrusive way to get the scoop on this redecoration, an irritating sub-thread of distraction to my thoughts about how on Earth I was gonna explain my presence in the cabin, best I could strategize being to let on I'd meant to ask for awhile, it'd kept slipping my mind ... except with no way of knowing when the change'd occurred, a wrong word to the incorrect person would have to be answered for, for real ... supposed the best first step would be to pop in a few other cabins, see if it was a general facelift or a localized alteration ...

As to the vent: opened it up, hoping there'd be telltales of recent ingress, but found nothing—or if something, not anything I'd know what. Closed the grate back up, attempted to familiarize myself with its appearance from all angles, stepped out for a cig, re-entered, removed the screws, screwed them back, not looking, stepped out for another smoke, a swig, returned, and tried to spot even the mildest difference—couldn't, but even could I, knew the method was moot as I'd nothing to compare *now* to from *before* ... maybe going through the motions would earn me an epiphany ... wheel spinning ... boredom ... cigarette ... swig ...

Took the room apart and reassembled it like a Lego set, drawers all the way out of the dressers, every last object turned over and around, traced fingertips along the carpet to test whether maybe, at some point, it'd been yanked up, glued down—don't know so much that I was hoping to find anything, though wouldn't have been miffed if I had, plus did feel I'd determined, conclusively, that though there were bunches of places Visa might've secreted his manuscript, the vent absolutely was the soundest, especially shoved back as it had been ... and if the stashing hadn't been 'casual,' there must've been a particular, calculated, paranoid desperation at play ... the room itself of significance ...

Looked up the details of that thug who'd stayed in Cabin Eight before my trip to *Sarnath*, learned his name was *Nils Dolphy*, studied the photocopy of his driver's license meticulously—not the guy from *The Foghorn*, though also not at all how I remembered him from the night he'd checked-in ... and not just because the license photo coulda been taken a long time ago, but on account of I still had an image of The Doc Cunningham Killer stamped on my mind, disappointed at my inability to disassociate from it at such a crucial time. Issue date on the ID was actually far enough back the card itself had expired a year before I'd accepted it, which perked me up for meaning it was probably stolen ... but quickly deflated when I had to admit how that not only wouldn't help me but made no difference at all, because the bully was nought to do with anything, either way ... except ... squinted at the screen and *tack tack tack* to the keyboard to pull up a few options ... discovered he'd not only stayed in Cabin Eight on the night he'd accosted me ... but a few nights back ... same time I'd returned from my trip ...

Fruitlessly typed some internet searches for *Nils Dolphy* then retreaded the worn flat investigations I'd previously made about all other 'persons-of-interest,' disappointed how I lacked the cleverness to uncover anything compelling—even with the 'new information' I possessed, names, addresses, possible whereabouts of Benjamin's murder, all which might connect this dot to this other, no search engine results seemed any less random than before and as many had zilch to do with the things I typed and hit Go on.

A sudden spike of anxiousness clambered up me, urgent desire to cover my tracks—but when I opened the browser's Search History, I not only verified how, in addition to everything I'd looked up since the starting gun still being in evidence, my co-workers nursed a healthy appetite for taboo pornography ... which meant I couldn't exactly take it upon myself to tap Clear All. If whoever else on staff noted the cache erased, they'd know they hadn't done it, use process of elimination to figure I had, and it was hop-skip from that to there being some reason for my having done so or, at least, to anxiousness over my having the goods on them. God only knew what strained interactions or over-compensatory retaliations might come of it were the manager the perv—fearing himself at hazard, that rascal might nix my at-will employment before I could say Boo ... one never could tell with people and their precious secrets ... especially when they seemed not to be keeping them secret ... sites for 'local hookups with hot MILFs in the area' were frequented often enough it only served to reason assignations were arranged on the regular ... which made sense ... motel to themselves and all ... joshed myself for looking down my nose at whoever it was, as though I were spending my time on matters of national scale and moral imperative.

I'd just downed a wallop from my flask, two minutes before, was out in front, simultaneously sucking a breath mint and smoking one of the unfiltered *Luckies* I'd found left in a room the previous day, when a car made its very slow way around the bend, pulling to a halt practically right up against me, engine cutting off, windows tinted but cracked enough I knew the driver was smoking, as well, wisps of blue-grey leaking out, quite gorgeous as they blended with the pea-soup green of the neon Office sign and the grime of the ambient illumination accenting a chilly mist tightening the air—did my best not to give the vehicle the slightest deference and also made no move to rush my cigarette, already irritated I might not be able to chain a second, per my wont. Had actually just taken out the pack, removed a tentative stick, when the driver's door popped open, fella got out, waved right away how I ought take my time, he'd be inside, asked was there a toilet—I felt lousy telling him there technically was but how it'd need my key, playfully shrugged toward the treeline if his business was nothing requiring clean up. Watched him take a leak and he pantomimed a doff of his cap as he returned across the lot from the dip down the gulch, entered the Office with the usual *ringaling*—had about half my smoke left and, feeling I'd done my good deed, took my sweet time of it.

'How you like your job?' he wanted to know once I'd joined him.

'About that much,' I deadpanned, to which he chuckled as I batted a hand to indicate I was kidding, told him I honestly adored it, just always felt odd about broadcasting as much, considering.

'Considering?'

'The job,' I moved my eyes like to indicate where we were presently standing.

'You think workers oughta be disgruntled?' This seemed to disappoint him, so I told him I'd simply observed how most workers were. 'I don't follow.'

'Since I don't tow the downtrodden line, feel myself a misfit, that's all.'

'You just wanna fit in with the peer group, is it?'

'Feel like I should's probably better to say.'

'*Better?*' The word puzzled him.

'More correct.'

'More *fitting*, do you mean?'

'Sure.'

'*Sure*—or *yes*?'

'Both,' I rolled my eyes involuntarily, started to tap things into the computer, get the Check-In forms cued, and gave a little nudge to the Guest Register to subtly prompt the show on the road.

As though none of that was happening, he tottered over to the empty coffee pot, lifted it, sniffed, and asked me what other sort of work I'd done in my life.

'Night security, out of high school.'

'Always at night?'

'Hence the job title.'

'Fair enough,' though he'd really meant to inquire whether I'd always worked at night, regardless of the duties.

'*Sometimes, not all the time ...* ' I half-said-half-sang in imitation of Dylan's 'Clothesline Saga' which, to my delight, he picked up on, and afterward we batted a few lyrics back and forth—seemed he'd seen Dylan perform live, one time, and *The White Stripes* had opened.

'Ages ago—another life.'

'Good life to've had,' I nodded, posture of down-to-business as he returned the coffee pot to its nest, reapproached the desk, leaned to the counter, blew a breath, a little embittered, and explained how, at the time of the concert, he'd been on a date which really hadn't gone well, making the whole experience a bust and a blur. 'Aha,' I replied, a raise of my hand both in solidarity and assurance I'd pry into the affair no further—set the Check-In sheet on the counter, turned it around, pen laid atop.

'No—I don't need a room. Just here *about a room*. Or rather about a *guest*. But really ... about ... *you*.' He paused, pointed with two fingers which were then tapped twice on the countertop.

Now chewing the remains of my breath mint, extra crunchy to appear unphased, I gave an indifferent gesture meant to express how I was, indeed, the party best positioned to help him with such matters. 'What's the shot, brother?'

Absolutely no build-up or establishing context, the man said to me 'You say you'd found this writing, here in the hotel?'

'*Motel* ...' I idiotically corrected, an obvious burp of nervousness no doubt how he interpreted it. 'Who did I say this to?' I rather stumblingly followed up, failing to backtrack to the more basic business of who was he, what exactly was he talking about, and why.

'I heard you said it to someone—didn't you?'

'I suppose I did, yeah.'

'You seemed not to know, few seconds ago.'

'I didn't mean I didn't know.'

'Then why'd you ask?'

'I was simply taken a bit by surprise at how you'd phrased the question.'

'How's that?'

'*Familiarly* ...' I said, segueing on the drop-off of the word directly into '... have we met?'

'Do you think we have?'

'Never.'

'Well, not until now, eh?' he grinned, paused, squinted, asked if I'd mind answering the question, at long last.

'Sorry—which question was it?'

'You say you'd found this writing here in the *hotel*?' he left the word uncorrected, which for some reason caused me to have a bad swallow, a few sips of coffee, and an almost involuntary reach for my flask. 'I don't mean to be rude—but who's asking?'

'Me.'

'On behalf of?'

'Someone.'

'Who is ..?'

'It's an alternate answer, depending on whom?'

Told him I'd need further context to know, but then threw my hands up, faux-what-did-it-matter, and somewhat groaned 'I found some writing in one of the cabins, yeah.'

'I'm Detective Judah Hellpop ...' he extended his hand and when I didn't take it winked '... do you want me to prove it?'

I admitted being personally indifferent, though supposed that'd depend on what else he intended.

Gave me a little finger gun, tsks sound as his thumb dropped the hammer. 'What was this writing, again?'

Air of genuine disinterest, explained as best I could how it'd seemed like some weirdo's innermost passions about a band. 'Like an extremely pedantic ranking of their entire, decades spanning output, the manifesto of a real fanatic was my impression, though I didn't exactly read it all.'

'Which band?'

'*They Might Be Giants*.'

'Never heard of 'em.'

'Prior to this manuscript, neither had I.'

'They any good?'

'Quite frankly, no. Only listened to a little of their stuff, but it didn't shift me.'

'Some albums you bought down the shop.'

'That's correct.'

'I hadn't been asking … did it sound like a question, just then?'

'You have an abnormal cadence,' I chuckled.

'Oh my gosh, I'll need to work on that.'

'It's not unpleasant,' I assured him, just made it difficult, in this instance, to know, definitively, what was a statement, a statement requesting response, a question purely rhetorical, one I was to answer, so forth.

He liked how I thought. '*A statement requesting response*—you consider that different than a *question*?'

'I suppose so.'

'Which room was the writing in—had you said?'

'If memory serves, it'd been Cabin Eight—though, no, I hadn't said.'

'Oh, *Cabin* Eight—these are *cabins*, I wasn't aware. But you found a typewriter in there, too—that help pin things down?'

Apologetically, I didn't catch his drift. 'Pin things down?'

'As to which *cabin*.' He imagined finding an entire typewriter along with a honking big manuscript was the sorta one-off I'd recollect where. 'Do you tend to have a good memory?'

'In my estimation, yes.'

'But you're not certain said memory always serves?'

'It was Cabin Eight ...' I sighed, nodding I got the hair he was splitting '... you have an odd cadence, I suppose I have a peculiar idiom.'

'*Idiom*?'

'Way of answering things—manner of expressing myself.'

Well, he didn't want me to be hard on myself, especially over something as inconsequential as that! As a matter of fact, now that he was getting the hang of it, kinda enjoyed how I conducted myself in conversation and wished a lot more people would adopt similar styles. 'Can you walk me to Cabin Eight—or is there a guest in there?'

Like we were a script, I knit my brow, leaned forward, gave an articulate stage-whisper of 'This is the sort of thing I'd need that proof for.'

'Proof?'

'That you are who you said you were.'

'Who had that been?'

'A detective, anyway ...' I squinted, overact of I'm-onto-you '... thought you'd said ... *Rosencrantz* ... or it might of been ... *Guildenstern* ...' put tongue-in-cheek to hip him I was being lighthearted though wasn't joking, per se.

Took out his wallet, badge, here was his card, I should hold onto it. 'Do you wanna telephone the precinct or anything—how thorough a protocol does *The Calico Bash Nitely* hold the marshals to?'

I waggled my hands, overly affable, admitted I was honestly maybe going about things more by-the-book than I tended to on account of a detective being on hand.

'Detectives make you act different?'

'More professionally ...' I could admit '... you might not believe it, but this isn't much of a job and one of the perks of that is it not being much of a job.'

As a detective he had detected that, yes—had once worked the laundry room of a gigantic hotel in an even more gigantic city, sort of establishment where the laundry room was big enough you forgot you were ever anywhere else or that there were any such things as anywhere else ... and so on he chattered while I escorted him through a brief bit of suddenly heavy downpour to the cabin in question, flapped the light switch, though it hardly made a difference, then moved to turn on the minty bathroom light which actually illuminated the room more legitimately.

'This fabled typewriter had been whereabout—on the bedcovers?'

'On the desk,' I pointed, absently moving for a cigarette, the detective noticing before I had a chance to decide against it, so struck my lighter, inhaling a drag as I leaned to the door, *patter-patter* and almost *thuds* of rain on the other side nearly vibrating me.

'The manuscript had been right there with it?'

'Near it.'

'In a folder, in a stack?'

'A document envelope ...' I nodded, like why hadn't I said so straight away '... like an inter-office envelope.'

'Except it was a *photocopy*?'

Nodded, but since he hadn't been looking it came off an odd pause, and he turned just as I said 'Yep, sure was,' training his gaze on me a few beats before moving on.

'You'd never seen the original—is that the case?'

'Never.'

'Never ever?'

'Then, either.' He tapped the top of the television rapidly for what felt like too long, so I decided to risk a 'Can I ask why you're asking?'

'Hadn't you just?'

'... just?'

'Asked.'

'*Asked*?'

'Why I was asking.'

'By way of asking if I could, yes.'

'That's all I'd been asking.'

'*Asking?*'

'*Saying* ...' he winked again while I made a dorky face of right-right-right, I followed his line of thought '... your peculiar way of speaking, again—I'm just enjoying it, you shouldn't be so self-conscious.'

'I suppose that's good advice.'

'Hey—does your memory serve how my job is to tromp around being a bona fide *detective*?'

'It does.'

'Who investigates crimes and the such?' Nodded, widening my eyes like he was getting to a punchline, but instead he asked 'But you don't genuinely believe it's a wise lifestyle to go lying to me like you've been—about something that, for all you know, is to do with a crime?' To go by the amused expression on his face, maybe that *was* the punch he'd set up—had found the perfect straight-man—but he didn't give me time to stammer a cough of reply before sitting to the mattress and going 'Hey, listen up—you didn't *find* any typewriter and you didn't find any photocopied manuscript *with it*. Here's what you did: got to work, once upon a time, after *someone else'd* found a left-behind typewriter, went ahead with waiting a good long while before finally your boss told ya you could have it, losers weepers and all. Here's something else: there was never any kind of manuscript *along with* that there typewriter. How come I know that's all on account of the woman who *actually* found the typewriter told me so. When she and I chatted. While I was detecting things. As I'm known to do. Now: do you feel like knowing what else I've detected, before we go on?' Once again, he left no pause for response, not even the nod I was too stiff to give. 'That you made a photocopy of something bulky, like a manuscript, maybe even a few copies—you don't recall that?'

I let out a very even, controlled breath, ten seconds long, raised my arms, flapped them down, hung my head. 'I'm terribly sorry—I have no excuse, don't know what I've been thinking, you're absolutely correct about everything—let me just explain as best I can, though I'm pretty sure all it'll accomplish is making me out to be an abject idiot.'

'Well, let's hold off judgment on a thing like that,' he seemed earnest in suggesting.

'I've kinda been fashioning a more romanticized narrative in my head—no idea why. Talk to myself—I'm that sorta guy, as you can well imagine—and tell people the story like how I told you, about finding the manuscript and the typewriter together ... but I don't know why I thought it'd be proper to keep doing that with a detective.' Plus, listen: if he wanted the scoop, no baloney, I'd had a bit to drink before he'd arrived, on shift, and was more exhausted than typical—but I'd be straight up, going forward, doubted I could help him, not that I knew what it was all about.

'Right this minute, it's about the manuscript.'

'Roger that—what about it?'

'Well ...' he narrowed eyes around me as though about to be upset I might be winding him up again '... where, you know, *did* you find it? *You* didn't write it, did you?'

'Certainly not. I legitimately found it.'

'Where?' he repeated.

Though I was loathe at it happening—knew how it made it seem I was reluctant and how therefore I'd been stalling on purpose like some jerk schoolkid—I couldn't help taking in another deep breath, cheeks puffed, then letting it out while going up on my tiptoes, down, raising my arms shoulder high, letting them flop, slapping my thighs lightly with my palms. 'I found it in the vent, partway between this room and the next. There'd been a leak, I'd looked into it—lookit, I know that sounds preposterous, but it's how it'd played out.'

He didn't find that preposterous, even a little. 'Where is it, now?'

'I've honestly no Earthly idea.'

'How's that?'

'It had been in my apartment—but I've recently been broken into.'

'The manuscript was *burgled*?'

'First, to be clear: I found a copy and it was that copy I'd copied.'

'Gosh! And the burglary ... *that's* why your place was all a mess when I'd gone by, a little while ago—the landlord let me peek my head in on account of being the law West of the Pecos and all.'

'Yes,' I answered, mouth dry.

'You hadn't reported this?'

'Hadn't seemed worthwhile.'

'What else'd been taken?'

I shrugged, at a legitimate loss, stammered and hem-hawed about nothing of consequence, seeing as I didn't possess anything matching such description—couple of CDs, movie or two, few bucks and the change jar it'd been in, then, for some reason, added as embellishment 'The manuscript was in a kind of chintzy lock-box with a bunch of other curio—only reason it's gone isn't particularly that *it* is, but because I guess whoever robbed me thought nice things were in there.'

'Well how about that! But hey, listen: could you do me a huge favor and ride down to the precinct—all it is, is there're some few items I want to gab with you about, a bit more in-depth.'

'Right this minute?' I rather balked, made a gesture around as though to communicate I was at work, he mustn't be absurd.

'It's kind of important—so if you need to call your boss, go ahead and do that, I won't eavesdrop.'

'Am I under arrest?'

'Do you wanna be?'

'No.'

'There any reason you oughta be?'

'Absolutely not.'

Well *phew!*—he appreciated that. 'Less paperwork, for starters. But why don't you make that call—I'll wait in the car.'

[*magnet axe woolen blanket 1997 calendar potato peeler*]

The reality of my situation wasn't lost on me, despite three long draws from my flask I'd taken in the Motel Office toilet before the ride over in the detective's car, a transportation choice which didn't sit well with me—having been in the front seat, on one hand, made me feel my being brought in truly was mere formality, Hellpop'd swing me back by *The Calico* after, easier than vouchers for gas money, mileage, but, on the other, steered a little too close to 'Car, what car, I wouldn't worry about it, no need for one of those where you're headed, pal.'

The detective was kind enough to pop an umbrella and hand it to me before he jogged a little ahead to get the station door, ushering me into the building at a trot as though this were some wacky romcom meet-cute we'd laugh about on our anniversary—he gave saucy little salutes to various people as we made our way through what looked exactly like the office portion of a car dealership, some returning them in kind, others quietly smiling, and one even blushed genuine crimson. Stopped at the vending machine for him to ask did I want something, it'd be his treat—'Provided it's none of them pastry thingamajigs on the top row …' not because he couldn't afford 'em, I must understand, but just because '… don't you agree three dollars is a bit steep for a *Zinger*?'

Told him 'Yes' about the snack cakes being overpriced, 'No thanks' about the offer in general, not that I was unappreciative of his courtesy, simply demurring how I was very regimented with my meals.

'Regimented in what way?' Laid out some utter hogwash which

didn't sound very healthy to him—though he supposed I'd probably chosen the term 'regimented' because I was well aware of that fact. 'Not that I mean you'd seemed to be putting on airs, no no—only on account of I seem to've picked up on how you're the sorta feller likes things to exist without no ambiguity. Are you?'

'Sorry—am I what?'

'Like that?'

'Like what?'

'*Unambiguous.*'

'I endeavor to be.'

He seemed surprised at so nondefinitive an answer, thought a beat, then supposed he'd actually been too hasty, there—what I'd said was the most honest way of putting it! '*Endeavor* is a word with far more candor than *try* and tons less pomposity than the phrase *I am*. We're off to a crackling start!'

Before I'd really processed our entering, I was seated in what I'd only at a stretch term an Interrogation-Room—felt like a set which'd either just been struck or was still being worked out, a space that didn't quite seem used regularly, random items stored in it, all only accidentally arranged to resemble a workspace. He'd be right back, once more asked was there anything he could fetch me—coffee went without saying, even if I didn't want it, and we could share cigarettes. 'Me with you ...' he clarified, adding '... meaning I'll let you bum mine' just in case I'd taken his clarification to mean the opposite, shook my head while he nodded his, promising me 'Two minutes, tops' before taking a bow, failing to note whether the amount of time mentioned was how long until he returned or how long he intended to keep me. It wasn't the sort of silence I preferred—could hear too much of the inside of my nose, feel too much of it, smell the stiffening membrane. Examined the items on the wall—job opportunities, *Crime Watch* hotline, things to remember if I'd been raped, random sheet of fingerprints, large wrinkled poster for the film *Upstream Color*, which I felt a peculiar need to get the story behind, maybe ask if I could have it if there wasn't one.

Soon enough, the door opened, a flunky type of officer set down my coffee, beside it placed a cigarette, and as he left I used my own lighter to get that going, the detective re-entering, pleased I'd made myself so at home, wasting no time, tone jovial, in practically serenading me with how eager he was to understand 'Exactly what in the holy heck you'd gone to visit Mrs. Strauss regarding, some little while back.' My face obviously betrayed recognition at the name, along with absolute confusion over this being Question One, plus a crinkle of anxiety over how I figured she might've gotten a burr up her skirt about me and decided to take out whichever frustrations existed in her life at my expense. 'Tell me what you're thinking, right there …' he waved a hand, leaning back, crossing his leg in a feminine manner, sipping his own coffee '… you appear to have what I will charitably refer to as *a look of particular concern* on your brow.'

'Not at all …' I countered, keeping calm but puffing my cheeks out again, vexation no doubt showing in my eyes for having done so '… I'm merely considering how there must be some vast misunderstanding. All I'd wanted to accomplish by way of my visit was the return of what I thought was her husband's writing. I've no idea why, but my doing so seemed to've rubbed her the wrong way—so much so she had the fucking police escort me across her front lawn.'

Regretted the profanity, but it appeared to amuse the detective, his demeanor totally relaxed—almost seemed he was about to drop anything official, we were just two chums having a wink of gossip. 'The *fucking* police, at that! Not even the *can't-get-laid-on-a-dare* division, eh?'

'That's what it said on the van,' I tried out as a joke, testing the waters, but only got deadpan in response and him writing it down.

'The *fucking police* is a sought-after position …' he said, let a beat hang long, then added ' … no pun intended …' without a hint of jocularity '… I tried the exam, failed it, but, in my opinion, my proctor was a bit too anal …' another pause '… no pun intended …' I chuckled because I hoped it was what he desired I do '… asked me if I'd mind being cuffed, the proctor did—I'd asked him *Hey, what for*? and guy told me *Extra credit*, so I had to explain I don't go in for backdoor helping hands … obviously the incorrect answer … so now I'm here, in the pee-wee leagues.' Took a pregnant pause, smiled as though he was waiting for something to dawn on me, but I didn't see the pun unless it was just pervy innuendo, totally non-sequitur, about underage shenanigans. 'How'd you deduce the manuscript was authored by who you wrongly assumed was Mrs. Strauss' husband, again?' he suddenly returned to business. I begged his pardon as my mind stalled out, chugged, and revved—remembered, for real, where I was sitting and what kind of consequences an arrest could have on my life, however brief and based on however lunatic a charge. 'Was the name written upon the manuscript you discovered?' he prompted, something near to pity in the softball, also a note of let's not make things too easy for him, please and thank you.

'The manuscript was signed …' I shrugged, but knew what a garbage thing it was to've said, too late to change to claiming the name'd been on the envelope, so faked a cough and picked up like the remark had been in preamble before giving him the truth '… though it wasn't anything legible, but since I found the thing, was intrigued by it, I'd looked into who'd rented the room once it occurred to me maybe it'd been written with the typewriter I'd wound up in possession of, but no help, there, the name used was bogus.' Described the impossible-to-believe sequence of events which'd led me to Hotel Detective's blog and, from there, to the News story about Benjamin, explaining how '… to me at the time, all the elements seemed to click how the dead guy, Benjamin, must've been my guy, the author—just got it in my head to pay a visit.'

'And to give his ex-wife a photocopy of the manuscript you'd pulled out of a wall,' the detective picked up, his tone a stubbed toe, my mouth opening and closing a few times while I couldn't think what to say. 'That wasn't a question, by the way,' he added, as though striking abject terror in my heart would help me build character.

'There only ever had been a photocopy,' I reminded him.

'What if that wasn't true, though?'

'What if ... what wasn't true?'

'A manuscript has to have an original, like how a chicken has to come from an egg, even if not from a chicken's.'

'I concur.'

'I'm asking: what if you *had* come across the *original* of a manuscript by a complete stranger's deceased ex-husband?'

Cut in to insist how 'I hadn't thought of it that way.'

'Which way had you thought of it?'

'Just as a thing I'd found—some manuscript, a copy of one—I didn't know anyone was dead.'

'People die every day, Marc!'

I began to insist I'd meant Benjamin *in particular* but—'Geez, I'm just joking!'—he knew what I'd meant, what with being in gainful employ as a salaried officer of the law!

'Anyway: you'd desired to keep possession of a facsimile of what you'd, by the time you popped round to meet Mrs. Strauss, discovered was her dead ex-husband's writing?'

Didn't much care for the way he was phrasing the matter, felt I'd been tripped up but also that it'd been my own fault. 'Still didn't know he was anyone's ex-husband—but for all intents and purposes, yes.'

'Why would you wanna go and do that, if you don't mind me being perplexed?'

'I'd grown attached to it—it was nifty and I'm the one who found it—childish things, none of which seemed they could possibly matter,' I spit out, rolling my eyes, fed up.

He conceded that what I said made a lot of common sense—didn't think I needed to be so up in arms, sorry he'd bothered me about explaining something so monotonous. 'Honest Injun, it'd been an off-the-cuff question, nothing more.' As though to smooth our ruffled rapport, he intimated how often he wanted to keep pieces of evidence from cases and crime scenes. 'Doesn't seem a bit fair to me how I can't, so I'm right with ya about holding onto a copy ...' leaned in like to share an unorthodox confidence '... lemme tell you about this one time ...' before sitting up as though the better had been thought of getting over familiar '... no, nevermind. But hey: have you ever watched the television program *The Flash*—the old one with John Wesley Shipp, like from when we were kids?'

'Yes ...' I said slowly, for some reason not wanting to betray how I thought I knew precisely why he was bringing that exact show up ... and more than a blip disquieted how I had several labeled VHS tapes from when I'd recorded the program in its original run at my apartment he'd only so recently visited.

'You know the episode with The Nightshade?'

'Yes ...' seems I'd been correct in my assumption about his association to the show and Hellpop must've recognized something in my expression because he lit up, snapping his fingers in celebration of finding a kindred spirit.

'Well, his little museum of curios from all his old adventures—remember?—that's what first made me want to be a copper!'

'No shit?'

'None at all!' He'd legitimately believed that once evidence stayed around long enough, it'd be up for grabs—even when they'd told him otherwise during his Academy days had figured they were simply giving the company line, but once he'd paid his dues a blind eye'd be turned. 'Now I will admit there's stuff gets auctioned, sometimes—though that's never strictly *evidence*—and I'm not gonna blow smoke, of course there exist bad eggs who swipe stuff, sell it to sickos who get their jollies off macabre memorabilia ...' he sighed long and melodramatic before summing up '... I guess it takes all kinds.' Straight into another curt pivot, as though our entire *Flash* interlude had taken place between parenthesis a reader ought feel free to skip over, he snapped his fingers-made-into-a-gun my direction then picked his ear with the muzzle of it, letting me know 'What I ain't so clear on's the following: Mrs. Strauss made it pretty gal-darned apparent you were to shove off—in no uncertain terms, I'd say, what with she'd had the *fucking police* summoned to underline the dictum, eh?' I was about to agree, fidgeting like a schoolkid, but he'd already continued, so I cracked my neck as though that'd been all I'd ever intended by my perking up and jitters. 'But then you sought out her kid?' I again opened my mouth, a natural hesitancy not of avoidance but of searching for how best to reply, and right away he told me 'That one was a question, just so you know ...' after which he took no pause before continuing '... her kid who's recently all of seventeen years of age, as you might be aware—is not what we adults term an adult, being my point, while you, just for example, haven't been a kid since *The Flash* was first-run during Primetime. Thing with a thing like that is: when a grown man approaches a minor, knowing full-tilt-boogie how the parent might take the liaison less than kindly, it's one of those occasions makes for *A Very Special Episode Of*, you follow me?' Lightly touched fingertips to the table, blinking in a startle, looked left-right left-right, then, totally different affect from the moment before, touched my hand to ask 'Had you told me what the manuscript was about?' Shook my head, trying not to flit my focus down to his fingers still on my skin. 'Well: what's the manuscript about, Marc?'

After a few uhs, told him 'Wait—no, yes, I did tell you.'

'Well: what's the manuscript about, Marc?'

'It's about *They Might Be Giants*.'

'What in the world's that supposed to be, again?'

'A band.'

'Terry's band?'

'No—they're called *Benny and the Roids*.'

'That's right ...' he comically smacked forehead with palm-butt '... so who're *They Might Be Giants*, you were about to tell me?'

'Just some band—some other band.'

'You like 'em?'

'Nope.'

'Well, blow me down!'

'Are you a fan?' I asked with marked sarcasm.

'Never heard of 'em ...' he grinned '... but I don't listen to music. Like talking to strangers, best steer clear.' He coughed, sipped his coffee, said 'Coffee' then winked until I nodded to make it clear I'd understood he'd actually said '*Cough-ee*' to which he flashed a thumbs-up. 'How do you know Terrance, if I may make so bold.'

'No, wait, listen: I *didn't* know—and don't *know*—Terrance. I'd seen posters for a band on the wall at his mother's house, observed someone had the same surname as his father, the author, so happened to call the joint on the poster, turned out there was a gig that night, decided to pay it a visit, since I was in town, didn't even know if I'd talk or anything, just wanted to check him out … which I kinda know sounds a lot worse, from what you were saying, but I simply thought I'd …'

'… maybe leave a photocopy of his murdered father's manuscript with him—not the original, because you didn't have that and, in any event, would've liked it too much and what'd the difference be.' My hard swallow seemed to be taken as a nod. 'An interesting point is this: why hadn't you just mailed the material? Don't you trust mailmen? I don't, by the way—but that's likely a quirk of mine and mine alone, so we'll just say I have reasons for feeling the way I do I'd rather not divulge and probe my psychology no deeper. What I meant regarding the subject at hand was: didn't you think you coulda mailed it, as an option—all the better to not freak anyone out and all?'

'I thought I'd already told you I'd thought of that—but maybe I hadn't … but, anyway: yes, I had.'

'Told me?'

'Thought of it.'

'I think you'd told me, too.'

'Then both!'

'Hey, settle down …' he purred unperturbed, moving a cigarette my way which I snatched rather petulantly '… could be you'd thought they'd have follow-up questions you'd be obliged to answer—that kinda thing doesn't much work in the format of a letter. Come to think of it: had there been questions you'd intended to put their way … or maybe something you wanted out of them?'

'That's outrageous!'

Well before I got outraged, he wanted me to view the business through the following aperture: 'You hadn't even brought the manuscript along with you to Mrs. Strauss or the kid—not really—as in you'd nothing on hand to deliver Mrs. Strauss, just a carrot to dangle, then with the kid had only dropped it with an employee of some pub after engaging in quite a protracted dialogue ... so when I put my mind to it, your intentions all seem rather curlicue. Can you shed some light on that?'

'Light?'

'Right.'

'On?'

'That.'

'What?'

'The conditions under which you'd give the thing up—or, to put it synonymously, the conditions under which you would not?'

'I haven't the faintest notion what you even might be driving at, detective.'

'Seeing as you didn't simply tender a copy to the woman you drove all the way out to see, leaving it up to her whether she wanted to cherish it, show it to her offspring, or toss it in the bin, I gotta wonder was there something required of her in exchange for the offer of it.'

Entirely fed up, I lost my cool, stamping out my barely suckled cig while demanding 'What in Christ's is happening, right now? May I ask, bluntly: have I done something wrong?'

Hellpop sniffled. 'That depends—did you kill Terrance Visa?' Just like that he put the question just that way—*whap!*—and clearly expected an articulate answer—just like that asked had I killed a child and expected me to respond without missing a beat, slapped the table, again, again, harder, harder, then glared at me until I finally squeaked out how I didn't understand what he was asking. 'Did you kill Terrance Visa?' he repeated, now placid, fingers of hands spread, eyes wide, twinkle of smirk to them, gazing my way like it was an obvious, even flirtatious, question to ask.

'Did anyone?' was what I managed.

Which surprisingly put him on what came across as a pleasant tangent, demeanor easing back to seem as though merely picking the brain of a revered and retired colleague he was glad for the insights of. 'Now there's a valid line of investigation! The theory young Terrance's death may've been accidental does have a lot to recommend it, you're right. He's a kid, first thing's first, and sometimes they do stuff by accident—then there's the troubled home life, dead dad, mom married to some monied schlub he can't stand so lives on whichever couches grown men he cozies up to in dive bars have on offer, so when he gets found dead, needle in his arm, not even just nearby it, and an alcoholic girl who had a fondness for him swears on her alive-and-kicking mother's grave Terry'd never ever tried drugs, it seems the miscalculations of an amateur could be to blame … or else a bad batch of brown sugar, et cetera, so forth … the lab isn't back about that yet.' But all that was neither here nor there, he again changed track to assure me. 'I do agree with you about how it might've been murder and might've been anyone—since I have you here, figured I'd nip that in the bud, seeing as you're someone, after all, and could be anyone, depending on who's asked.' It was the *timing* of it all—the timing's why I was sitting where I was, let him be honest. 'Terrance and that bartender chick had a sort of faux-sibling relationship, you might not know—she and the dead kid had read a bit of the manuscript, found it a hoot and all, and the dame mentioned it really appeared to've done Terry a heaping helping of good, thoughts of his old man, the banner times of yesteryear, melodrama and maudlin out the wazoo. You might not understand a thing like this, but the divorce'd been lousy with acrimony and Mrs. Strauss hadn't been keen on letting pops see kiddo, even before he'd shuffled off. Which I find sad. Do you find it sad?'

'I do.'

'Do you find it *familiar*?'

'Apparently, you know I do.'

'I knew you ought to, considering—but to get it down unambiguously: do you?'

'I do.'

'I do, too.'

There was another pause while he got a new cigarette going, offered me one, I accepted, lit up, and we both took drags in silence.

'Oddest thing you ever heard, Marc: that manuscript you left a copy of got up on its hind legs and walked away ...' Hellpop told me, adding '... *post-mortem* ...' with a trill of his fingers as though to suggest such was technically speculative but seemed conspicuously apparent '... broad couldn't find it amongst the boy's possessions and she hadn't kept it for herself—no one has a clue where it'd been spirited off to! Unfortunately, in her young, guileless grief, she'd asked mama Strauss about did *she* have it and—by Golly!— this gets ol' mater's blood boiling! Had that visiting scamp Marc Limoncello the unmitigated gall to impose himself upon her teen-aged son after she'd made it abundantly clear he wasn't to have interactions with her family, for real? Then there's talk of this *manuscript*, again, and of her dead ex's favorite band—sheesh! She was sick to her teeth, let's make no mistake about that, Marc, really on the warpath! This is all on record, having been poured out bitterly to a policeman she was acquainted with, one who knew from being there she wasn't joking about telling you to take a less-than-proverbial hike—so he reached out to our department, professional courtesy, my boss whispering to me yeah yeah yeah he knew it a tad outside my purview but might I have a quick word in your ear. The long and the short is it'd turned out to be my pleasure to—because it sure does look mighty funny, from the outside.'

No hesitation, I fairly sniffled 'It does.'

But that'd been neither a question nor a statement requesting response. 'Here's one, though: you'd stayed in town.'

'Town?'

'*Sarnath*. Dead man's town, dead kid's town—not their slogan, I'm only putting it that way for context. After leaving off the manuscript, you spent an entire night and day there, plus the evening beforehand. When'd you leave?'

I didn't recollect the date, sorry, but the night after seeing Mrs. Strauss and Terrance. 'The afternoon, at any rate.'

'Not the night after the night of that afternoon?'

'No.'

'Why stay even that long?'

'No reason.'

'None?'

'At all.'

Snapped his fingers a few times and wagged a finger at me, expression like I'd been trying to pull a fast one. 'Oh! Before I forget to ask: what clip were you talking about?'

'*Clip*?' I was one foot off the merry-go-round again, felt without reference but too rattled to be ill at ease.

'Said you coincidentally came across a clip about Benjamin Visa being dead ... but you didn't know anyone was named Benjamin Visa yet, did you?'

The bastard now let me sit in silence, drank his coffee, ate a few pizza flavored chips, offered me one—I took it, ate it, and answered him in a more tentative voice than I wanted because as I did so grew to realize I'd already explained it before.

'That's right ...' he munched, wave of apology '... but you know the guy you're talking about, dude with that blog, he died, too.'

'I'd come to be aware of that, yes.'

'Before or after your personal visit to Mrs. Strauss and her son?'

'Before.'

'Wait—really? Are you some kinda True Crime loser, into the bargain—I'd never've had you down for one of those, Marc!'

'I promise you, I am far from it.'

'Goodness me—all that story you'd told! Find out a guy's dead, then the guy you learned about the guy being dead through's dead, you're not even a fan of the music the two seemed to so clearly have in common, but decide it best to circumvent the United States Postal System, take all your days off work to drive ages away, all with it in mind to gladhand the surviving cast of characters—the *until-recently-surviving* cast of characters, some of them, turns out—and no one sees you again until you're back drinking on the job!'

'Am I under arrest—can I please get straight on that?'

'Yes—yes, indeed, you most certainly are.'

'On which charge?' I blurted in unconscious imitation of a dozen direct-to-video scenes.

'For the time being, none ...' Hellpop followed suit '... you are a person-of-interest in an ongoing homicide investigation, amongst other things.'

'I'm going to prison?' I sputtered, bewildered, mind in a wind tunnel, numb but understanding the impact was going to hit soon and hit hard.

'Naw, not prison—just *jail* and just for *awhile*.'

'What's awhile?'

Barring something unforeseen? 'You'll be free as a bird, in seventy-two hours.'

*the first in line to see
the missing head*

[*the monochrome martinet*]

As it panned out, I was held in police custody a touch less than twenty-four hours—which was more than twice plenty-long-enough and then some. Three meals were served me, the first practically right when I was clanged into lockup, the one served to other prisoners only a few hours later skipped over without remark, then standard lunchtime, dinnertime, though all I ate from each was the biscuit, drank the what-passed-for-coffee, and felt bashful each time I handed over my tray, watched the uneaten content tipped into a trashbin, worried each time a new meal was brought that I'd get lectured over how being wasteful or unappreciative was the sort of baseline character trait frowned upon in a place like this, not to mention made a fella give off guilty vibes, a true index some crook was rotten to the core—the existential anguish of 'be a good houseguest' was whipped to its thickest and I kept looping my mind around, trying to psych myself into believing local customs trumped medical conditions and self-preference, both. The worst was the horrific sense of time and space, of being embedded in the moment I was in, conscious of every physical inch of it and of me, how impossible it became to let myself become distracted by anything, let alone to invent, untether, think, daydream—tried to pepper my thoughts with blasé bromides such as 'travel broadens the mind' in order to tilt where I was and what was happening into a cultural moment of experiential value or an event witnessed from a distance, a moot trial I'd obviously come out the other end of unscathed, be able to novelize, so no point not romanticizing it while in progress ... but such effort only made things worse, the tension more compacted. The idea I'd ever have to tell anyone about what I'd been up to, the manuscript, the 'detective work,' let alone my having to do so by way of justifying an incarceration, grew me nauseous, at several moments on the actual verge of calling out for a guard, demanding I be seen by a court appointed physician with regard to a simmering panic attack—Viggo … his mother … Christ Jesus, my throat constricted over how she'd respond and what she'd do with the news … my sobering mind conjured up an onslaught of arguments which'd be leveled my way, each one painting me in a more irredeemable light. I didn't even call *The Calico* because the night I'd been picked up bled into my days off, so why make that bunch think even less of me than they most likely already did—not that every last washout who worked there wasn't some declension of ex-convict or on recommendation from this or that halfway house, except the housekeeper, who also worked busing tables at the duckpin alley, but she'd grown up in a cult famous enough to've been featured on the Nightly News, once upon a time, and had only come to us post-reprogramming … I needed to believe I possessed some face to save, a posterity worth fretting over … slept briefly, sitting up, because I felt lying down equaled considering myself done for.

When told I was being released, I didn't exactly know how to conduct myself, asked was I to further consult with Detective Hellpop or was an escort shuttling me back home, to which I was responded a piteous glaze of eyes and a breath which translated to I'd be back in no time if I kept thinking in such imbecile terms—kept further inquiry to myself, including any question regarding which circumstances had shifted to allow my being sent on my way … was I cleared of whichever suspicion, did someone owe me an apology they were skimping on? I wasn't exactly relieved as I used the restroom off to the left of where my exit papers were processed and when, as I signed a few things I hadn't bothered examining, the woman working the desk told me 'Your lawyer's waiting out front, he said to say' I just blinked, all but certain there'd been a monumental snafu and I'd soon be accused of 'jailbreak under false pretense' or some other such rubbish crime that'd help truss me up but good, caulk over the unlawfulness of my having been brought in, to begin with—not to mention being pranged with Civil charges from whoever's lawyer had actually sprung whichever lout, made to pay out big league for shuck-and-jive mental distress caused by my scofflaw impersonation, a seemingly opportunistic nature pegging me a flimflammer, through-and-through.

For a moment, I reckoned I'd better be sneaky about how I exited the building, just in case the legal beagle waiting in front would do a double take, send me back—but at three in the morning it wasn't exactly gonna be a railway station outside, so no method of blending in sprang to mind except ones which'd seem tremendously conspicuous if noticed. Then it occurred to me how whoever the attorney was'd have no idea about me, one way or the other, so the best bet'd be to stroll out as though I hadn't a care in the world, worked there, had been visiting someone in the capacity of assisting them back onto the straight and narrow—stiffened myself up into pious posture, hands in my pockets, like the primrose path was wide and idle for a bloke of my fine breeding. Shock to my system when a slender chap waved, called me by first and surname, asked how I'd slept, and held across a packet of fancy cigarettes, colored papers, a nice mint-green unfiltered poking out my direction which, without a word and in no hurry, I accepted, declining a light to instead tend to with my personal Bic, after which I waved away his offer of keeping the rest of the pack—regretting it as I took a long drag, had a look around at the blank of the witching hour, pavement and sundry surfaces powdered with what seemed more like hail than light snow.

'*Crusted* is the better word ...' I for whatever damn reason vocalized, the man taking the statement in stride, glancing to where my last blink had fallen, nodding thoughtfully enough I got the impression he totally knew what I'd been referring to—must've also been acutely aware of the once-over I was giving him, my hairy eyeball far from subtle: his suit struck me as flippant, especially considering where we were and when, something about the coloring of the jacket and pants, the shirt, the tie, the pocket square, and a sheen to the fabric paired with the shine to his shoes reminded me of a condom wrapper, an impression so distinct but oddball I almost told him to his face, wondering would he laugh and confess that'd been precisely what he'd been aiming for, thank me a lot for being the first person who'd noticed it and taken time out to appreciate the care he put into appearances.

'Do you want something to eat?' he asked, shrug like nothing was nothing.

Told him I didn't think anywhere was open, but he pointed out there was a joint directly across the street from us—I'd forgotten we weren't near *The Calico*, weren't even in *Laampray* going by the signage on the station house. 'I'm new in town, so you'll pardon my bluntness I hope ...' I blew out a slow breath of cig '... but what exactly do you have to sell me, here?'

No beat missed, he half-whispered to me 'I'm one of those creepy faggots who springs bums from the clink in exchange for favors of a perverted nature, as seen on TV ...' held deadpan long enough for actual concern to show on my face before laughing bulbous and extending his hand '... Nathan Jehovah ...' he held a grin high even though I blatantly waited several beats before giving his paw the most perfunctory and unfriendly of taps '... I think you were briefly acquainted with my nephew, if I got this correct?' I squinted while he explained how 'Of course, young Terrance isn't my *nephew* in any sort of *bloodline* way of viewing the world, but I've always thought of the kiddo in such terms of endearment, no brood of my own, do you see?'

'Are you really a lawyer?' I needed to know, gut suddenly tight like against diarrhea, really giving a think to making an about-face, demanding I be put back into the holding cell, snug and secure.

'Sure.'

The monosyllabic response didn't put me at ease. 'You bailed me out?'

'I *lawyered* you out,' he corrected.

I didn't know what that meant, if it meant anything, and he pointed out we weren't moving yet, which he felt was quite silly, seeing as a well-balanced breakfast awaited. 'Or at the very least something scrumptious enough to make you temporarily not care how obvious it is you'll regret every crumb.'

Where such repast awaited was a run-of-the-mill greasy spoon, cops loosely littering tables, the few other patrons, I imagined, local newspapermen or sidewalk-seller folks waiting out a last few hours before their daily business got going and, under different circumstances, I'd've been positively enchanted by everything the place had to offer—its humid dinge, mop-water lighting, jukebox set on Oldies which always felt magically generic despite being known adoringly beat-for-beat, coded mumbles as meal orders, plates not cleared from tables with any urgency once patrons had toddled out with belts loosened, tips left either too much or miserly … yep, in my youth I'd have attempted to make such venue my haunt, though always woulda felt an imposter, same as I still felt anywhere … *except in the holding cell* came a thought unbidden but mostly accurate … I'd not felt 'at home' there, per se, but so very appropriate I didn't yet know how to feel being out.

Once coffee and a doughnut were brought for me and an omelet meal was placed in front of Nathan, space-aged silver coffee pot set at table center, my savior said through a mouthful of hashbrown 'Fan of *The Giants*, are you?'

'Not at all.'

'Not a little?'

'Less and less, as it happens.'

'You're a man plucked from a million …' he chewed the words, eyes raised in a kind of gawk at the curio of my taste.

'Am I, though?'

'Perhaps we run in different circles, is all.'

'No doubt …' I rolled my eyes, though didn't know if my agreement proved a point or undercut one '… I guess that song 'Twisting' is alright…' I shrugged, offering this engagement out of courtesy and on account of it was the only title I could recollect—he sang a little of it, patting the edge of the counter as instrumental, looked at me like to verify we meant the same piece. 'That's the one …' I sighed, suddenly no longer fond of it even as much as I had been.

'What about ...' he furrowed his brow, massaged the Dogue de Bordeaux wrinkles in a gesture of *think think think*, then rattled off '... 'Sleeping In The Flowers' ...'

'No.'

'... 'Spoiler Alert' ...'

'Nope.'

'... Take Out The Trash'?'

'Never heard it.'

'How about ... 'Wait Actually Yeah No'?'

'... okay ...'

'You are fond of 'Birdhouse,' at least?' Stared expressionless and reached for the pack of smokes he'd set out while he sang a bit— screwed up my face, shook it like something smelled worse than it looked and his face, in turn, contorted itself into Holy Smokes! but mirthful. 'You are just as peculiar to me as most people'd term buttons cute! How've you gotten involved, then?'

'I don't have any involvement.'

'In?'

'This.'

'What?'

'I don't know.'

'Then how do you know?'

'It seems fairly obvious, from my point-of-view.'

'Which is?'

'Lookit: if you're a lawyer, I'm certain you've been given access to all kinds of a dossier which told all about what I'd been in holding for better than I ever could, so why not cut it out with the pat-a-cake and get to your point?'

Instead, like I hadn't been as curt as I'd made concerted effort to be, he wiped his mouth, sipped coffee, wiped his mouth again, took one more fork-cut bite of omelet, and gave me a little speech which struck me as very much pre-rehearsed. 'As for myself, I am a lifelong fan, though that's not the word I prefer. Believe me, Marc, I've met *fans*, the rabble who dub themselves such with cookie-cutter pride, even admit, through a blush, how I began as one, as is only natural, larval and naïve, but, no, I cannot endorse most of them and stopped attending live performances a decade ago due to finding such company altogether disgraceful—the perennially stunted hangers-on who, even at fifty, hold hands like fifth graders, claim they love the music for its playfulness, its antidote to the Bacchanal of most rock-n-roll, whatever such verbiage's even supposed to mean, and who dress up as characters replete with adopted personas cribbed from liner notes or wiki-excerpts of interviews, as though they're the ones pure, innocent, and studious enough to get it. I find the same features present in most Lovecraft fans, quite frankly—abject bores who latch onto the most surface level, front-and-center aspects of an Art, overpronounce it, miss the guts beneath the epidermis, entirely, but tut-tut others for being no more than skin-deep, nicknaming themselves all the same obvious referents as they strut in purloined ownership of the stuff ... though, worst of all, are the deep divers, the analysts, the play-pretend scholars, collectors of factoids who set up lifeless mausoleums of television appearances, fan photos, and oral histories, entirely missing the pulse.'

'We're still speaking of Lovecraft, are we?' I quipped after a long breath of cigarette upward to one side.

He winked at my fatuousness, apologized for the previous rant, as he supposed it was neither here nor there. 'My own connection to the music came through Benjamin—who you know of but never knew. He blushlessly considered himself a very big fan of the band, indeed, and I was a very big fan of his. In ways I cannot rightly express, we became quite inseparable—this was in seventh grade, you understand, was that sort of inseparable, lived at each other's kitchen tables and slept in piles on bedroom floors, our minds overlapping rambunctiously. I'd none of my afore-seethed opinions of other listeners of *They Might Be Giants* in those days, of course—the songs and reactions of others were sounds to listen and riff along with and over time became the soundtrack to my unconscious. Do you apprehend what I mean? Perhaps you aren't the sort who could ... to explain as best I can: I'm something of a mathematician, even moreso than I'm something of a lawyer, and for the years it took to become these—starting as daydreams and imitations of television programs, through to slogged years at University, then padding in the murk for stable employment which wouldn't leave my soul tasting of bilgewater—I would think of my life's events as though little movie trailers, set always to *Giants* songs, the most random of which never failed to go lock-step with various breakthroughs I'd have on professional or research fronts … without even realizing it, for example, while I struggled with my dissertation to secure doctorate, would introduce myself at functions always as *Dr. Worm* … as I was not yet a real doctor, you see?' He paused as though for camaraderie, but soon gave a crestfallen tsk at the realization that if he'd made a reference, there, it was lost on me, took a further beat to light a pink cigarette and summon more coffee, then picked up with '… I wouldn't have stayed interested, though, same as I'd never have become interested, if not for Benjamin. He was forever on about them and yet, contradictory as it sounds, I can think of very few times he brought them up—other than during our early days, can summon no memory of him specifically conversing with regard to the group, their new albums, so forth.'

I nodded and he nodded back, so felt the conversation ball was in my court but didn't exactly care to do anything with it. 'You were a good friend of Benjamin's, then?' was all I limply managed, a lacquer of unintended sarcasm to it he either didn't notice or didn't hold against me.

'Oh, we were the very best of friends—a trio inseparable, as I said, until we weren't. Things happen in life, as you no doubt are aware, from which there is no going back.'

Annoyed at another stranger insinuating knowledge of my failed personal life, I pursed my lips in almost genuine curiosity, rolling my hand like to stir up further context, asking 'What had you meant by *trio*.'

'Benjamin, myself, and Sullivan—ever since middle-school …' but he stopped short, must've noted my involuntary change in expression at the mention of the name *Sullivan* '… you know him?'

'I've heard of him, I think,' was the best I could put it.

Though it was abundantly evident from his shift in posture that Nathan was keen for further explication of this vagary, for whatever reason he staved off asking direct follow-ups, and instead, like 'Take Two, action!' had been called and he was the consummate professional, returned to the expository narrative about the lifelong bond between he and Benjamin. 'We were far closer than he and Sullivan were ...' it seemed important to him I understand, the point belabored for nearly ten minutes with a series of anecdotes and minutia presented as though courtroom exhibits—a presentation brimming with aspects unspoken, I felt, some element not being blurted first and foremost due either to decorum or feeling I'd not be simpatico enough to take his side bullishly. Why he needed to so thoroughly, yet in so peculiarly underhanded a manner, paint Sullivan in a negative light was beyond me and grew tiresome, double quick—told him I couldn't care less, then gave a look of consideration, amending my pronouncement to 'No, I actually might be able to, if you really want me to give it a go—pray continue.'

'I don't much care for your tone.'

'I don't much care what you care for. Is bail refundable—if you recall, I didn't use my one telephone call to summon you,' I sniped, sitting back, eyeing the last of my doughnut but feeling it might send mixed signals to reach for it, right then.

'I *lawyered* you out,' he reiterated.

'Then I guess we're even, in the eyes of the law.'

He giggled at that far more than I felt was warranted, waggled a finger my way in mock-chastising, told me he'd changed his mind. 'You're growing on me, tone and all—I find you fascinating, in several ways, quite frankly.'

'I bet you say that to all the girls.'

'*Not all boys are the same but some boys are the same ...*' he replied with a cheek twitch—clearly another quotation or reference or paraphrase he knew would be lost on me, this time seeming rather to like how it was—then switched conversational gears to how, as a matter of fact, I'd been correct when I'd suggested he'd been given paperwork containing summary of my situation, material he'd taken it upon himself to explore in a thoroughly scrutinous manner—wondered would I mind his asking a few contextualizing queries.

'Am I being charged?' Again, now seeming to insist it important, he told me he'd lawyered me out of any legal bind, but I shook my head. 'For this ...' I groaned like going capsized, gestured my hand back-and-forth over the table between us '... attorney-client consultation or whatever such a thing'd be known as in the trades.'

'Marc, I'm not really *your* lawyer, just *a* lawyer—unless you *want* me to be your lawyer ... except, in that case, you couldn't afford me ... though we might be able to work out a deal.'

Pleased with myself for how long I'd kept from grabbing his bourgeois lapels to cram a proper 'What is it you fucking want, man?' down his throat, I was now precisely on the brink—the assault to my psychology from the previous night's interrogation, the hours in a holding cell, it was catching up to me, then add in the violent realization that nothing which'd happened to me for quite some time was being treated as the game I'd considered it or the misunderstanding it obviously must've been, no matter how little I understood and regardless how less it concerned me, and the result was the forfeit of my tether. I was bone tired, simply wondering how I was going to get home ... then felt triple-drained at knowing the only way I honestly had at my disposal was the barely-not-being-throttled man sitting across from me poking a fingertip to his plate to dab up crumbs of bacon and potato char.

'What I read in the report hadn't given me any indication you might be aware of Sullivan,' Jehovah broke in, no doubt noticing the glaze over the bloodshot of my eyes and, seeing no reason not to, or maybe not looking for one, I told him to get me another doughnut. 'I'll get several,' he gestured as though this went without saying, and once he'd ordered them, I gave him the scoop concerning how *Sullivan Shallcross* had been the name Benjamin's room at *The Calico* had been taken out under.

'Simple as that,' I puffed air out one cheek, smiling at the waitress as she placed doughnuts at center table, waiting until she'd moved off to snatch one, over-chomping the first mouthful of cake and tight chocolate icing like a gloat I'd gotten something over on an opponent.

My remark seemed to've struck Nathan deeply in some private way—a distinct mix of very particular emotions, while equally a single indeterminant one, paced in the crow's-feet around his wide eyes: surprise, melancholy, betrayal, suspicion, confusion, nostalgia. The change to the atmosphere was striking—not enough I regretted telling him, but almost enough I felt like pressing him with a taunt of 'Penny for your thoughts.'

Eventually he nodded, said he'd neglected to request that the waitress bring a bag for the doughnuts—'Would you like a lift home?' he vaguely said like to nobody then stood before I could answer and I watched him stroll all the way to the restroom on the clear opposite side of the place, around a corner which seemed an optical illusion from where I sat.

It crossed my mind how easily I could leave, scurry down a few streets, duck in someplace or behind something, wait out a few hours ... but also struck me how pointless it'd be to do so—the man obviously knew where I lived and worked and I'd no viable way to get myself to either without him. Assured myself I wasn't interested in anything from the weirdo beyond such transport, though argued how it seemed there was a case for someone pointing out otherwise ... I confessed to a kind of draw toward his story, the details he was providing, all of it enticing, stoking something in me uncomfortably close to the clinginess of a first date about to end, kiss not yet a foregone conclusion. 'You're in shock, you're fatigued ... I explained it before ...' I whispered, felt the thousand perverse implications of where I was sitting and who with circling me, sniffing at the edge of my periphery. Too late to run, nowhere to hide, the fact that I was in the company of Nathan Jehovah and that sitting with Nathan Jehovah, under the circumstances I was, felt organic, drained all imperative, all volition from me—regardless whether I desired it or detested it, understood myself sat plop where I most needed to be ... which wasn't where I preferred to be ... was where I preferred to not want to be ... any such consideration purely semantic as I watched Nathan stop at the counter to retrieve a bag for the doughnuts, held a hand out for the pleasant, white-waxed, thick sack as he arrived, then placed the treats inside, one by one.

I didn't flinch when he patted my shoulder on the way to the door—felt so unfortunately myself I had to laugh.

[*accidentally in a coal mine it was found*]

After ten minutes driving, snow flurries abating, picking up, abating, no word passing between Nathan and I, my heart further sank at the sight of a road sign reminder that this was gonna be a forty-five minute drive, another symptom of how shook up I was, somehow I'd not at all registered the distance the detective had brought me the previous night and even the name on the station front hadn't really screwed the point consciously home—as we made the turn onto the main road leading to *Laampray*, I grew unable to maintain my cool without some kind of anxious prattle, so asked after the music on the radio.

'I'm surprised you don't know this album,' Nathan scoffed in a cheery way.

'I don't know any,' I explained as though for the millionth and final time.

He chuckled, seemed about to say something else, changed his mind to explaining how what we were listening to was called *The Escape Team*, the specific track titled 're-Pete Offender,' then gave some rap about how Benjamin had always harbored mixed feelings about the project. 'He felt it being so consciously a *concept album*, having so concrete and definitive a *function*, so to speak—linking itself directly to an accompanying comic book, so forth—somehow drained from its overall merit, diluted its oomph, despite the songs themselves possessing all the same esoteric touchstones and absurdist underpinnings of any *Giants* offering. Which isn't to say he found fault with the artistry on display—far from it! The song we just finished, which was his avowed fave on the album and which he spoke of alongside greats from even the most highly regarded discs from the boys, is a prime example of how the verve and cartwheeling inventiveness they possessed would fit itself to any container—in my opinion this being even moreso in evidence with 'Mister Mischief Night' and 'Juan Postal,' which I can tap back to, if you're keen.' He was moving his finger to the radio to do just that, but I told him, in all vowels around a mouthful of the last available doughnut, how it wouldn't be necessary—as though never having intended to actually waste time playing me anything, returned both hands to the steering wheel and kept on speaking, technically overlapping the last smecks of my declining his offer, the moment before. 'Each individual song on *Escape Team*, according to Benny, would've been a gem were it to've appeared within another album's listings and, depending on which album, several may even've been the best on tap, regardless, would garner more individuated attention and processing than when all so directly to do with each other, building blocks to a little diorama, details in a miniature. The combination of the songs and artwork—while conveying what it set out to, no question—alas was a tad too precious and, in my friend's eyes, somehow affected the tunes even when they were heard by someone with no understanding of any trivia else. I agreed wholeheartedly—perhaps not surprisingly—and also supported the sentiment that, scattered amongst the band's output, these all would've been delightful character pieces, their kinship a special treat to uncover by attentive, curious-enough listeners, a secondary world certain individuals might've sorted out for themselves, built histories and connections regarding while never knowing for sure if such was the intention or not. I remember the conversation well, Mister Limoncello, because it suggested how purposeful a schematic might be at play, directly beneath the noses of an audience who'd never peer beyond the surface gloss presented so quantifiably, a clue of sorts which put other observations Ben made in a more focused light—how certain pieces sharing iconographies and predilections were disseminated across decades while these were bundled together served as a *pointer*. In the same conversation, Ben explained how he had to put an album titled *Glean* above *Escape Team* just slightly in rank, for while *Glean* was also too self-contained for his taste, not abstract enough the so-easy-to-sketch out a through-line in evidence—indeed, he somewhat derisively thought the Johns had watched *Eternal Sunshine of the Spotless Mind* and decided to reproduce it as a marginally veiled, fragmented musical—at least that album swung wide in its venture and any connective tissue had to be induced by an active audience. The two albums proved a *sequence in quality*, a *progress* he didn't speak of in depth, on that day, but which got my attention, my own wheels taking turns they couldn't be spoon fed.'

As it would've been impossible to express to the man how little I cared about any of what he was saying, I merely endured it and eventually, after a bit of coughing out dryness from his throat, he mercifully altered tactic to asking if I could give him further insight into the structure and content of the manuscript—I remained silent, though, couldn't shake how there was something off about the guy, a quality difficult to put into words of one syllable, he seemed up to something and the fact he was helping me out of a jam tweaked him the more dubious still. Well put together, articulate, implacable, polite, yet each second spent with him I felt myself in the presence of something squirming, as regardless of what he said, his words were ropes made of buttered eels and the impression given off by them was that there lurked something he wasn't letting on about, an undercurrent he desired to express but couldn't make blatant until he'd sorted out something about me—he seemed not *manipulative*, almost *childish*, in fact ... *wimpy* might even've been the correct term ... I got the impression that he felt, were his cards put on the table, he'd lose even though I'd already folded my hand. This assessment was reinforced when, as though the words had been held back but no longer could be, in good conscience, he blurted: 'Sullivan Shallcross is a *liar*—whatever impression else you may have of the man, please take that to heart. I know how he comes across, which is however he wants depending on whichever purpose he'll conveniently leave off divulging. Lord knows what leprous distillment he might've poured in your ear about me—about all of us, in which manner he might've perverted our history—but none of it's to be trusted. That charlatan's nothing to do with Benjamin—not for ages and whatever he alleges was between them, in epochs bygone, is no more than a screeching figment of his monied imagination. I could give you the blow-by-blow of his every travesty, but shalln't be petty—sufficed to say, he has neither connection nor rights to anything of or belonging to Benjamin, however dearly we all once held each other. This is a man corrupted, Mister Limoncello—he'll work hard to portray me as a misguided zealot or a …' he took a pause as though the word were particularly distasteful to utter '… a *numerologist*, but I am the furthest thing from either! I surely admit him capable of spinning a yarn that even I might believe—of crafting phantasmagoria I shamefully didn't do more to pierce the veil of when it might've made all the difference—and well I know that he can couch points in a way I at times envy, construct fanciful vistas out of elements and sights true to the natural eye … but he is a cheat, a false-friend, a betrayer. If he moved you to believe he was intimate with Benjamin, in any present capacity, he has baldly deceived you—there hasn't been so much as telephonic air between them in a dogs' age and umpteen times he'd been turned out on his ear. You've no reason to believe me, of course—you have every reason to distrust me, no doubt!—and I know what you're thinking about me and you're absolutely correct to be, Marc: where did I come from, who am I, what am I doing here, what're you to me?'

He went silent abruptly, an almost audible *clunk* to it, while I chewed the inside of my cheek and looked out the window, strong instinct to remain clammed up the remainder of the journey … except to not counter such a rant was a kind of tacit acquiescence to whatever point Nathan felt he'd proven, would no doubt reinforce some truth in his mind—logic didn't matter, everything was down to how this man, specifically, would interpret the stimulus provided him. No doubt he could do a real number on me were I to cross a line, how he'd 'helped me out' entirely illustrative of the power he had to raze my life to the ground—the menace he represented was uncanny, despite I might've been conjuring it from whole cloth.

'I've never met Sullivan Shallcross …' I finally said, turning to Nathan directly '… never've so much as spoken peep to the chap. I cotton from what you've said why you figure I might've, but he's just a name, in my experience, and I'd thought him to be a fake one. Even when I looked it up, no Sullivan Shallcross appeared to have the measliest connection to anything—not that I knew what things there were to connect or to which they'd possibly have connection.' Huffed, patted my knees, shrugged shoulders high, huffed again, patted my knees. 'Lookit: I am just literally nobody, okay? I've got nothing to do with you, with Benjamin, with Sullivan—I seriously don't even like this band of yours, think they stink, if you want the hard word. I appreciate you getting me out of a bind … but all this other business you're on about is Greek to me … it's a ride I just want off, you dig?'

He nodded, sighed, and told me flatly that he believed me when I said so but equally didn't—wanted to but couldn't—and tried to put a jovial bent to this impasse by framing it thus: 'We're in it together, for a bit—though there's worse things to be, probably.' Next, he prodded me with a recap of what he'd learned from the detective's notes—how they'd hipped him that I'd claimed to've found the manuscript at the same time as a typewriter when I'd anything but, for example, and he wondered, somewhat rhetorically, why I'd lied to the police about such a strange crumb of minutia. 'I suppose I want to know what's the genuine truth—need a way to suss inside from out.'

'I just lied, Nathan …' I tried to ebb his energy down '… seemed easier than relating every last curlicue—sometimes people're numbskulls, you know?'

'Or perhaps people want what they say codified by official record—you see what I mean?'

'I don't.'

'In case someone else ever looks into it.'

'Now I even less. Listen …'

He held up a soft hand which translated to he wouldn't, explained gravely how he couldn't be careful enough about every particular, and barreled ahead with all kinds of gimcrack theories concerning how, even though I'd been witnessed at a photocopier, it didn't mean what I'd photocopied was the original manuscript—after all, I was claiming it to've been nothing of the sort—so, by extension, any further photocopies couldn't be treated as substitutes for an authentic original artifact. 'See it from this angle, if you will: you *might've* discovered a hand-written original, typed it up, and copied that, maybe made changes to what was written, here or there, even accidentally, while transcribing—songs in a different order, that sort of quirk.' Not that he was making an accusation—nothing of the sort!—obviously, though, if someone else had possessed the original, before me, it might've been they who'd molested it as he'd only just postulated. 'I've never laid eyes on this manuscript, original or duplicate—that is my primary source of tension, you must understand. I can well imagine it, had known it was going to be written … but other than that, it's all too much to blithely take a third party's word on, no questions asked. Instead, you must take me at my word when I stress how it's of paramount importance that I learn whether there still exists an original, whether you know its whereabouts, and, if possible, that I obtain it.'

If there were, indeed, only duplicates, he desperately needed to scrutinize their pedigree, nail it down utterly, compile a chain of custody tick-to-tock from copy to copy-of-copy, as at any stage, even after replicas existed, alterations may've occurred before being replicated further, for whichever reason—most imperative was that, whatever version or versions existed, he be the one to examine them first.

'Before Sullivan has a chance to,' he added, almost apologetically, seeming to cringe at how the words made him come across some fanatic basted in colors of crackpot, a looney-bird nursing a carnival grudge instead of an honest man with an agenda to take at face value.

'Don't you think he's had that chance—my apartment was burglarized …' I ventured cautiously, not wanting waters to get choppy.

'How could that've been Sullivan?' he asked, perplexed. 'You allege not to know the man—how would he have any inkling of you?'

'I'm asking if it was *you* who burgled me, actually ...' but I could tell halfway through speaking these words that the man hadn't a thing to do with the incident, knew of the trespass only from whatever he'd read about it in the capacity of 'being my lawyer,' his mind already churning with as many noiac suppositions as my own.

'It was only a copy that'd been absconded with, correct?' The mask of his face in the rearview betrayed nervousness enough to let me know I was yet being probed.

'There's only ever been copies.'

'Not possible.'

'There's only ever been copies to steal, then.'

'How many exist?'

'Just that and the one left with Terrance.'

'Both stolen.'

'Who said that one's stolen?'

'Where is it, then?'

'The kid maybe tossed it in a rubbish bin, burned it—all things considered, and not to come off crass, his state of mind wasn't up to factory specifications, was it?'

'You think my nephew killed himself?'

'I dunno ...' took a pack of cigarettes from the dashboard '... maybe ...' got one to my mouth '... *inadvertently* ...' lit it even as I asked '... do you particularly think he didn't?'

'The timing seems strange,' Nathan said quietly enough he almost just breathed.

'Does the timing ever seem apt for a teenage overdose?' I volleyed back, inhaling deeply.

Unphased, he amended his statement to 'The timing seems *especially* strange.'

Holding in my drag, I ventured 'Maybe you killed Terrance ...' let it out slow '... hadn't that ever occurred to you?'

'No ...' he chuckled '... but I have considerable inside information making such proposition silly.' He pushed in the car lighter, reached for the cigarettes I'd tossed back on the dash. 'Maybe Sullivan did—hadn't *that* ever occurred to *you*?' Odd emphasis to the question, like still rooting out whether I was in some kinda cahoots with his nemesis.

'I didn't know Sullivan was a real person until about five minutes ago, as I've already told you,' I put a fine point on the matter, almost a growl. 'Is that what Sullivan is to you, now—a former friend, a liar, and a child killer?' Nathan numbly shook his face, which I didn't like the feeling of, so figured I'd better drop even the banter-esque antagonism—put a somber cadence to my voice, turning toward him to say 'If you think your nephew was murdered, I don't see how I'm the guy to confide in.'

'As a lawyer ...' he quipped '... I foster an innate distrust of policemen, if what you're suggesting is that I try floating unsolicited murder theories to them without evidentiary basis.'

Likely unaware of it, his driving was incrementally picking up speed, eyes more on me than the road—regretted hopping to this track, my knee bouncing, rather wanted to wend back to the manuscript, find some way to wield it, shoo him outta my life. Took a drag, then simply shoehorned 'Nathan, the truth is what I found at the motel was already a photocopy, okay? From it I made a few copies, just because it was neat—I was gonna share it with people for a kick, a story, a party favor. In total, there was the quote-endquote original, the copy for Ben's wife that wound up with Terrance, and one more. Both that one-more and the faux-original were in the strongbox that got lifted. You wanna know the weirdest thing? I'd even considered putting the one I'd first found back in the vent—got to thinking it was so goddamned bizarre an item to've buried that no doubt, one day, someone who held legitimate claim would come prowling around.'

The vehicle had slowed during my recitation and, following it, Nathan lapsed into contemplative silence—the car lighter popped, his cigarette was lit, he inhaled, exhaled, and asked 'Is that the truth?'

'Why the fuck wouldn't it be?'

'A moment ago you'd told me there was only the original and the copy—now two's become three.'

'I'd meant two copies plus the original copy.'
'Even when I'd said *both*?'
'Had you?'
'Decidedly.'
'I must've thought we both meant the same *both*.'
'Meaning both *copies*, not the *original*.'
'Yes—but also meaning the *original* was always a *copy*.'
'Which you'd considered returning to the vent from whence it came.'
'Correct.'
'Did you ever?'
'No.'
'Who else have you talked to about this?'
'Oh for heaven's sake—can you just let me out, right here!? Seriously, fella, I have all day and don't mind the walk—and you're fraying my last nerve. It'd been mighty Christian of you, springing me from the clink, but all I want's to get back to humble living, unbothered by whichever cloak and dagger you and this band's blasted fan club have cooking.' It was lunatic how no one would simply take me at my word—my story made as much sense as anything in Nathan's head, for starters, plus, from what I could tell, he knew nothing at all—soon my temper had the better of me, coiled into an aggressive curiosity, stovetop orange. 'Let me ask you a few questions, while we're at it. What difference is there if it was a copy I found or an original? For all you know—and you said as much yourself—yer buddy might've penned it out longhand, then typed the bugger— maybe *he'd* made mistakes doing that, never noticed—such things happen, right? You haven't seen the manuscript, man, but I have! Lemme assure ya—it's a three-hundred page, self-indulgent geek-fest, scribble scrabble corrections all over the place, literally a ponderous transcription of the same convoluted blather people fart on about when it comes to any band, any record, if you poke around enough, the sort of tedious, pedantic faff that fills the void of the world wide web's every nook and cranny. Nathan: it was his personal, overly wrought, nonsensical poetics about a buncha songs! I

mean, what do you truly effing care? I could understand you if this was a matter of your best pal's snuffed it and you want some totem to cling to, but at the same time I feel obligated to point out that if your darling Benny'd wanted you to have custody of this treatise of his—original or otherwise—he'd have licked a few stamps, not snugged it in a literal hole in the wall at some last-ditch motel in a town you've never even heard of!'

I abruptly cut off when I recalled the envelope which'd accompanied Benjamin's writing, NATHAN JEHOVAH typed on it, in my slot at the Post Office, contents still uninspected—the very Nathan who that'd absolutely been meant for sitting behind the driving wheel, less than arm's length from me, clearly intrigued by my sudden silence … if that's who he was … wanted to ask did he have a card, could I see his license and registration, but—boy oh boy!—wouldn't that come off peculiar, at this juncture? My mouth went dry and my eyes flitted to the radio, shocked at no tape deck, then remembered whose car I was in, averted my eyes, closed them, and a moment later had to think of something to say in reply to his asking me if I was feeling alright.

'Everything's fine …' I unimpressively burped, then thought Hell with it, knew asking'd clear up the weird pause plus seem perfectly unconnected to what I'd been ranting about, by now, so went '… may I please see some identification?'

He simply gagged a guffaw of nicotine. 'Now you're getting it, eh?'

'Can't truthfully say that I am, is my point.'

He hocked up a few more chuckles, worked his wallet out of his suitcoat pocket, and tossed it for me to inspect at my leisure. 'Trust needs to be earned,' he intoned with a last cough and a thump to his chest.

Everything appeared legit, had a solid flush of cash money, credit cards, photos of family, his business cards were even plenty classy—made me realize in a glum way how I'd never even owned a proper wallet, just the odd flap of leather that'd been part of one I'd once found in a desk drawer during a shift as a temp sorting files for a realtor. Handed it back his way, but he told me just to toss it on the dash, though I oughta take his card, first—I did so, simply to not make any more an ass of myself, and really felt depleted, less-than-zero, a brackish current of wanting some answers but only because getting them was probably the swiftest way of attaining the competing desire of being left alone. This idiot wasn't gonna be done with me until he got what he was after, so why not give it up—take him to the original, the letter addressed to him, the cassette, fork it all over, and let him knock himself out? I really couldn't answer myself except by admitting I didn't think he *deserved* it—some tarted up loser couldn't swoop in, bully me out of my finders-keepers-fair-and-square on account of some jabberwocky and hijinks nothing to do with me but which'd, by now, really put me through the wringer and likely held consequences still to come. Oh sure, I hand it over, he goes away—but flash forward a jaunt and all of a sudden it's me talking to detectives about overdosed kids, harassment, and murder most foul, and all I can do by way of explaining myself is rattling off this weird little episode with Nathan which not even I'd expect someone to believe were it told them!

I was surprised when, referencing the final lines of my abated tantrum, he soberly told me '... you're absolutely correct: if Ben had desired to send me what he'd written, copy or not, I'm sure he could have. But he didn't. You're not wrong to be cautious. So I find myself in an impossible spot—quite an ironic one, all things considered. I have to wonder *why didn't he* and also wonder if he honestly did. Do you see what I mean? You claim what he hid away was a copy. Perhaps it was. Could he have sent me the original, in that case? Could the package have been intercepted? Did he hide the original, someone else find it, alter certain elements, hide the copy you found knowing somehow or another I'd come across it—had you just happened to be that *How*. I feel I would *know*, Marc, if I could see it, hold it—but maybe I wouldn't. I admit I find it difficult to stomach Sullivan's name being part of this, but you know as well as I do how it'd been used to rent the room. I can't know what that means. The more I think about it, it could mean anything. No matter, though—this isn't something I can let go. No one involved in this will ever let it go. Which now includes you, I'm sorry to say. Even if I believe you, man, my belief won't do either of us any good.'

His unforced emotion caught me quite off guard—as did the rather rollercoaster trip from sentiment to philosophy to what came across practically a threat … enough of one, anyway, I felt it best to invite him inside when he pulled into the lot of my building, an unprompted courtesy he was either pleased with himself over having tricked me into or alarmed by … I was too exhausted to differentiate such nuanced shades of what didn't matter.

He wordlessly followed me down the stairs, eyeballing the stale narrow hall in an especially skeptical way, so much I broke the silence with 'I promise I'm not taking you to the kill room, this is just where I live'—hoped it got across how much he didn't need to consider me, how not of his world or any world I was, gestured around with jokes about not being able to offer much by way of hospitality, had some crap coffee I was about to brew, the bread stale but likely still in the good way. Clearly not listening, he'd drifted to the typewriter immediately upon entering the squat, slowly inspected it with tilts of his head, one fingertip caressed across the keys, roughed in his hair, after—glancing around a bit more, seeming rather awed at how little there was to glance at.

[*what nonsense are you speaking, broom*]

While Nathan was occupied using my toilet, I put some coffee on, refilled my flask, downing two tilts which were immediately replaced, then treated myself to an additional mawful direct from the bottleneck for the trouble—lit a cigarette to convince myself I was getting my head wrapped snug around what'd be the best play to make, but when I heard the *kebang* of the flush realized I'd been looping a repeat of certain vague preparatory phrases, nothing more ... *Look, I get where you're coming from, but ... Hey man, I'm not gonna blow smoke and say I can fathom your passion or anything, however ... I don't wanna speak outta turn, but if this Sullivan guy beat ya to it, that oughta be easy enough to verify, yeah?* He re-entered the room with a distinctly different air than previous, bowels not only moved, bladder thinned out, but primly freshened up, all around—hair combed and slicked back with copious tap water, scent of baby powder he sure hadn't filched a squirt of from the bottle I didn't own.

Salesman direct and funerary somber, he asked if I'd indulge him just some brief while longer, as there were some items he felt it important I become cognizant of. 'What I impart may sound peculiar, but without the appropriate context, let me assure you, you're no more than floundering around at the edges of something intricate and inexorable—a matter of grave importance which you'll not be left alone about, even were I to bow out and never return.'

He meant the Sullivan character, I assumed, and he without sniff confirmed as much, adding the words 'at the very least,' but right away apologized for the creepiness of them, reiterating how there was no way he could expect me to trust him or to trust anything, at the present moment, insisting I understand how his situation was identical—he couldn't take me at my word about matters directly concerning the manuscript. 'Neither could Sullivan, if he already hasn't,' he tacked on ... no apology for the far creepier creepiness, though I didn't bother drawing attention to that.

Nathan's hope was how, once I'd heard him out, we could arrive at a genuine meeting of the minds from which we might attempt a more frank and unguarded discussion of specifics it seemed only I possessed knowledge of—the *Bulliet* helped me figure out it'd be best to let the guy make whatever case, as despite it possibly digging me deeper into whichever little fantasy realm he existed in, it might ingratiate me and thus get him to toddle off for good. I'd allow him forum to speak his piece without interruption, comporting myself with the utmost attentiveness and courtesy, and therefore he'd be seasoned to believe whatever I decided to do next, as well as being teed up to respect how I wanted to be left well enough alone—considering himself heard by a non-combative audience, tensions would ease from his system, whatever ludicrous path he was following, it'd be unquestionable that I'd turned out to be a thoroughly investigated dead end, so whatever new mystery he invented for himself to focus on would be none of my business, and I'd be remembered fondly as the one man who'd been of open mind enough to lend a hand in aid, friend, never foe.

He took a seat on the duct-taped comfy chair while I moved to the desk to retrieve more smokes—I'd intended to sit, as well, but strategized it best to not go that easy on him ... the queer fish wanted to work, it seemed, so I'd begin with signs of patronizing skepticism, arms crossed, pacing as though only half paying attention, from there ease drip-by-drip into a benign, polite curiosity, nodding and on the verge of encouraging comment at whatever was said, then eventually I'd take my seat, a symbolic gesture of joining him at his eye-level, the vantage from which it'd seem most intimate when we had our final chitchat.

I offered a swig from the flask, which at first he declined, then thought the better of—motioned for it, caught it when lobbed over underhand, rushed a rather full swallow which seemed to hurt him more than he'd braced for, coughed, stood, coughed doubled over, retook his seat and refined posture, holding the flask out to me, which I accepted, taking an automatic kiss from it in the same motion.

His hands held up, palms facing me, thumbs touching, he chewed on his lower lip, then let arms drift slowly away from each other as he worked to establish the atmosphere: I was to think about Objectivity—not as mere abstraction, but how said notion was perceived through the aperture of an individual opinion. 'Subjective Opinion, Objective Truth …' he pronounced, closing one hand into a fist '… Subjective Truth, Objective Opinion,' he added, closing the other, arms dropping afterward, hands folded like a doily over the knee of his crossed leg. 'Objectivity, Mister Limoncello, but to do with the human mind, heart, soul—pray, you shouldn't get confused with the notion of Objectivity as it pertains to the physical senses or the sciences, full stop. What we are discussing is horribly tangible, let me assure you, but let's never mistake it for a fungible commodity.'

'Heaven forfend,' I couldn't resist quipping, but didn't feel bad as a tad bit of snark at the get-go was part of my alleged plan.

Nathan seemed more amused than affronted, bowed his head, begged my pardon, knew how he could sometimes come across. 'There is so much weight to an atom …' he dove right back in '… a certain bridge can withstand X amount of pressure while another bridge Y—*an object in motion will remain so until* and were a pendulum let go inches from your face it'd swing back to no nearer. Such things and countless others are physically objective—but what of objectivity in opinion? Certainly, you'd posit there exists no such monster—as any halfway rational person would! All opinion is subjective, not only by definition, as is fashionable to say, but by nature. Certainly, there are semantical gainsayers who might sophistically attempt to refute this by pointing out how countless batches of consensus might be observed daily on matters mundane to almost farcically esoteric, all manner of seemingly near-universal agreement concerning certain points-of-view. But ask enough people, for example, *Is this shirt I'm wearing yellow?* and you'll soon enough come across those who genuinely wouldn't agree—let alone how, even if all agreed on Yellow, if one were to alter the term to Saffron or Flaxen or Lemon or Blonde, suddenly we'd be thrown into the deep end, realize we call *Yellow* objective when it is anything but and that, even if it is and we were to consider those other designations as fixed, we'd soon discover every last one of them tethered to nothing firm. We confuse *opinion* with *perception* and even *perception* we re-confuse with our own versus that of our countrymen. But, returning briefly to science, we long ago discovered that Objectivity must be well-tempered with skepticism, thus did Geocentrism lead to Heliocentrism which begat Galactocentrism, you see?'

Chuckled how I ought probably fetch my thesaurus and some Aristotle to cover up I'd no idea what Heliocentrism or the other two meant, though as the bourbon warmed me felt I got the gist. 'Old concept gives way to a new, yeah yeah yeah, I once read some of *Flatland*,' I waved him to continue.

He gathered himself in, as though there were muscular difficulty keeping himself on one stable point despite doing so being essential to his success, and returned to the notion of the yellow shirt: 'There would be those who'd disagree about the color even when one-hundred-thousand others were in effortless, amicable agreement. *Naysayers* we'd dub them, poor souls at the mercy of some softness in their psychology—for even if, in their hearts, they not only knew but believed my shirt was yellow, they'd never be moved to admit as much, would turn rhetorical cartwheels to convince even themselves they had a point apart from impudent nose-thumbing. Such recalcitrance, such absolute showcase of subjective will, is at the heart of what I intend to speak of. For any person might have an instigating bent in them, be possessed of composure and sense of purpose enough to say *That shirt is not yellow* despite painfully feeling it the yellowest goddamned thing they'd ever laid eyes on! Even concerning something so rudimentary and irrelevant, even with the gradations and synonyms of coloration taken away, the human heart, when surveyed writ large, would never arrive at objective consensus of Yellow, or at least none which could be definitively determined, regardless of our suspicions! An honest auditor, a scientist, must forever take as given fact that someone was telling the truth when they spoke as contrarian, as only the Other could know their own mind's eye and comment on their rationale for calling Yellow anything but.'

The bourbon made this first day of class lecturing grow tiresome, quick. 'Yes, quite, I follow—please, get on with it,' I rolled my eyes, keeping my smile bottle tight but my posture relaxed, wondering whether he might've been testing the waters with this seventh-grade twaddle to gauge my sincerity.

Another bow of apology, he punctuated the air with his hands in such way as to express we were moving to matters particular. 'What can be made of a personal reaction to a work of Art—specifically to a musical composition? No doubt you understand how, for purposes of this exercise, I want you to think of *They Might Be Giants*, despite your apparently limited familiarity with them. You have listened to a little, correct—is there any full album, perhaps?'

'*Flood* ...' I shrugged '... went through it the entire way, probably twice.'

'That'll do nicely! A series of twelve tracks, all quite different from one another but sharing a harmonious continuity. What do you think are the odds that any fifteen people would agree, definitively, to a ranking of the songs, Worst-to-Best—but not only agree, be willing to voice their agreement, with full throat, no mitigating factor or hem-haw, and furthermore not only proclaim such consensus, but persist in doing so, with increasing enthusiasm, when they heard others carrying on in exponentially hyperbolic terms, no instinct to correct or dampen down or bring up how there were different strokes for different folks so they mustn't go so far as to claim to be speaking for everyone, same as they'd not want anyone else to speak for them? How about if fifty people, five hundred, ten thousand, so on, even with some skepticism in them to begin, studied the rankings and then listened to the music anew, in the order prescribed, then agreed, absolutely positively, that the designations were correct, and went so far as to assert they could imagine no way, even theoretically, that anyone could see it otherwise?'

He finally stopped, motioning for my actual reply, which thankfully was precisely as he'd desired it. 'That would never happen, not on your life.'

'Even if it did ...' he clapped, seemed about to stand up directly into the first hop of a jig '... eventually *some* person was *bound* to disagree, even if just because they'd begun to feel disquieted over the sight of millions upon millions of their brethren being lulled to lockstep. Such fundamental revolt against organic conformity and capitulation is well documented in history—even in mathematics such principle is demonstrated.' While I couldn't speak to the math part, precisely, I agreed how book-learning and street-smarts had this natural disinclination in common, so far as I'd ever experienced. 'Let us then expand the experiment to every last album, every last song by *They Might Be Giants*. There's more'n a couple ...' he winked '... and we're including all varietals, from Demo Tapes to Television Theme Songs. What become the odds of universal agreement on, first, the rankings of the albums, second, the rankings of the songs within each, and then, finally, the songs, down to the very last, pitted all against each other?'

'Beyond astronomical!' I declared, actually enjoying myself, despite all—this certainly hadn't been the direction I'd expected Nathan to fall off the turnip truck! I was still wary of a sudden veer into dangerous lunacy, but for the time being eased giggling into the desk chair, legs crossed, to listen on with intrigue.

'Please, spare no effort in conceptualizing it, constructing the model *in abstracto* as one might the notion of two parallel lines eventually touching—or else think of Zeno's arrow, of the sum of an infinite set! If every human being on Earth who engaged in the question directly, after listening to the properly ordinated music however many times they chose to, were to agree—be it in part, about the contents of a single album, or in total, about the album ranks, the songs within each, the full spate of everything, battle royale—if every Tom, Dick, and Harry who took up the challenge wholeheartedly came to be in honest rapport, not a niggle of doubt amongst them, that would be something, eh?'

'It'd be something if that many people agreed on the ranking of any two songs ...' I conceded without prejudice, but if he was suggesting that, were infinite people taken into account, such a thing could go down in even the wildest outskirts of the most fevered imagination '... no, nope, it's an immutable fact that it'd never.'

Here he seemed jolly pleased, leaned forward, rubbing his hands—I'd apparently touched on a favorite digression. '*Infinite people*, Mister Limoncello? Now there's a concept! Certainly, we agree that there haven't existed *infinite* people up til now, yes? I'm not being glib, merely pointing out that, even if we discounted every grubby unknown who'd toiled and died unrecorded in humanity's history, and even if we took into account theoretical humans existing off planet in some glory of sci-fi pulp made manifest, there's only so many of them there could ever have been, counting from the Big Bang onward—true or false?' Still seated, he wriggled around toddler-like, apologized after pausing for some yoga-esque breaths to get centered. 'What I desire your measured answer about is twofold. First: Do you truly believe the human race will ever near infinity? In all seriousness, granting no end to the universe, gifting eons yet to our race, we will indubitably come to an end—you must see this, Marc!'

Swigged my flask, making a succinct *Mmn* noise he appropriately took for 'Fair enough.'

'Secondly: Don't you see how it's too rhetorical to discuss *anyone who might possibly* listen to all the music in the manner described? Of course, by the time the race yields to oblivion, X number, at most, would have engaged in the proposition, X number would have chosen not to, X to have done so only approximately, the rules not followed—and moreover, those who existed before the music was composed would null the experiment, so we couldn't rationally include *everyone* to begin with et cetera. *All who'd listened* would yet be a vast, but finite, set—and such would be the only number which need reasonably be explicated. *Of anyone who had—tangibly, not theoretically*—listened, all had been in outspoken solidarity—that is what alien archeologists would see as fact, in the same way we assume fossilized footprints mean single civilizations, ignoring how true it is that if we only discover one footprint of a civilization of millions it makes, from this same evidence, perfect sense to conclude five other, equally vast civilizations, lived concurrent without leaving so much as toejam behind.'

'Yes …' I nodded into my next cigarette '… the same as we can nitpick the syllogism of all men being mortal yet still know it true.'

'Precise!'

'Though not everyone would agree with us,' I winked like spoiling his joke.

'And those who don't, Marc, we both know would fall over themselves to let anyone in earshot know all about it!' he countered, as though glad I'd been puckish.

At any rate, I had to admit how if something as conceptually impossible as he'd outlined were to be evidenced in reality '… it'd be staggering, extraordinary, positively otherworldly.'

He nodded, motioned for the flask, took two measured swallows, motioned for the cigarettes, traded the flask back for them, caught the light when I lobbed it. 'Once a threshold of the extraordinary happens …' he was having trouble getting a flame '… a thousand people, a million so on …' finally got lit and inhaled a long drag '… even you yourself said it'd be uncanny for five people to agree about two things, did you not …' let the smoke out so thin it hardly colored the stale air we sat in '… can we agree it'd be safe enough to start thinking we were onto something and that what that something seemed like was exactly what it was?'

I didn't see why not. 'And what is it we'd be onto, exactly?'

'*Objective Subjectivity*.'

I repeated the term.

'That's how I refer to it …' he intoned with posture going unwittingly religious '… though I doubt any pet-name could do it justice. If such were so, Mister Limoncello—absolute provable consensus on a scale so outright bewildering—would it not contain a direct contradiction to one of the most fundamental sureties in existence? Not just agreement, but an ornately passionate insistence of the objective truth of something which all logic and reason, all lived experience and conceptual constructs, demands must be subjective, would threaten to uproot all we think of as human, I daresay! And something as protoplasmic as that has no choice but to contain the calculus of some application.'

'*Application*?' I coughed after squishing a quick swallow of *Bulleit* down.

'If the data were before us—nothing piecemeal or small scale enough it could be dismissed as a freakish one off—if proof there existed an Objective Stance of this nature were held in one's hands, it must follow that from such could be discerned an Objective Stance to any set. The content of Benjamin's manuscript we, for sake of argument, will grant contains this—thus, if one were studious enough, one might apprehend an underlying principle of enormous power which could grant not only objective insight into specific affairs but map the way to structure dialogue none would speak or act in defiance of. No, it wouldn't allow one to *choose* the truth, so to speak, but being able to see an inarguable truth and thus have means to proclaim it makes irrelevant the need for choice. Take something so paltry as my own profession: if all of the facts of a case were gathered, and if there could be explicated some formula for the ordination with which evidences, opinions, notions might be presented which would, without fail, garner an exact response from all in audience—a judge and jury, reporters communicating out to the public and so on—it would gift an enormous advantage to whoever possessed it. I couldn't, in this example, use it to sway the public to my own subjective stance, but could identify the objective opinion which would be embraced by all and align myself to it with abandon. Now think larger than that: how a formula might be hit upon, a mechanism through which to observe the Objective Stance entire societies would take on issues minute or gargantuan!'

I let the man bask in his cliffhanger pronouncement the length of stubbing a cigarette out on the desktop before ruining the climax with '... I'm sorry to go ahead and deflate the chances of this, Nathan, but I feel I'd not be a true buddy if I didn't point out—brace yourself, okay?—that I didn't enjoy one goddamned thing I'd heard by the group you pin so much of your hope on.'

Thankfully he'd not taken my remark as snide—quite the opposite, he pointed at me as though we were on the same page. 'Don't you understand that is entirely my point?' My wide eyes and silence betrayed I must not've. 'Let's keep our example to the music of *They Might Be Giants* and Benjamin's ranking of it, shall we?' I nodded, now nibbling on my left pinky nail, befuddled. 'Personal preference would have nothing to do with it. Whether an auditor enjoyed or outright loathed the music, irregardless of where their personal favorite tunes wound up on the list, despite all passions this way or that, whatever it may be, every last person who, in fact, engaged would, as if by magic—but demonstrably not by magic—come away with an absolute belief in the sanctity of the *ranking*.'

Now I did get where he was coming from—one step beyond the outer limits of the twilight zone! Reckoned it best to calmly, succinctly sum up, so nodded a few times as though chewing the matter thoroughly before swallowing to deeply digest its nuances in order to buy myself time, fearful a foot in my mouth could blow the gaff on my insincerity. 'If a ranked list of the albums and music of *They Might Be Giants* ...' cleared my throat '... or anything ...' coughed, unscrewed my flask '... but that's what we were talking about ...' took a glug '... was to be compiled ...' cleared my throat more forcefully '... and if somehow all of humanity—or all of whichever sampling of humanity, young, old, this country, that, these beliefs, these others, those affiliations, their opposites—listened to the catalogue in order, Worst-to-Best or Best-to-Worst, and were found to be in absolute agreement as to the Objective Truth of the ranks of all tunes, it follows that their in-common subjective opinions added together as like until infinity ought rightfully be equated to a fundamentally Objective Opinion, the existence of which would prove the possibility of Objective Opinion, overall. That is: if there was one, there ought well be all manner—the world is numbers, fella graphs any set of numbers means patterns're gonna emerge, from those patterns one can choose positions to secure alliances and perhaps, eventually, have everyone on the same path, and wherever said path leads, de facto, would be where all, even if only unconsciously, yearn to be. The secret engine of the world would be obtained and, from it, all manner of understanding could be derived—a richer, more nuanced take on ourselves, a locus of control over others, or else a sort of spiritual straight line from one harmony to multiple to, perhaps in the end, harmony-writ-large as it came to the hearts and perceptions of all mankind.'

He adored how I'd put it, thanked me profusely—wished he'd written that down!

'And what you're today, in this apartment, suggesting is the list your friend Benjamin typed up in Cabin Eight of *The Calico Bash Nitely* where I hump the graveyard shift would be such a thing?'

He nodded. 'There will, from the raw data, be devised a mathematical method of representation which will prove applicable to all creatures, great and small—despite the seemingly arbitrary starting point, a Universal Law of Opinion will be derived.'

'As was the case with urine for alchemy, an apple for gravity, or whatever led to our understanding of electromagnetism?' I didn't ask this with any hint of challenge—by now a lush, semi-drunk propelled me, and giddy as a lark I wanted to be certain I was on the same page with my guest, even if about to not only decry the man a bus-stop wing-nut but crown him the single biggest dork I'd ever had the pleasure of making the acquaintance of.

He nodded, again, watched me light a new cigarette, motioned for the pack, and I almost flirtatiously chucked it at him as he laughed, then pretended I was gonna pelt him with the lighter to make him flinch, at which he laughed harder—once his smoke was going, he set lighter and pack on the floor between us, making a gesture to let me know he was redirecting. 'I'm not blind to your skepticism—it not only lingers, but I'd wager has grown. If you'd be so generous as to suffer through a touch more of my imposition, I'd be quite keen to explain several things which might aid you in comprehending my own lack of any—if you'd permit me, I'd like to tell you about my friend, Benny Visa.'

I was all ears, I promised—switched which leg was crossed in order to prove it.

[*exact dimensions and the shape of the state whose name*]

Nathan had his first encounter with Benjamin Visa when the two were twelve years old, during an afterschool audition for a chintzy, two-act theatrical abridgement of *Dracula*—initially, Ben had sheepishly announced his intention to read for the part of Van Helsing, but the bull goose of the Theatre Squad barked that the role was already taken, so he'd mumbled how he'd have a crack at playing 'Jonathan Harker or whoever the main character is, then' such remark roundly guffawed at by all gathered while the lad stood befuddled, after a moment piping up to inquire who the main character in the particular adaptation might be. When the chucklehead in charge put on a garish show of incredulity, hamming up the quip 'Uh ... *Dracula*, dude, hence the name of the play' the poor kid became the subject of a pecking party of antagonism before having his earnest cold go of an almost dialogue-less sequence giggled through, whereupon he'd been dismissed without so much as eye-contact. Nathan admitted he'd joined in with his fellows lambasting Benjamin's best efforts at coming across a vampire after the audition had concluded, but found himself viciously regretting such capitulation acutely over the following weeks—when it was announced that the understudy position for the titular Nosferatu had been awarded to Ben and further mean-spirited jibes were swift in coming, always behind closed doors, he'd decided enough was enough. 'It was the afternoon of that casting announcement when I approached Ben to apologize for my part in the insensitivities, outlining in detail all I'd personally said and making no effort to spare the reputations of the rest. Benny told me I shouldn't give the matter another thought, as nothing in the world could be less important. Though it was obvious he recalled every detail of the humiliation he'd been present for, that every new piece of information I'd hurled at him had struck nerves, and despite he was aware there'd be ongoing character assassination which he could do nothing to alter the groove of, it was nonetheless as though what I spoke of was a fact from a million years bygone or else one of countless, entirely fictional, qualms a person might develop in their own mind, no need to get bent out of shape about. I insisted myself upon him, though, proclaimed I'd been an utter asshole, and that he should tell me so to my face, there and then, even punch me square in the nose if he felt like—though I quickly altered such invite to the arm or the abdomen.'

Nathan stubbed a cigarette and, for a long moment, seemed as though attempting to get his mental bearings—I wondered if the *Bulleit* had the better of him and, if so, what price I'd have to pay for the derailment of our tete-a-tete.

'I know it seems as though I'm making a mountain of what amounts to an incidental moment in a young life and one, all things considered, of little traumatic uniqueness. But there had been a look on Benny's face which I'll never forget—I see it in my mind's eye, even now—shock and a kind of doubt at himself mingled with shame, as though being cleverly and appropriately dismissed by a party in more knowledgeable authority than himself. It'd been that same expression I'd noticed a flit of when he'd stood in the classroom to throw his thespian hat in the ring—shy as a rug and stranger to stagecraft, he'd no idea who'd be considered the lead in a script which hadn't been furnished for review in advance, therefore had proceeded from his familiarity with the source novel, alone, which I only later came to learn contained no single protagonist. As a matter of fact, he was spot on: the vampiric count was scarcely in the blasted play and the roles of Harker and Van Helsing were, indeed, the spotlights—both had been closed to him, *a priori*, because they'd been snatched up in backdoor deals by the darlings of the troupe, making their corralling and mockery of him all the more heartless and calculated.'

Such was a quality which forever remained with Benjamin, I was told—no matter how confident he presented himself, how cocksure, cavalier, and uncaring of the opinions of others, he always, without fail, assumed everyone in whichever room he stood was more educated, crafty, worldly, and from the ground up more *correct* than himself—a random passerby riffing for the first time on a subject they'd never once thought about before in a manner which didn't align to his own view would reinforce what he deemed a proper distrust, call into question opinions and positions held most dear and personal to him, no matter if they were based on lived experience or expertise.

'Benny always struck me as something of a Conduit to another realm of perception ... but things weren't meant to strike me that way, Mister Limoncello! I was Nathan Jehovah—Mister Mathematics—therefore all was to be proven empirically and even when a lover cheated on me I'd soothe my wounded pride with statistical analysis. But the longer I knew Ben, the more he was revealed to be the most peculiar of conduits for almost idiotically unsullied Socratic communication one could dream up. Here was a man who neither needed to be taught nor sought out mentorship or correction—almost like the plague, he'd avoided formal education and yet would always stumble into the exact knowledge needed for whichever occasion. More than that: he'd float opinions *ex nihilo* or make jokes entirely off the cuff which he'd discover, to his surprised delight, were part of the collective knowledge or the popular idiom, glib inventions he'd feel certain were fatuous and faulty notions all his own he'd instead discover to be holy precepts to practitioners of multiple art forms or immutable scientific laws. I know what I'm saying sounds strange—and yes, such happens with everybody, now and again—but with Benjamin it occurred with uncanny frequency and on multiple, wholly unrelated fronts. He'd less-than-zero interest in the sciences—in mathematics, least of all!—while still attending school would never study, and after dropping out promptly forget all formal proficiency he'd accumulated. It was no matter—when first presented with a great mystery, which myself and several colleagues had spent years building the scaffolding from which query could even be posed, over coffee and cigarettes he'd approached it from some oblique angle, playfully spouting off what would seem the most preposterous way forward to anyone with investment in the matter ... but those same people felt tickled by a truth and suddenly made breakthroughs which, while far afield from anything *specific* Benjamin had so jubilantly espoused, would nevertheless claim themselves indebted to him for. In University, I'd fairly burned with jealousy when such events would transpire—at times my contemporaries found publication with papers built from some faff Ben'd thought of about Time or Evolution since six years of age which he'd imparted by way of showcasing what a nitwit he was over beers after my foolishly choosing to introduce him—and I seethed all the moreso when Ben stepped away from each encounter, happy as Larry, non-cognizant of my amazement or of how bowled over were my betters. From philosophical chestnuts such as pondering *what came before the first thing* to dissection of the implications of infinite infinities, this shirkaday rascal could hold his own, in good humor even when struck down in spite, with people who it seemed ought never give him the time of day! I once observed him teaching a youngster the game of chess with entirely the incorrect rules, yet the strategies he'd devised, when squinted at, were, in fact, quite ingenious tactics, simply expressed in bozo terms! What I mean is: he'd made it all up about how the game was even supposed to be played, but someone deeply involved in the pursuit apprehended what was honestly present in the guts of what he'd so dopily pretended to be driving at and, armed with this perception, went on to achieve acclaim in their sphere. None of which is to say Benjamin, himself, was a prodigy, a savant, or a success—to the contrary, he was as far from any of those things as you can imagine! A contradictory mechanism, through-and-through: ambitionless, lazy as a carp, the most uncurious man I'd ever encountered, awash in curlicue impressions of the world, unable to differentiate between a correct assertation and a flagrant falsity, finding equal value in all ... and, I daresay, living blissfully despite having no excuse to be able to, stirred discord and acrimony in many of those closest to him.'

'But not you?' I couldn't help asking, grinning despite the last thing I wanted was to suddenly tip the hand of my impertinent slant on what was being said.

'Never me. The truth was, the more pathetic Benjamin's life became—because there was no other word for it—the more my feelings of kinship, reverence, and adoration grew. The man was a glorious imbecile—incapable of acting in his own best interests, a glutton for being taken advantage of, an almost clockwork entity lost to rational living—yet at the same time, was entirely able to tend to the tasks associated with everyday life in a way which seemed imponderably serene. Our life paths and core beliefs couldn't have been more dissimilar—only a single thread of outside reference connecting our souls: *They Might Be Giants*. The music was the single interest the man perennially entertained—the only interest which seemed passionate and deeply held, his own, and not to be trifled with. His mind was always most lucid and nakedly expressed through discussion of this song or that, his feelings on one album over another—but despite being wholly referenced to the music, such passions had little if anything to do with the band, in the popular sense. It was arresting, spooky even, how he could quote lyrics at just such a time, framed in just such a light, they'd be more pertinent to matters they seemed utterly alien to than the most incisive and evidence-based exploration from an expert speaking in appropriate jargon.'

Benjamin's opinions regarding *The Giants* were also the solitary item Nathan'd never known the man to be moved from his stance on, the lonesome precept he'd witnessed his friend hold the conversational line over and—which was equally as striking—the exclusive adjudication he'd witnessed his friend being deceptive about, nodding at those who expressed contrary takes in such a way as to make them believe he'd come around to their viewpoints but which one in the know, such as Nathan, understood was him being patronizing.

'He'd even belittle others, behind their backs—speak in the most libelous, embittered tones to me in confidence. Otherwise, I might've cut bait with him many times, even accidentally! It was something in this fixation, this focal point of his true nature, which compelled me to remain in contact—I came to understand I never wanted the man out of my sight. In my own researches, before abandoning the academic world, private sector mathematics, and turning to Law full time, then afterward and on until the present moment, I confess to a penchant for seeking out solutions seemingly otherworldly—perhaps there is some kernel of truth in Sullivan's catcalls of numerologist and Confidence Man, yes, that is fair. These inklings, Marc, had first stirred when seeing Benjamin's face at that audition—I felt touched by a current of understanding, a truth more substantial than any other, convinced more of the same would be found where there seemed none only by distrusting the lessons embraced through community, looking at any educated persuasion I might avail myself of always partway askance. *Numerology* is going too far, of course, and there is no whiff of shuck-and-jive in what I mean, either: I sought to utilize, methodically, the inexplicable only when it truly *was* inexplicable, but never to seek out matters to debunk for the sake of puerile satisfaction or personal advancement—to move toward what seemed thoughtlessly the truth yet should not be and then to gently test its mettle.'

Perhaps he picked up I was losing step with him, the narrative becoming far too in-referenced for an outsider to find scrutable, because he took another distinct break, standing while lighting a cigarette, sitting back down with a posture indicating we had moved back into our current intrigue.

'When Benjamin called me, Marc, when he reached out before he left his family, before his disappearance, before his death—when he told me what he was doing, when I heard the pure certainty, the absolute imperative pouring from him, I understood he was going to accomplish, somehow, exactly what he stated he would. Benny Visa would definitively rank the entire output of *They Might Be Giants*—not to do with opinion, but with ironclad truth. What I'd no way of knowing was that I was saying goodbye to him and that his work—his singular expression, his inimitable offering to mankind—would be lost or else made forever dubious by a confluence of circumstances I'd never have envisioned but which, my God, suited the man perfectly.'

Not in the manner Nathan likely had intended—and no doubt the *Bulleit* was batting clean-up for him—I found myself genuinely moved by this turn in narrative, came quite near to tearing up, at times, on account of the dead earnest, all business timbre which couldn't help but betray an anguish over a lost friend, an ache which could never be articulated directly, needed fable and fancy, almost religious iconography to come to any semblance of terms with. Here was a guy who'd been unable to reconcile a personal loss—maybe the last who'd ever spoken to Benjamin, truly—and then been presented a tangle of mysterious loose ends to tie up which he'd contorted into a Quixotic quest to complete in homage, a man who was wounded and needed closure—but someone who, because of that very thing, I needed to treat as an interloper, a threat. After all, even through my tipsiness, I'd noticed several shifts in the alleged straight line I was being fed: first, he'd made Sullivan Shallcross out as a figure to fear, then he'd spoken esoterically about what was more-or-less nonsense, unless viewed as symptomatic heartbreak over the death of a friend, which, in turn, had morphed into a maudlin appeal to emotion—there was something of the puckish huckster to him and, yes, his mentioning he'd been dubbed such by a person he was vilifying seemed tactical, in and of itself.

The bottom line was: I needed him out of my life, toot suite and irrevocably, had to sever ties in a manner which would safeguard me against further intrusion—there remained no way I'd be compelled to dispatch him the original manuscript after all I'd endured, of course, as I'd no loyalty to the dingbat and it'd be no betrayal even if I did, not to mention that if suddenly he received the genuine article he'd know I'd been lying to him, initially, which wouldn't sit well, might even raise his ire ... he'd conjure fresh doubt regarding the seemingly authentic draft's pedigree, appear at my door again, if just to have the hard word with me about what'd I think I was playing at.

Knowing I might live to regret it, but even more aware I was likely going to live to regret everything, same as had been the way I'd lived my life since fifteen, I told Nathan I intended to strike a deal with him—no doubt he suspected what I was going to propose, seeing as he must've calculated out how I yet had possession, or at the very least knew the whereabouts of, the manuscript in some form, original, photocopy, whichever, but, if so, he betrayed no telltale. His part of the bargain was to leave me alone—I didn't need any trouble because I had that of my own, by the boatload. There was to be no further contact between us—or between myself and any associate he might employ—beyond one further instance, which I did my best to explain cogently and without ambiguity, my claim and my terms going as follows: 'There'd never been any original, not so far as it has to do with me, but I produced multiple duplicates, beyond the ones I've already mentioned, one of which I sent to a friend of mine. I'll not divulge the person's name, but it's that same copy, or another copy of it, I'll provide. You'll have to be patient. Go home. Don't call me. I'll reach out only once, after I've sent the document, in a manner of my choosing—one which'll require your personal signature, thus allowing me notification of its receipt. That's it. The end. You never darken my doorstep, again.'

He digested my proposition with nods, lip puckers, the usual—I could guess some of the things he wanted to say, so decided to nip them all in the bud by telling him 'Listen ... you want to know why I made such a to-do, back at the start, why I didn't just hand it over—and you deserve as much, I fully admit it. Here's the scoop on that: I'd gotten mixed up in something I've no part in, then you show up, right after I have the scare of my life, and start talking about some relatively out-there this-and-that. I was arrested, Nathan—no idea what I'd do had I wound up charged with something, and even if that Strauss woman had pursued baloney harassment claims it would've sunk my battleship for all day, no fooling. In a blink, my life was turned upside-down—a touch of curiosity had beaten me black-and-blue, so my instincts told me to just keep schtum and wait for it all to go away, you know? Figured I'd be left alone if I could prove my orbit to certain questions entirely incidental and the best way to do that was to put on a dum-dum routine—I didn't see the difference between telling the detective I'd been the one to find the typewriter and the manuscript together rather than telling the weird and gnarled truth, for example, and that'd bit me on the ass proper—then right on the heels of figuring a young man deserved to make up his mind for himself what he wanted to do with some writing his dearly departed dad'd left behind, I learned the kid's dead and suddenly here's you, his kinda uncle, claiming to be a lawyer and you're buying me breakfast and you're driving me home after interrogation and a night spent in lock-up ... so I'm thinking that before sunrise a garrote wire's gonna get involved, okay? To top it off, you start asking about other copies of what I'd given away and had been robbed of me? *Forget it, Jack ... it's Chinatown*—that's what I needed to think, is what I'd told myself. But turns out you're a man hurting tremendously from the loss of a brother and wanting to do the right thing, *in memoriam*. Listening to you speak—not of this admittedly far-fetched mumbo jumbo you're floating about Benjamin's list of some song titles containing an Objective Truth or the key to reality itself, but of the friendship, the love you shared with Benjamin—put a lot of what I've recently been going through in a kinder relief. Whether I think what you think about Benjamin's manuscript is immaterial—what I can't deny is it's to do with you, for real, and with me, not a bit.'

I must admit I was righteously proud of this speech—no retelling can do it justice—I didn't oversell it or gobble the scenery, it wasn't Oscar bait, wasn't amateur hour ... but considering how utterly false it was, yet how unerringly genuine it came out, put a spring in my step. 'Do we have a deal?'

All business, he told me I was to dispatch the package to him at the law firm where he worked, rather than using his residential address. 'Of course you may do so via whichever courier service makes you feel most comfortable.' As further condition, he insisted that it be made out in care of *Delmont Bruges*. 'You should put a separate package, addressed to me, inside the package for Delmont.'

While this might sound unorthodox, I was to rest assured the manuscript would be placed directly in his hands, within minutes of receipt.

Try as I might, I could find nothing to object to in this proposal—even the fact that someone else would sign seemed inconsequential—and, despite a bourgeoning curiosity, I made no inquiries into the reasons behind the insisted particulars. Meanwhile, Nathan had taken out one of his business cards, jotted pertinent details on its reverse, then placed it on the desk in what I took to be a sign that, even already, direct interactions between us were over, interactions, *in toto*, to promptly follow.

I vowed to myself I'd act in no hurry—make no move to retrieve anything from the Post Office for at least a week, as the manuscript was safe as could be and waiting awhile would make the off chance of my being observed come off like I'd, as explained, contacted my buddy then waited the requisite number of days for him to zap something my way which I'd then re-routed Nathan's ... though if I were being watched, how would I ferry the original someplace I could make copies, one-hundred-percent certain no one'd be the wiser? ... such a task was far more of a challenge than it had any right to be ... too much sat dependent on chance ... easiest thing seemed to be spending time driving around in such way I could verify no one was tailing me ... except if that went wrong, which it could in any number of ways I doubted I was clever enough to foresee, I'd be quite the dead duck ... the simple act of driving in a demonstrably aimless way while being tailed made it a cinch my pursuer would sniff I was trying to test the waters ... if I were willing to get up to such skullduggery, they'd up the ante ...

Oh, what in Hell was I on about!? As much a lunatic as this fellow came across to me, he'd not behaved rashly—more than being harmless, even, he'd done me a good turn. What percentage would be in it for him to tack a shadow on me or arrange a tap on my phone—how could he, even? Were he a villain, certainly he'd see through my ruse of 'contacting an unnamed friend,' understand the aim was to get him as far from me as possible—indeed, he'd know right well

I had a copy, if not the original, someplace relatively near at hand. Were he the violent sort, why hadn't he trotted out the rubber bat or the phonebook, the pillowcase full of oranges, as he could've easily done from the start—one glance at me was all it took to confirm I'd spill my guts about anything under the stars or sell out those closest to me, no more cudgel required than a modestly well worded threat I'd be smacked in the snout were I to resist. Quite frankly, his balderdash philosophies had shook clean the feeling of being caught up in anything creepy, because compared to the jabberwocky this loon had spouted it wasn't the least bit farfetched that Benjamin's murder'd been nothing to do with the man personally, that Hotel Detective lost his life in a legitimate car accident, and that poor Terrance was a dumb kid who'd used too much of a needle—I wasn't involved in any intrigue, Nathan Jehovah had shown up purely in hopes of getting what I was going to send him for understandable, human reasons, if paired with a bit of bonkers-worded grief.

[*plain as the lie on your lips*]

Some days passed by in joy and gladness ... not hardly—the vacuum I once again existed in threw me for a loop, the void of a life back to normal. After navigating a ridiculous amount of redundant steps to courier the manuscript to Nathan in a manner which made me feel completely clear of it, my exhaustion took center stage, mind stem-to-stern milky, disinterested even more than it tended to be, sleep broken or else barely existent, whichever VHS I popped in to pass out in the glow of cycled all the way through twice, three, four times while I remained awake for every reiteration—I attempted exercise, one night, but all that accomplished was getting me buzzed enough I couldn't sit still, wound up walking for an hour in the cold, hoping to freeze myself unconscious.

I'd shown up for work on a night I wasn't scheduled, a desk clerk I'd never met before glancing up at me in an aloof manner which made me feel only partway present. 'I'm Marc Limoncello—I work here,' I'd decided I ought to explain—he'd never heard of me and when I inquired how long he'd been on staff it sounded impossible, but I had to admit I'd no way of knowing ... his name was on the calendar, after all, as were two others I must've seen before but couldn't recollect. 'How many people work here?' I asked him. He answered, but seemed confused as to the intent of my question—hadn't I been there way longer than him? 'I work nights,' I replied as though doing so didn't paint me an idiot, but thankfully he took the remark as a sign of solidarity, giving a fist pump I took to mean 'Yeah, that's why I don't know anything, either—what does a motel even do during the day?' Gave a quick peek through the Guest Register, but no idea what for, then asked the guy if he needed anything from the gas station—he wanted to know was I buying and, aiming to magnanimously save face, I shrugged 'Sure,' learning, in that case, I could bring him this, that, and a pack of *Lucky Strikes*.

On the drive, I reworked my finances—needed to knock it off with the *Luckies*, myself, switch back to *American Reds*, save beaucoup bucks and get that honest to goodness flavor of ground glass back in my lungs, plus *Bulleit* oughta be downgraded, as well, seeing as it was an undeniable twenty bucks cheaper per bottle to go with *Zachariah Smith* and while I was at it why not spring for one of those big jugs, save myself practically double in the long term, seeing as all I did was pour the poison in my flask or drink from a plastic juice cup … the Liquor Store staff knew me well enough not to sneer if I suddenly purchased in volume and it'd likely make them feel less like thieves, in the long run! I'd been running two packs of smokes a day, two bottles of bourbon per week, thus a conservative estimate revealed, at the very least, I leaked almost five hundred smackers per month—six grand a year … which I decided was impossible … I couldn't've wasted even half that much on two of the most nonessential items imaginable … took the avowed stance to decidedly *not* alter my habits, just to prove it … would reassess once all the evidence was in. Halfway across the parking lot of my building, realized I'd not stopped to get stuff for the *Calico* clerk, so drove back out to the gas station, the motel, and told a lie about having had to take a phone call that went long—new guy seemed not to give a hoot, either way and, not much feeling like driving home all over again, decided to ask him if he ever noticed anything weird.

'Weird?'

'Overnight, you know?'

'Other than it's curious *The Calico Bash* is even allowed to be a place, I never much pay attention—mind my own business, you know?'

'Good policy,' I nodded, genuinely liking this dude.

Both of us lit up in the Office and I made as though it was a funny anecdote to tell him all about the guy who'd gotten aggressive with me—did a big impersonation, yukking it up about what a coward I was and how I'd been looking over my shoulder, ever since.

'Waitaminute ...' he paused me a moment to get his mind's bearings on something '...waitaminute ...' he muttered, blinked, abruptly turned the Guest Register around '... just ... a ... sec ...' he built the suspense like Agatha Christie then finally tapped his finger and said '... *Nils Dolphy*—was that the name?' I swallowed, uncertain how best to respond, but turned out the question'd been rhetorical. 'That guy wrecked the joint! Smashed the television, punched a hole in the wall!'

'You're putting me on,' I vainly hoped.

'Cabin Eight?' he asked to which I nodded. 'Surest thing you know, man.'

'Why hadn't I heard about that?'

He didn't exactly follow '... was it the sort of something you'd hear about?'

Almost said 'I'm in Cabin Eight, all the time,' but stopped myself and gave it a real tick of thought—the new bureau, different television, the painting nailed to the wall to cover a hole instead of fixing it up was just the sort of shortcut the establishment would take after a ruckus.

Didn't want to think about it but couldn't think of anything else—a feeling of sensational dread overtook me, one which lasted all that sleepless night while I smoked a paced circle of my basement room, and the disquiet intensified as I discovered myself disappointed at having to admit there was no reason to believe the man's actions had anything but Jack Squat to do with me or the manuscript ... even though he'd been in Cabin Eight a second time after I'd visited *Sarnath*, our initial encounter predated every active interaction with parties connected to my foray into noir-ville ... no one would've known about the document on the night Nils Dolphy entered my frame of reference ... but still: couldn't he've come looking for Benjamin's writing, once, thinking he'd known where to find it, discovering nothing instead ... then been hipped, during my trip, to the fact a copy'd definitely been uncovered, therefore the original must be there ... told to have another, thorough look ... become furious when it truly was missing and, in a fit of pique, taken it out on the inanimate world around him? A dozen ways this scenario made zero sense demanded I let it drop, but I *wanted* it to've happened—after all, it did give a lot of weight to certain lingering loose ends. For example: while it tracked about the police questioning me, how exactly had Nathan become privy to my involvement, able to be on hand so shortly after I'd been arrested?

Stalking doom reared its head, again, when I popped in at the *Video Grog* that morning and Oldtime Dougie casually inquired whether the guy who'd been looking for me had ever got in touch.

'What'd the fella look like?'
'Ordinary.'
'What does that mean?'
'Like anybody.'
'Like me?'
'Naw.'
'Like you?'
'No—like somebody else, you know?'
'Could you humor me with adjectives?'
'Oh I dunno ... like a little *weird*, but that makes him hard to describe and, either way, it was awhile ago, and I've seen other people, since then.'
'When ago?'
'Awhile.'
'A long while?'
'Naw.'
'A short while, then?'
'Kinda.'
'How short?'
'I can't remember, man.'

Asked had it been on the date of Dolphy's second visit to *The Calico* and he still had no idea. 'But the guy wasn't well-dressed or anything ... like a detective?'

Like nothing was nothing, Dougie replied to this with 'Naw, he wasn't that detective—I take it you never met up or it'd be you remembering not me. Hey, whatever happened with the detective—you were in trouble or you were a witness or what?'

Brushed this off to press him about 'The other guy you're talking about—before or after the detective?'

'Felt all about the same time, more or less.'

Which I supposed was fair enough. 'What did you tell him?'

'The detective?'

'The other one.'

'Just you lived somewhere around, didn't say where, you worked at the motel, otherwise I'd seem like a liar—I like to steer clear of other folk's private affairs.'

What I wanted was to make some continuity fit flush, a narrative line wherein Nils Dolphy'd shown up in town looking for me, been tipped I worked at the motel, gone there after the manuscript, found it missing, smashed the room, then smashed my apartment, afterward ... but that didn't *quite* seem to work out ... it was a better match to imagine it'd been Nathan who'd asked around ... though that *also* didn't gel, sequence wise ... but it's not like it was just gonna be some altogether other guy looking for me, out of the clear blue sky ... one who'd then not found me ...

Pulled into a parking lot and mumbled a cigarette, intent on getting to a fine point '... Nils was after the manuscript, but before I'd told anyone about it ... totally disconnected, random ... Detective Hellpop is accounted for ... Nathan only coulda been *after* my visit ... or else learned shortly after I'd seen Mrs. Strauss ... I'd stayed on that extra day, driven back ... except in that case: why'd he not reveal himself until after I'd been arrested ...'

No matter how I sliced it, there appeared to be a third person who'd come around asking for me—and more unsettling was how Mister X remained an unknown, the single person out of three who'd no reason to be looking for me who hadn't made contact.

I'd entered my apartment, sighing under my breath, stripped nude, taken a swallow of bourbon, then slouched into my lounge wear, had a swig or two more, and was on my second cigarette when I noticed the blinking of my answering machine: Viggo, not even fifteen minutes before, had left a quick message—if I was free in the next little bit, give him a call, but if not no worries. Got some sausage and biscuit in my stomach, washed it down with another swallow of *Bulleit*, peanut-butter crackers for dessert, and eyed through my fridge for some string cheese I apparently thought I still owned, then stood in the shower, mind roiling lower and lower with this question of who in Christ's had been asking after me ... I was easy enough to find, if one had their heart set on it ... maybe Dougie's mind had just splintered the single encounter with the detective into multiple incidents ... 'That could happen ...' I sniffled, washing my face a fourth time '... chemically, psychologically, synapses, sure ...' or else the damned portly coot might've only meant the detective when he'd asked his question, then, for whichever reason anyone does anything, said it was some other guy to make it seem like he hadn't been prying—after all, he'd never even brought up the detective's visit back when it happened, only followed up about it, which might've felt unmannerly, thus he'd invented a more innocuous, imaginary person he knew I'd not have met as a clever way of getting politely around to what he'd actually been curious about ... 'Everybody's playing games ...' I spit onto my toes ... or they weren't ... only I was ... '... though maybe not, too' I had to admit, blowing my nose into a soggy washcloth which smelt of mildew.

Remembered the message from Viggo and it struck me I'd intended to ring him back, as requested, but'd let my mind wander, so dialed the lad up, straight away—after greetings and my asking about what some noise in the background was, which he explained simply as 'Some idiots I have over' while clearly moving into another room, shutting a door behind him, he dove in with thanking me so much for '... putting me onto that band!' Apparently they were the greatest thing since calling a triangle *isosceles*, in his humble opinion—gush gush gush he spouted off about how he'd started with 'one of their current albums' but then 'lost a few days deep down a rabbit hole of listening to almost their whole catalogue, online' which'd finally wended him round to their early work, the quality of which'd just about flipped his little lid like he didn't even know what!

'It's insane how much they've changed without getting technically worse—though nothing will ever compare to the Holy Trinity of *Self-Titled, Lincoln*, and *Flood* ...' he proclaimed, on the breathless heels of which he tripped over himself to add '... *John Henry* might even go second on my list, if it came to a gun in some hostage's mouth, I admit ...' but he sorta felt the output was '... a perfect one two three four—none worse than the other, per se, just a clear line of lighter-shades-of-perfection' comparing it to the early films of Wes Anderson.

I'd gone silent without realizing, nerves jangled not only from the unbridled and unselfconscious enthusiasm the kid was careening his words with, but from how he was already framing his love in terms of hierarchy, discussing ordination, ranking, explicating which whiskers-of-a-degree would separate what from what—moved toward the typewriter, for a moment wondering why the manuscript wasn't present, blip of panic as though I'd miscalculated and remained with no copies, but shook my face when I remembered the Post Office box.

Viggo'd picked up on my remove, even with his mile-a-minute jabber and the phone-line to disguise me. 'What's the matter?'

'Absolutely nothing ...' I coughed '... I'm thrilled you're digging the music, though admit I've not had much of a minute to give it any kind of proper listen.' Told him I agreed about *Flood* being superlative, especially one song, but demurred how I couldn't recall the name—he rattled off a few titles I could tell he thought went without saying were unforgettably whizbang, but I shrugged how 'Naw, it wasn't one of the Titans.'

'Do you happen to remember the track number?'

Lied, again, claiming I owned it on cassette, which he thought was the coolest thing ever—got the impression he was reading the listings, in order, off the back of his own copy of the album, so just said 'That's the one!' randomly to seem with it. He gave me a 'that's interesting sound,' admitting how, in his view, my pick would be lower down the pecking order. 'Not that anything on the album doesn't hold its own and trounce all comers else, a cinch!' His friends were gaga over *The Giants* too, by the way—though they dug what he was already referring to as 'their more mainstream stuff,' which he derisively clarified as 'the ones even people who don't know the Johns know about.' For his money, the best was never that sorta thing, and propounded how he harbored reservations about sharing a viewpoint with 'the fandom,' a tint of satire to his voice when he admitted 'The big big whoredom scares me, you know?' as though I'd be hip to whatever the words were in reference to.

Hearing him pontificate with such zeal, as though to the manor born, his life already anciently interconnected to some damned nerd-rock which seemed Hellbent on colonizing every facet of my existence, brought all the anxiety I'd gone through in recent days galloping forward and then some—I wanted to start an argument with him, correct his taste, outright command him not to listen to the shit anymore, point out how I was his father so didn't have to explain myself when he'd snipe in protest.

I was in the midst of this rising disquiet when he cut off from relating to me, in whooping detail, the sensations of first listening to a certain tune to ask 'We're still down for this weekend, right?' Trying to allow myself a moment to regroup, I attempted to get a cigarette lit, but stayed silent too long in doing so, his tone indicating he'd connected this silence to the previous, which must've been loitering in his forebrain, a tickle of unease his own. 'You're not coming out, are you?'

The manuscript would be arriving to Nathan during precisely that time and I'd intended to be around, hawkishly monitoring my phone for delivery confirmation, plus I didn't want any noise in my head while around my kid, not to mention didn't think it a terrific idea to be in his presence if I might yet be under surveillance—I mustn't ferry any infection into his life, be seen with him at some critical juncture ... thought of Hotel Detective, of Terrance, and it all got too eerie. Say someone did follow me, heard my son enthusing about *They Might Be Giants,* wanting to put together a tier-list of their work, then heard me playing along, batting ideas around with equal vigor, and suppose word of it got whispered back at Nathan—it'd take that skunk all of two-times-two seconds to reckon the double cross was in! Being round the bend he'd deduce, based on his own faulty wiring, how the reason he hadn't been given the original was my child'd been gifted it—that it'd been Viggo, not some nameless friend, who I'd waited to receive a photocopy from! To a madman, it'd follow as the night the day that, now armed with insights into what Benjamin had produced, me and my offspring were gonna be the ones to unlock the mysteries of the universe, horde 'em all to ourselves—when whatever he expected to happen because of the writing didn't happen, would get revved rabid to have his mitts on the *real* text, jet right to the source ... same as he might've thought Terrance had it, he'd think Viggo did and, in no time, would at least have to satisfy himself.

All this trilled migraine in my head over a handful of seconds then sat humming, louder, louder, while I told Viggo I didn't think my meeting up with him was a good idea, at the present moment. 'We'll sort something out for later on, I promise.'

'Why isn't it a good idea?' came the sound of teenaged heartbreak not even pretending it needed to be polite. 'Jesus fucking shit, dad—I put this all together and jumped hoops to be able to get free without whiff of it getting back to mom, so what're you even fucking talking about?'

'I can't exactly explain—you'll have to take my word.'

'Fuck your word—that's what I had taken! You go on all day long how if I need you, no problem, what do you care, name the time, the place—now, the first fucking time I take you up on it, plus do all the work so you don't have to just act like a goddamn adult with mom, you crap out!'

'Hey listen—I'm not crapping out, kid. I have some troubles, just now—completely unexpected and poorly timed. I'm sorry about it—and having to put off getting together's the last thing I want—

but I literally don't think it's advisable for me to go down there. For real, man—for your sake. I am being an adult about this by making the hard call—what do you think, I'm saying *No* to disappoint you out of malice, that I want you angry at me? Come on and just understand it isn't personal—I hate having to do this.'

'The fuck does *it wouldn't be advisable* mean?'

I blurted how it might be dangerous, then repeated the word emphatically. '*Dangerous*, alright? You just have to trust me, a minute.'

'*Dangerous*?' he mocked back an impersonation of my graveness, hardly able to keep a laugh of contempt out of his voice, one which sounded so borrowed from his mother I involuntarily bared my teeth. '*You*? Involved in something *dangerous*? Which you can't tell me about and have never once mentioned squeak of yet all of a sudden means you can't …' he cut off with a sigh I wanted to hang myself from.

'Vigs, listen …'

But he wasn't having it—not that I could blame him—and took me to task for living in my pit a million miles away, to begin with, instead of doing anything responsible to get my life up and running in a way maybe I wouldn't have to be out of his—doing whatever it took, even with no guarantees, instead of guaranteeing each and every day there was nothing else to do. 'Are you drinking?'

'Drinking?'

'Right now—are you?'

'No—we're talking.'

'Or doing whatever, again?'

'*Doing whatever*—what's that mean?'

'Oh can you just come off it—don't you know how bogus you sound!? You're my dad, but—what?—you can't afford a weekend with me in two years? You don't even need to afford it, because I fucking afforded it for you!'

'That's not fair—and it's nothing to do about affording it.'

He made a sound of dismissiveness like industrial dish steam. 'What else makes sense? You do or don't have a job, right now?'

'Of course I have a job.'

'I don't, dad—yet magically I could afford to arrange things!'

'You think I wasn't gonna pay you back when I got there, slip money in your fucking dirty socks if I had to?'

'I can just skip the fest, come out to see you—fine, let's do that, instead. Or is it too dangerous?'

'It is. Too dangerous. Do not come out here!'

He told me to provide him with one detail—just one speck of specific-sounding information—and promised, after I had, he'd lose the attitude, take me at my word, wouldn't even sweat it, and look forward to seeing me once I'd sorted whatever it was out, glad I'd had his safety set as top priority. Sure, there was a lot of sarcasm in the way he was phrasing it, he knew that, but straight up demanded: 'You must be able to divulge one morsel of context about what sort of danger you're in, or about why it'd be a hazard for me to spend a few days at a Film Fest with you—one fucking specific, come on.'

'Anything I tell you is going to sound crazy,' I said, flat, hoping it would count.

He retorted coldly how nothing he could conceive in his wildest imagination sounded crazier than what I was already saying, so I oughta wind up and pitch. 'I'm not even asking for a cogent narrative, just a *hint*.'

I couldn't bring myself to say 'I can't,' so all of a sudden was saying, in a put-upon tone mixed with almost an affable deprecation which must've sounded monstrous from his end of the line 'A hint? Okay ... it has to do with *They Might Be Giants* and I never should've told you about them.'

After a devastating silence, he forced a virulent fake chuckle, followed by the crackle-breath words 'The actual fuck did you just say to me?'

'You wanted a detail. That's the detail. The music. *They Might Be Giants*. I never would've told you about them if I'd known what I was mixed up in.'

'I'm getting off the phone.'

'Viggo, waitaminute ...'

'I'll wait all the minutes, you don't gotta worry on that front.' But he remained on the line, sounded gutted, the over-loud breathing and overlong pauses between each of a child desperately waiting for the grown-up to say something sane and stabilizing. 'You're on drugs, aren't you—I can tell by how you talk. Fuck you, man.'

'I'm not on drugs, Viggo …'

But it was too late for me to communicate anything—some deep-seeded, personal narrative, one buried and hoped and prayed against for God knew how long, had the kid's helm. 'You never even did drink, did you—it was fucking smack or coke or whatever, right?'

'I did drink—and I still *do* drink but not like *that*—I mean, I never *drank*—I still *drink* alcohol, a little bit, if that's what you mean, but I've never been a *drunk*.'

'Yeah, I get that now. Being a junky's so much better.'

I swore to him I wasn't drunk, nor was I on drugs, then blurted 'Fine—I'll come see you, alright?'

'Oh, wow—golly gee thanks, mister!'

'What do you even want, then? I said I'll come out …'

'It all of a sudden isn't too *dangerous* to come see me—what happened in the last twelve goddamn seconds?'

'It *is* dangerous.'

'Just not *too* dangerous?'

'It might be—I don't fucking *know* how dangerous it is or it isn't!'

'But what—you'll risk it? You'll endanger my mortal soul if it'll shut my trap about how you're fucking high as shit right now, is that the thing?' I'd no idea what to say to that and told him as much. 'It doesn't matter—I'm hanging up.' There was a long pause, after which he silently, shyly, brokenly said '… I fucking always *knew* mom had been right.'

'What?'

'She'd even softened it, probably—and Jesus, look how long you toyed around with me while all she'd been thinking to do was keep you painted in a better light.'

'I have no goddamn idea what you mean by any of that or why you're saying these things to me, Vigs.'

'I always knew when she said ...' but he went dead in a way there'd be no other words in the wake of.

Which didn't stop me growling 'Said *what*? What, Viggy—your motherfucker of a fucking mother said what?'

'I'm just gonna hang up.'

'*Why*?' I hissed, unable to keep myself from treating him as though he was the one hurting me, my voice more unforgivable than a slap.

'Because you're either lying or about to tell me mom's a liar and I don't feel like hearing either of those things.'

Click.

The End.

I didn't even bother voicing the 'I'm sorry' I couldn't dredge out of me into the air of the empty room the telephone receiver crashed to the wall at the other end of.

[*no taxi could take you, no trains going by*]

It would've been, and would be, easy to see how I'd behaved as a wake-up call, cop to having gone off the deep end, soused far too often, the plot lost so utterly I'd disappeared down a briar of some indeterminant nature, needed to get my head straight, snap out of it—yes, I wanted to believe it'd've been simple to've gone back on what I'd said, called Viggo again, apologized, told him he'd been correct about everything, assure him I'd taken his feelings on board, fessed to the weirdness I'd allowed myself to become involved in, promise I'd be at the festival, participate in the gift he'd poured his blood and sweat into obtaining for us ... but nothing is ever simple when nothing is even exact. Oh I lacerated myself thinking on it, attempted to work up the head of steam required to drive out to see him, without notice, pictured myself refusing to leave his mother's porch until I was permitted inside and we'd at least negotiated or else he'd been forced to watch me dragged away in cuffs—but the more time I spent in such contemplation, the clearer it became that I hadn't done or said anything wrong. My instincts had been protective, had been *fatherly*—I'd taken into account matters my son couldn't know or understand, not due to his removed perspective and lack of context, but because of his age. The situation he and I now found our relationship in wasn't my or his mother's doing nor anything so obvious and finger-pointing as that—it also wasn't my fault for having gotten mixed up in what I was mixed up in right when I was. The less I told him the better, was a matter of fact—it was immaterial whether or not he understood it or even felt there existed a reason he ought attempt to.

For the first time in a very long time, I called out of work—not directly to my manager but rather to the young man I still referred to as 'the new fella' and who was more than glad for the extra hours, would pass on word of the illness I claimed to be suffering. What I was in need of was a detox—not from the *Bulleit*, per se, though I'd do my college-best to pace it out a tad better than I'd been managing in recent weeks, but rather from 'my situation.' I made one jaunt to the gas station for the requisite supplies—sausage biscuits, frozen pizzas, a couple share-sized bags of gummy *Smurfs*, coffee for the pot, filters too, three-for-four dollar loaves of bread, saltine crackers, Ramen soup, peanut butter. I'd not exit my basement room, not even take smokes out in front, and permit no contact of any kind with anyone for any reason—the one exception being if Viggo were to leave a message, I'd be at his beck and call. Furthermore, I'd keep the room lit only by the paltry bulb above the kitchen sink and the glow from television—didn't matter if all I did was sleep for two days straight, though my plan was to keep my mind nostalgically occupied by going through tapes of television shows and movies I hadn't revisited in ages, *The Irish R.M., Millenium, Strange Luck*. Needed a concentrated expanse of familiarity, the experience of treading well-trod boards—figured after enough of that, I'd come away reinvigorated, returned to my old self, hopefully even get a little bit of motivation up me to pursue a viable hobby, something as simple as starting to collect comic books or old *Shadow* pulps, again, perhaps adopt a pet cat of some kind, a Tabby, a Tortie, a Manx, someone to talk to, get on the same wavelength as … normalcy: I could and would find a path to it.

Hard to tell if it went well, even for a second—perhaps there were starts and stops, ups and downs, but by the time I became preoccupied with whether I should be reaching out to Viggo such preoccupation overwrote whatever'd come before, became all that was happening and all that'd ever seemed to've been, even casting memory back to a time before it seemed to contain the possibility of such thoughts. There I vaguely existed, in the dark, pacing, *Rumpole of the Bailey* filling the room, scent of crumpled noodles coming to boil, Parmesan cheese sprinkled atop, stirred, sprinkled atop once more to harden into a crust like halfway-pot-pie, spent cigarettes down the sink gullet, gnashed by the disposal after a squirt of soap for odor control, flask emptied, refilled, body flopped in the chair—no, better yet just make myself a nest on the floor!—*VR Five* playing, *Briscoe County*, Richard Greico in *Marker*, Sir Mix-a-Lot was *The Watcher*, *Kung-Fu: The Legend Continues*, *Time Trax*, pizza with rising crust, sausage and pepperoni, cold water from the same gallon that'd been in the fridge over two years, refilled maybe not quite a thousand times, though perhaps more ... why not call my son ... or call his mother—not give up the game how Viggo and I'd been in communication, just explain I had something important to tell the boy ... it wasn't as though I'd been denuded of my legal rights or was devoid of the humanity required to elicit empathy ... maybe he'd already opened up to her—that was quite likely, in fact ... chances were he'd spit it all out in order to be washed clean of me ... so maybe it was time to go ahead and blow the gaff, to stop doing everything I did in secret, consequences be damned ...

My inner play-pretend forked preposterously: What if I died, for example—choked on a chomp of sandwich, set myself on fire due to a spill of booze near the heat of the stove's tawny coil, simply suffered an unexpected malady which wiped me out, *kabang*! How long until my son would learn of my death—would his mother tell him immediately when she was informed or hold off due to some rationale she'd feel proper, claim not to've known, herself, whenever he came to discover my fate, later in life ... 'Your father died when? Oh no, oh my gosh!' would be a perfectly believable scene, coming from the woman. It wasn't as though the news of my passing'd be akin to winning a sweepstakes—I wasn't even proactive enough to sport a life insurance policy, though defended such defect by pointing out there'd never truly been a reasonable time to've figured I'd have occasion to die. But if I were kidnapped—what about that? If that thug Nils Dolphy finally kicked right through my flimsy room door, dragged me by gunpoint to an area undisclosed—if I was plugged, my carcass left out in the sun, how long would it take for anyone to search for me and for how long would they do so? Would Viggo wonder if the danger I'd spoken of had anything to do with my disappearance—if my remains were found left in a swamp below the underpass, murder unquestionable, would he blame himself for not taking me seriously, or would he scoff, deem any strange timing coincidence, indifferent bad luck the way Terrance might've done about Benjamin?

Yes, it was two-days-and-change of a grindingly loopy, no-good-for-anyone head I fruitlessly endured—when 'the new fella' agreed without protest to let me return to work on the third of the nights I'd requested he cover, it was as though I was being spat back into circulation. Terrifying how familiar the sight of my slop-bucket car and the cardboard outdoors surrounding the claptrap establishment I dwelt in seemed—I recalled how, as a young man, a kid still Viggo's age, sometimes I'd exit a place I exited five times each day to discover everything around looking like it never had before and might never again ... now, it was hard to bring to mind even a memory of remembering what that feeling had felt like ... which may've been good, I told myself ... might've been appropriate how the sight of *The Calico Bash Nitely* evoked the word *home*.

Straight from bang, I noted how the parking lot was plumper with vehicles than usual—must've been one of the semi-frequent family reunions going down somewhere in town, *Calico* picked for lodgings through the shrugging rationalization 'How long will we really be in it, you know?' Cabins Seven Eight Nine all had cars and trucks in front of them, plus a rickety motorcycle might've also belonged to Six, tough to tell from how it was up on the sidewalk, leaned to the building façade, the owner likely quite fearful of the coming sleet my radio'd informed me all were preparing to endure the doomsday of—the bustle made me happy, especially the idea of Eight being booked for so blasé a purpose as I didn't need to go sniffing around in there and, better yet, now I couldn't. Oughta keep things professional for a month or so, because no matter what else'd been going on in my head, it did remain true how, in the days spent locked away, there'd been no oddity, no attempt to contact me, no kooky series of events to read into—if I could get a few solid shifts under my belt which went likewise, it'd amount to proof I'd induced my recent travails far more than I'd ever deduced them.

Two hours into the worknight, however, second tilt back of *Bulleit*, seventh cigarette, and inside from out front into the frosty Office, heater on the fritz, I happened to crane my head for a peek at the Guest Register—an idle check for whether it was time to flip the page, automatic gesture, no forethought. Not trusting I was seeing correctly for things being upside down, I spun the ledger and centered myself over it—halfway down the three-quarters filled grid, clear as the lingering chill running my nose, the name *Sullivan Shallcross* was inked quite *ker-splat*, computer telling me he was the current occupant of Cabin Eight. My stomach knotted and I wheeled around, bumped right into another cigarette and tottered in hiccoughs of lighting it with a Bic that didn't wanna fulfill its function toward the door, through it, outside—my vexation centered on: how on Earth could I return to work only to discover, practically within minutes, someone'd left the damned Register opened to the page with that name and how in Christ could that'd even gone down except for I must be losing my ever loving mind!? No sooner was my cig lit and the flippant humidity of the recent rain crawling around under my shirt than I flicked the barely dragged from stick away—car crash of embers as the twig hit the trashcan, a few dozen more as it bounced then extinguished across the wet pavement, query line of grey-blue rising from the puddle it halted in—and it occurred to me that, no, it was the *current page* I'd been looking at. Confirmed: *Sullivan Shallcross*, Cabin Eight—he'd arrived the day following the detective whisking me away for questioning.

Absentminded a new ciggie to the crease of my lip and lit up right there—blinked and blinked and rubbed my eyes at the name like my mind simply wasn't recognizing another moniker very much *like* Sullivan Shallcross but which wouldn't be, upon closer inspection, something which'd resemble the name but re-assemble, all at once, into the name's polar opposite just as soon as my brain caught the kink in its processing, after which I'd laugh myself queasy about my initial reaction for the rest of my life. Instead, the clarity of the penmanship, the stiff yet slightly curved formation of the all-capitals made it occur to me there was something else off—flipped back through the register until I found the entry from the previous year: completely different handwriting, not a sniff of similarity in fact, almost impressively so.

At that very moment, as the crème of uninhaled cigarette curled over my cheek to tickle the underside of my nose, a man named Sullivan Shallcross was present in Cabin Eight of *The Calico Bash Nitely*—a room receipt confirmed he'd remain so for a week yet and had paid for such privilege up front, in cash, a large asterisk on the printout of his registration slip I'd no idea the meaning of, no indication what it corresponded to, zero notations on the paper, front or back ... just another of far too many curiosities, a spice of emphasis to an already more than surreal little caper.

The computer told me how not only was this guest called Sullivan Shallcross, but the stay directly linked to the previous entry for the man—which, sure, coulda been a technical bloop of some kind, but also, and more likely, could mean what it meant: it was *the* Sullivan Shallcross who'd presently rented out Cabin Eight ... except it couldn't be ... *that* Sullivan Shallcross, our previous guest, was dead ... and because that Sullivan Shallcross had *actually* been Benjamin Visa ... it possibly meant now this was Sullivan Shallcross, *proper* ... or else that someone else was using the name pseudonymously ... or any number of twists and turns else ... but: so what? Not only was I not gonna do one damned thing about it, it wasn't to do with me—even if it was something connected with the manuscript, a continuation of the narrative I'd briefly, by accident, gotten a bit part in but which I was now free from, whoever was in the room was only there because *there* was *here* not because *I* was.

I paced triangular behind the locked door of the office toilet and insisted to myself I'd let sleeping dogs lie, that to do otherwise amounted to no less than willfully entrenching myself, becoming complicit in the misery ensconcing me, no mitigation—there weren't even questions I harbored a genuine desire for answers to.

What could I need to know—the less the merrier, that's how I saw it! I'd simply come in to work, do my job, give this a week and the spectre would've vanished—supposing I'd not decided to take back tonight's shift, by the next time I'd have clocked in I'd never have known about Shallcross being on hand, or, if so, by the time I did he'd have been gone. All I had to do was act like it was already the week-from-now it might as well have been ... 'All in favor?' I flushed the toilet I'd not sullied ... 'Carried unanimously.'

Back outside, swig, smoke, another, another, another of each as I ambled off toward the dumpsters then strolled along the lip of the gulch as though in blithe thought, lengthening how far along I went by a few steps with each yo-yoing until I was around in back of the joint enough to have an eyeline on the cabin in question, whereupon I alternated squinting down into the woods at the skeleton of an old *Family Fun Center*, which nature and frisky teenagers had reclaimed, and casting little glances toward the motel's front—even in the murk and from such distance I could tell the long car parked outside Eight was dented up beautifully, paint at least three different colors all of which were synonyms for *incorrect*, a junker which looked like a worse-for-wear taxi from a movie circa the middle nineteen-eighties, and as I ventured nearer in oblongs I hoped appeared meandering, saw its gorgeous speckling of knife-wound rust as well as a notably different colored pane for the rear driver's side window than the rest. Through the passenger side door, I could make out various litter, though none of it trash—novels and notebooks, a few articles of nondescript clothing, the jewel cases for compact discs, what looked like an empty shoe box, a snow shovel down on the floor with some unidentifiable stuff trundled around it. The front passenger seat had what appeared to be an open, emptied knapsack sitting in it, plopped square overtop a silly amount of loose CDs, all down-facing—several cans of energy drink coated the floor, what were probably empty packs of cigarettes dotting the dash ... license plate revealed the vehicle to be from well out of state, the exact hodgepodge of lettering somehow random looking enough to make itself seem Venusian.

I'd kept wary, flitting eyes to the cabin window probably too often to seem as innocuous as each flit was meant—lights out, curtains more like thick heavy blankets clearly all the way drawn, nowhere from which a head could be peeking through, not even a sliver of eyeball ... as our cabin doors had no peepholes, it was unlikely I'd been espied, but I crept off to loiter in front of definitively unoccupied rooms, all the same, chaining a new smoke going, no closer to having defined a next step than I was to justifying taking the step I just had against my own counsel. Sullivan might not actually have been in the room at that time, of course—odds were he'd been lurking around in the abundant darkness, taking detailed notes on my movements since I'd arrived, had desired to clock my original reaction to organically discovering his printed name, let it prove something or at least be distinct enough he might jump to a pre-determined conclusion with full confidence. '... except he'd not known I'd be on duty tonight ... nor that the Register would be on the appropriate page ... nor that I'd have any reason to've inspected it ...' I puff puff puffed what felt like a clever few kisses of nicotine outward. More and more, I considered the possibility that Benjamin Visa never had taken the room out, in the first place ... Shallcross certainly could've been the occupant from a year ago ... could be he'd already possessed a copy of the manuscript and had typed a duplicate to hide away, one which had all the earmarks of an original ... had wanted to make certain alterations to selected pages, as Nathan'd feared might've been done ... was back on account of some communication concerning all that'd transpired ... no doubt it was Sullivan who'd been the party asking around town about me ... though why any of those very plausible items ought be concerns of mine I curtly told myself 'Shut Up' about ... 'You shut up ...' I countered '... I'm not gonna be able to stop thinking about it, anyway, so the smart money says think about it in spades!'

If I was being observed, a lure being baited, it'd even make sense why the penmanship in the Register was so different than before, whoever'd taken the room wanting it for as damn sure as possible I'd see the name, be curious, confused, spooked—which is precisely what'd gone down! If events hadn't played out that way, I'd bet bottom dollars there would've been some Plan B snare in the offing, perhaps several enticements else simmering to summon my approach, each designed to make it come off as though everything I did was of my own volition. I might've received a ring from one of the cabins telling me there was something the matter with the coffee pot, could I bring another, so I'd have to ask 'Which Cabin?' and be prompted by the 'Eight' to look up who was in there ... or else a wake-up call request, to which I'd posit the same question or else 'Which name?' ... whatever ploy might lead me to check out the computer or the ledger to verify was child's play, the more shots taken, the more certain the cumulative effect would land true.

Nodding staunchly, I decided this theory was something I oughta devise a method to test—needed to think like someone stalking me not like me being stalked. If the point of keeping the room was to surveille me, Sullivan, or whoever it was, would check regularly who stood stationed at the desk, no way around that—might discover I'd called off, but would have little way of knowing for how long. If there'd been chatter about me with 'the new fella' it probably would've been mentioned when I'd called to ask if I could have the shift back—'Oh good, this guy's been asking about you'—or else might've been reported back—'*Psst* ... Mister Shallcross, that guy you told me to tell you about'll actually be in tonight, after all' ... though it was tough to imagine I'd have been inquired after by name or anything so blatant ... same as he wouldn't try to bribe my home address off someone, he'd avoid any memorable show which might come back to haunt him ... plus, I had no grounds to understand why Sullivan would want to watch me, to begin with ...

I'd lost count of had I taken one or two swigs so had another and called it two-definitely when it popped like bacon grease how Detective Hellpop might've been overseeing the ruse ... though the very next moment it struck me quite bracingly that I was getting far far ahead of myself, over-paranoid to the Nth ... not to mention how moot a point it'd become to be clever ... if I truly was being watched, how I'd behaved would've already clanged every alarm klaxon on Earth for whoever my observer was and I'd been at it for hours without them making approach ... therefore, my safest course remained to do nothing else, that night, and to go about my business in the coming days, playact an aloof, even implacable calm, enjoy my days off, then continue treating my existence as humdrum when next I arrived, putting on a show until someone either made a move or didn't for a long enough stretch I knew they never would on account of there being nobody who would.

The advantage I held was, up to that point, my actions could be ascribed to something far from involvement, even to a gumshoe with preconceived notions about me. 'I've been through all kinds of a lot, lately ...' I whisper-snarked like as though to Hellpop in response to a pointed interrogation '... and then I'd suddenly encountered that name, so of course I'd reacted strangely and absolutely I'd pawed around a little—and with good cause, it seems, eh?'

When it became clear I'd gotten a grip on myself and moved on, whoever was keeping tabs would either consider whatever matter dropped or else be moved to escalate—regardless, their doing whatever they did would be nothing to do with a choice I made. I wasn't gonna offer myself as a game piece, anymore, and that was my last word on the matter ... such resolve lasting all of three-quarters-of-an-hour, perhaps less ... and it was no more than a full hour at which point I ventured back outside, now beneath drizzle, alternately scraping my toes at the ground and bobbing like a fighter in a bruise-scented locker room psyching himself to take a dive.

I'd no legitimate call to knock on Cabin Eight's door, but anything could be doctored up as an excuse if the Sullivan Shallcross in it turned out to be either coincidence or literally someone without inkling of my existence—I considered printing out a phony note I'd pretend to've found waiting for me on the Office desk, one I'd only just noticed, a complaint of a funny smell or an irritating sound from the room next door, could someone look into it, thanks. If this Shallcross was nothing to do with me, worst case scenario went: a bleary guest would wonder what the devil I was up to for approximately thirty seconds after I'd proffered an unexplained 'Sorry about that' and slunked off—what else was some weirdo gonna do, make a federal case out of not having had a smashing stay at *The Calico Bash Nitely* in the enchanted isle of *Laampray*?

'And if it is the Sullivan you think it might be and he is here about you?' I regretted asking as I aimed myself for final approach ... having to meekly admit how I didn't have the faintest idea.

[*mister love maker heart breaker number one*]

'Marc Limoncello, as I live and breathe!' were the first words out of Sullivan Shallcross's mouth, the cabin door hardly opened—it was clear as lark song he'd been awaiting my arrival, the overdone expression of boisterous welcome, wide arms and stepping back as though I'd likely bear hug him something I got the feeling he not only'd rehearsed a few times but figured I'd be appreciative of. The room's interior was junked but also seemed done up like hyper-particular set-design: pizza boxes flapped open, only bones of back crust remaining alongside crumbles of grease soaked napkins the delivery joint's branding could still be discerned on in a touch of clever product-placement, equally artful were various energy drink cans in two rows atop the television, an almost-circle more of them on the desk, one on the floor, ashtray plump already and being squeezed down by the stub he'd used to light his current cig in the interim between my knock and our face-to-face. As for the man himself, I'd expected nothing and even still he was nothing close to it, an almost egregiously drib-drab fella, the sort you'd mistake for quite literally no one yet still always remember in detail—other than his mustache being a smear of meconium black, in stark contrast to thinning hair, cinnamon brown, eyebrows clear cropped, he was the Platonic Ideal of nonentity and I joked by calling him 'Mister Nemo' as I gave bowing-head squint to his extended paw, a grin betraying he didn't understand the joke though knew I'd meant one, glad I'd started the ball rolling with a fatuous moment of mirth.

He ushered me in, told me to sit wherever I pleased, apologized for not being a better host, only had tap water to offer, and mentioned he hadn't used either of the plastic-wrapped cups left by the bathroom sink so there was no need to be wary of the cooties he genially fessed up to probably having a raging case of. 'What're those cups for, anyway?' he wondered in a paly way. 'Seems if they were for drinking, they'd be somewhere else that wouldn't inspire any confusion.'

Felt odd about entering the room so freely, but told him 'I just work here, so how would I know about cups and plastic?' then reminded him we'd never met.

'So what brings you?' he inquired in response, making me feel caught.

'I was about to ask you the same.'

'Were you? Why on Earth?'

'You make an excellent point, but also know my name, meaning maybe you'd better be the one to explain—who's fooling who, here?

'We seem to have mutual acquaintances, Marc—I was curious how come.'

Replied how if he knew we did, he only could by knowing why '... so seriously, could you get to whatever's your purpose here?'

'Did you know *Benjamin*?' He emphasized the name, waggled his hands, tilted head to-and-fro, did a little circle where he stood, arms wide, gestures all indicative how we were talking about when the now dead man had been a guest disguised with the Shallcross name.

'I'd not even known to know Benjamin was Benjamin. But to answer directly and hopefully lead by example: No, I did not know Benjamin, in any way, shape, or form. Until this very moment, truth be told, I hadn't any way of knowing whether Benjamin had actually been a guest in this fine establishment—from my perspective, he well coulda been Sullivan Shallcross, you see?' He nodded like I'd made an extraordinarily striking observation, then, as though to keep us from getting bogged down in parliamentary red-tape, spoke a summary narrative of the leak, my finding the manuscript, so casual about it I almost wasn't alarmed. 'How is it you know any of that, Sullivan?'

'Mutual acquaintance,' he replied, tongue-in-cheek tone like hadn't we already covered that ground.

'Which?'

'Well, when you put it that way, maybe not a mutual acquaintance! I'd heard it through the grapevine, then—how's that?'

'Which?'

'Which what?'

'Grapevine.'

'I thought there was only the one.'

But I wasn't up for games of Miss Mary Mack, sighed to signify so, at the same time realizing I also wasn't down for leaving, since I'd already gone through the trouble of showing up—lit a cigarette from a pack I saw on the bedspread, feeling depleted by where the hands on the clock had come to. 'What brings you to *Laampray*?'

'What's that?'

'Here.'

'Thought this was called *Calico Bash*.'

'It is—I meant the town.'

'I meant the town, too.'

'Then it isn't.'

'Then it should be. *Calico Bash*'s a name deserving of a map—who's ever heard of *Laampray*?'

'You, somehow.'

'I'd really no idea.'

'What brought you to this room, then?'

'You.'

'What else?'

'Benjamin.'

'What else?'

'Is there?'

'I'm asking.'

'So am I.'

'Chrissake, could you do me the favor of a straight answer? I'm nothing to do with whatever there is to have something to do with, so I think it's the least you could do!'

'Okay—but in that case a guy's gotta wonder how come you speak so fluently, as though you are.'

'I don't begin to know what that means.'

'You've spoken with Nathan, haven't ya?'

'Have I?'

'You haven't?'

'I have.' He turned his palms up as though there-we-had-it, *ollie ollie oxen free*, a gesture which deeply vexed me. 'He spoke to me, is better to say.'

'You spoke to each other is best, though?'

'He started it.'

'Why was that?'

'For someone so well informed of my comings and goings you seem curiously not, when it suits your mood. Except I see right through that, so here's what we'll do: you tell me why it was, then maybe I'll tell you something else.'

'What would you have to tell me?'

Shrugged. 'Maybe nothing. It'll be for you to determine once you've heard it. Or you can hazard a guess, piss off, and leave me to my work.'

'Work?'

'Here.'

'Desk won't jockey itself, eh?'

Not even bothering with appearances, I took my flask from hip pocket, downed a squishy swallow, held it across. 'You're free to use one of the mysteriously purposed cups from the sink if you're worried about more cooties, of course.'

He took the thing, told me booze would sterilize whatever buggies lurked on my lips, took two quick tilts, handed it back, much obliged. 'Nathan bailed you out.'

'*Lawyered* me out.'

'Double quick, too.'

'Anything else?'

'No doubt you talked.' I'd just told him as much and told him as much. 'Touché. But what had you scamps gabbed about?'

'Do you really not know?'

'I'm not omniscient.'

'Does no one you know really know?'

'Not other than Nathan.'

'So why not ask him?'

'I'm already here.'

'I have his telephone number—you're telling me you don't?'

'Sure I do—and that would be another solution, you're an everyday problem solver, you are! But you're still already here, too, so certain steps'd be redundant—don't you agree?'

'Does that matter?'

'You were only a minute ago asking that bushes not be beaten around.'

'Touché.' Took another swig, looking left-right like there was a chance I wanted someplace to sit, then, starting with my back to him, lazily related how his good pal had strewn about a load of horse hockey. 'Don't go getting me wrong—he was the very pink of courtesy, a gentleman through-and-through, bought me breakfast, and I appreciate breathing non-confined air, as much as the next man, just much prefer doing so without philosophical discourses on the importance of a band I don't even care for.'

'You're not a fan of *The Giants*?'

'Is that so curious to you?'

'It's anecdotally and statistically odd, at least. Which albums have you listened to?'

Told him '*Flood* and the one with the octopus on it.'

'Which?' he rabbit-wrinkled his nose.

'Is there more than one?'

'I don't think there's any.'

'The one with the same name as a found-footage horror film.'

'That doesn't help.'

'With about ten zillion tiny songs at the fucking end!'

'*Apollo 18!*' he snapped his fingers like a plucky kid detective figuring out who'd stolen the bullied kid's lunch money since it hadn't been the bully just faking they hadn't.

'That's what I said,' I stubbed my cigarette on the table beside the telephone.

'You've hardly given them a chance, my good man! They've been at it almost as long as you've been alive. Wait—how old are you?'

'Forty-four.'

'Been at it as long as you've been alive,' he amended.

'Well hoop-de-do and dickory dock for them if they've improved over a lifetime, but I'll survive without verification.'

'What's your tipple, music wise?'

'*Tony Coca Cola and the Roosters* hit my tickle spot.'

He laughed and, to my honest delight, acted out a few minutes from *The Driller Killer*, seemed to expect I'd join in with doing the background singers' *Oop-sha-doobies*. 'But seriously ...' he frowned, giving up trying to coax me '... I'm trying to break the ice.'

Rattled off some names of music groups, hoping it'd get us out of our loopy deadlock—it didn't, so I opted for a firm redirect. 'I was told you're a fan, though.'

'So I am.'

'Big time, so the story goes.'

'And from way back. Benjamin, too.'

'So what was that he'd typed up—the fan club bonus?'

'I've no idea what he typed up. Seems to me few people do, if anyone does.'

'Well, there's bound to be someone,' I sighed again, took out one of my own cigarettes, lit it with the lighter by the ashtray, leaned to the wall by the television.

'There's you.'

'I don't count.'

'How's that?'

'On account of I barely skimmed it.'

'Then why say there's someone did more?'

'There have to be others.'

'Agreed.'

'Ask them.'

'Sadly, it doesn't seem that I can,' he said, paused like stifling a sneeze, coughed rather severely instead, went to the bathroom, ran the tap, slurped some water, gargled. This oddball intermission was a good thing, too, because his response had seized something up in me—I moved back toward the room door, verifying it hadn't been locked and latched at some point my attention had strayed. 'What was it you were going to tell me?' he asked cheerily as he re-entered the common area, chaining a new smoke lit from the one he picked up which I hadn't noticed he'd dropped and left smoldering on the carpet.

'Tell you?'

'You'd said it was a take turns kinda proposition we were in, hadn't you? I mean, there's something I could maybe guess you could tell me but which, having been forthcoming, I'd prefer to not have to.'

'I have one more question, first.' He nodded I should feel free. 'Though I have a sinking suspicion I'm going to regret asking it …'

His eyes widened, blink blinked, lips parting with cigarette at a dangle. 'Why the devil would that be?'

'Because it's about did you kill Benjamin and his son.'

'What about did I kill Benjamin and his son?'

'The part about did you.'

'Certainly not. Though, more importantly, I don't follow you.'

'You know they're dead?'

'Certainly. Though, more importantly, I don't follow you.'

'You know somebody killed them.'

'Somebody killed Benjamin, yes, I'm aware of that … Terrance, however … while dead … I thought was on account of he slept through the Afterschool Special that woulda made all the difference …' he took a pregnant pause, looking me up and down, genuine curiosity wrinkling his eyes '… wait … *you* didn't kill Terrance, did you?'

'Jesus Christ, no.'

'Did *someone*?'

'I'd thought maybe.'

'Me?'

'Maybe.'

'Why go thinking a dreadful thing like that—I didn't even know you, til now!'

'It had been shabby of me, in retrospect, please accept my insincere apology—though I'm only giving that on account of I suppose thinking it really doesn't make sense.'

'Sense?'

'Considering.'

'Considering?'

'How if you'd killed Terrance you'd be the one with the manuscript.' Ah—okay—he followed me—but seemed very uncertain about something still and I admitted how '… being an unconcerned third party for a living, I sometimes get a little confused.'

'With what?'

'What's going on.'

'Which is?'

'I'd hoped you might tell me.'

'Is why you knocked?'

'What're you doing here?'

'Came to see you.'

'Why?'

'About Benjamin's manuscript—hey, aren't we going in kind of a loop here? I want it on record that, if we are, it's you looping it and—well!—that doesn't jibe with wanting to get to whatever my point is.'

'What *about* the manuscript?'

'Where is it—I'd been hoping you'd know.'

'As it so happens, that's exactly what I was going to tell you.'

'I would've guessed that!'

'You should've—woulda saved us a week.'

'Where is it?'

'With Nathan.'

He stood, passive, taking this in, inspecting me—slowly lilted head left-to-right, right-to-left *crick-crick-crick* of neck popping as though it were growing spikes, then shook his head, hung it, and sighed how he was certainly sorry to hear that.

'I'm indifferent to hear how you're sorry to hear that—have you been in town long?' I pivoted to, figuring it my turn to turn a table or two.

He shrugged. 'About as long as you know right well it's been, no more, no less.

'Taking in the sights, are you?'

He actually was a fan of duckpin bowling and, while I might not care for my hometown, told me it boasted a very fine little Museum of the History of Antiseptic—he was a sucker for bumpkin passion projects like those. 'Why're you changing the subject, though?'

'Was I?'

'You were.'

'What'd the subject been?''

'You can't remember?'

'Would you believe that?'

'Try me.'

'Did you believe that?'

'Yes—I usually wouldn't, but in your case I'll write some allowances. I've been keeping an eye on you.' Vocal change to the last sentence, hurried in the beginning and then slow, ending with a marked pause to make sure I'd picked up on the intent of the melody.

'An eye?'

'On you.'

'Your own?'

'Both. Peeled.'

'And what is it you've gawked me getting up to?'

'Not much of anything, give-or-take.'

'Sounds like me—but also the sort of lucky guess someone'd make just from a first glance.'

He supposed that was true enough. 'But keeping an eye on you hadn't been my original intent. I'd been quite keen to chat, as the two of us are currently doing so enjoyably—though keener still to chat in the manner I sincerely hope we finally will.'

'You could've just knocked.'

It had crossed his mind. 'But you didn't seem the sort who welcomes company.'

'I'm not the sort who welcomes being voyeured, either.'

'I'd erred on the side of what you didn't know couldn't hurt you.'

'But now I do know—so where does that leave me?'

'Unhurt—as I reckon you can see for yourself.' To put his cards on the table: he'd been standoffish and conducting his own inquiries—but such could only go so far and he'd no bent for criminality. 'Figured it best to wait you out. There are particular queries I need replies to and *unforced* seems the best way to go about eliciting them.'

'Is *unforced* what the kids call *coerced*, nowadays?' He didn't follow. 'Why not just have your hired goon shake me down?' I bluffed, tone serious enough it wouldn't seem so but easy enough to re-color with a roll of my eyes.

'Hired goon?'

'Nils Dolphy.'

'Who's that?'

'Some thug.'

'A notorious one, this neck of the woods?'

'You tell me.'

'You'd have to tell me, first—then I could quote you.'

'You don't deal in thugs, eh?'

'Sure don't, nor goons.'

'Lend me a grain of salt and I'll take your word with it.'

'What would I be doing with a thug or a goon?'

'I didn't know you enough to know.'

'You do now?'

'I don't. So a thug doesn't seem any more far-fetched than a goon, which doesn't seem far-fetched, full stop. You're dead set on making this interaction between us quite a little screenplay, after all.'

'Am I?'

'How'd you even know about me—about any of this?'

'How had Nathan?'

It wasn't at all a bad question, actually—which I mistakenly let show on my face, mugged for a minute, then suggested Nathan was a friend of Benjamin's family, so my guess was he'd heard about me through them.

'Or the grapevine.'

'That does seem a viable option.'

'It's where I heard of you, after all—and of you and he.'

'Why'd you ask, then?'

'To scrutinize how you'd answer.'

'How had I?'

But Sullivan no longer seemed interested in role-playing cops-n-robbers, drooped his shoulder, arms dangling limp as he plopped to the lip of one of the twin beds. 'I can't imagine he had anything nice to say about me.'

No reason to deny it, I didn't. 'In fact, I'd been cautioned not to trust a single word you might say were you ever to say any to me.'

'About?'

Took me a moment to comprehend the question. 'Him, I suppose. Or anything, I guess.'

'About him or *anything*? Seems the second item would've sufficed, so he probably mostly meant the first, wouldn't you figure?'

'I see your point—while at the same time don't give a tinker's cuss.'

'What libels did he libel?'

'Said you'd branded him a *numerologist*—which I only know was incendiary on account of how he explained it.'

'Which was?'

'Kinda with heartache, to be honest,' I couldn't help but chuckle and the remark seemed to strike the man poignantly. 'You two were ... *buddies*, weren't you?' I asked but more quoted *Dark Place*.

'We were—and he's right. Though he brought that particular pet-name on himself—haven't you talked to him?'

'As previously established.'

'Then I'm sure you must've noticed.'

'He seemed more of a crackpot than anything specific.'

Sullivan nodded, then seemed to consider something a moment, twisted his mouth as though apologizing for being pigheaded, and told me 'But certainly he'd call me *something of a Mystic* … and be correct about that, so far as it goes.'

'Mystic as opposed to?'

'Philosopher. Student of the World. Believer.'

'He didn't call you any of those.'

'But he did call me *Mystic*?'

'He did not.'

'I find that quite hard to believe—though seeing as the last of the designations I'd mentioned was a long time coming, I suppose I would.'

'Fascinating, I'm sure I'm in no way sure. You can either make the retelling brief or else skip it altogether, no point making a fuss on my account.'

'What I mean is: for the longest time in life I'd have demanded to be known as a Skeptic.'

'You expect me to believe that?'

He snorted in amusement before pressing on, relating how, curiously enough, it was the same thing which'd made him dub Nathan a Numerologist that'd tilted him into the camp of Believer. 'As a matter of fact, it was Nathan who was responsible—odd as that may sound.'

'No odder than anything else, Sully. Lookit: you've kept an eye on me, we've met, how about we shake hands, wrap this up—a gag's a gag and all, but unless there's legitimately something I can do for you, I think the day can be called.'

He'd be much obliged if I provided him the manuscript.

'Nathan has that, now.'

'No no, not that one. We want the negative, Mister Veil.'

Doffed a pretend cap to the reference, grinning how much I adored *Nowhere Man*—though kept to myself how I wondered if he already knew that from my hand-labeled VHS tapes so lovingly preserved—then took the reference-game a tap further with an allusion to *The Prisoner*. 'Then it's just a little matter of my resignation, eh?'

'*Top state secret confidential why why why ...*' he kept it going, glorious giddy clap to his hands.

But unease was getting its teeth in me, so I cut to the chase with 'There is no original. There never was. I told Nathan as much, too.'

'If there's a copy there's an original.'

'That's exactly what your old buddy said.'

'He's not my buddy.'

'I said *old buddy*.'

'So you did.

'Which he wasn't?'

'Which he was.'

'So I was correct.'

'And he was correct.'

'About?

'Copies having originals.'

'I suppose so.'

'To which you'd replied?'

'*Or at least at one time they did.*'

'Clever. How'd he take that?'

'In the manner intended.'

'Which was?'

'*Clinically.*'

'And what else had the two of you spoken of, regarding manuscripts?' I sincerely didn't follow, showcased by a furrow of my brow, a half-squint of one eye, a little click of my jaw. 'Come come, Mister Limoncello ...' he murmured, busy with a cigarette.

'Nathan put on a jolly maudlin song and dance. I took pity. Told him if he went home, left me alone, I'd mail him the manuscript.'

'The manuscript?'

'The exact duplicate I'd found.'

'How'd you know?'

'What?'

'The duplication was exact.'

'I didn't.'

'You said you said so.'

'I did.'
'But you didn't.'
'That's right.'
'And you mailed it.'
'That's right, too.'
'No—I don't believe it.'
'Believe what?'

'Any of it. Not to worry …' held hands up as though I was over-reacting to a physical threat despite I hadn't altered my posture '… I've zero intention of strong-arming you. I simply know certain things you don't—things I'm not-shy-of-certain Nathan knew, just as well, and, indeed, likely claimed to know far better than me.'

'Things such as?'

'Benjamin. Who I imagine he told you I was estranged from.'

'He'd phrased it differently, but sure.'

'He made claim that the true dramaturgical dyad was comprised of the two of them, I a measly hanger-on, out for my own buck?'

'In fairness, he was also the first one to tell me you were anything more than a pseudonym.'

Sullivan grinned, stood up, dusted his thighs, and then, in a very warm and direct manner, stated he truly wanted me to come around to telling him where the manuscript was, of my own free will—would be aghast if anything he did or said caused me to act rashly. 'As a matter of fact, I sincerely desire you to be my witness.'

No idea what he was on about, I did my rational best to explain to him how all I wanted was to be left alone, so he oughta take matters up with Nathan—there were a few too many moving parts to whatever their little grudge was, in my humble opinion, and I had more than enough going wonky in my own life to spare a minute tending to any of them.

'There are matters which exist of far greater importance than whatever petty hiccoughs you're experiencing, Marc.'

But enough was enough—I stood with a cutting gesture of how our audience had reached its terminus, demanded he admit I'd been forthright in playing along, but he'd better understand I was going to report everything that'd passed between he and I and between Nathan and I to the police, which'd mean any further contact would carry appropriate consequence.

'Marc ...' he rolled his head so his neck cricked and cracked again, gazing at me almost piteous, a genuine sadness and yearning for understanding in the voice.

'Sullivan, listen: I get it—Nathan explained all about the secret code and the power to cloud the minds of men so they cannot see you or else a super-cool trick'll let a bloke bend the will of a jury or a populace algebraically ... or whatever! I'm not interested. It's jabberwocky.'

But I must understand—he wholeheartedly agreed—and with hands laced into a kindergarten pose of beseeching, went 'You mustn't think me of a mind with Nathan about that lunkheaded rot. Clearly my erstwhile friend had been allowed to plead a case, so—with further promise that afterward I'll leave you alone should you still desire it—might I be afforded opportunity to do likewise?'

Unscrewed my flask slowly, chuckling when he perked up as though my doing so was a gesture meaning we were gonna share, took a swallow, closed it up, and quipped how he might've left me at least a slice of cold pie.

'We could order more,' he suggested with the magnanimous thumbs-up a deadbeat dad might flash were it his every-other weekend—an offer which tempted me, but seemed that taking meant I'd be okay with whatever his spiel was running even as long as the cook time, let alone the interval until delivery.

'Naw ...' I finally replied '... just hurry up and let's get this over with ...' the little twinkle in his eyes, seemingly at my exact choice of words, making me quite wish I'd not.

[*pass round a picture of a mobius strip*]

In a sudden bolt of sensibility and guile, I mentioned offhand to Sullivan how we ought step outside to continue our discussion, as not only would the crisp nick of the night air keep me better focused, but if we remained in the room I'd grow distracted by thoughts of unattended job functions, as well—what with the occupancy a click or two higher than usual, told him I reckoned it'd behoove me to keep line of sight on the Office, bare minimum. 'Nevermind the telephone …' I added with a dismissive brush of one hand so as to pepper nuance into the deception and thus better secure the sale '… as I don't tend to answer it regardless, always figure if a guest's that up in arms about whichever trifle they'll eventually pop their head out to grouse in person, otherwise no harm no foul.'

Sullivan made no objection, simply explained he needed to use the powder room first, a chore he tended to with both admirable and somewhat bewildering speed, after which he gathered up a fashionable coat, one which didn't at all befit the state of the room or what I still assumed was his junkyard ride parked in front, and motioned me out, mugging an expression of almost genuine curiosity as to why I hadn't started on my way without him—I'd thought about doing precisely that, but figured it best to overemphasize how I'd no rush to be rid of him, nothing patronizing going on, my end, I'd wholeheartedly accepted his offer to speak his piece in the spirit it'd been expressed, so if it did break that he got riled up even he'd have to admit it was no fault of mine … of course, if the guy did become volatile it'd be little matter who he deemed responsible, but in those moments of silence, I felt crafty enough a tactician I'd bet I coulda designed a popular board game.

My gambit, indeed, proved savvy—several of the cabins had people standing out front of them, doors opened to cast polygons of light out every which way, cigarettes, chatter, television or radio from interiors turning the seclusion of the lot into a public space I wanted to take full advantage of. Peered in through the Office window only briefly, while getting lit a fresh cig, then gently drifted toward the most illuminated area of the lot, beside the dumpsters, skirting the lip of the gulch slanting precariously down toward the abandoned *Fun Center* so the two of us would remain in eyeline of as many witnesses as possible and for as long—I'd keep placid, imperturbable, so that if Sullivan betrayed any sign of agitation it'd be magnified, my vague hope being that even giddy enthusiasm on his part might be mistaken as something more sinister when mentioned in some stranger's recap of what, to them, would be only a squinted at pantomime.

Sullivan picked up a small crag of asphalt and flung it into the wooded area, all manner of far too much bustle resulting, then swiveled his head to give me a look like we were young partners-in-crime, segueing from an almost flirtatious grin into saying 'Nathan and I, you must understand, while it has to be admitted were cut from the same cloth, had branched out into what you might call two *sects*—or if that sounds a tad too radical, just say we saw things through fundamentally different apertures.'

'I daresay,' I quipped.

'Than each other,' he'd meant.

'You don't say,' I carried on, though Sullivan seemed not to notice or else was almost horrifically unbothered by the crank-yank.

If I wanted him to simplify it, he'd do his best: 'It's interesting you'd spoken of Nathan in terms of philosophy—*philosophical discourse*, I believe you'd mentioned, though I suppose doing so was meant only in derisive jest or merely to turn a phrase. In truth, and unfortunately, Nathan never had much of the philosopher about him. Such was at the heart of our schism …' he fished out his cigarettes

'… or better say *split* …' seemed to utilize the pause of getting his lighter struck to deeply contemplate vocabulary '… but, no, both sound too harsh …' gave another beat of consideration, let out his drag and continued '… he is Math and Science while I am Philosophy—and while many would point out these all started as one and the same, many others would point out on the double-quick how they certainly didn't remain so for long. Even when Nathan branched off into Law, there always seemed something of an abacus to the man—no, Marc, humanity rather eluded my old friend.'

I've no idea was it coincidence or if he'd picked up on my trick of utilizing the parking lot as a display case and so wanted to assure me he wasn't looking to thwart any safeguard I'd invented, but Sullivan took a seat on the stump of a streetlight, stage center to the bulk of milling guests, and began to speak more theatrically, voice stentorian, wide gestures of arms, hands casting finger shadows several directions at-a-time. 'Not the first song, but the most impactful, I heard by *They Might Be Giants* was over the telephone—it wasn't the first Benjamin had heard, certainly, nor was it the first he'd shared with Nathan—and what was most unique about it is that it was played to me over the telephone, yes, but not by the service the band offered, known as Dial-a-Song, which itself was nothing fancy, you simply rang a number, waited until an answering machine activated, its message whichever tune the band'd decided to have on offer for whichever number of days. It was a song Ben had just come across, having learned about from a random encounter with some stranger's internet posting—a discovery he'd been bowled over by and shared between us on a rainy afternoon, each sequestered in our basements. He'd held his phone to the speaker and I'd listened a half-dozen times to a song about a diving board, about a swimming pool—the one could see the other, the other could sense the one, each with no conception of what they, themselves, were, no comprehension of the other's origin or intent, but both with an innate, unquestioned understanding that their purpose was joint and, therefore, so was their possession of the other. It was a love story, do you see?'

'Sounds like a hot ticket,' I said instead of telling him I didn't.

'Oh catchy as the day is long, rest assured!'

'Wait here—lemme put on my green dress and some socks I can hop in.'

'When simply explained, it does sound a bit abstruse, I admit ...' he laughed.

I sighed, anxious he was gonna start singing, and to cut him off at the pass told him 'I don't know that word so I'll have to take your word on it.'

He gave me the eyeball, up down, like he couldn't sort whether I was playing dumb—eventually, apparently, satisfied, he puffed a long drag as though tracing a shape with it and resumed: 'Well brainy young lads were we—and brainy young lads fall in love with brainy young bands and sometimes with brainy each-others. Head-over-heels was the case for all three of us—and how! Well ... *more-or-less*, I suppose is the more truthful expression. *The Giants* were a lifelong infatuation for Benjamin, to be sure. Nathan, frankly, always struck me as harboring only a topaz adoration. For myself, I confess there was attachment beyond the music—and though I fervently kept up with news of the group over the years-turned-to-decades, doing so was more symptom than disease. But I won't belabor that, as not only do I suppose you heard an earful about it from Nathan before, I've also no interest in disabusing you of whichever way he attempted to slander me with something I don't think capable of being wielded for such ends. Sufficed to say, it wouldn't be going too far to proclaim that Nathan had loved Benjamin *for a purpose*, while I'd simply loved him. Again, I shalln't roll your eyes with sentimental particulars, shall simply admit, in candor, how you strike me as a thoughtful enough sort of fella to understand that rifts such as those which developed between myself and Benny often have the opposite-of-rifts as their impetus, and how interpretation from outsiders not attenuated enough to view the world in such terms often have their blanks filled in quite scurrilously.'

What he said genuinely warmed me—I felt he was correct about my constitution and wanted to find a way to express what I'd gleaned was his meaning. Thought of how Benjamin's estrangement from Mrs. Strauss had long predated this manuscript and, no doubt, was steeped in a specific sour of acrimony—was certain I now had the context in which the woman'd uttered the word *ghoul* ... except wondered if I was making up tall tales, again ... she'd said *ghouls,* after all ... which suggested several people lumped in together ... knew I mustn't let myself connect dots which didn't exist, as doing so equaled playing myself into hands I wanted nowhere near me ...

'This notion of Benjamin's—this thunderbolt concept which inspired the manuscript he finally spit out—hadn't started as anything grand, rather was conversational banter, fun-and-games kicked around. *Is 'Tryptophane' a better song than 'Lie Still, Little Bottle'? How can you even say that? Well, I disagree!* So forth so on so on so forth. The thing with Benny—as it was with all three of us—was that we were only ever keen to speak to one another, in general, and about *They Might Be Giants*, in particular. We couldn't be arsed with fandoms and factoids and concert tees—mostly because Benjamin was vociferous in his insistent absolutism when it came to opinion. The poor bastard practically flagellated himself whenever his own feelings on a tune altered—for any reason, especially those outside his direct control, and most frequently because a new song would upstage one which'd sat high in his esteem for ages. He'd grow despondent as the band's prolific output showed no sign of flagging—often seemed pushed past exhaustion in the face of the music's quality remaining undiminished while budding outward like twinkling yeast. Of course he might, as many did, point out an overall decline in X quality which, even if counterbalanced with a notable improvement in Y, equaled an absolute lessening in their work—he understood that, as with all things, there was a trend toward stagnation and, from there, a procession to the void, but the glacial pace of their entropy was a source of barbed consternation. I found it adorable—my feelings toward the man left little choice in that—how his vexation in learning they'd provided a song to a soundtrack or released some set of venue specific melodies was worn like a war wound, the pride in his misery apparent if one knew where to look. What ate at him most—seemed at times to incite alarming rage!—was the indisputable fact that, regardless of any overarching downslope, each and every album, as well as any collected handful of new offerings gathered from disparate one-off sources, contained works utterly top-notch, songs on par with their greatest. What this meant, to Benjamin, was the notion of finding a Definitive Order in the rankings of their work was folly—not abstractly, not merely because they kept on going, but practically, *explicitly*. Plenty of artists continue to produce well past expiration date but, without fail, these artists become not-themselves—stubborn autumn leafs refusing to untether from their freezing branches, they metamorphose to eyesores, never remarked as lovely when finally they do fritter to the chill winter's uncaring floor. Even if, out of the blue, a has-bin experiences a rejuvenation, manages to produce a seminal work long past when even diehards would believe it possible, there's a clear demarcation, a way to delineate it nothing to do with them in the terms anyone means when they're spoken of. *The Giants* were a galling exception—in his eyes intensely, this intensity parroted in Nathan's, my own peepers viewing the matter as largely irrelevant. To me, it was a quirk how, all of a sudden, a new album dripping with tracks he'd determine ranked above so many others already tabulated—many of which he'd have considered *enshrined*—moved him to lament. I'd play along in his bemoaning how his life's pursuit was a mug's game, his passion project nothing but the model ship of a hobbyist, his experience no different than that of a hack writer compiling an off-the-cuff internet listicle. What he sought was a grand unifying theory, you see—what I sought was the man seeking one.'

I followed him insofar as his friend sounded like the third person in as many weeks I'd never want to spend a minute of my alone time with—but when my remarking such received an honest-to-Christ glare from Sullivan, I glugged twice from my flask and conceded 'Yes, it's a drag how he died before the band did and thus his life's work can never be complete.'

Was that the shot, here—Benjamin's manuscript was being ridiculously sought by this man so Benjamin might live on, Sullivan or

Nathan would selflessly tend the fire until the band retired or kicked the bucket, would, every year on Benjamin's birthday, raise a glass and act as though he were there alongside them, convivially discussing their hot takes on whichever new offerings had arisen during the interim months, assuring his ghost that he'd shuffled off at the most propitious time, as—boy oh boy!—it would've been a downer to watch his beloved pet dilapidate to rot and ruin?

Sullivan motioned for the flask, took a drink, another, then squinted at me, wary, confused, or both. 'I thought you'd spoken to Nathan. Gotten to know the man's *philosophies*, as you called them.'

'Nathan was a nutbag ...' I sniffled into another swallow as the flask was gingerly passed back my way '... but I figured he probably did his thing on his own time, you on yours, and there might still be something mutual in your outlooks.'

'Ah ...' Sullivan motioned for the flask back '... no ...' nodded thanks as he prepped for a swallow '... nothing mutual ...' breathed after the drink seemed to've stung him too bitterly. Let him go back a bit: 'Nathan fancies himself a man of Science, Marc. You got the idea, I can only imagine—reckoned he could alight on some universally applicable data set in Benjamin's obsession. I promise you, there's plenty good reason he came under this delusion—indeed, I grudgingly admit there is something intoxicating to the idea and, so you'll best comprehend, shall endeavor to explain it, presently, but we'll let such business sit by awhile. How we've arrived where we are happened like this: when out of the clear blue sky, Benjamin announced he'd had a breakthrough, when his passion turned outrageous enough he'd declared he was leaving his life behind without preparation, sequestering himself until his work was completed, Nathan had gone a little funny in the head. There'd been some ... *altercations* ... which Benny made me aware of when he reached out—I'd not interacted with Nathan directly in ages, nor he with me, doubted he knew how much Ben and I kept in touch. Anyway: when Ben left home, abandoned it all, declared he was going to write it all down, once and for all, Nathan felt ... left out, abandoned ... *wounded*, I'd go so far as to say. Then when Ben never came back

… when his grisly fate was revealed … Nathan felt … well, I don't know what he felt but a fair word for it is *lost*.'

All fascinating, I admitted, but deemed it only honest to point out how little I cared. 'Illuminating as this flashback is, perhaps the cold equations could be stuck just a touch closer to.'

'You think like Nathan—cold equations. That's how he saw it—saw everything—mingled with maybe some megalomaniacal notion of there being power to harness in this dream of an Absolute, a force which could light a city or raze one to the ground, so to speak.'

'Fuck's sake, guy—I'm all but done with this. I gotcha: Nathan's a kook but Sullivan knows better than to harbor the dream of the mad monkey …' I was startled dumb when he flashed an eager thumbs-up at my reference—blinked and asked him, utterly skeptic, whether he'd heard of the movie.

'It was released under the title *Twisted Obsession*, yes?'

'Yes, it was!' I had to laugh, an ugly, ungainly, unselfconscious blat.

'Hence I thought you'd been making a very esoteric and deep cut joke at my expense.'

I assured him no joke had been intended, but that I sure was chuffed he'd picked up on the citation, the two of us digressing into a chitchat concerning the obscure and, so far as he explained it to me, much maligned motion picture in question, a poor reception he couldn't for the life of him fathom and neither could I—but I soon grew to feel I was being led by the nose, lulled into an unearned chumminess which would guarantee the outcome he sought … the one I was becoming more dead set on denying him.

Noticing my cigarette was nearly done, he offered across one from his pack, getting it revved before handing it to me—I accepted the gesture, not betraying I hadn't cared for the practically stealing a kiss level of sneakiness in it, some trace moisture on the paper where I inhaled, not even a filter to make me feel buffered from his lips. My next question might've had a touch of hardly buried snark to it.

'Why hadn't you assumed Nathan'd killed Benjamin?'

'I had …' the photo-flatness of the statement rather numbed me. '

… except: he didn't appear to have possession of the manuscript, at that time. You see?' A playground shrug up and down.

I didn't see—was beginning to feel genuinely ill at ease again, doing my best to disguise a glance toward the motel, wanting to reassure myself I still had an audience who, if all went South, might report me and my cause aright to the unsatisfied.

'Of course, I still thought he *might've* killed him …' Sullivan continued, my attention snapping back to him '… as obviously a great variety of things *might've* transpired: Nathan'd done poor ol' Benny in, wrongfully assuming the manuscript would be in his baggage or glovebox or trunk, only to learn far too late how it wasn't. Or else: he'd accosted Ben, crazy eyed, froth on the mouth, but Ben'd not had the manuscript on him, at the time—Nate'd made demands, Ben in no mood to relinquish anything to him, full stop, and perhaps claiming he'd not managed to compose anything, to begin with—Nate wouldn't have liked this one tiny bit, a Schizoid rage ensued, Ben tortured in vain hope the writing's location might be extracted … or whatever damned thing else, you know? My pet theory became: Benny hadn't so much left home as been coerced to depart at Nathan's gunpoint, dig it? Shanghaied to this pit of a motel. Told to complete his task. Maybe he'd escaped—a pursuit, an accidental death repurposed to look like murder, body dropped elsewhere …'

'Please stop.'

'Well, just let me finish!'

'That's the opposite of *please stop.*'

'You're the one who asked.'

'You might observe how unmoved I am by my agreement on that point.'

'Oh gosh, Marc, I'm nearly done—can't you bear with me?' He practically bowed a gesture of apology for getting off on his macabre tangent. 'None of those things happened, I don't really think—couldn't have. If something had been written, Nathan wouldn't need to go looking for it. If Nate'd known about the motel, nothing would've been found in the wall, months and months later—copy or otherwise.'

I couldn't disguise an almost giddy sense of *Gotcha!* when he said this—jumped at the opportunity to, as though lording it over him, ask 'How did you know about the manuscript being found in the wall?'

'The grapevine ...' he said so much like saying again I felt it was at least the third time I'd asked.

'Oh, right, that ...' I took a seat on the lamp-stump he'd previously perched on '... do go on.'

Seemingly starting down a new track of narrative, Sullivan related how it hadn't surprised him to learn about my motel being where Benjamin had holed up to complete his work: the funny thing was, he'd once been a guest, as had Ben, the two of them, together, having once upon a time taken an impromptu cross-country train, accidentally debarking in the town apparently known as *Laampray*, not *Calico Bash,* and taking a room—he gestured at our crowd, but I think more specifically at Cabin Eight—spending two full days in the area because it'd been so grungily romantic to them. 'Ben had declared the burg, and your place of employment specifically, *the very last place anyone would ever look for anyone else.*' Sullivan seemed to regret the memory of those words not having occurred to him at the time of Benjamin's disappearance—especially now having learned his own name had been used to register, he felt perhaps Ben had expected him to turn up, awaited him as long as possible, assumed there'd be a phone call to inquire was either Benjamin Visa or Sullivan Shallcross a present guest and, when it turned out yes, it would've been counted on he'd drop everything, travel there, posthaste, to be part of events, as they transpired! He felt, certainly, Ben would still be alive had he done so—a failure, a regret, a catastrophe he was to blame for ... because something had never settled right about the entire affair to him, yet *The Calico* had never once crossed his mind. 'To think how, all that time, what Ben had written had been stashed away for someone to discover. For me to discover, I think—after all, who else? Nathan knew nothing of this place, do you understand—it was a part of Ben's history and mine, nothing to do with him. This is why I believe my friend had presaged disaster, taken cartoonish precautions with his beloved work out of fear he might not make it home—would not be permitted to, somehow—that our little in-joke about the motel and my name in the Register would eventually lead me to what he'd accomplished ... as it had, regrettably *post mortem* and, though I hope not, altogether too late.' But that would be up to me—not because he said so, not because I said so, but because, from the moment I'd entered the narrative, I'd become a meaningful, essential component of the outcome. 'I'd not known what to make of you, frankly, because from the time of your first peripheral involvement onward, it seemed a lot had gone left-field, simultaneous, all with you as a fulcrum if not a dead center. At first, I'd seen you as no more than an obstacle and I'd strategized to behave much in the manner I've come to understand Nathan did and most likely continues to ... but the more I cogitated, the less you seemed a lock to pick. You were a Gatekeeper. All the evidence pointed to it. I hadn't recalled a scrap about the times Ben and I'd spent in the room he'd chosen as safe-box, right when I most ought to've, after all, and thus the manuscript had been discovered by you, investigated in a way I can only deem ... *peculiar* ... and which would, without fail, bring it to Nathan's attention before mine. But you hadn't relinquished it to him—not really, Marc, as you know I know—though you'd had every reason to and absolutely no reason not. You'd embraced Nathan ... but wouldn't go so far as trusting him. It followed that you'd been waiting to do likewise with me—to weigh my case against his, as it were. You're here for a reason, as I am, as Benjamin was, as is even Nathan. Because if you aren't, Marc—then why are you?'

I shrugged, took a sip from my flask, offered it across, but he declined and so I took another—then, sheepishly confessing he could do with some coffee and a toilet, unaccustomed as he was to sharing booze in the dead waste of night, and grousing a bit about the shrewdness of the cold, the failings of his aging flesh, Sullivan wondered politely if we might return to his room, or at the very least to the Motel Office.

'Bourbon's meant to keep you warm,' I sneered in a chummy way.

'I must not be doing it right ...' he chuckled, now motioning for more, which I was reluctant to give, so near to empty '... and I admit when I was a young, cancer-free lad I'd thought cigarettes were supposed to do the same.'

'Figured the whole world's pants were on fire, did ya?'

'Or that it was a failure,' he sniffed, puppy-looking enough I relinquished him a drink and nodded my head meaning a return to his room would be fine. He took only the slightest blink of the *Bulleit*, having been courteous enough to sound the contents out with a shake of the flask, returned it with a nod and, as we got to the curb, fished his room key out, and told me 'I truly am in your debt.'

'You'll forgive me for treating that as a threat ...' I shivered from the sudden warmth and beige light of the sepulcheric cabin '... or else you can pay me back by forgetting it.'

[*manifestos at my summer job*]

Sullivan's supplicant attitude struck me increasingly as genuine, though as it did made me all the more wary—it was one thing to not know what someone's gonna do next, a whole other nightmare to pick up they'll do whatever you say but you've no idea why. He now returned from the bathroom area where he'd splashed hot water on his face, took a seat on the edge of a bed, and motioned as though to be certain I was ready for him to continue his sales-pitch while I took my place at the desk chair, rolled my hand he ought finish out with a bang, and drained the last juice from my flask in a single mouthful-and-a-half.

'There was reason for Nathan to believe as he did, I'd remarked, before—quite a rational rationale behind why someone of his mathematical bent had latched on so tightly, despite Benjamin's inner turmoil about none of his rankings ever amounting to a quantifiable truth because of the unavoidable occasion of fluxion, new material displacing old ...' he paused for me to nod how I remembered where we'd left off, yes, no need for a refresher, thanks '... over the years, Ben compiled rankings of particular albums which he'd revisit from time-to-time—while new albums might overtake old, likewise with songs, the ranks within each closed-set he considered inviolate.' To explicate this point, after a quick back-and-forth reinforced my passing familiarity with them, Sullivan referenced *Flood* and *Apollo 18:* 'The nineteen tracks on the former were ranked, in the containment field of the album—for the latter, he ranked not only all eighteen tracks, counting 'Fingertips' as a single offering, but again ranked all thirty-eight tracks, each portion of 'Fingertips' given its own entity. From there, he showed how he might develop a second, entirely cogent and unalterable list of the two-set: All the songs on *Flood* plus all the songs on *Apollo 18* against each other, both ways of treating 'Fingertips' undertaken separately. I'm certain you get the idea how, from there, Benjamin could add in other albums, mix-and-match these three, four, five albums, or else a definitive rank of some three dozen tunes culled from nine separate albums, so on.'

Nodded but held off remarking—realized how little I wanted to interrupt, now that we were back inside and I'd begun to relax. With the talk of bloody murder and catch-kill in the rearview, seemingly not to rear up again, I admit I found what he was driving at worthy of focus—it was charming even if I wasn't quite charmed.

'This sort of listing went on while Ben, Nate, and I remained thick as thieves and persisted while life took us in separate directions, Nathan and I developing our differing perspectives.'

He still hadn't explained any 'differing perspective' to my satisfaction, it occurred to me, and I almost interjected to state as much, reminding myself, just in time, how little I was supposed to care and how much bruising I'd be cruising for were I to start inducing avenues of digressive discussion—I did listen with more sense of suspense, however, wondering if he was gonna delve into such subject matter in-depth, anxious I'd not be able to stop myself prompting him to, if not, even at the cost of inviting him to stay on longer.

'Nathan was always terrifically interested in the lists, practically began to commission them—Benny was never hesitant to provide, either. It sometimes unsettled me how he might seem to've hardly given consideration to *The Giants* for stretches at-a-time, but the moment Nathan even hinted at wanting to discuss rankings or have written codifications presented, the man would drop everything, sweating blood until he'd jotted matters down in the manner he considered correct. Say there was a set of albums, A-through-F: as each variant was scrutinized—A vs B, A vs C, A vs D, A vs B vs C, A vs C vs F, et cetera so forth—and as rankings could be made definitive for all, Ben grew more fervent in insisting there existed no way his mind might be swayed or that he should ever design to countenance *gadfly arguments* concerning the topic of rank, in general. That is: there were songs objectively better than others and, because such was so, all it took was the appropriate embrace of the core of such concept to arrive at objective ranks, overall—the number of items being considered doesn't change the fact that concrete relationships are actual. What he became fascinated with most rabidly was two-fold: first, how the top ranked album never altered and, second, how he could never find anyone who'd actually agree with him that the album he proclaimed top-dog was correct—as, though he openly admitted it was a controversial choice, bound to draw argument, in his mind such arguments ought be set over the flame, boiling off opinion to reveal the truth as he saw it.'

'This'd be *State Songs*?' I said, looking around for a lighter.

'You've heard it?'

'I haven't.'

'He still ranks it Number One?'

'Seems so …' I remembered this easily but made like it was trouble to recollect while scratching at my Bic '… he'd scribbled something about how solo or joint offerings didn't matter.'

'Scribbled?'

'Typed …' I corrected with a *piff* of smoke '… explained how parts of the same entity are the same entity. Quoted *Hamlet*.'

'Which *Hamlet*?'

'Is there more than one?'

'Which passage?'

'*Father and mother is man and wife, man and wife is one flesh and so …*' scratched my ear while explaining I knew the rest of the line, but his buddy'd truncated it there.

'The diving board, the swimming pool,' he nodded, very much to himself.

'Whatever you say—but you're losing the hook you've worked so valiantly to only barely have in, eh?' I opened my eyes wide enough to get the point across I was about to consider time to be a wastin', so maybe we oughta toddle ahead?

It took him a moment to unmoor himself from whichever reverie either my words, the drink, the late hour, or some combination of the three had briefly sunk him into, but once a cigarette'd been borrowed off me, he soldiered on: 'Unbeknownst to either Benjamin or myself, for years Nathan took the lists proffered him and, with them, conducted various *research*. In online forums he'd post them, often presented as video uploads he'd pay others to narrate—any venue or format he could think of, he'd entertain, though was always cautious his name be kept out of it. Sometimes, the studies he undertook were strictly controlled, participants selected, rules explained: after an audit of whichever music, repeated at regular intervals over this or that amount of days, subjects were to state, unambiguously, whether they agreed with the rankings presented. Just as often, however, he'd simply release the rankings into the wild and collect unsolicited public response as it rolled in. Another method was to seek out people well familiar with the work of *They Might Be Giants*, certain to have hard-baked opinions he'd scrutinize in advance, asking for their rankings of albums other than the ones he'd later probe them about, choosing only those whose opinions didn't naturally align with Benjamin's—and still other times, he'd gather groups of folks based solely on the criteria that they'd never heard of the band ...' he gave me a cordial thumbs-up which, strange as it sounds, made me chuckle in ease '... and have them listen to the songs in album order, then random order, then all sundry orders else, finally asking them to rank the tracks ... once they had, he'd present them with the rankings Ben'd come up with, requesting they state whether they stuck with their own rankings or conceded to his.'

Sullivan leaned forward, voice lowered in enthusiasm, rubbing his hands almost lasciviously as he continued—clearly I'd betrayed how this part of the affair actually piqued my interest: 'Here's the fascinating consideration, Marc: if there were ten subjects in such a study, it was very seldom any two would come up with the exact rankings, even little clusters scarcely matched up flush, yet, without fail, no matter if discussed in private or in groups—where argument was all but certain to occur, due to the mercurial nature of human psychology in social settings—when Benjamin's list was presented, the agreement would be immediate, enthusiastic, and unanimous. *Unanimous*, Marc, even despite people's favorites getting lower placement than they'd deemed appropriate—and this went the same when *Giants* connoisseurs were confronted, under whichever guise such conversation transpired. As you can guess, this absolute agreement also occurred with regard to any of the groupings of songs taken piecemeal off multiple albums. The long and the short repeatedly proved to be: no matter what Benjamin decreed, the communal response fell lockstep.'

'That's quite a thing, to be sure ...' I nodded as though meticulously digesting all that'd been imparted '... but to not agree with you too quickly ...' I crept ahead in faux-hesitation, both because it was an obvious thing to point out and because I personally wanted it argued '... it all sounds a tad too pat, Sully. As in to say, I'm sorta gonna have to call *bullshit*.' If he was telling me, with a straight face, that Nathan was so single-mindedly obsessed with his concept, I'd tell him, straight to his, how it went without saying the kook'd be of a mind to manufacture the requisite evidence to plead his case convincingly. 'It'd be simple: never *actually* conduct the group tests but *claim* to've done, or else *alter* the results in whichever reports he presented in whichever forum—or else the trick'd be pulled by moderating the comments, eliding any he didn't care for, either because they were directly contradictory or on account of they introduced a tickle of hem-hawing or sophistics. It wasn't as though this donkey-act was peer-reviewed, eh? Heck, your old bosom buddy could even've been so crafty and delusional he'd cobbled up umpteen dummy accounts online to pepper in hundreds of responses, as though elicited from all corners of the globe—it's crackpotism of the classic kind!' I wasn't even arguing against there being occasions wherein clumps of consensus had organically formed—such was bound to happen, now and again—nor did I know how any trickery'd *specifically* been pulled, but Sullivan wasn't seriously saying he believed this codswallop, was he? Any school kid could point to all manner of crackerjack sleight-of-hand artists—not to mention explain in detail at least a half-dozen delightful camera tricks all pains were taken to have come off as unbroken, unmoving shots '... but at the end of the day, the card'd been marked in advance and chosen by a confederate and the elephant'd not even moved, let alone had Lady Liberty vanished.'

'I'm right with you, Mister Limoncello, have no fear.'

Told him I wasn't sweating it in the least, but kept to myself how the only exception to that was how he'd taken to considering me simpatico—the moment the charlatan started referring to 'he and I' as 'us' I'd crack him square in the jaw and let the chips fall where they might.

'Let me assure you: I've privately done due diligence so far as debunking Nathan. However: each time, I became all the more flummoxed. The online comments weren't moderated, for example.'

'How do you know?'

'I took the time to create phony accounts from which I'd post gobbledygook statements—nothing about either agreeing or disagreeing and sometimes spitting out insane or inflammatory pronouncements, way off topic—but each and every time *ping!* they'd show up, straight away, automatic, and not one's ever been taken down.' He'd also looked into other commentors' profiles—most were deliriously active internet folk, littering their two-cents across websites like hotcakes, expounding on all manner of business, making jabbering jackasses of themselves quite proudly on topics from geopolitics to who-wore-it-best, and the names in many could be traced to actual occupations, addresses.

'I get the picture ...' I motioned he ought cool his jets '... it'd be staggering to manipulate, but that doesn't mean it'd be impossible, especially for an individual unconsciously invested in laying a deep, deep groundwork in which to cocoon his most fundamental delusions.'

He had to agree, of course, though emphasized how 'Even with much elbow grease spread over an embarrassing amount of man hours, all appeared kosher,' and gestured me to stay seated as though I'd been on the verge of storming off, patting the air in third-grade eagerness to be allowed to finish his turn. 'Next, I'd taken to cribbing the posted lists, conducting my own studies in mimic of what Nathan'd done. The results were the same. *Always*. To call it uncanny wouldn't be at all a stretch, even making allowances for some amount of foul play ...' but more important was '... right now, Marc, you must be thinking to yourself: Sullivan, instead of randomness, instead of conducting your own inquiries, why didn't you post contradictory opinions—would that not kerplunk Nathan's whole scene? You're thinking I'm suggesting to you there's some magical reason I couldn't bring myself to announce a disagreement publicly, even if I harbored one—moreover, that I couldn't fake one because some force compelled me not to. But it was nothing of the sort! There'd simply be no percentage in it ... because I did agree with the rankings, you see? If I wrote a false opinion, I'd know it to be false—just the same as I could *assume* some of the people's *agreements* were false. All inducing a contrary stance'd accomplish would be getting matters all tangled up, making *rhetorical* what I wanted to keep *clinical*.' I must understand: he was well cognizant of all the squirms Nathan would employ to inch then bound away from logical argument—had wanted something indisputable, a rebuttal he could get his mitts around and really wield. 'By this time, I'd come to believe—do you see? Was deeply convinced Benny's rankings *were* absolute. As insane as it felt to my rationality, the proposition had to be treated as Truth—it'd go against everything I held stock in, even polite skepticism, to ignore the evidence in front of my own face and which every ounce of my ingenuity had tested and tested and tested but never reverse-engineered.'

It'd been one evening spent going through the contents of some old boxes with his wife when he'd come to comprehend the depths of this belief and how it differed fundamentally from Nathan's—in an old spiral notebook, one which he and Ben had shared for a year but which Nathan'd never laid eyes on, there'd been a volley of commentary concerning the rankings of a group called *The Cramps*, the volume passed to each other in the back row of class, he recalled it all so vividly. 'This album against that, the songs on each, so on—

one entry crossed out, another corrected, that, this, this, that, no, yes, yes, no, endlessly and endlessly for pages and pages and for memories of verbal conversation further, either between us, in the flesh, or in my own head. We had never agreed. *Never.* Not on one song. Not any album. I still don't. How could it be? Because Benjamin didn't have any supernatural knack to always know the Objective Truth, of course! Rather, *The Giants* rankings, for whatever reason, were a band apart. No code lay buried in them, Marc, no schematic which could be applied to anything but them. Nathan had looked upon our friend as a Conduit through which all manner of insights and inventions would travel—in his limited way of understanding, such was perhaps the nearest he could come to an apprehension of the true reality of Benjamin. He was a Medium. Of one thing, only. The One True Thing. Why must we imagine that because a seeming impossibility exists in one place, under one set of conditions, it follows that there must be a way to make such impossibility not only possible elsewhere but commonplace? Why rush to replicate, to manufacture, to peddle—no matter what motive he might've given himself, Nathan's task was self-centered and would be fruitless. In his heart, I imagine he must've known as much, but it'd become too comfy cozy a deception to bury himself beneath, a Linus blanket with which to take the edge off his mortality, no different than many find in all manner of poppycock else. Wouldn't it be tranquil, after all, to live your life perpetually envisioning yourself on the verge of *Eureka*? Fidget with one more digit, observe a little click further and all the Universe would come together, the result being how yours would become a name enshrined in the posterity of mankind or, at the very least, you'd die knowing something you'd brought to light had now imbued and enriched the existence of all who'd come after. *As sad as a scientist*, I heard a poet once say—there have never been truer words.'

Sullivan stood, a rakish tilt to him as he conjured a cigarette and moved toward me to pluck up my lighter. 'What I believe, Marc ...' lit up, inhaled, exhaled '... is that what Ben discovered ...' took a deep drag, held it, let it dribble out mouth and nose with the words

'... is *singular*.' My own smoke had gone out, so I sorted a replacement, Sullivan moving toward the bathroom area, hitting the light switch to give himself more stately a stage for what I tensed to know was the Big Number. 'Absolutely unique, Mister Limoncello—a concept which hadn't so much occurred to him as found the appropriate aperture to pass through. Nathan sensed this, to be sure, but that dolt couldn't see outside his own eyes, still filters all experience through opinion, not willing to give himself over. A numerologist, then—possessed of the outrageous notion that the unbridled nonsense of human communication made pictorial can have numeric schema. A man of mathematics would never believe such twaddle and so I say, again: he became a *numerologist*. Those monkeys, those typewriters—say for as long as you please what they may produce, but we know, despite some abstraction of infinity, there will never come a random mashing of keys which'll show flawless replica of Shakespeare. What words are isn't random, but resists randomness, violently. By all means, build yourself a supercomputer—go ahead, ask it how many combinations of attempts it might conceivably take to even reasonably assume such a volume would be randomly produced and the gadget'll spit out a number it'd take you three-times-three lifetimes to even pronounce let alone fathom. But what it will never say is *It might well be the first attempt*. Ask your machine, next: what're the odds of *Two Gentlemen of Verona* being immaculately replicated three times in-a-row by sheer randomness and hear it beep *Not bloody likely*. I say if that couldn't be, then such could never be random! Yes, I simplify the matter to a bit of a fault—but only because I implore you to understand how my belief isn't in the mock-science vein of Nathan's. My old friend would purport that both Benjamin and the music are random, non-essential to the underlying truth of discovery: if not Benjamin, someone else—if not *They Might Be Giants* then *Experience Unlimited*, *Snap!* or *Matchbox Twenty*. Again—balderdash! For not only is it singularly Benjamin, singularly *The Giants*, it is singularly Ben's *perceptions of their music in its totality* that's important. You can see for yourself how no final ordination might be arrived at while Flansburg and Linnell yet draw breath—and what would it mean if one perished, but the band yet lived on in Dan Miller, Marty Beller, so forth? Due to the faulty way Nathan'd comprehended Benny's innocent statement of what he was aiming to render and the sudden, overwhelming imperative to have it accomplished, he'd retreated into himself, imprinting his personal reality onto what was actually happening—a ponderous emergence so much more sprawling and fundamental than he could embrace! Yes, he saw how perhaps it was irrelevant if further music was produced or released after the manuscript had been rendered, but only because he assumed the numeric code necessary had reached the appropriate threshold to be birthed—further data might even be superfluous, Pi had revealed itself to be neither non-repeating nor non-terminating! He superimposed all this on Benjamin—*assumed*, Marc, he *assumed*! But I? I *understood*—and I *understand* that I must remove myself and my opinions from the matter, approach with belief in what I'm approaching: an inimitable, living, impossible occasion. I, the first and single person to understand it to be completely what it is, complete it being that! The experience of my giving myself over is the spark which gives life to what I will experience by doing so. I am, therefore, an impossibility amongst impossibilities—I can only happen once and, with me, in this microscopic timestamp, can something so singularly alive find life! What Benjamin produced the igniter to isn't something that all can share, plug into, or draw information from—no!—it is an occurrence which'll never repeat but which'll forever be part of all else—a Big Bang, as it were, the first breath of a new radiation, the one and only time God's fingertip'll reach down to allow one man to step upon it and be moved not out of human experience, but to remain human, and to exist as such, in a realm no human has rights to.'

I'd sat transfixed by this performance, though the alcohol sluggishly coursing me did most of the going along with it on my behalf—when Sullivan doused the toilet light, returning to his bed-lip perch, I realized I was both trembling and somewhat perspiring.

He was quiet for a solid minute, during which he relit the cigarette he'd lost track of during the monologuing, afterward touching my knee with three fingers, briefly, gently, the digits pulled away casually, as though the gesture were a custom we shared. 'I need to have the document, to know it is precisely what Benjamin composed, because I doubt he understood exactly what was happening, knew merely that it couldn't be stopped. I believe he foresaw his rather gruesome demise—again, a seemingly impossible thing, straight out of the pages of *Spooky Times Quarterly*, I know—and that he not only foresaw, but accepted. His reaching out to me proved he desired a partnership—perhaps Nathan was needed too, as I've explained before, but what was between Benjamin and I was altogether different than what'd passed between the two of them. I believe I made Benny uncomfortable, if you want the truth—and I believe he felt why that was, resisted it, until he realized the futility. Why leave a trail for me to arrive by? Why include me at all? Because, in his bones, he apprehended there was something happening far larger than himself, inexpressible to anyone, a compulsion to produce what he did and, in so doing, create a path which only the one who might use it could.'

I stood up, though had no idea why, a jolt as though at having spotted a grotesque insect making its way up my leg, a tentacle—Sullivan blinked while I tottered, feeling increasingly foolish and bashful.

'You regard me as out of my mind …' he said, watching me as though curious would I sit down, but not curious enough to deem it of importance '… and I'd do the same, were I you. But see, my pulse beats temperate, as yours …' he grinned, for some reason thinking more *Hamlet* would soothe me '… it is not madness I have uttered.'

I tried to get a cigarette going, but my hands were palsy, laughed at how ridiculous it was not to be able to still myself, chuckling '… I'm honestly not afraid of you or anything like that …' then suddenly found myself devoid of language.

Sullivan lit me a smoke, put it to my lips, likely would've moved it to and from them in a nursing gesture if I hadn't wrested my head and taken a few paces toward the door. 'I assure you, Marc, now that you've heard me out, I'll impose upon you no further and would never think to apply one grain of pressure. I don't believe coercion to be necessary. This reality, whatever it is, has been in the offing for a period of existence I cannot comprehend—be it millennia, a split second, or the last nineteen months, all are incomprehensible. What I ask you isn't to hand anything over and certainly isn't to join me in some farcical crusade of Mathematic mumbo jumbo, no—I want you to be my *witness*. I believe that to be the very reason you discovered the manuscript. I'm no fatalist, merely see what I see—and it fits too well to be anything other than the truth. You are an Arbiter, Mister Limoncello. A being wholly impartial. What I will experience, and what results from it, would take a Believer—so let Nathan have his test subjects agree in perpetuity and *ad nauseum* about Benjamin's rankings, he can use whatever computations he pleases to render fractal art to his hearts' content, but even if he conducted studies with Benny's full list, had the thoughts of those musical fanatics and those of strangers to it entirely lined up to tick boxes … none of it would be anything to do with what's *happening*. Plant a seed in asphalt, it will not grow—plant that same seed in fertile earth, what it births will twine and grow and even its death will last forever, for that seed will become synonymous with Earth.'

I hadn't noticed he'd removed his coat until he was slipping it back on and gently moving toward the door with me. 'You believe you have nothing to do with this and are correct, in a certain sense. Yet here you are. Knowing all you do and knowing the one path to be free of it: will you take it?' He touched my shoulder like a priest, a politician, or an honest janitor might. 'You can keep the paper and ink once I'm finished, if that's what you're worried about. Do with it as you choose. All I ask is that I be allowed my coupling. I invite you to play chaperone, in fact. But more important, I assure you that no one will trouble you about this again, afterward—afterward, there will be no one to do so.'

[*strategies for hangman, cat's cradle, origami*]

True to his word, at least for the moment, Sullivan ended our dialogue with a courteous nod and almost bashfully suggested I probably oughta head back to my station, as he could only assume there was something required of me to justify drawing a paycheck—'However little,' he quipped, I think referring both to requirement and rate-of-pay. I could tell he could tell from my narrowed eyes I wasn't exactly sold on this bill of goods about next steps and conclusions being all up to me—decided to just tell him so. What he proposed was a deal, in that case—explained how he intended to keep his room for another few days, as I may've already been aware, so if I came to my final decision before he took off, I ought feel free to let him know, no need even to knock, I could ring him from the front office or from home, though he certainly wouldn't look down his nose at my company. Conversely, if by the time he'd checked out we hadn't touched base, he'd ring me—'Might you be so kind as to provide a contact number?'—proposing we meet at some nearby restaurant he named, surprised when I confessed to never having heard of the place. 'It's incredible pizza pie, right in your backyard practically! Oh Marc, while I empathize with why you might prefer the habits of a hermit, you really oughta get out at least enough to nab a slice.'

Brushed off the bogus chumminess and wanted it from him direct: 'How's this gonna go if I don't return your call or show up for brunch?'

'That'll be that.'

'Indeed. But what's *that* and what's *that*—that's what I'm curious over, you grok?'

'Golly, I'm not about to do anything rash, despite I openly believe you have ready access to the original manuscript. No doubt you've taken some manner of precaution against me or anyone forgetting their manners … and if you haven't, I sincerely invite you to satisfy yourself with some safeguard over the course of the next several days.' He reiterated his stance: I didn't have a choice in the matter, was what I was, and his lot was to respect the reality of it. 'You're not under threat from me, Marc, and I wish you'd embrace that.'

He was leaned in the frame of the open motel room door, body language that of patiently scooting me on my way—I began to feel awkward for lingering, but wasn't ready to be budged, quite yet.

'Lookit …' he shook one of the last cigarettes in his pack out for me to enjoy '… if you'd truly wanted shut of things, you'd have banged those shutters down, ages ago …' I patted myself for a light, but he'd already taken out his '… given the original manuscript to Benjamin's family, kept only a copy for yourself, relinquished it to Nathan …' smiled as I accepted his well-timed flame '… or burnt it to a crisp.' My not having done so only served to bolster his case and, whether I wanted to aloud or not, he felt I'd admitted as much in my heart—all he requested was a promise that I'd reflect heartily on that very thing, for only in contemplation of it would be found the compass to best guide myself. 'There's a question you need to ask and it's one only you have the answer to. If you up and do something unfortunate—destroy the manuscript, sink into hiding, whichever nonsense you might conceive in that dime novel noodle of yours—it'd be down to me to reassess, making due with what else I might, be it a copy or contacting Nathan or some as yet unknown avenue which I've no doubt would present. It'd profit me nothing to throw a tantrum, do me no good to get on the wrong side of the law and thus doom any possible path forward—since I have belief, it's best to believe in it, wouldn't you agree?'

The soporific gravel of his speech made the solid points he proposed come across all the sturdier—in certain moments, I had the striking suspicion he already knew exactly where the manuscript had been secured, made no move for it strictly on account of how he honestly did regard me as integral to whichever daydream he existed in ... I couldn't settle on whether that calmed me or kinked me all the more anxious, but was able to break off from our encounter without another word.

Entered the Motel Office as though waking fitfully after a long sleep I hadn't intended, spent an hour in a sludge of thoughtlessness, glanced up every twenty seconds or so, always uncertain of my reflection in the oily interior glass—a few times made ridiculously abrupt moves to shoulder the door open in order to prove to myself there was no one lurking on the other side, forehead just far enough away from pane it wouldn't disturb the images I'd see from inside, eventually able to relax when, despite the still overcast morning, it became light enough outside I could see from the counter across the lot to the hunk-of-junk woodland.

I've no memory of the end of my shift—what I'd said to my relief when he arrived, if anything, whether I'd appeared inebriated, beleaguered, how long it'd taken to convince myself I was in tight enough control to drive, all those files are lost. When next I became conscious of thought and action, I was stood at the gas station, realizing my mind had wandered and I'd filled the tank entirely rather than squirting only the five bucks I'd intended to, a glissando of rage rattling me which ended in my choking down a blurted curse with which would've come a kick to the pump or some further scene I could afford even less than the petrol—sat in the car, numb thoughts churning *chuggachugga* down a single track until a honk behind me and the attendant's glare from the shop window parapet made me realize I needed to get a move on.

It'd been only a few days since my answering machine had blinked the message about the package I'd sent to Nathan being signed for—no further contact from the man, as promised, which I surmised ought just about equal The End of that thread, at least so far as I was concerned ... though I understood there was never an absolute assurance nobody would behave idiotically ... set my resolve stern that, if push came to shove, I absolutely would transform the manuscript into flame into ashes—*foosh!*—sweep it out onto the pavement behind my building along with the shards of the smithereened cassette and I'd be honest about having done so when I told Sullivan such was my *decision* ... whether he did something retaliatory would be at his own hazard, I could promise him that! Because—yes, by God!—I *would* take precautions ... type up my account of all that'd been going on in my life since I'd unearthed Benjamin's wretched screed ... send copies to the newspaper, the police, anywhere I could think of to assure the narrative wound up on file, names named, the whole shebang, just in case anything drastic went down ... better yet, I'd run the risk of producing one more copy of the manuscript, give *that* to Sullivan, let the bum cry his eyes out over there still being an original I'd make it a point to never let him lay a finger on ... what I'd do was mail *that* to *Officer Picador* to pass along to *Mrs. Strauss*—see how far making a request would get anyone, then!

It remained true that if I hadn't found the manuscript, everybody'd have zilch—and since there was absolutely no difference between the original and the copies, whatever Sullivan and Nathan had to hash out between them to verify they'd both received identical keepsakes was none of my concern. Once the jockeying for ownership of the real McCoy was removed from the equation, for all I knew there'd come a fine rekindling of the strained friendship between those lads—a silver lining for somebody other than me, my good deed for the day.

Except, now I wondered ... was it true no one ever would've found Benjamin's work? Sullivan's little memory walk about a train trip might've led him, eventually, to *The Calico Bash*—there was circumstantial evidence enough in support of that having been Benjamin's hope, and the letter for Nathan might've been included to indicate his desire for the estranged friends to come together. If Ben and Sullivan were as close as Sullivan suggested, it wasn't beyond reason to imagine the former might've known his buddy would make symbols of everything—just in the way I'd been dubbed The Arbiter, the presence of a message for Nathan might've prompted a similar fabulation of events and the characters populating them. On the other hand: the whole spiel about the train trip, the motel, the intimacy coulda been hot air—not to mention, the man sorta had a point about me. Suppose I hadn't been the deadbeat boozer humping a graveyard shift at precisely the joint Benjamin'd shacked up in, during this particular time and the period leading up, the little sad sack who collected baubles left behind and possessed the proper aesthetic to covet an obsolete typewriter—if anyone else had found the duct-taped package, they might've chucked it in the garbage without even peeking inside, plus there were thousands of ways, at least, it coulda been found earlier on by some guest who'd have disappeared into the ether, no chance in Hell of ever being tracked down. If so, Sullivan might well have shown up, searched around, found nothing … Christ—if I'd not investigated that random leak myself, just passed it off to the manager's uncle-in-law or whoever he was, that's who'd have been custodian of the precious tome and were we truly to suppose such bumpkin would've done diddly with it so far as returning it to the owner or next-of-kin, made others aware it existed in any way shape or form? It'd taken me ludicrous amounts of digging to even sort out who'd written the damned thing and had I not driven out to return the bastard to the family, neither Nathan nor Sullivan would've ever heard peep—which, come to think of it, I still didn't quite understand how they had! My involvement truly did seem to merit the role Sullivan'd bestowed me—at least if looked at from his overall askance view of life, the Universe, and everything … but the longer I spent in such reflections, the less comfortable I became. Here I was: arguing on Sullivan's behalf—the man'd boozed me up and wormed his way behind my eyes! What was I suggesting—that I'd all along been fated to participate in whatever nonsense he was making up as he went along? Since when—before meeting, marrying, divorcing my wife, had it been written in advance I'd ditch out on Viggo and repeatedly come up short for the kid? *The Arbiter!*? I mean, there was no getting around how that's precisely what I was—but only on account of Sullivan'd fashioned the batshit narrative that way, introduced the term, and treated me accordingly.

If what both of these recent maniacs had explained as their intentions was true, I'd done my bit—given the one all he needed to fulfil a mathematical obsession, so what harm in providing the other what he needed, to go ahead and act as his witness to … whatever it was I was meant to bear witness of?

If Nathan were to discover I'd been duplicitous with him, by the time he did so he'd also know precisely where the original could be found and be able to take it up with his former best mate! Was I legitimately in fear there'd come any sort of—what?—physical reprisal over this poppycock when literally nothing which'd occurred suggested any such chance in the cards—quite the contrary, in fact, if I were to discount the dithering of my own paranoid delusions! I took myself to task, right out loud: 'Once and for all, Marc—this is over and done and you're nothing more to do with it!'

Spent an entire day-and-a-half in something of a Novocain daze, making every attempt to stop dwelling, assigned myself practical matters to overcome—tried to convince myself to purchase a cellular phone, for example, at least a pay-as-you-go one, they weren't expensive and even if I'd hardly use it would still maintain my landline. I wrote the question *Why not just do that?* on a note I had taped to the fridge—dozens of other such context-lost queries already there, what was one more?

Even if I felt settled—yes, fine, destroy the manuscript—the particulars of final disposal found ways to stir up the silt bed of disquiet … after all, I'd first have to retrieve it from the Post Office and how could I trust the world was a safe enough place to risk such a thing? Thoughts of this nature irked me—feeling I might yet be under observation, that some intrigue would mousetrap when least I'd expect. Worked to convince myself there was no reason to consider such eventualities, but couldn't shake the sensation of surveillance, would write out on paper an exact sequence of events proving how most of what I'd gotten mixed up in was truly my own fault and how even the more dramatic bits were nothing to do with me—I wasn't even 'mixed up in' anything, strictly speaking … and I'd then tear these lists to shreds, soak the shreds in water, and bury the pellets I fisted the remains into deep down the greasy guts of my kitchen trash.

By the end of the second day following my tete-a-tete with Sullivan, the angst had only intensified—I paced circles of the square apartment, bundled up in smoke, the only illumination a slight bit from the bathroom, its door left open hardly a sliver. Lack of sleep wouldn't help me sort anything, but try telling that to someone who couldn't pass out, beg borrow steal—in fact, as insomnia lengthened, I felt inches away from a breakthrough, with every go round of the eighteen-by-eighteen cubby I called home I got one step closer to freedom, I could swear it!

Eventually, it struck me where the imbalance in the equation originated: I'd made only three copies of the manuscript, one of which now resided with Nathan, second stolen, the other left with the bartender girl for Terrance—and that one'd gone missing. Part of me'd been unconsciously presuming Nathan really had it and that same part of me that Sullivan did—and they still might, but such truth'd require everything one, the other, or both'd said to me turning out to be some sort of elaborate put-on. In slow-motion I wanted to probe it: If they'd known about, even already *had,* the copies and were *only* interested in the original, how would matters have played out … believing me to be in possession of the genuine article, perhaps they'd pretended not to know about copies simply to gather up intel … had approached me one at-a-time, not wanting to risk anything too over-the-top unless the clock came to last-ditch … it was an odd proposition to consider, but what about my life, lately, hadn't been odd—what about my life, ever?

When I really held myself to it, why in Christ's had I decided to take it as read that both Nathan and Sullivan weren't in cahoots—only they had said so, after all, and who were they!? Their contradictory, joint efforts made so much more sense when viewed as a ruse to shake out of me what they sought—come on, now: the one shows up right after the other, the first on the heels of I'd been arrested as a favor to the estranged widow of the manuscript's author, the other mere days after I'd not given the first exactly what he'd hoped for? I wasn't suggesting they were fiends in the cinematic sense—no!—my life wasn't a fiction in which desired objects could be obtained through the commission of violent acts, willy-nilly—Nathan and Sullivan were just geeks, in no way immune to consequences ... and even if they thought they might be, weren't insane enough to jump to such pitch without at least entertaining a few preliminaries.

I needed to back up, forget all about Nathan and Sullivan, awhile—what was my oldest unanswered question? *Why had the manuscript been hidden?* No way to know—so what was the second oldest? *Why hadn't Terrance had the thing around—where had his copy run off to?* I tried to sound it out: The possibility existed he'd given it to somebody—but ... inside a week ... naw ... I removed that from the list of viable options because *unlikely*. He might've destroyed it ... but again—why? Was I suggesting the drugs he'd died from were definitely a suicide or allowing they might've been an accident—if he'd opted for self-harm, was the destruction of his father's creation a component of it, had receiving the volume acted as trigger? Not that I knew the kid, but nothing about him'd struck me that way—not to mention, I was certain Mrs. Strauss would've raised holy Hell, had me hauled in for more than cutie pie questioning and rink-a-dink charges any Nathan Jehovah could finagle me out of. Terrance and the girl had spoken of the manuscript with each other, read from it, the object well en route to becoming a treasured touchstone—that information came courtesy of the police, obtained in the course of an official investigation, so didn't seem the sort of thing I oughta go around doubting ... except: *why not?* After I'd visited Mrs. Strauss, Officer Picador had put a bug in Detective Hellpop's ear to roust me—there'd been no kind of official reason, it'd all been prelude to a shake down! How was I to explain Nathan popping up from out of the ether, posing as my lawyer if not as a little scene, all pre-arranged ... Nathan tracking back to Picador tracking back to Strauss ... except Strauss couldn't have had anything to do with it, because I'd flat offered to give the lousy thing to her ... and if Picador had involvement, why hadn't he even asked to see it ...

because I'd already mentioned it was a copy ... *had* I already mentioned that?

Any of you ghouls ... any other ghoul ... any ghoul ... whatever Strauss'd said, a version of the phrase insisted itself into my thoughts, once again—at some point, I'd ascribed the origin to News reporters or bloggers like Hotel Detective, then'd got to figuring it was down to her disapproval of the possible intimacy between Benjamin and Sullivan which may've led to the dissolution of their marriage ... and maybe that was it ... she wanted the manuscript, same as anyone, but had no idea where Benjamin'd hid it and didn't trust my bit about only having found a replica ... sounded too fishy, like a ploy Sullivan might pull to try worming it out of her if she had possession of the original ... so I'd been put into a laboratory experiment ... Strauss, Picador, and Nathan, working together, were already in possession of the Terrance copy ... wanted to see what my motivation was, where my loyalties lay, whether I really was just some schmuck who'd found something, as advertised ... or ... something ...

None of which explained Sullivan arriving, as though an independent variable—but maybe he really had only heard whispered rumors through that grapevine of his, needed to be certain it wasn't a trap baited to throw him off the trail ... I didn't like how clunky that nuance felt, though—when eliminating coincidences, even one coincidence left was ten too many. Not that it much mattered—smoothing things down too aerodynamically was as much of an issue as not enough and nothing was ever smooth when magnified to know what it really looked like.

I also couldn't focus exclusively on Nathan and Sullivan, wholesale ignoring the possibility there might yet be an unnamed party in play—someone who'd killed, perhaps killed and killed, desired the writing for reasons altogether nothing so nerdy and esoteric as those who'd already come knocking, hats in hand. Such menace might be keeping a strict eye on me—all the more for having witnessed my interactions with both Nathan and Sullivan. For all I knew, such stalker was a person Nathan and Sullivan were well aware of and harbored suspicions I was in league with—these were obsessional fanboys, at the very least, and perhaps a touch more, to judge by their monologues, while I was still a mutt from a motel, pretending I didn't know diddly when meantime I certainly didn't know squat ... and one who was giving himself the creeps.

Where, when, and how had conspiracy-to-commit-murder really gotten into my head—drip-by-drip and none of it my own invention! I was caught up directly in Sullivan's noias, because they were the freshest and all centered around tangible, in-referenced characters—himself, Nathan, Benjamin, a group intimately connected ... but their nonsense ideas about Objective and Subjective were theirs alone, had to be, because who would make up such inanities as part of an elaborate scheme? Without *that* narrative thread there existed *nothing* to make the manuscript either *meaningful* or *poisonous*—and that thread was self-terminating. Say a murderous fiend had been after Benjamin's writing for whatever purpose—I was proposing they'd taken the manuscript from Terrance and killed him in the process, right ... and I suppose it'd also been this monster who'd manhandled my living quarters, clearly in search of a possible original, that they'd gotten my name and address from the cops in *Sarnath*, made a beeline to *Laampray* to trash my joint but good? Then what? Kept me under some kinda twenty-four hour scrutiny to suss out what I was up to with Benjamin and Nathan? Even if that made sense it didn't make sense—and how was I supposed to know that it not making sense didn't make the most sense of all!?

Fatigue burped up all sorts of possible 'loose ends' I'd scribble into lists, read back, find no reference in, the trains of thought, the questions incomprehensible—I was scouring minutia but couldn't for the life of me think why. Blinked in the vague light at the following, for example:

> Detective spoke to copy shop clerk—knew I'd used Xerox—if date and time were provided, was there a way to determine how many pages I'd printed?—If a 'killer of Terrance' obtained the kid's copy, couldn't they've learned the page count, concluded there had to've been three copies plus an original which'd produced the Xeroxes?

I felt insane, increasingly, as the night swirled round and round, sinking lower, shrinking, but never seeming to tighten—hadn't even registered I'd gotten myself skunk drunk until I was leaving my apartment for more cigarettes ... realized I was pretty far gone when I'd decided to drive yet had presence of mind enough to park a distance off from the gas station so I'd be able to approach on foot, thereby seeming responsible, were anyone to ask, and was even glad for the drizzle having wetted my coat fully, as little touches such as those truly helped sell the illusion: 'Yep, he'd been drinking, but clearly he'd walked, officer, guy with his head on straight, that's Marc Limoncello!' *Presence of mind*—was that what I was calling this, staggering like a school kid, trying to come off more together than I was to some fat-bottomed night-clerk who couldn't care less and was probably high as a kite or about to be, themselves? Was halfway back to my car when it caught up with me how I'd engaged in a whole conversation about something, said interaction having concluded in my purchase of a small, overpriced plastic bottle of crap booze no stronger than stale maple syrup—a concoction I promptly downed while leaned against the cold hip of my car, squinting at Christmas lights on some house across the road from me, as though waiting for the sun to rise ... *apart*, they say ... *at the seams*, they say ... perhaps I was just resistant to things feeling normal ... didn't like what normal was ... what my normal was ... because when it turned out nothing had ever been happening, how the Hell did I intend to explain or excuse myself ... and who in Hell did I imagine questioning me about anything when not even I would and there was nobody else?

*for both erasing it
and also for writing it down*

[*no eyes at all, not even one*]

I woke on the floor, a fact which slowly dawned on me—my floor, at least, which seemed a good sign and probably also the best it was gonna get. After several moments trying to sort out if this positioning of my body or that would best keep me from feeling I needed to urinate, I recalled how I'd slept on the floor, on purpose—then lay thinking what an odd way that was to put the matter ... why say *slept on the floor on purpose* when *had decided to sleep on the floor* came across far more civilized, even sophisticated ... smecked the words aloud through gummy chapped lips to prove as much. The back cushion of the comfy chair had apparently served as pillow and, at some point toward the beginning of the night, I'd been underneath a blanket which now tangled for dear life around my left calf—closed my eyes which made the sound of chewing cornflakes, brought on a sensation of being capsized, and drifted me into a little dream of being late for work, showing up, apologizing while still pulling on a shoe I knew wasn't mine and hoped I wouldn't be held accountable about ... opened my eyes to the feeling time had passed, but no idea how much or from which point ... looked around the ceiling for a clock, knowing there'd be none, looking around anywhere within lazy eyeshot, next, still knowing just as well ... closed my eyes *crunch crumble crinkle* and drifted off again, but this time it didn't seem for as long ... had another dream, far more apropos, cinematic: showing up to work, once again, manager casually reading from Benjamin's manuscript to a woman and her kids, all three saying 'Hi' without looking up as I felt confused until noticing another copy of the manuscript on the chair by the punch-clock, relief washing over me when I recognized it as mine. 'I'd left it there …' I explained to myself as I remained flopped on my apartment floor, fully awake, then struggled myself standing, said 'Sheesh' when I won, pressed my weight down against a foot cramp, the breed which didn't give up without a world war—all there was to do for the first twelve minutes of my life, that day, was be in pain and annoyed at it.

Turned out when I asked the microwave that it was late into the evening, sorted how it was still Tuesday by some counting on my fingers, which was more good news—I hadn't lost a full day, wouldn't even show up late to work if I managed to shower myself, coffee myself, get it together. What sleep I'd achieved certainly hadn't counted physiologically, but I could steal catnaps in various cabins—joint wasn't suddenly gonna be a-hoppin-and-a-boppin, all night long, plus what was the worst that might happen if someone found me asleep at the desk? I worked there, they'd see that, they'd get it—if there was one worry I didn't have about *The Calico*'s clientele it was their being tattletales.

Cleaned my teeth with a brush I really ought to've long ago already eventually replaced—the bristles seemed fanned away from each other so sidewise I giggled at pretending they'd had a series of bitter falling outs and hated how they couldn't afford new apartments for another few months—rinsed my mouth with dull mint antiseptic, the sort which cleans but doesn't change your breath so costs dollars less per bottle. Next up: stripped nude and spun the shower dial to hot, giving the same glum appraisal of my nudity as I always did, in tones of *National Geographic*—'This specimen is skinny the way a blobfish would be if we realized how much, really, it could let itself go—as though a blobfish were printed on taffy and given a pull—but experts maintain the best way to phrase it is non-blobfish related: *this man looks like a popsicle stick with only barely a little left on it*—as in to say: *like a popsicle but not a popsicle at all*.' That sorted, swallowed a half-handful of discount ibuprofen and stepped into the heat and steam of the water, the only amenity my room had and that only on accident—water couldn't go anything but near-to-scalding, so if such wasn't yer cuppa, it'd be a negative selling point among the countless many a basement squat boasted ... not that it was my cuppa ... I simply could get used to anything, just about, and could get used all the way, when left with no choice.

I supposed a part of me regretted tying on such an inelegant drunk, the previous night, though another part, of equal or lesser value, felt it'd been for the best—a period of blankness could only be a net positive, as my present, unconscious fixation on trying to sort out what thoughts or events had filled up the numb cavity of nighttime overrode any other concern, would hold my attention until next I slept, and, with a little luck, when I awoke after that things'd have regained equilibrium, a hangover always making it feel like a week had passed instead of a day.

Because I couldn't recall when last I'd fed myself, and due to flits of memory suggesting perhaps I'd regurgitated quite a bunch sometime during the overnight, I opted for four microwave sausage biscuits, despite it emptied the pack and I'd probably forget to pick up more on my way home—survey said I owned bread, peanut butter, and a whole box of microwave sausage links which'd been in the fridge the three months since I'd realized I'd bought the wrong kind, *Maple flavored*, whatever that meant, though maybe I'd like 'em, by now ... point was: worst came of worse, I had provisions enough for one more night on planet Earth.

I smoked a cigarette and paced around while I broke fast, the room putting on a drabber show than usual—but I supposed *drabber* felt more correct than *still-drab* because the latter suggested some kind of effort expended toward maintaining however paltry a degree of quality and, well, just look around. Considered doing some exercises, except it'd be too uncomfortable with the sausage grease settling in me, the chewed-up mock-biscuit hardening to concrete almost immediately upon contact with stomach acid—maybe tomorrow I'd focus on fitness, before passing out in the morning do some abdominal crunches, that'd be smartest, shock the muscles when they least suspected just like the professionals recommend ... it'd feel like not really doing anything apart from something pointless before sleep ... even if I could motivate myself into five, ten minutes of physical activity before bed I'd come out ahead, in the long run ... pretend I took a little swig of bourbon just before doing my routine: I'd likely hardly notice what I was up to but still reap the benefit ... my head could swim me through the first few days of discomfort and, before I could regret it, I'd find myself knee-deep in a healthy habit—so things were looking up, by God!

Which meant, quite obviously, that's exactly when I'd notice the message light blinking—pulled my hands away from massaging my brow and the bridge of my nose and there it was, *One*, blank, *One*, blank, *One*, blank, a coquettish game of Hide-and-Seek played with utmost passive aggression. Knew just from the look of the two digital sticks composing the green numeral there was a worse headache than the one I was nursing, right at my fingertips—finished my last meal, smoked one more cig, enjoyed a tilt from my freshly refurbished work-flask, because hair of the dog and all, took a final blink of procrastination, and *click*.

What fresh Hell was this: my ex-wife's voice was *soignée* in more than its usual cadence of wit's end over being forced to stoop so low as gifting me direct contact—the exasperation was specific, so whatever was up went deeper than some mildly irksome bloop of Viggo's adolescence which'd require both parents' signatures ... though she didn't spell out what, precisely, the shot was ... took royal pains not to, it seemed to me, considering I'd no idea what it even might possibly be. Listened as she repeated a few times how she 'didn't care' and that 'your life is your life' then overrode such elegant points by insisting how 'at this point' she felt she had 'an actual right' to know 'what was going on'—seemed she'd been made aware how I'd been speaking with Viggo quite regularly, despite what I 'damn well know the arrangement to be' and was cognizant how long it'd been going on and 'everything about it,' which she copped to being upset about in spite of admitting 'you are his father and he's getting older, so whatever—he can make up his own mind about involvement with you,' then stressed how I might've 'behaved like an adult and just broached it' with her instead of making parenting into 'cheap cat-and-mouse games more than it's naturally turned out to be, without help.' After an eventual steadying breath, she explained how 'because it affects Viggo' it was honestly quite imperative that I return her call, as soon as I was able to—'Because now he's scared ...' she said, but corrected to *upset* '... and frankly now I'm scared ...' corrected to *worried* '... and want ...' *deserve* '... to know what's happening ...' then, after a long beat, morphed into the timbre of accusation I knew so sensuously ' ... no, why am I mitigating on your behalf, again? No, Marc—your son is fucking *scared* and I'm *pissed* and you goddamn *need* to call me back!'

I re-played the message three times, hoping tails could be made of it even if heads couldn't, but every word felt exponentially cryptic and I seethed a bit more embittered about the Viggo stuff, each lap around—knew I should've called him after our previous argument, should've jaunted out to see him, even if merely to be turned out on my sorry ass, owed that boy a genuine apology ... but when all was said and done, what in the name of the great good Lord could this message possibly mean, all of a damn sudden!? I was sure I got the overall picture, no problem there: Vig had been in a dumpy mood due to my cutting out on the Film Festival, suffered doldrums which'd likely become apparent in his interactions with others—with his mother, most of all—and, in the interim between then and the present message, he'd either spilled the beans or else had them wrung from him, emotion which'd been stewing in a damp place'd built to a dam-burst, a torrent of confession, in the direst possible terms, impossible to stop once it got going. I could only imagine how it'd've seemed, occurring as though from thin air—who knows if he felt a need to tart up something about being frightened by what I'd said to him to diminish his fear of punitive measures for having been in touch with me, full stop, or if he'd actually grown convinced of whichever dreadful bogey and needed a grown-up to intervene.

Their time, it'd be an hour later than where I lived—which didn't make right-that-minute an unreasonable moment to call. She'd be loitering by the phone, I'd be willing to wager, expecting me to ring around then—I'd appear considerate enough to've waited until her day's responsibilities were in the can, responsible enough to've used the period before going into work to tend to familial concerns or whatever she'd wind up dubbing this fiasco. Obstacle was: it'd be disastrous to venture contact before I'd gotten a gauge on how impaired my indulgence had left me—for heaven's sake, Viggo'd gotten all mixed up about I was a drunkard-turned-druggie, so the very last thing I oughta was even have whiff of such things in my voice … probably oughtn't have already thrown back a swig, either, or the other one I'd downed after listening to the message a final time. From the malignancy in her voice, it hardly mattered if I called at a stupid hour of night—she'd expect as much of me and might even appreciate it, see it as my working family into my day-to-day instead of offloading it to the hours most convenient for others but clearly the most generally useless to me. Indeed: my phoning earlier than a reasonable person would while still being me would come off disingenuous, a low-key form of gaslighting, tilt the woman a thousand times more suspicious of my being on the spike, the pipe, or snuggled down at the bottom of a bottle of red-devils. It was clear from a country mile the hot water I'd be wading into, so I'd take advantage of long distance to prep some cogent talking points—her not being pleased with me for how I'd been in contact with Viggo was fair enough, seeing as a deal was a deal and I'd flouted the Rule of Law, perfectly understandable the piper awaited his payday. Every last funny detail of the most recent conversation I'd had with my son had probably been pried from the lad to explain his abrupt decision not to attend the Film Fest—indeed, it'd most likely blown Vig's cover story in some way I'd never be able to sleuth, made him seem as though up to some legitimate no good behind his mother's back and, thus, whatever doom and gloom he'd spouted about me saying strange nonsense or turning to drugs had been filtered through emotional distress mingled with maternal instincts stirred around with some acrimony for matters there was no need to enumerate or re-litigate.

Scared was such a my-ex-wife kind of word to use—retreating from it to something reasonable then insisting it back into the mix out of pride in her own felt point-of-view just precisely her style! 'And just because you're scared doesn't mean there's anything to be scared about, darling ...' I snorted aloud '... I mean, let's play pretend that I'd told you I was scared about this-or-that—I sincerely doubt we'd ever drop everything to conduct a heartfelt pow-wow until my every imaginary goblin was slain!' Yep ... now I was screaming at my empty wall—therefore: not the right time for a telephone interaction. I needed to at least not be furious, and, better still, to not even be angry, not *come off* angry—knew if I tried anything right that moment a cake-icing veneer of polite 'What's going on, dear?' would crumble to astringent tangents in ten seconds flat. I'd take a few minutes, while I could, to expend all that sort of venom on the vacant apartment—get myself dressed, approximately clean shaven, maybe even wait until way late into my shift to roust myself toward the plank-walk toward predictability.

Noticed the cassette box was open, left near the radio—for a moment panicked as though I'd been burgled, again, but discovered the tape in the slot, all accounted for. Which meant I'd been listening to it last night ... or had intended to. Since the television wasn't on, there was a reasonable chance I'd passed out with Benjamin over the speakers—except my radio was the sort to let a cassette play in perpetuity, an automatic flip mechanism I'd never gone to enough school to sort the science of ... since it was stopped, I'd either never started it or else had at some point shut it off, on purpose ... neither moment was present in my living memory.

Pressed Play and mid-sentence heard:

> '... exist two types of Perfect Songs and beneath Perfection lies a whole Phylum of Exceptional, dizzying arrays of Terrific and Gollygee-that's-goods! Context clues'll let on which Perfect you mean. But Perfect vs. Perfect? In the clutch, only one Perfect wins. The same Perfect? Every time? Has to. Evolution, baby. Can't. Checks and balances. Same as how all manner of intricate factors differentiate Coleoptera from Lepidoptera from Hymenoptera, Solid Gold Hits differ from Masterpieces from Classics from merely Top Shelf Greats and

so on down the pecking order. Separating Perfect from Perfect is a delicate operation ...'

The words felt both as familiar and foreign as headlice—had I, by now, listened to the entire cassette? Sure, in the car, several times—not enough I'd memorized any, no, I could hardly remember what'd just been said, if put to the test ... but could I've listened to it enough I'd recognize it, generally? I simply didn't think so—to me, the words might as well be different each time the cassette wound round ... for all I knew they were ... and for all I knew was all I knew.

'... First type: propulsive and irrepressible. Requirement: getting stuck in your head. Then there's Perfect's second genus. Ploughed you flat, no problem there. Dragged you gleefully over the waterfall, each and every time. But while these melodies impacted, they never truly adhered. Such songs needed to be playing to exist. While they did? Owned you outright. But once you'd crossed that bridge, my friend, the ghost was gone, its power would end. Certainly both Perfects deserved the term. From there it was eye of the beholder. Those which needed to be singing themselves for you to sing along might seem a sniff inferior to the ones you'd summon to your lips after ten years, no effort. Then again, the quieter ones might seem all the more noteworthy for their humility ...'

Another jazzy jostle of recollecting how it was probably not recommended to keep this recording around shook me bad—it was only a copy, of course, but what if someone did take it upon themselves to break in, again? Seriously, it'd open a whole new can of worms for Nathan or Sullivan or whom-else-so-ever to discover an audio element to proceedings, one it'd appear as though I'd been playing it close to the vest about, refusing to divulge while promising copies of Benjamin's written work—an entirely new series of leprous intrigues would blossom for this caravan of ghoulies: *Is the tape the original, one of a set, why hadn't I mentioned it?* Plus: throw into the bargain how, if I gave the original to Sullivan, say, and afterward Nathan got wind of it, that nut-bar might get it up his dork head I'd handed over nothing but a partial to Sullivan while keeping a more comprehensive original all to myself or else had given the full original away, sure, but kept a copy along with other previously unknown goodies—either way, the conclusion he'd reach was I believed his hogwash and was angling to decode the secret of the pyramids myself, get all hot-to-trot about acquiring every goddamned trinket, all versions, any previous ceasefire brokered between us discarded with prejudice! What I oughta do was copy the copy ... it was sixty minutes, both sides counted ... transfer it onto a ninety-minute cassette ... put fifteen minutes of music before each ... secure it in the box of one of my old mix-tapes ...

Stopped cold, took a drink, thoughtless, lit a smoke that way, too—because that's how the tape was in the player to begin with: I'd literally made all of those considerations and acted on them, before ... so why didn't it feel like I had? But I couldn't even hold myself to concentrating on the questions I needed to pose, let alone the ones I didn't want to, as a torrent of further, previously addressed, concerns and the wise-ideas I'd decided on cotton-balled my head, pressure building migraine between my ears: Why not just destroy the things, anyway ... why hadn't people stolen all of my stuff if they were gonna take the trouble to steal some of it and it seemed easier to do and lazier not to ... were thieves so fundamentally slothful they'd not pocket the brass ring when it was already in their sweating mitts—especially bandits who were also lamebrained fanatics with single-minded interests! Not that I oughta be thinking about thieves or about anyone ...

Took a breath when it struck me how I'd legitimately begun to perspire, though soothed any concern with a gentle reminder that the state of me was nothing to worry about—I was rickety on account of the booze, the smoking, baseline of feeble body. I wasn't nervously breaking down or even as out of it as a first glance suggested—not by a long shot! What'd do the trick was another shower while I still had the time—ran the water but never stepped under it, kept glaring at the cassette, not comfortable leaving it behind when I departed for work, just on principle now, though my car wasn't a secure location, either, and I couldn't very well keep it on my person if safety was the principle concern. Nevermind it'd always been around and never once gotten molested—I couldn't go living in the Past as the Past is what led me to reminding myself of that!

Was I supposed to—what?—bundle it up in a plastic bag, toss it in the dumpster outside or use duct tape to latch it underneath, retrieve it, later on—conduct the same ritual, on a daily basis, from now until Kingdom Come? For all I knew, my trash got truffled through on the regular—that was exactly one out of all sorts of things a weirdo might do if they didn't find what they'd sought out anywhere reasonable! Imagine if Nathan employed some podunk P.I. or else Sullivan tapped some crony thug in the area to keep tabs on my comings and goings—if suddenly there's a cassette of Benjamin talking which I'd never said peep about being espionaged out to a random location accessible to the public, it'd have all the earmarks of a delivery dropped for pick-up, evidence of some ongoing correspondence with an unknown quantity! If I were a maniac, I'd be champing at the bit to leap to the wildest supposition—and since Nathan certainly was and Sullivan no different, it was clear I'd not have a leg to stand on when it came to explaining myself.

'Oh, that tape? I just didn't want it anymore, that's all, felt like the ol' home and hearth was becoming a tad cluttered, ho-hum,' I playacted trying to sell the line, burst a laugh I regretted bursting for what doing so implied, then snatched the cassette up and furtively scanned the full expanse of my room around—which didn't take long nor lead to any solution ... not, I reminded myself, that I had any reason to think about any of this, anymore ... though also reminded myself I'd little reason to think *that*.

It was wretched, existing as two things at once, the cursed sort required to have notarized motivations for the boundless things I never did or even considered while the honest rationale for the things I did would be viewed as yawn-inducing, filed away without audit—how was my life, out of any, suddenly everyone's but my own, why couldn't what I desired it to be be something left up to me? I'd crammed my entire existence into a Universe no vaster than a postage stamp and no sturdier than a soup cracker and here was the thanks I got in return—even the act of giving up something which had to, must be performed according to the terms and conditions of complete strangers to me! Did I really have to explain why I couldn't explain myself when nobody actually cared how I would or that I couldn't—I was a goddamned exercise in a vocabulary book, so far as the wide world was concerned, an example to be conjugated every which way *and* loose by anyone who I ever happened to cross paths with.

Shut off the shower and stared at the grunge outlining the tiles, the two empty bottles of shampoo, the comb I'd dropped in the tub a month ago and never been able to work up the oom-pah to bend down to pick up despite my daily concern about slip-and-fall—took stock of the dripping still life as steam coiffed itself around me and tried to think of one good, solid word to describe myself but earnestly came up dunce. What was I—and why was I the only person who couldn't name me?

[*charming witty drunk gate-crashing parasite*]

Sullivan Shallcross was still checked in at *The Calico Bash Nitely*, or at least his junked-up car remained an eyesore in the lot, now the only vehicle on the motel's rear side—perhaps it ought to've unsettled me but it didn't ... although I couldn't quite put my finger on how come. Decided it was nothing more complicated that knowing his being elsewhere would mean I'd no idea where he was, plus would indicate he'd not kept to his word so I'd have no reason to imagine he intended to, later—problem there was: seeing as he had honored things, at least so far as this went, made me have to consider how the reason why was wily, a feint so I'd be soft-cudgeled into making my final decision to his face. I didn't want to think about that, though, nor should I have to—there was an accidental safety in the manuscript and original tape being locked up where they were, the box key down my back pocket, and if I desired extra protection, easy as pie I might walk toward the gulch, toss it away. The P.O. Box was rented out for the year, one of my only sound financial decisions, and when my term expired it wasn't as though the Federal Government handed out the contents of mailboxes like freebies to any random passersby—if civility broke down and Sullivan went Mister Hyde on me, I'd tell him exactly where he could find what he was looking for, no threat need be applied, from there, he'd either have to break in or arrange for me to acquire a duplicate key, the latter requiring an in-person visit to the Post Office which, in turn, meant *escape route*. What was he gonna do, waltz onto Federal property with the beak of a blunderbuss spreading my ribs, count on me to fake a passable enough smile to explain away the shiner I'd be sporting—was he about to kidnap and threaten my family, willing to act as trigger man if I decided to turn States Evidence?

An hour into the shift sloped into two, anxiety cooling to congealed boredom which prompted a vague curiosity—looked through my wallet for the business card Sullivan had scribbled some website addresses on, spent awhile poking around a selection of the venues where both of my tormentors had posted various working-versions of Benjamin's rankings, throughout the years, wanting to see with my own eyes how underwhelming this mumbo jumbo was, certain I'd hit on proof enough Sullivan was blowing smoke about the degree or the pomp of whichever agreements, at the very least find responses worded dubiously enough to be properly considered ambiguous. True to his narrative, though, the sites I checked out had a whole slew of respondees and every speck of commentary whooped, hooted, and hollered in support—easy enough to spot how the illusion was meant to work, though: these being listings Sullivan'd jotted meant they were ones he'd vetted, passed along as though casual so I'd not get wind they'd been hand-crafted to keep me from growing more skeptical.

I satisfied myself a bit by pulling up random ranking lists presented by strangers, but in no instance did I come across anything I'd remotely label *consensus*, not even when there was a general sense of agreement in the audience interactions—indeed, I encountered many examples where no more than a handful of people posted remarks which baldly showcased a lack of hive-mindedness, vehement counter-arguments, to boot. Most interestingly, I came across zero lists composed by anyone else with the exact ordinations Benjamin had enshrined—in the short probe conducted, found no two lists the same as each other, either, though some veered near to being. It honestly was quite peculiar, as random chance ought to've insisted there'd be one, if not several, direct matches—though no doubt there were ... just because fifteen, twenty minutes, an hour of limp browsing didn't yield me proof positive meant nothing when the eternal, ethereal sprawl of the online world was taken into account, let alone when adding in how all sorts of people made similar lists, privately, pen and paper, posted in closed groups, verbalized in chit chat, written down in spiral notebooks, so on.

To further bolster my belief, I navigated to a page displaying the songs from an album entitled *The Spine*—one of Nathan's meticulously controlled experimental groups which, according to Sullivan and proved in a description, was comprised of participants ranging from life-long, die-hard, self-described aficionados, to Dick and Janes from Any Street, USA who'd boastfully avowed they'd listened to nothing but Classical music since prior to exiting the birth canal and who found the very concept of Rock Bands downright icky. There were well over six-hundred responses to the test subject's thoughts on the Official Rankings, all left by readers who'd stumbled upon the site over a span of years, some brief and to the point, some essay length, all not only agreeing with the order but many expounding upon the details of precisely why it was undeniably correct—indeed, some of the longer items read similarly to excerpts from Benjamin's manuscript, and even the agreement responses had sub-responses agreeing to their agreement!

I signed up for an account which'd allow me to post my own comment, took a swig from my flask, stared at the screen, and thought about a game I'd played as a child: laying in bed in the dark, letting my eyes blur at the ceiling, telling myself I was paralyzed, couldn't even shiver no matter how much I wanted to, the point being to will false belief into reality—sometimes, it seemed to work, and I'd remain supine, first euphoric at my victory then growing terrified I'd succeeded so well I couldn't un-succeed for trying, for ten minutes at-a-time truly unable to move, twenty, my brain refusing to end things at some unconscious level.

Blinked, shook my face, waggled my arms, my legs, took one more swig, a deep breath, then slapped out a vicious disagreement—really laid it on thick and, insult to injury, posited an alternate order.

> Placing the crown on 'Wearing a Raincoat,' right off the bat, is an embarrassment—on an album boasting 'The World Before Later On' and 'Prevenge'!? Who's fooling who, here? Lemme explain to those eating paste in the back row (and if this whole list is a prank, sorry,

but I fucking take this kind of thing seriously, and can't fucking stand a wind up): bottom rung are the woefully overrated 'Au Contraire,' 'Stalk of Wheat,' and 'Bastard Wants To Hit Me.' Top Tier are (as aforementioned) 'World Before,' 'Prevenge,' then come 'Thunderbird' and 'Memo to Human Resources.' I'd even argue those last two could be swapped—but 'Thunderbird' edges out 'HR,' if we're being sticklers. Only some dry-hump who never heard a song before is gonna go with 'Experimental Film' anywhere other than position 12 out of the 16 (calling it Number Three!!?? Methinks your dribble bib's on too tight, sir or madame!). 'Spine' and 'Spines' make up the middle (who cares which is which, but I say 'Spines' is the better of the markedly undynamic duo). Bottoming out the top chunk we obviously have 'I Can't Hide From My Mind' and 'Damn Good Times,' then the last dribble (and really just by process of elimination) is 'It's Kickin In.' Topping out the lower rungs (in descending order): 'Broke In Two' and 'Museum of Idiots.' Keep in mind: Top Dog on this middling album is *maybe* worth a charitable *Seven*—but only if you hear it in the right mood or just came into some money or something. Everything from 'Thunderbird' on down's a *Five*, at best—anyone who in good faith contends that half the songs couldn't be lost without ever being missed needs to *explain* not just clap along like you're happy to've found friends with the same lack of guts you were born with a bellyful of. Honestly, even ranking *The Spine* is malarky (what's it, like the third worst of their albums—and EVERYONE agrees with that, it's barely a nose above *Mink Car*, ferchrissake!) but if you're gonna do it, at least LISTEN to the fucking tunes and exhibit a modicum of discernment. I wasn't even gonna type this, but it's been bugging me for days and every last person I know agrees with me (even if a few like 'Damn Good Times,' best of all). Get a clue, please, and don't go calling something *definitive* like someone's not gonna pull your card, okay?

'Take that Objectivity!' I cackled as the comment, in its entirety, appeared for public consumption, straight away, rewarding myself with a swallow of *Bulleit* as I melted from sheer relief, cigarette to my mouth as I chuckled so heartily I had trouble lighting it—gave a squint to make sure I hadn't dreamt the action, re-read my thoughtless remarks, grabbed a key to Cabin Five, then moved to the Office door, through it, outside, strode the lot. I needed to lay down, get my head settled on ending things ... but what things—there was no thing, never had been, it was all the same preposterous nothing as always! Benjamin and his manuscript, Nathan, Sullivan, Philosophy, Mathematics, Mysticism, Numerology '... Conspiracy! Murder! Mayhem!' I bellowed while flopping to a twin bed. I was an absolute moron—still a kid holding pigheaded inside my unlocked body as though immobile. Well screw Nathan and Sullivan, both, I certainly wasn't gonna take sides or play favorites—if I was The Arbiter, I'd be a magnanimous one, treat all as equal, provide Sullivan precisely what I'd couriered Nathan ... I'd produce one last copy of the writing, destroy the original, and nobody would get the cassette or ever know there'd existed such a bauble! Such was the only path toward truly being shut of the matter, removing myself from the equation while, at the same time, equaling the rest of it out—such had occurred to me countless times before, but finally seemed to've taken root.

Thinking in this way, I revisited another childhood nighttime experiment, this time attempted to convince myself how instead of being on the bed looking up at the ceiling, the bed was on the ceiling, gravity securing me to place in it backward, looking down at the floor—felt the world seem to reorient around me, for a brief moment did indeed believe the polarity of everything'd reversed, then, exactly as I'd always done when six, seven, eight abruptly altered the rules: gravity was normal and, thus, I ought plummet downward to the floor which remained the ceiling-flipped. As it had back then, my body kicked in a sensation of weightlessness, my eyes opened, and before I could truly register how I'd felt myself falling, was too familiar with the sensation of not having done so to summon the so-recent memory of what I'd experienced to mind—*experienced, dreamt*, no difference, just as one cannot recall a sensation of pain after it'd been endured, or truly recollect a taste without tasting again, all I had of Past or Pretend were approximations, lies I could tell myself if I felt like it, nothing more.

The nap worked wonders—waking, I took a moment to smooth out the bedcovers, then started up a smoke, peeked out the window while treating myself to yet another, slinked into the chill night, and made a loop all the way around the building, Sullivan's car still present and, though it was impossible to tell, I imagined there flickered light from his television just beyond the shuttered curtain.

I discovered a vehicle parked outside the Office, but didn't sweat it—most likely the person'd only just arrived, because who finds the front desk of a joint like *The Calico* deserted but is so intent on a night's stay they hang around … besides which, if it was such an individual, they'd have no choice but to accept my not being on post was a predictable consequence of being exactly the sort of person that was.

Detective Hellpop was seated in my chair, glanced up in an offhand but friendly way as I entered. 'I was gonna send out a search party,' he winked.

Scoffed at his remark with a shrug, claiming all I'd done was walk a lap of the grounds while smoking, took my time of it '… kinda the equivalent of a lunch break.'

He admitted to busting my chops, confessing he'd arrived all of ten minutes prior, didn't have anywhere else to be, anyway, and certainly wasn't gonna grass me, no worries. 'I'm not a narc, after all. Plus: it seems it'd take a heckuva lot more than not doing your job to lose a job like this.'

Demurred how if anyone could manage it, though '… that happy bastard is me,' big point of two thumbs at myself.

'Thought you weren't a fan?' he said then coughed into an elbow wrapped round his face. 'You hike the Damascus Road, since last we met, have yourself a come-to-Jesus moment?'

'Fan of ..?' I ellipsed, knowing he could only mean one thing but without understanding why he would.

His unblinking eyes remained on me while his head cocked in a way which made it seem on twice as straight. 'Isn't that what you told me?'

'Fan of …' I prompted again, though acted as though I'd put it together the instant his attention drifted to the computer screen, even before he gave a tap-point at it '… oh, of *They Might Be Giants*?'

'You guys smoke 'em peace pipe or what?'

'I'm not a fan. Why?'

He read my comment off the screen, grinned how I sure was arguing with the denizens of a pretty buzzy hub for an innocent bystander, then segued into an anecdote about initially disliking this or that band, over the years, until quite all of a sudden he'd realize what a stubborn little whelp he'd been, ready to admit he not only liked the groups but always had and loved them, into the bargain. 'Hence I thought somewhere on the way to Tarsus your name had changed, so to speak.'

As he flicked the screen and leaned back, I shrugged. 'I'm not arguing with anyone.'

'Well, it reads like you are, that's for sure! They are with you, *definitely*.'

As he said this, fished out his pack of smokes, lit up as though I wasn't there, taking idle drags as though on desk duty in place of me—even poked through some of the drawers same as I might've to seem occupied while a guest waited on a taxicab. Painfully curious about what he was referencing, I moved around toward my seat, Hellpop graciously freeing it up as I did, slowly drifting into the customer portion of the Office while I inspected the monitor—discovered how, in the past hour-and-change, there'd already been *twenty-eight* responses to my posting, many quite virulent, tagging me with every epithet under the sun, including a smattering of ethnic slurs I'd no idea why they'd include, my education level lambasted, and it being questioned in the most derisive terms possible whether I understood music at all, doubt duly raised as to whether I possessed anything bearing even superficial resemblance to a soul! Other posts were more civil in their voiced disagreement—several claimed they liked my list just fine and admitted how it fit more with their 'personal faves,' but the same people, afterward, took time out to remind me the rankings I was commenting beneath were 'like, *actually accurate*, if you really aren't just talking about yourself.' Variants on that sentiment were in evidence and two people'd posted their own 'old rankings' to gently showcase why I ought not be treated as a pariah—after all, it was possible I'd misunderstood what the presented material was positing or else had misworded my harsh reply, multiple parties courteously requesting I respond, by way of formal affidavit, to concede that the ranks presented in the original experiment were absolutely sacrosanct.

Realized I'd fallen into a snare when Detective Hellpop's gaze was coolly on me as I looked up after being absorbed in reading over everything—couldn't see myself, but had to admit I looked pretty goddamned invested, plus it was evident as the nose on my face I was signed in and the comment I'd posted had been offered up earlier that very night. With no way to distance myself, I let out a long breath into 'I actually dislike the band, more than ever. If anything, I'm morbidly fascinated how anyone could have their wig flipped over such niche faff.' Went with the likely story I'd simply been trolling people, aim being to get a bug up their britches, but good—had obviously succeeded, as the screen showed three more comments hitting and the blinky dots of a few others, forthcoming. 'I don't imagine my music taste is why you're calling on me, though.'

'You have a terrific imagination,' he slapped cigarette pack to palm and took a seat in one of the shabby cushioned chairs next to the coffee pot and pile of ancient magazines—picked one up, opened it over the knee of his crossed leg, air of genuinely perusing while he asked me how things had been going with me.

'Things?'

'How are you, I mean.'

'Same as usual.'

'How is that?'

'Well enough.'

'Compared to?'

'I've heard tell people have troubles their own, so never like to boast about mine.'

'Good lesson to've taken to heart ...' paused to light up a fresh cig, flagrantly using the coffee pot to stub his previous in '... but out of sheer curiosity, would you, just between we two, say you'd been doing well?'

'Well enough.'
'How well is that?'
'How do you mean?'
'Enough to be actually well or not quite?'
'I've been fine.'
'Which isn't synonymous?' he wrinkled his nose confused, still pretending to read the magazine, licking a thumb, turning the page.
'I've been fine and dandy.'
'Well, that sounds fine and dandy!'
'I like to be precise, so I'm pleased to hear you say so.'
'You sound sarcastic, though.'
'To who?'
'Me.'
Didn't see what I was expected to do about that, a sentiment expressed with a shrug of my eyes.
'Do you have an alibi for last night?' he asked with two fake coughs right afterward.
'Alibi?'
'Right. For last night.'
'I was at home.'
'Cool—what I'm asking, though, is do you have an alibi?'
'I was in my apartment.'
'You ... do know ... what an alibi is, don't you?'
'I do.'
'Cool—what I'm driving at is: do you have one—you understand the question?'
'I do.'
'Understand the question?'
'Yes.'
'Have an alibi?'
'All I can do is tell you where I was.'
'So, you don't.'
'Have an alibi?'
'Yes.'
'I guess not.'

'You need to guess?'
'No.'
'It's just your idiom.'
'Right.'
'No—that was one of my statements not requesting reply.'
'Is there some reason I ought have an alibi to provide?'
'There typically is, isn't there?'
'You'd have to tell me.'
'You'd think so though, right?'
'It'd depend who was asking.'
'I'm asking.'
'Then sure, yes—I imagine there's good reason I hopefully would.'

'Fabulous imagination,' he complimented me, again, flipping the magazine page, not having looked up once.

Several new comments had appeared—I gleaned enough to know I was being squarely raked over the coals, by now, called coward and worse for remaining mute, unwilling to engage beyond my aggressive opening salvo despite a green light showing my avatar still active on the forum.

Closed the tab while Hellpop fake coughed a few more times. 'Let me just ask, again …' he fake sneezed '… do you have an alibi?'

'Alibi for *when*?'
'Don't you mean for *what*?'
'No.'

He nodded with genuine respect, told me 'Most people always get that wrong. *Alibi* is, indeed, a word meant to account for a period of time!' Wiggled a limp thumbs-up, closed the magazine, set it down, stood, lifted the coffee pot with now his two cigarette stubs in it, frowned, set it down, looked at me, said 'For Saturday night.'

'Which Saturday?'
'This past. Few days ago.'
'What happened to last night?'
'You don't have an alibi for it, you said—or suddenly do you?'
'I don't.'

'What about for Saturday night?'
'I don't.'
'You weren't at your apartment?'
'That isn't an alibi, I've heard tell.'
'Depends.'
'On?'
'Was someone else there, who else that was, and what they say, if so—things of that nature.'
'Oh.'
'So: do you?'
'Nope.'
'But you were at your apartment, you'd claim?'
'On Saturday?'
'Yes.'
'Yes.'

'Well that's all cleared up then—*phew!*' he clapped and did a little shuffle of stunted dance-club boogie as headlights arced into the lot, splashing over the both of us through the dingy window. 'Not that I'd ever have worried about it, were I in your shoes. I don't have an alibi, myself! I don't guess a whole ton of people do, if you think about it. For all kinds of stuff, really. I was only asking you since I'm here and you're here and, at this point in the game, I've gotta.' I swiveled my head his direction, but before I could breathe in to exhale something along the lines of demanding an explanation for the insinuation in his last remark, he told me he'd been listening to *They Might Be Giants* quite a bit since last we spoke. 'I've become something of a superfan—lemme tell ya! They don't seem to know how not to be catchy, you gotta grant 'em that!'

'Agree to disagree,' I supposed.
'You don't like ... what about 'Brontosaurus'?'
'The song or the dinosaur?'
'Song.'
'Never heard of it.'
'Dinosaur, then.'
'Neither,' I absentmindedly replied, to which he sighed.

"'Canajoharie'?'

'Dunno what even *Joharrie* is I'd need a whole can's worth.'

"'Alienation's For The Rich'?'

'Is that one of your things that isn't a question or is it you're asking?'

'Sheesh!' He wagged a finger and extoled the virtue of giving '… those Johns a fair shake! They work hard, fella—what do you ever do?'

'Things which interest me.'

He scoffed out his nose. 'No, I just don't comprehend how you could call yourself *not a fan* if you haven't even listened to them—not the way I'm talking about.'

'Not doing things is how I define myself mostly, as a rule.'

'Touché,' he supposed. But I must see what he meant—in his opinion as an amateur armchair psychologist, my resistance belied a passion I simply felt shy about. 'For myself, I feel I can only *start* to consider myself a fan, despite boasting myself a *super* one, only moments ago! Thing I've noticed about opinions is: people cling to them, even when, from the outside, you'd never guess why. Like alibis, you might say—or maybe not like alibis, you might say, too.' Follow his thinking: a lot of people will not only name their favorite of something, but declare it definitive—but such was no more than folly, and he felt bound to say so! 'If it came down to a Pearly Gates situation, those folks'd trip over themselves to fess up how their own opinion of favorite changed the more they listened to whatever it was, eh? That it used to be X and then became Y, reverted to W, then all at once hopped right to Z! Might say they'd heard twenty out of two hundred songs, certain they knew the best—but if Saint Pete pressed for their final answer, you and me both know there're gonna go on in a drivel of they'd listened to something that was, at one point, new to them which'd dislodged an old favorite, but they still felt queasy not calling the old-favorite *favorite* because of duration and nostalgia and scooby-do-be-doo. They'd become resistant to being surprised, is all—shaken up, rekindled. Which is a real pity, I'm sure you agree.'

'What're we talking about?' I scrunched my face as though he were the sort of person I had power to dismiss.

'I was hoping you might be able to tell me.' He'd provide more context first, of course. 'We'll require some privacy for something like that, is all.'

I nodded, paying more attention to the sound of a car door out front finally opening and closing, the crunchy approach of footsteps, the next moment's *ringaling* of the door opening and my manager stepping in, nodding to me then to the detective—the two confirmed introductions before Hellpop waved me to come join him, while at the same time the manager rounded the desk, patting my shoulder in a gesture I'd hope would never be meant for me if from someone like him. 'It's fine …' he sighed into his seat '… you take care of what you gotta take care of.'

Blinked at the man, unsettled by the genuine empathy in his voice, considering I was privy to at least several squares of his own checkered past, then turned my attention to the detective, who giddily motioned for me to hop-to-it. 'I'll do my best to get him back to you in one piece,' he remarked, more as though to a general audience than to anyone, held the door open, and patted my shoulder ten times worse than the manager had as I trundled on through.

[*hitchhike boogie, hypocrite bop*]

It was a different Interview Room than before but felt the same, despite being obviously far more official—seemed I'd been there more times than I had, than anyone had, too many to count, so just called it far-far-too-many. Rather sterile, exactly the way television had taught me, except with a quality of lighting and damp chill the late night flicks and shows in syndication had conditioned me to associate with a Medical Examiner's domain—the glaring difference, one which made me terrifically anxious, was a digital clock, two spaces for the military hour, two for the minute, two for seconds, and three for flickering fractions of seconds, indefatigable slot machine windows. The surrealist touch of this display, overlarge, front-and-center, made it seem time was counting down instead of up—no, that time was getting larger, bloating instead of twirling cyclic. The previous room Hellpop had dragged me to has smacked of cinema verité, documentary, while in this one I felt washed in the colors of direct-to-pay-Cable torture-porn or like I was in a Canadian co-produced nightmare—the only missing component which would've locked in the latter impression was the presence of an odd light source, vaguely green.

  Hellpop opened the door and I listened to him finish off a casual conversation with some female colleague I got no glimpse of—at first I thought it was a put-on, that he was speaking to himself in a hammish, theatrical style meant to unfoot me, but eventually could tell the woman was simply softspoken, perhaps keeping her voice down out of an expected decorum her colleague had charisma enough to get away from adhering to. Their exchange ended with a laugh and his promising he'd actually show up at some pub or another—yes yes, she could promise everyone, he was turning over a new leaf, no more Mister Stick-in-the-Mud—and once he'd entered, loitering just inside the not-quite-closed door, looking through the papers in a file folder, he chuckled at something, moved his foot to allow the click of the latch while he cleaned his ear with the tip of a pinkie finger, wiping it on the outside thigh of his pant as he ambled to the seat across from me. When he looked up, it was with an air of my having finally shown up after he'd been kept waiting. 'You're absolutely certain you didn't wanna soda pop? The last three people I'd interviewed all wanted soda pop, down to the man. They called it *soda pop*—not even *a* soda pop—and frankly I thought I was going out of my mind! Because, here's the kick: none of them knew or were remotely connected to each other—different crimes, different cases, one just a person-of-interest who I'd rolled out the proverbial red carpet for. Hey—guess when's the last time I'd ever heard someone ask for *soda pop* before those three.'

'I've no idea, detective.'

'Hence I'd suggested you guess.'

'When you were little.'

'Good guess—but no. Never! Nor had I, even one time, had the question put to me, personally. Have you?'

'I don't think so, no.'

'Except just now.'

'Well, if we're gonna be all technical about it …' I tried to get us on friendly terms by grinning this with a breath down my nose meant to convey *aw shucks, you know I'm always here to help.*

'At any rate …' he changed lanes, trilling four fingers on the table while he spoke '… could you let me know a little bit about what sort of trouble it was you'd meant you were in?'

'Trouble?'

'That's the stuff.'

'Which sort of trouble?' I mugged how he'd lost me.

'Sort you'd told your son you were in all kinds of—or some kind of but a bunch of it, at any rate.'

'Told my son?'

'You ... do have one?'

'I do.'

'Called *Viggo*?'

'Yes.'

'You told your son Viggo you were in all kinds of trouble or one kind but a bunch of it, didn't you?'

'I did ...' I began tentatively.

Barreling right overtop, Hellpop explained 'What I'm paid to wonder, and sometimes just do in my spare time for free, is: what the heck kind of trouble was that?'

'You spoke to my family?'

'Would that make a difference to your answer?'

'It would affect the attitude in which it was provided.'

'Isn't it obvious I've spoken to your family?'

'It is.'

'So my answer to your rhetorical question would affect your attitude toward my actual?'

'Why were you speaking to my family?'

'Point of order: they'd been speaking to me.' I provided an impassive glare to this which he got the drift of then, I suppose to grease the wheels, he told me how it'd gone. 'Went: your ex-wife, upset over something that son of yours had intimated to her, had telephoned you. Left an urgent message. Not heard back. This had led to that to word got round to me ... which brings us to a moment or two ago, wherein I'd asked what sort of trouble you were in.'

'My ex-wife spoke to you, today?'

'Yesterday, as a matter of fact—or, considering the hour, two days ago.'

'I don't see how such a thing's possible.'

'Could you explain why in the world that is?' he blinked, utterly bewildered in what almost seemed a pleasurable way.

'Can't you just come to the point?' I squirmed.

'Well, I sure could've before you'd said something so darned intriguing! That was quite a way you'd put the matter! Holy bones—

you know the sort of fella I am, if not personally then professionally, so can't expect I'll gloss over a morsel so lip-smacking!'

'You said she'd left me a message—that she hadn't heard back?' I sighed, rolling my eyes to which he nodded, pat. 'That message was left only today, detective—hence the impossibility of the narrative you just now presented.'

'Was it left *today*?' He blinked, genuinely perplexed, looked at the table like there might be notes pinned to it which'd clear things up.

Meantime, I realized I wasn't at all certain. 'Wait …' I held up a hand.

'When had she left the message?' he now asked, paly tone, ready to correct a sophistic miscue.

'I told you today … but … when had she said?'

'Friday.'

'This Friday?'

'Last Friday—though you'd probably meant that.' My face likely betrayed how I was realizing such timeline might well've been accurate—explained in a mock-up of amiable embarrassment how I didn't always look at my answering machine. 'Nobody *always* looks at their answering machine—we're busy people, after all,' he waved a hand as though telling me I mustn't go so hard on myself.

'You're right—I don't regularly look at it at all, except by accident.'

'How often, by accident?'

'Well, maybe I regularly do—I didn't mean *accidentally*, per se. Just not *frequently*.'

'Not *habitually*.'

'Not *as a rule, upon entering the house*.'

'*House*?'

'My *apartment*.'

'*Apartment*?'

'My *room*.'

'In the *basement*.'

Nodded, let out a cross breath, then succinctly broke it down how people seldom rang me—threw up my hands about how I didn't know how to explain my unconscious predilections when it came to checking for telephone messages, really!

'Oh gosh—I promise I wasn't asking you to do a thing like that! And lookit: maybe she'd left *another* message, today, one you were thinking about.'

Shook my head, apologetic, humble. 'No no—I'm certain the only message she'd left had been the one you're referring to.'

'Did you call her back?'

Shook my head, shrugged.

He raised both hands as though no explanation was necessary. 'But may I ask you why you're such a liar all the time, though?'

The boyish curiosity in the question halted me—watched him light a cigarette, inhale as he kept an air of 'simply curious' in the slouch of his posture, the cross of his legs. 'What do you mean?'

'You *have* an alibi for last night …' he told me flatly, squinted, unsquinted, seemed perplexed how I wasn't concurring '… in the wee hours, anyway. You were at some service station. Bought cigarettes. Sprung for a bottle of cut-rate hootch.'

Bubble-bath crackles of memory plipped and plopped. 'Sorry …' I nodded '… you're entirely correct—I had been, yes. Couldn't get to sleep for trying. Went out for smokes and such. So, there you have it: my alibi.'

'For last night.'

'Right—tonight I'm here.

'You were drunk.'

'Last night?'

'Tonight?'

'Last night—yes—I was. Hadn't I already said so?'

'I'd surmised, at any rate. Plus: already knew because someone'd tattled to me and showed off a spiffy black-and-white video of you being so.'

Lookit, I was confessing smack to it, what else did the man want from me? 'Drunk, out of cigs, fresh air, exertion might help, hence a walk, bought another bottle on impulse—one of those nights.'

'The sort you're lying about, even still?'

'I hadn't *lied* about it, once—I'd *forgotten*.'

'The sort you're still being perplexingly evasive about—is that the better way of phrasing it?'

'It's quite obvious I'd wound up a touch more blotto than I'm comfortable with, detective. But to the best of my admittedly flimsy recollection, the stroll I'd taken hadn't been anything to write home about.'

'Where's home?'

'It's an expression.'

'I am well aware that it is—one of them idioms you speak so fondly of and in. But out of curiosity: is home your room in that basement?'

Knew I snarled a bit at the remark—wished I hadn't, but what was I supposed to do about it after I had except reiterate, with over enunciation, how '… the trip … to the store … had been … uneventful …' and ask could we leave it at that.

'Went home. Fell asleep on your floor at some point.' I nodded, hoping he got the drift it was meant to be for the last time. 'But there you go, again,' he tsk-tsked.

'Where I go, again?'

'Lying.'

'The fuck do you mean—I woke up on the floor, so it serves to reason I'd gone to sleep on it.'

'No no—you're on *teleologically* sturdy boards, there, absolutely! I often sleep on the floor and that's precisely how it goes. Plus: even if you'd slept in a bed, to begin with, and then fallen to the floor without any say in the matter, you'd yet have no choice but to wake up on it, after.' See how reasonable he was being—never one who'd resort to Nazi-ism over specifics. What he'd meant was I hadn't walked to the service station '… not all the way. Which I know on account of a citizen I'm under no obligation to name had wondered who that was parking a car sidewise in front of their trashcans, middle of the night. They and a neighbor of theirs witnessed you allegedly *stumble* out of said vehicle, allegedly *stagger* away—and one used the term *sashay* to describe how you'd returned, a short while later. Before loitering. Driving off. The idiomatic expression *Four sails to the wind* had come up as well, you might be pleased to know.'

Okay okay okay—I recalled all of that, now, more-or-less. 'I still wasn't lying—it'd simply been a rather bad night.'

'Drink driving is fairly serious stuff ...' he was afraid I'd have to pardon him for not tee-heeing it off '... people can get hurt, Marc. I've known some who did and I've jailed others who were on the wrong end of bumpers, you know?'

I could well imagine. 'Had I hurt anyone?'

'Last night?'

'Isn't that the one we're talking about?'

'In conjunction with other things, sure.'

'What other things?' I asked but suddenly welled with frustration, blurted 'Forget it!' and all but growled how he didn't need to answer—slapped the table, huffed an unguarded angry breath and demanded 'With all due respect, I'm going to have to ask to speak to a lawyer, at this point.'

'To ... *a* lawyer?' his nose crinkled, quizzical.

Nodded, arms crossed.

'Or to ... *your* lawyer?'

'*Any* lawyer.'

'Why *not* your lawyer?'

'I don't want to trouble *my* lawyer.'

'Nathan Jehovah.'

'Correct.'

Hellpop pursed his lips, told me he doubted Nathan'd be troubled '... in fact, I don't much see how he could be.'

'Well maybe I don't wanna be charged a fee when I think there's a free-trial version available.'

'It's *financial* ... the reason you don't wanna trouble Nathan?'

'Jesus—fine! Please call Nathan!'

Shook his head, shrugging as though at a loss. 'It won't do any good, calling.'

'What in Hell are you—why's that?'

'Nathan Jehovah's dead… ' was all he meant '… but—geez!—if you insist on it, I'll go ahead and call the man. Seeing as though he's toes up, though, do you want me to do that on the telephone or can I just holler—it'll amount to the same.'

I couldn't process this but was beginning to get a feel for exactly what it was I couldn't—moved to stand, sat down, declined another offer for soda pop, accepted a cigarette, a light, stood up, paced a minute, sat back down. 'Nathan Jehovah is dead?' I asked, two fingers held up like I wanted a direct answer, no curlicues.

'He is.'

'Since when?'

'As early as middle-day Saturday—more likely since Saturday night. This Saturday. Or last Saturday, just to keep it clear. Three days ago. Or four, considering the hour.'

I made a gesture like stifling a sneeze, meaning for fuck's sake could he cut it out with the cute bits, then nodded harsh, nod nod nod, paused a beat, nod nod nod. 'Hence you'd asked for an alibi off me, eh?' Hellpop ran tongue over front teeth, regarding me as though we were drifting from what he'd understood to be a shared point. 'You thought I might've murdered my lawyer, is it?'

Even deeper confusion wrinkled his eyes and the twist of his lips—seemed to be using the pause of getting his own cigarette revved up to calculate some equation. 'Was he your lawyer—like, for real?' he eventually asked.

'You know he was.'

'Hadn't you only met him after he'd finagled you outta jail, few weeks back?'

'He's still my lawyer.'

'Not legally.'

'What's that supposed to mean?'

'That you'd never procured his services in any official, documented way.' I took another cigarette from the pack that'd been left on the table, despite knowing full well my current was going strong, then took another, arranging them both primly in front of me while

Hellpop explained he could get me another lawyer, an *actual* one. 'Do you still want that?'

'What happened to Nathan?'

'He got stabbed to death.'

'Where?'

'Several places. Fatal one down his throat, through the mouth.'

I blanched, tensed against nausea. 'I mean ... was he killed ... around *here*?'

Hellpop blinked, looked left-right then behind him, moved as though to ask clarification from me, stopped, nodded as though he'd cottoned to my meaning. 'In Florida.'

'Why would you've thought I'd killed him in Florida?'

'Why would I've thought you'd killed him in Florida?'

I didn't answer and Hellpop didn't press me to—could tell he saw every turn of the creaky wheels behind my eyes which'd led to the click of my previous query: my ex-wife's call, I'd seemed missing, afterward, unaccounted for until Sunday night, Monday morning, spoken of trouble, drink driving, soused interactions ... gave a thumbs-up to prove I was with him, though none of my considerations had been spoken aloud.

'Why would you think I'd have thought you'd have killed him, here, there, or elsewhere?' Hellpop leaned back, now with a more predatory bent, but one which seemed benign in an out-of-sync way.

'Television tells me detectives mention people're dead to people they figure may've made 'em that way.'

'I saw that episode, yeah—hey: what did you mail to Nathan?' Gave him a stare and he held it. 'Before he died.' Doused my present cigarette and gingerly got one of the other two going. 'I'm just curious.'

'I doubt that.'

'Okay—I'm curious, *too*.'

'I've gotta hunch you're dicking me about, Hellpop. If you know I mailed something you clearly must know what.'

'I don't—though I have a guess.'

'You should go with that, then,' I snorted, but regretted doing so immediately, because doing so seemed far less clever aloud than the triumph it did in my head—my anxiety had me feeling soaked in swabs of alcoholic gauze.

'What is it about this band?' he redirected, as-though-casual, in such a way as to emphasize how non-casual a redirect it was.

I let out a growl, banged the table *bam bam bam!* 'For the last goddamned time, man: I've no idea about the motherfucking band! I find their music—what little I know of it—trite and too precious by a yard. I'd found a manuscript about them—written by someone who felt the polar opposite of me—and wanted to return it. Is that a crime?"

'For the last goddamned time, man ...' he said serenely and then slow-motion banged palms to the table without causing a sound '... no, it isn't. But ...' he whammed a fist down hard, jolting me '... you hadn't just *returned* it, had you?'

'I'd made every attempt ...' I started, then shook my head, slapped the table again '... No! Actually, I fucking had done—to the author's son!'

'The dead one?'

'Not at that time.'

He nodded his concession of this point, then twinkled the fingers of his free hand while taking a drag on the outbreath of which he said 'But you'd left out a whole bunch in the story you'd told—where you'd found it, under which circumstances, the fact you'd spent a good long while looking into the matter, beforehand.' I took a deep drag myself, not bothering to disguise my caginess. 'I know you'd looked into it, Mister Limoncello—otherwise how else would you've learned who'd written the thing?' Just sighed, didn't feel capable of making a clean breast of the matter when there was no urgent need—he was obviously savvy, didn't even remark my silence as he kept on with his summary of events. 'You looked up—at this very computer ...' he gestured as though we were still sat in *The Calico*'s office, kind of eerie how it cinematically set the scene: I felt myself there, stepping into a stylistic rendition of events depicted just shy of how they'd been presented earlier in a flick '... all manner of things. This name. That. Combinations. It'd been very apparent the hunt was on. You say it was for the author's name? Okay. Something you wanted to learn so badly you listened to all kinds of music, read a dead crime blogger's account of Benjamin's murder, looked up further materials on that morbid subject—do you follow my drift?'

'Yes,' I barely peeped when it became clear he'd wait for my response before moving on.

'Then, after all that, you still made an in-person visitation.'

'Yes.'

'During which you'd claimed the name had been on the folder you'd found the manuscript tucked in.'

'Yes.'

'For what reason?'

'Does it matter?'

'Probably not.'

'Then why ask!?'

In a flash of theatric anger, Hellpop slammed both fists to the table, gripped the side of it, shaking it so the legs bashed repeatedly into the tile, the horrendous racket of this display clanging about in echo as he yelled 'Because a lot of people who seem connected to each other are all varieties of dead while you're going out of your way to be cryptic and outright deceitful!!' I was shaken to the point of palsy as he sat back down, leaning toward me, voice sharp as a number line. 'You'd better understand, Mister Limoncello, that I'm no pretend policeman from TV Land—as a matter of fact, I've worked long and hard to achieve my rank and the respect of my peers along with it—so can tell you, from lived experience, that the way you're comporting yourself isn't in keeping with someone who feels themselves un-caught-up-in some spooky shit.' He leaned back, eyeballing me derisively. 'Are you a cuckoo? You seem like a cuckoo, man! You come off like a wash-out who cares more about their obsession with a pop group than the deaths of several people occurring in the course of as many weeks as there're corpses to revenge.' Returned to a completely neutral demeanor, he took the last of the cigarettes I'd laid out in front of myself, lit it, then fished the pack from his pocket and pushed it across to me. 'Do you have an original copy of this manuscript everyone's so zany for?'

'There is no original—not that I've ever seen.'

'Not everyone thinks so.'

'Not everyone anythings.'

'But some people do,' he pressed on, undeterred by my flippant remark.

'Some people anything, too.'

'Maybe you do have an original, get it? Maybe wanted it to sure seem like you'd never.'

'I'm not following you …'

'Or maybe someone *else* was hip to you had an original but didn't exactly want that fact known to certain parties.'

'Now I'm not, even more …'

'You got yourself in cahoots with someone, I think. No clue what's at the bottom of it—not yet. About this manuscript, though—the original. There's someone out there and—boy oh boy!—they wanted it bad and all to themselves—but there's also someone else who so-did-they. One of those two knew about you and needed a story circulated, the kind which'd get printed on official stationary. Story'd go: you'd found a copy, only, and you'd returned it to the grieving family.' He looked so proud of himself—like I was about to be cornered and would bawl to him all he desired to hear. 'Then someone needed to make it look like they'd come knocking on your door, see? All hot and bothered with trying to pry the original off you. Alack—there never was an original, you'd proven so conclusively, and off they'd tromped, dejected, nothing to show for their trouble but a copy of a copy.'

My throat had gone dry to the extent I couldn't respond—the whole affair grinding to a halt while Hellpop pointed out this was precisely why I shoulda wanted a soda pop and we waited through me coughing and swallowing sufficient spit to get even keeled enough to speak without irritating hacks of interruption. 'What're you asking me?' is all I could honestly think to ask, though.

'Do you personally *know* Sullivan Shallcross?' he asked, demeanor now altered entirely from his previous thriller-flick *gotcha*.

Involuntarily stiffened up, looked smack in his eyes, which equaled affirmative.

'But you ... *don't* ... have an Alibi for Saturday night?'

The emphasis on the contraction was a terribly attractive lifeboat—doused my present cig and took another from the pack to disguise my hapless indecision, or at least hoped it covered up my desperately waiting for myself to just instinctively do something I most likely shouldn't. Blinked, my tongue extended a little, felt the growth of my moustache on it while tracing gummy lips, back and forth. 'This Saturday?'

'Last Saturday.'

'Saturday just passed?'

'We should've been calling it that all along!' he gave a rah-rah of approval with both fists, like a cartoon who'd won a championship.

Figuring whatever I might be in the thick of I was in thicker than I'd be able to sort out without all kinds of surprise shit hitting unbeknownst-to-me fans, I flatly said 'I was with Sullivan.'

'Sullivan who?'

'Shallcross.'

'Sullivan Shallcross, you with him—just to be clear.'

'I was with Sullivan Shallcross.'

'So you *do* have an alibi,' he rolled his eyes, a playact to conceal whatever his emotion legitimately was over this tactic I'd taken.

'Hadn't I just said so?'

'With you, I can't quite tell whether that means much of anything.' But: so we could never dream of saying we weren't on the same page, he wanted me to distinctly state whether I'd been—in person, sharing physical space—with Sullivan Shallcross on Saturday night, speaking out the day, month, year-of-our-Lord.

I told him I had been.

'Where?'

'Here.'

He gestured around '*Here*—what?—being *interrogated*?'

Didn't let this phase me. 'In town.'

'This town?'

'My town.'

'Which town?'

'*Laampray*.'

'Where in town?'

Rolled the dice, but kept it like I was finally unburdening myself of a weight. 'At my motel.'

'You were with Sullivan Shallcross at *The Calico Bash Nitely* on the date I'd just now inquired about?'

Nodded, said 'Correct' and then said 'Absolutely.'

'Wow! So you must really *really* have been, then!' stuck out his tongue and reached for his cigarettes.

'To put it mildly.'

'Had you been drunk at that time, as well, forgotten about it?'

'Nope.'

'With Sullivan Shallcross, undrunkard, at *The Calico Bash Nitely* on the night previously established ... doing *what*?'

'Talking.'

'About?'

'*They Might Be Giants*.'

'Well, knock me over with a chickpea—now how about that!'

'Does he say otherwise?' I asked with a petulant sniff.

'Would he?'

'No idea—just thought it'd be nice to know.'

Hellpop lit a smoke, flicked the pack hard enough it landed in my lap, then seemed to perversely enjoy three slow, long drags before he told me 'I suppose that concludes our business quite handily, then—didn't need a lawyer after all, so guess it doesn't much matter about Nathan, to you.'

'I don't understand the implication there, detective, or your snippy attitude in general. I've done nothing wrong, as you've obviously satisfied yourself of, and have been entirely forthcoming.'

'Is that what what you've been goes by?'

'Look—I'm free to go?'

'You've never been freeer—but could I ask you one favor, before you skedaddle?'

'You can ask—depends on which favor, whether I'll grant it.'

'When whatever happens to you happens ... will you please remember, kindly, my telling you *I told you so*?'

[*in lieu of my coming conniption*]

My dismissal from Detective Hellpop's custody was perfunctory and swift—no personal escort back, instead I'd been summoned a taxi, paid for by voucher, dumped out at *The Calico* by a driver chagrined at being right he'd be receiving no tip. Most likely, I was something in the ballpark of traumatized because I felt perfectly fine, even ahead of the game, like I'd scratched a Lotto luckily or otherwise proven myself worthy of admiration—had a fatigued cigarette for a treat while stood beside my car, deciding whether to pop inside before heading home. Raised a hand to the Day Shift clerk, inquiring whether he'd been asked to come in early and while he told me 'No' with a dubious head tilt, it caught up with me how my sense of time was out of joint—it was hours since I'd been carted away, the man I presently addressed nothing the least bit to do with such narrative, merely a dude working his own grind with his own spots of bother. Rather wanted to sound him out over whether I'd been gossiped about, but not only was the answer 'probably,' even if he told me 'no' and 'no' was the truth it'd make no difference, so we just gabbed a little bit about nothing at all while I attempted to manage my sea-legs—felt rather as I often had back in grade school, or when in hot water as an adolescent, like there was something which was supposed to be done, an order I ought conduct myself according to, an exact method to climb the rungs of toward the happy restitution of the status quo ... but, no, didn't much reckon there was anything along those lines waiting in the wings concerning my present circumstance. It was honestly a dreadful knowledge which crawled through me, despite its semblance of serenity: if I so desired, I could walk away from literally everything, unencumbered and unbarred, same as I could any day—not meaning my current little intrigue, only, but absolutely all I'd ever known. After awhile, I'd simply be someone else, somewhere else, and it'd hardly matter to me who or where, my Past or my Anything interchangeable with somebody else's, be they real or fictitious—so much of my life already didn't belong to me and even more had been forgotten that, regardless if I stayed where I was and told myself remaining meant the world, it'd merely be one more thing I'd claim, impossible to verify. But *The Calico* Day Clerk was no one to speak to of philosophical pitfalls—guy was likely more well-read than I was, first of all, so it'd never get past formalism or him calculating how many years I hadn't gone to college.

Stepping back into the lot, I immediately rejoined the plot—I was being observed, had to be: *ringaling* the clerk'd be answering a call from Hellpop or else sending an e-mail or else would be doing either thing later on, some cabin not legitimately rented but with all the formalities tended to, name in the Register, the computer, a policeman or third-party dick keeping tabs on me—Hell, maybe it was paid for, in vouchers doled out like with the taxi ... what was obvious was how I hadn't been left to my own devices, never to be tapped on the shoulder, again.

Sullivan's car was gone—which made sense, it'd been his last day, check-out time was soon, so he'd likely just got an early move on, what with my not manning the desk, anyway. If he kept to his promise, I could await his message about a meet-and-greet at the Pizzeria I couldn't remember the name of ... but felt so drained ... sick to the teeth with it all. Knocked on the Cabin Eight door, heard nothing, took a beat, tried the knob, and when it opened stepped inside to the pleasant aroma of shower steam, aftershave—all the bedclothes were gathered up and left on the floor, as guests sometimes did, a habit which I always nodded at because it made a ton more sense than the ones who made the bed themselves, as though doing so was any help to anyone.

Drove home vaguely giving another attempt at working out how

Sullivan'd ever gotten wind of me, felt reasonably certain his 'grapevine' consisted exclusively of Officer Picador, maybe a few other parties with odds-and-ends connection to Mrs. Strauss or Nathan, but I also yet reckoned any prattle of grapevine was ruse, misdirection—like a quick-change artist grifting the new kid on the till, he'd gotten more out of me than I had out of him, his each deception equaling three secrets of mine purloined. Knew I'd been dressaged through *somebody's* well-orchestrated rat maze, at any rate, though supposed what Hellpop'd been driving at was I'd partnered with Nathan or Sullivan, element of a long-con to play one or the other into one or the other's hands ... just couldn't suss which way he'd meant it or how'd it'd work if it were the reality I knew it not to be. Seemed he figured I'd colluded with Nathan to make it seem I'd only ever found a copy of the manuscript, which I'd then sent to him ... but that Sullivan hadn't bought into this ... still believed I had the original, under lock and key ... had murdered Nathan to eliminate all copies, regardless ... or paid someone else to ... using me as his alibi ... and would soon pressure me somehow ... menacingly have me fork over the original, and now single-remaining, copy of the document ... Sweet Christ—even trying to sort out how that'd all work or wouldn't couldn't hold my steady attention for more than a moment!

'This, that, this-that—who fucking cares?' I grumbled with foot depressing the parking brake, lurched out of the car, lent a cigarette to some obviously underaged lad whose parents and movers were ferrying bulky items out of a rectangular box-van, new tenants to the ordinary rooms, upstairs—pleasant enough kid, he asked was I his neighbor and when I responded by describing myself as the deadbeat who dwelt in the basement, he beamed at me, proclaiming how lucky I was.

'That's my dream-life,' he sighed all but lovelorn.

Which made me chuckle—as it'd been mine, at his age, as, at one point, I'd hoped it would've been Viggo's ... and that he'd actually achieve it but in the way it was meant, as a dream, not the way it went when achieved purely by accident and misadventure. Asked the kid whether he dug a band called *They Might Be Giants* and was surprised when he knew them—claimed he liked them alright, but such stuff wasn't much his true style, preferred *The Kinks, The Kooks,* and *The Count Five* so I left him with the rest of the pack and a silent finger-to-lips 'Shh.'

Had a shower, some maple-sausages, which were Hellmouth abysmal—even two links at-a-time folded in bread and hardly chewed—a swig of *Bulleit* direct from the bottleneck taking the curse off. Found no messages waiting and wanted to ring Viggo but knew I'd only get his mom—wanted to call her but also didn't so didn't.

A knock came to my door just as I was drifting off in the comfy chair after fruitlessly staring at my stacks of VHS in vain hopes I'd discover the exact right thing to distract me—groggily rolled my eyes and croaked 'Just one minute' like whoever was there had rights to me and I oughta feel ashamed for not being spiffed up and ready.

'I knew I could count on you …' Sullivan said, first thing, touch to the knot of his necktie like he'd only right then finished getting it snug '… or rather, I wasn't the least little bit certain—I must say, you certainly do give a man faith in faith.' Looking over my shoulder in a manner which, in a movie or in a different life, would've been endearing, he wondered 'Are ya gonna invite me in?'

'Would it much matter?'

He claimed not to follow me and I was too beleaguered to bother even a fart of resistance—ushered him over the threshold, flicked fingers curtly that he could sit wherever he liked, tsking when he chose the comfy chair, flopping to it as though dry beat at the end of a long day coaling the mine.

There was a part of my mind which briefly contemplated the consequences I'd face for murdering the man, unprovoked—if just in the middle of handing him my flask for a swig I were to slit his throat or something dastardly like that, a deed done in the coldest of blood and no going back on. Of course, I had no means to accomplish the task other than man-to-man combat, but overlooked that part of the

What-If to probe the principle at its base: if I *did* have a gun or an *implement* of some kind, what would happen if I wielded it? Detective Hellpop clearly suspected the man of something—as did I, quite frankly—and here he was, in my windowless apartment, no chance of witness, so I could darn well claim anything I felt like'd gone down, after the fact, paint it like he hadn't been invited over but instead kicked my door down, do the requisite damage myself once he was neutralized, wrap the gun in his hand, briefly, *post-mortem*, and blast myself but good somewhere a faker wouldn't dream of, the kneecap, the hip, before tossing the weapon across the room to dent the wall, suggesting I'd gotten it away from him after some scuffle ... would the detective look into such a calamity far enough as to reconstruct the scene with models, prove droplets, spatters, or powder patterns meant I was full of hot air?

Such jimble-jamble of bargain-bin potboiler grab-bag pinballed between my ears all in a manner of seconds while my back was turned—segued quickly to what on Earth I'd do if Sullivan, in fact, had aims on ending my life ... I'd probably not be discovered for days ...weeks and weeks ... if I didn't show up to work, the manager'd just assume I was in something deeper than he'd reckoned, tend shifts personally until a replacement could be sorted, mail my final paycheck, hardly a thought given it ... my ex-wife and Viggo might call ... but also might not—and what good would a call do? When it earned no call back, that'd be interpreted as my kiss-off—good riddance to bad rubbish, so far as they'd be concerned, and learning me dead, official, Vig's mom'd move on even more than she already had and, as for Viggo himself, sure, it'd hurt him, haunt him, but everything I'd ever done and hadn't already did that, no doubt, and maybe my death would even a little bit less. '... not that I want you to kill me,' I grinned at Sullivan, interrupting whatever it was he'd been saying, which I'd been paying zero attention to. He begged my pardon as I extended my flask, gave encouragement with a tap of my nose—'*You will not die, it's not poison*,' I drawled in my goofy-best Dylan voice, this bringing a chuckle and a gesture of cheers from the man.

He took a long swallow, another quick tap, wiped his mouth after a cough. 'But seriously, I didn't catch what you said.'

'*Not that I want you to kill me.*'

'Aha ...' he gestured for the flask back '... in that case, I had caught what you'd said ...' took a tilt '... and in that case: what the devil are you on about?'

Told him 'Guess' in a little impersonation of Detective Hellpop, with hope I'd be able to glean from his reaction whether or not he'd ever been spoken to by the guy, but no dice—he likely supposed I was simply dropping in another esoteric Pop Culture reference, one he'd no connection to, so I just opted with going 'I mean—of course you spoke to the detective. That's what he meant about all that alibi business he sweated me for. I'd confirmed it—which is what you meant by knowing you could count on me. See? I'm hip, Sully, I'm with it—old dog new fleas, as they say.'

He shrugged like all I'd just uttered coulda gone without, then took a put-upon breath, tummy extending a bulb, sinking with a grumble. 'I suppose you still think I killed Benjamin and Terrance ...' snapped his fingers, maybe honestly right then updating files or perhaps only playacting it for effect '... and now probably also that I killed Nathan—to complete the set.'

'The notion had occurred to me.'

'I was literally a guest of your delightful motel during the commission of whichever crime snuffed ol' Nate—I think you know that better than anyone.'

'You must forgive me for having no way of verifying that whilst being intelligent enough to know, even if you didn't croak your former frenemy with yer own bare mitts, ya easy breezy coulda sent instructions for someone else to do the dude dirty.'

'You have some goofball impressions of my personal character and the ways in which the world works, my friend ...' he took another sip of *Bulleit*, wiggled the flask to offer it back, lobbed it gently when I motioned him to, then held up a hand he was good when I moved to toss it back after my own tilt '... not saying people don't kill people—with reason, without—but I sure don't go in for such shenanigans, myself, and neither do I cruise to ruin my natural life getting tangled up behind bars. I genuinely recommend you calm down and get both feet on firm ground, Marc—life's complicated enough without complicating it.'

'So who killed Nathan—who killed Benjamin? These were your childhood besties, your soulmates in whichever esoteric nonsense brings you your jollies and, frankly, you're coming across disquietingly blasé about their rather shock-horror demises.'

With a directness I felt cowed by, he told me it was unbecoming to make assumptions about him—whichever inner devastation he presently weathered and how he went about enduring its throes was no business of mine. 'Keeping wits about me and head above water goes far beyond homage. As it stands, with Nathan gone, you are my final, far flung Hail Mary at putting any stamp of meaning to anything—and barring meaning, at the very least providing a meaningful cap to the lives and personal passions of my dearest friend and my erstwhile one.'

'You reckon someone else killed them?'

'It kinda goes without saying, wouldn't you say?'

'Coincidentally?'

'How else?'

'Considering my situation, the timeline, the whole nine—you actually expect *me* to believe that?'

'What I like about you, as I've explained, is your disbelief, Marc.'

Knew exactly where this was heading—self-defense murder plots flickered in me again, palpable enough I had to disguise my discomfiture under a muffler of blathered redirection. 'You know all of your theories are precious podunk nonsense, right? I'm not being a jerk here, fella, but I've no doubt you've heard yourself yap enough to've picked up on what you come across like. I'm gonna spell this out plain and tall, pleading your forgiveness in advance: you three were piddly twerps who gathered round their loser campfire, telling tales of testing and verification, all under the guise of being non-interventional and meticulous, a buncha lonely dweebs cobbling up some holly jolly mythology—but then none of you exerted an ounce of effort in questioning any of your basic tenets with the slightest lick of gumption. Well Sully, I hate to burst your bubble—though maybe it'll aid you in finding the closure I honestly think you need—but this crapola postulant that *nobody disagrees with Benjamin's song rankings* you've spent so much time convincing yourself you'd subscribed to on an evidentiary basis has been debunked. By me. Mere hours ago. Though I have to believe you'd done the same as I had—that Nathan had, as well—or else encountered it, many times over. I'd been able to disagree with the listings, no sweat—zero magical, philosophical, or logical threads encumbered me from the ability to nimbly type out the words for all the world to see. I will fully admit, it was jolting how much aggressive counter to my contrariness occurred—and in short order!—but even while there was much of it, there were others who came to my defense. If that happens but once, your whole religion's *kersplat*—isn't that the bitch of it? Well, it happened, man, and just like that. I am sorry, in a way—but in another just need you to know about it and to never come back once you leave here, today.'

'Which album?'

That was it, all he asked, nonplussed, like there was no possibility of substance in anything I'd spouted off about, his tone that of a teacher gently correcting an obvious mistake, one redressed a billion times before in a million others, a rite of passage, all part of the educational process, I'd see it soon and maybe emend the same glitch in a student of my own, one day—I stammered then finally remembered '*The Spine*.'

'Terrific album! What's your favorite song off it—your personal favorite, not what you consider objectively the best?'

'I hadn't even listened to the fucking album!' He shrugged and, fine, I took his point. 'But people defended me.'

'Noble of them—what'd they said, do you recall?'

My limited understanding of computers had me at a peculiar disadvantage—was it possible he was already privy to the content of the thread? Figured anything he'd set up for me to investigate he might've done so with it designed to send him indication anytime interactions took place—most likely likewise with anything Nathan ever had—all of which, no doubt, he'd directly interacted with under some cloak of disguise.

'Let me tell you what whoever'd defended you *hadn't* said, Marc: that whichever alternate order you may or may not've posited was correct. Now, let me tell you a few other things. There's no way to know if they'd even read Benjamin's proposed rankings—no way to know a whole lotta things! Coulda been punters who'd dove direct to the comments, as many these days have a wont to—bottom line being, all they'd said, if they'd said anything near what you claim, amounted to *you should be allowed to blurt the merest idea if by random whim one occurs to you*—a reference you likely don't pick up on, but which isn't surprising coming from the crowd you're referring to … and, by the way, no one ever suggested otherwise, not Benjamin, not Nathan, and never myself. Quite the contrary! Having a preference, a passionate favorite, doesn't disappear in the face of an indisputable fact.' He gestured to my VHS collection—I felt in an accidentally familiar way which revealed he'd been in its presence before—and told me 'You might absolutely adore the film *Naked Massacre* …' my impression of his slip-up deepened, except the title was visible on the box-edge and he might've glanced it earlier, recalled it despite not having faced the tapes directly, right that moment '… but you'd not say it was Objectively a better film than *Brubaker, Enemy at the Gates,* or *5150 Rue Des Ormes*.'

I didn't say so … and had to admit it to myself as he continued to bulldoze his point.

'Opinion is based on interaction, not rhetoric. Subjectivity is born of Objectivity. You cannot have an opinion of something you've never experienced—not truly. Whoever had taken your side, therefore—even if they did know the album and had been comparing it to Ben's ranked list—couldn't be said to have taken your side because, Marc, listen to me, though you know it far better than I: You … have … no … side.'

I wasn't ready to submit to that, actually—he was correct to an extent but was growing recklessly grab-assed with his explanation to the point I felt patronized. 'Fine snakes and ladders ...' I granted him '... but can't you admit how, by your own logic, the project is defunct? Benjamin is essential to the content of Benjamin's manuscript, it can come from no other, but Benjamin's manuscript is extant while Benjamin is expired—*They Might Be Giants,* meanwhile, live on! Probably have other albums, crates of unreleased material waiting in the hopper! So even if the whole band were exploded by terrorists at eight o'clock tomorrow morning, what good is Benjamin's list? Are you going to turn into Nathan, now? Think yourself able to divine from Ben's existing opinions some formula to properly rank, distill the truth as accurately as he would—will you be the one to number all that comes now which your dead pal can never audit? I honestly feel for you, Sul—but this has long since dribbled over the line of rationality into, if not grief, outright insanity! All that aside: none of its to do with me—I'm nothing to do with any of it ... so what are you doing here?'

He took a long pause—there was something in his face I wanted to be recognition of how thoroughly I'd defeated him ... but it wasn't. 'Marc, do you know how you can prove to me that you're nothing to do with this, don't have aims on the manuscript yourself—can make me go away and never ever return?'

He looked across at me serenely, zero argument left in him, no threat of any kind—whichever flaw he understood deep down existed in his fairy tale was of no relevance whatsoever, so why was I persisting in my stance of condescending little prick? Clapped four fingers into my palm, a gesture of 'throw me the flask,' before I remembered it was in my own other hand '... alright ...' took a swig '... alright, fine ...' another '... alright, fine, yeah. Let me get my coat. This has probably all been my fault, anyway—everything tends to be.'

A look of concern for me crossed his face, but I wanted none of his pity—snarled at him, though it was meant for myself, no idea why I'd said what I'd just said and deeply regretting it. A tremendous anger welled in my chest, cramped my shoulders, knotted my stomach, my ears ringing, clogging, clearing, clear but the world remaining *una corda*, regardless—pointed at the radio on the desk and told him the cassette inside was important, too. 'Nathan'd never known a thing about it—came with the manuscript when I'd found it, but I never mentioned it to anyone. Help yourself.'

He spun in the chair, stood, moved to the radio, ejected the cassette, held it, looked at me. 'What is it?'

'It's Benjamin.'

'Reading the ...' but he could already sort out, as I once had, that it couldn't possibly be what he therefore didn't finish asking.

'It's him ... talking. I dunno what it's supposed to be, but it's there.'

'*Talking*?'

'About things he thought about ... while working out the list, I imagine.'

'It references the list?'

'I don't fucking know, Sullivan!'

'The tape is *original*?' he held it up like pulling a switchblade, eyes like two more he'd use were this some stunt.

'It's ...' but I didn't even remember '... a dub, maybe. I'd meant to leave it for Terrance but forgot it was in my car. Either way: I'll get you the goddamned original when I fetch the manuscript.'

'The manuscript?'

'Yeah.'

'The *original*?'

'So far as I know—yes.'

He stared at me until satisfied I wasn't bluffing, gaze then drifting to the cassette which he'd begun absently pawing, mouth drifting almost amorously agape, no longer registering my presence at all, I was certain—*yeah ... I thought ... if I owned a steak knife, I could end this, here and now, no issue ...*

It saddened me how almost-beautiful the moment was—the two of us buried, both men far far far from any plan.

[*nothing but air, with your hand in the air*]

I closed my eyes as I depressed the parking brake, opened them, checked the side mirrors, the rear—here was such an ungodly ordinary looking day, so rudimentary the strip mall the Post Office freestood at the corner of, so pasteboard the mildly overcast sky overhead, colors from the funny pages of the nineteen-fifties on all my eye could see. I allowed the song playing on the radio to finish, 'Sea Cruise' by *Frankie Ford*, the next, 'Hi-Heel Sneakers' by *Tommy Tucker*, the next, 'Codeine' by *Donovan*, avowed that when commercials came on I'd get out of the car, though decided I'd meant when next they came on, I'd go instead ... *Jay and the Americans* 'Come A Little Bit Closer' ... *Gerry and the Pacemakers* 'How Do You Do It' ... *The Andrews Sisters* 'Boogie-Woogie Bugle Boy' ... *Nervous Norvus* 'Transfusion' ... Watched traffic pass on the road across from me—*whish whoosh th-thunk* of a truck that didn't deign to slow for speed bumps and any two vehicles of the same color I assumed housed the same driver. Counted the contents of the spaces around me, compared it to the number of patrons entering, exiting—the van and two cars which never departed were likely employee owned and sat empty ... though it'd be a simple affair to have a pinhole camera unobtrusively mounted ... just as elementary to be strategically posted in any of the office buildings or restaurants I could see nearby but couldn't see into ... or in an adjacent lot, outfitted with a professional grade zoom lens ... sure, I understood Sullivan'd been ravenous to listen to Benjamin's cassette without a precious moment wasted, but not to the extent he'd risk me doing something he'd live to regret ...someone had to be tailing me.

Though, on the other hand, I allowed how the revelation of the cassette may've served as proof enough of my good will—why even mention it, let alone present the bugger unprompted, if only to give me breathing room so I might execute some underhanded prank? On the other other hand, its existence—*presto!*—was something I'd previously fretted over quite righteously—Sullivan seemingly permitting me to roam free was a cinch to be the signal to whichever cohort was on call to proceed with whichever contingency such a turn of events required ... on the other other other hand ... Sullivan might simply have trusted me, in general, kept his word, felt this was me keeping mine, an agreement among gentlemen.

None of which discounted Hellpop and the sundry police henchmen no doubt at his disposal, as those staunch civil servants not only hadn't stopped investigating murders, but had more reason than ever to clock my every move—two deaths, perhaps three or four, was nothing they'd play it loose about, promotions were built from such, nevermind how, promotion or not, they were gonna be asked about outcomes by bosses and the inquiring minds of the Free Press so better have something clever to say for themselves. Now that I'd confirmed an intimacy with Sullivan, they'd likely wanted to see with their own eyes what I'd meant by it—for all I knew, the fix was in, everyone playing their angles: cops might be in my apartment, having already turned Sullivan to their side, sometime *a priori* cornered him into painting me the culprit, he now serving as tool to run me aground. The man could've claimed to be under threat or any outrageous gambit else—might've presented a narrative which indicated my going for the manuscript proved something untoward, once and for all. In exchange, they'd let him keep possession of it— or at the very least award him supervised access to review the document. Or he might yet be in cahoots with some agent among them—Officer Picador revealed to be the insane creeper who'd killed for this prize, more than once, starting with Hotel Detective when that poor geek'd gotten within even ten miles of too close, Hellpop and others all part of a cabal, running interference or else dutifully doing so by doing what they ought to be doing in the line of duty while with wool over their eyes ... whatever way it went it'd end with proper parties obtaining what they'd hunted, verifying it to their hearts' content, plugging me, and dumping my sorry carcass somewhere like they'd done with the others, the deed pinned on a patsy who'd never know what'd hit 'em.

No matter what spikes of paranoia I might invent, retrieving and turning over the original was the only play left to call—Jesus, it wasn't as though I was on the verge of a revelation or wanted to be! Going through with this hand-off was my purest desire—I'd be shut of it all, free as a jailbird was nude. For some reason, thought of something I'd once been told about teaching a horse to live without food: First day feed it the full meal of oats, subtract one oat per day, no way it could tell the difference first day to second, second to third—repeat this no-difference long enough and eventually serving it nothing would suffice. I'd always aligned this to the feeling of wanting one moment more one moment more one moment more— to Zeno's propounding how if there's always halfway there's always halfway-to-halfway, always more time hidden in time hidden in time, and therefore it could never be too late ... but it was—and I not only knew it, but knew to be glad.

Yet I couldn't shut down the niggling voice in my gut that whispered hoarsely how relinquishing the manuscript was an error—it felt not only mine but, by now, felt me, and though I'd no intention of doing anything with it except having it, the ache I felt crossing the parking lot was intense. There were other factors, as well—perhaps there were only other factors, no want at all ... maybe just an instinct toward self-preservation ... even plankton sported those, I'd be willing to bet! I hadn't let go of the notion that Sullivan was a killer, for instance—even if Hotel Detective and Terrance'd met fates not of his design, dying on purpose or accidentally through sheer luck-of-the-draw, the fact that Benjamin and Nathan were extinct by way of explicit and inexplicable violence left Sullivan the only feasible suspect, no call for him to show his hand until he'd fondled the manuscript with it. It always was plain enough how the reason I was ready to relinquish might be on account of the self-same instinctual sense of threat—correct or incorrect, nulling Sullivan from the equation still left the possibility somebody else, ready and willing to slay, was lurking out in the weeds. Whether they wanted the manuscript or not, I'd no way of discerning—their motive might be Nathan-centric, based around Benjamin, to do with Sullivan, one leading to the other to the other and, from whichever demented perspective, I might now appear part of a chain which warranted erasure. The more distance I could honestly put between myself and the artifact, the better—as it might, even in my vaguely sketched scenario, be interpreted as putting distance between myself and all actors in the production. Regardless: with a preponderance of evidence demonstrating the manuscript sat at the dead center of whichever concentric circles comprised this macabre affair, washing my hands was wisest—no longer could I let myself entertain the childish notion that lying would suffice were I accosted, no more 'from someone else's point of view what difference was there whether I'd found the manuscript, itself, or merely a copy.' Mathematics suggested I'd discovered and replicated an original—were some leather-gloved fiend to crop up, hold me at knife point, I could honestly squeal 'Sullivan Shallcross has it!' and that ability made it most likely they'd toddle off to verify before gutting me like a halibut, since I'd make the most sense alive, just in case. Yep … the fact I'd be able to, under threat, give a lusciously detailed narrative of where, when, why, how the exchange had taken place would buy me a ticket out, temporarily, at least … I hoped … insofar as I hoped it wouldn't be necessary.

 The Doc Cunningham Killer might've been observing me even as I shouldered through the heavy Post Office door—a solid chance Sullivan might never get what he wanted, the McGuffin snatched out from under him right at the moment of triumph. All it'd take was to wait until the material was removed from my mailbox, a hard shove to tip me sideways, the catcall of a blunderbuss perforating me from behind a shady coat pocket or a shiv snipping my femoral, culprit beating feet off thataway, only to ever be identified as a blur of grain captured by closed circuit camera—even if an assailant just purse-snatched and split, leaving me mootly alive, that'd be Sullivan's battleship sunk. Maybe he wouldn't buy it, even had he accompanied me, witnessed the crook scampering off—perhaps he'd assume I'd orchestrated a phony pickpocket, only the time I'd not have remaining left to prove out how this wasn't so.

I briefly considered telephoning Sullivan, waving him into the Post Office—he'd discover me standing in line, in witness of dozens, whereupon I'd display the original, permit him to verify every page to his complete satisfaction, then ask to be allowed to keep it if we could go make a copy, one he'd absolutely know hadn't been altered a tap. Too late, even if I actually wanted to go that route—it'd sour any good will, turn me into a flagrant instigator, sewing noia right when I was promising nothing was lodged up my sleeve. Since he hadn't accompanied me inside, he'd have to allow for the possibility I'd left something behind in the mailbox … in fact, it seemed fishy he'd been content to wait at my place, cassette to audit or no … almost as though seeding the world for an opportunity to keep a delusion functional when whatever he hoped for went up in smoke …

Why not stop off and make myself a replica or turn over the original and ask that we swing by the Copy Shop, he could watch me do the duplicate, keep a dupe of the tape, to boot—would that seem suspicious? How could it, if I explained I was fearful, needed insurance on hand in case someone else came knocking … not, I'd have to grudgingly admit, that having duplicates would've helped Benjamin and Nathan draw breath a day longer than they had were my delusional insistence on a masked slasher in the wings proven true … whoever such blurry assassin was, it'd be an altogether different game they played … didn't want the original, but rather to destroy it along with all copies … eradicate the manuscript from existence … why in God's name they'd host such desire I was beyond the point I had energy to fathom—and if I was asking the question, I trusted it was one which nobody probably ought be.

It was so paltry a feeling to remove the envelope from the mailbox—the act slapped me in the face almost sternly enough to clear my head. One-hundred-sixty odd pages of double-sided newsprint paper, typed all over, then scribbled on variously in green, closed in a store-bought manilla envelope—it was nothing, an artifact which only held meaning to three human beings, so now was only of value to the one of such trio still vital on Earth ... except my eyes fell on the envelope included with the hidden package ... addressed to Nathan Jehovah ... specifically ... the only item personalized ... nothing tagged for Sullivan Shallcross ... but Sullivan'd been the one to've shared the motel with Benjamin, sometime in their young days of roaming, his the name used on the ledger ... the theory that such had been meant as an unmistakable pointer, in case the worst befell Benjamin—a last leap of faith—did carry some currency ...

There had to be a reason for both of those facts—if the entire caper was Nathan-based, it made sense to assume using the Sullivan name was for verification purposes, as Nathan, perhaps, had been informed of Benny and Sullivan's stay ... except ... why not just leave it someplace for Nathan with direct Nathan-centric context were it, indeed, meant for him, exclusively? Likewise, if the materials were intended solely for Sullivan ... why include a sealed document meant for Nathan? If the two existed from each other across a vast schism, Benjamin may've aimed to force a conditional reconciliation upon them—something I'd no way of being privy to which'd make Sullivan require Nathan and vice versa ... but with Nathan dead, Sullivan would have everything ... meaning he could read whatever had been written for Nathan ... and I couldn't begin to crack what use the specific words in whichever letter might be!

There was bound to be an honest explanation, though, however unsatisfying, however multipronged—concrete, unalterable, certain events were more than superficially connected to others and would turn out to link in hyper-specified ways undivulged to me, ever, the manner in which I saw it, or wanted to see it, having no jurisdiction over reality. One indisputable fact was: Benjamin Visa had taken pains to arrange it so that *somebod*y might uncover his manuscript, whatever his doing so was meant to achieve—another: Whoever its intended audience was, I wasn't—my opinion on the worldviews of

Nathan and Sullivan as irrelevant as my disinterest in the music a dead man had not only enthused over for a lifetime but felt important enough to abandon his family over without explanation, even if for only ten day's worth of typing.

I swore to myself that I didn't want any of this noise in my head for one moment longer, but couldn't stop it resounding, nor could I remain in the Post Office, having already loitered far too long—if he didn't already think I was sorting out a double-cross, another ten seconds and Sullivan'd get the creeps but good, I could feel it in my joints.

Though no one could've been watching, I huddled myself over as I slipped the envelope into my inside coat pocket, folded in half, in half again, tucked against the flap of leather I called my wallet—my legs felt like numb pegs, rubber shudders up me with each foot to asphalt as I tottered my way back to the car.

I needed to be comfortable removing myself from the tangential importance I'd acquired—back to being nothing to anybody, or to being someone who would have to dutifully climb my way out of a pit of my own creation, long predating Benjamin Visa and his infatuations, and whose possible re-embrace by others would be entirely up to them. I needed to become tentative, my worth interpretable— I was something, but it wasn't down to me to determine what. This was impossible to accept, though—for ten seconds of chuckling, it was easier to imagine actually making a detour to the *Dollar General*, buying a block of butcher's knives, shoving one then another then another then all-of-however-many into Sullivan's torso before fleeing into a life of oblivion, an exile wherein I was the commander of something, the possessor, the only man who could grant or deny or give meaning. Better yet: a life in prison—oh, such definitiveness held an attraction! Limbo, after all, could never last forever—life where the hammer might always come down was life which always could change. Permanence might be preferable, after all this time and miscalculation—just put a fine point on me and have done! No one would disagree, unveil their bleeding hearts in a plea for my betterment, orate how I deserved a second chance or was worth reconnecting with after a fuller appraisal, seen from eyes of a different age. I actually understood Sullivan, Nathan, Benjamin, for a moment—Christ, let something in this pointless din be now and forever! This song here, this song there—better, worse, deal with it, because it's irrevocably so ... shut the voices and the questions and commentary up, please and thank you, kindly!

Road to parking lot to stairs to corridor to key-to-latch to turn of knob to Benjamin's voice playing to Sullivan, emotion on his face.

'... *Certain People I Could Name* is a luminous offering. Poignancy: top marks. Melody: quite toothsome. Vocals: so primly weaved in it feels like listening to ballet rehearsal. Verses: Solid, inventive, slipping a toe over the borderline of Inspired. On first listen, you'd go to the mat declaring it worthy of special distinction. Subsequent listens, nothing substantive changed. Typical *Giants*. Compared to non-*Giants* material, song was beguiling as the scent of a forest fire. But throwing down with other *Giants* stuff, it was more akin to glancing through the window at a neighbor's Yule log. Nothing to sully its jacket, get a grip! But it takes no risks. Demonstrates no gumption. No get up 'n go. Has aplomb. Lacks kick. As to explicating what tipped *Dark and Metric* over *(She Thinks She's) Edith Head* ... Kick was something *Edith* had oodles of. Aplomb to beat the band, rough-hewn though it may be. Was *Edith* as sophisticated as *Metric*? Quite honestly, yessir, it was. Couldn't be arsed with making sure everyone knew how much, on the first go round. That's all. Takes that risk. Shows the gumption we're talking about. Seems a digit more does not such qualities warrant, though. Nor a decimal, neither. All songs are Eights. How to parse an Eight from an Eight. Again: the boner of the Ten Scale. Trio of Eights—which beats which? This here's an Eight-point-one, this other an Eight-point-two? Then what? Eight-point-three-one versus Eight-point-three-three versus Eight-point-so-on versus Eight-point-so-forth? Fractals of Ten Scales inside Ten Scales inside Ten Scales? Codswallop! *Edith* being an Eight, same as *Metric*, was pristine illustration of such Scale's pitfalls. Play both tunes back-to-back, you can't deny the spiritual difference. Remained unquantifiable how the scuzzy lo-fi verve of *Edith* carried the currency it did. Priceless if ineffable. Also absolute ...'

He turned down the volume of the tape when he saw me lift the folder, undramatic as a prediction failing—I simply placed the object down on the arm of the chair, stepped away to lean on the counter, poured some *Bulleit* into my short plastic cup, sipped it, downed it, lit a smoke, watched. Tears filled his eyes as he examined the introductory pages—he wiped them with the back of a wrist, not batting a wink my direction even once as he leafed through every sheet lovingly, too swiftly to be reading, here or there stopping, though not, or it didn't seem so to me, with it in mind to verify anything, either. Something in the tenderness with which he caressed the document, his fingertips as though to a naval for the first time after a timeless desire, communicated to me the only confirmation he required had been attained and was to do with intimacy far removed from the words written—perhaps the typing had been done onto a paper stock beloved to the lot of them back when they'd first met, or some history more personal to it, a ream Sullivan had gifted Benjamin, way in the Past, which the dead man had, for no real reason, promised to one day compose his masterpiece on … I'd no way of knowing, would never ask, but even the fact there were two absolutely blank final pages seemed meaningful … I reckoned it was the way Benjamin had always done things. There was such sentimentality on display, in fact, that I became emotional, too—the fondness displayed made me long to be longed for in such a fashion, remembered, cherished for my every nuance, to inspire the need to be known absolutely, have acquired friends, loved ones who'd never be fooled by or satisfied with a replica, would demand that a replacement in-name-only was less than a replacement and a replacement an abomination to even theorize, couldn't allow for the possibility the soul they'd held so fast to their bosoms might ever be defined or memorialized as other than what they saw it as, knew it to be … at this stage in my life, could it be possible to stoke such devotion in another … was that supposed to be a joke—of course it could not! Were all to go South, my death to transpire under the most grisly and mysterious of circumstances, it wouldn't stir an obsession such as I regarded in Sullivan—even in my own son, it'd hit like a newspaper article, at best. Nothing I'd ever had hand in might prompt another to seek out and preserve the truth of me—I'd be summed up, instead, by the rhetorical *What is truth anyway?* and by fingers to chins, pretending to ponder. This would do and if not this, that—I was a song which could be listed at any rank, one agreed about without being listened to, once.

I envied Benjamin the pain he'd brought into the lives of those he'd never thought to've hurt—envied Sullivan having such ache instead of the torment I'd inflicted on those I'd wanted nothing but wonders for but from whom I'd filched the chance of even the most mundane comforts. Knives crossed my mind, again, how if I attempted to slash with one I'd fail, how I'd root to be dispatched by my intended victim because I'd be saving something for not saving myself, attaining a last chance at sympathy, to exist as a regret: 'The fool, he hadn't needed to do that—if only we'd explained ourselves better—we let him down, may he forgive us for it.'

The tape clicked, flicking me out of my maudlin reverie, began silently spooling out the content of its opposite side—likely this spoken-word material served as a secondary verification concerning how to interpret the writing, instructions for how to unscramble it into its correct order, which no doubt differed from what pains had been taken to have presented as absolute. From what I'd heard, that'd make sense—certain portions of the manuscript were included only to be disincluded, or else phrases corresponding to some spoken dictums were to be searched for within freewheeling descriptions, a codex which'd unveil the appropriate order to the proper audience. Benjamin had wanted to take no chance that his work could be purloined by a stranger—only those in the know would be aware how to apply his seemingly off-the-cuff insights about Studio Albums versus Singles versus Demo Tapes, gleaning from the subtext of his anecdotes concerning when he'd purchased an album and how many times listening it'd taken him to decipher a lyric not printed in whichever liner notes what to take at face value, what to invert, what to wholesale ignore. Yes, the two items combined had to both be essential to whichever final purpose—probably why the dogged insistence on actually acquiring the original, no ifs ands or buts. If I'd never let on about the cassette, Sullivan might've thought a map-key not found in whichever copy had been removed—such made miles more sense than believing the trouble had been undertaken to retype sections or swap material around … yeah, I was nothing to do with this muddle … and was probably the better for it, regardless how lonely that left me.

As though a mind-reader, Sullivan glanced up, eyes still wet, and said to me 'Don't you see how you were meant for this, Marc?' through a bubble of mucus stuck in his throat.

My chest tightened—I wanted to say something in reply, merely nodded, almost brought a palm to my heart, but halted, closing the hand to a fist I then worked into my neck as though some stray pain had stolen my attention.

'Thank you, Marc …' I remained unable to express myself, verbally '… what you've done—what you've defended without reason or stake, what you've preserved without belief in—is more astonishing than even witness can make it for you. But I do, genuinely, want you to come with me …' I parted my lips, nothing more '… I cannot cajole you to and would never try—but I feel you were born to this as much as I was or was Benjamin.'

'Born to ..?' I managed.

To which he shook his head softly. 'Bear witness, Marc.'

Bear witness to what? I didn't ask. Knew he wouldn't have told me, then—could tell that was precisely what *witness* meant.

[*protozoa, snakes, and horses have enlisted in the forces*]

I've no idea what I'd expected, but as we snaked down a private drive approaching a gated entrance to an estate I couldn't yet make out the residence of, it became clear Sullivan lived in an opulence I'd never have guessed—we hadn't spoken for nearly an hour, had been on the road more than six, snug in the same beat-to-death junker the man had parked in front of *The Calico*, stopping only once for gasoline and a cheap bite to eat from a Truck Stop *Roy Rogers*— coffee and a medium order of fries for him, nothing more. We parked briefly, vehicle left idling while he exited without a word, walked the short distance to unlock an imposing chain holding shut a wrought iron portal—upon his return to the car, we pulled through, onto a paved road from the previous gravel, stopped for him to lock up behind us, then pressed on.

The home was just shy of palatial, outwardly in a state of elegant disrepair—he glanced at me a number of times, grinning, no doubt at the questions clearly all over my face and alert posture, but remained silent. I felt Mars away from anything I'd ever known, transported, both comfortable with this and numbly terrified—the latter feeling only increasing when, as we parked in a lazy diagonal partway on some untended grass beside an overgrown fountain with at least two dozen tombstones flanking it, he asked 'You don't have a cellular phone for me to tell you to hand over, do you?' Shook my head. 'You aren't a luddite …' he sniffed '… so what's the explanation for you, exactly: a hipster, a man jammed-out-of-time?' He confessed to being appallingly fascinated with what he'd glimpsed of my lifestyle—the assortment of obsolete odds-and-ends I'd hoarded around myself, cathode-ray television set, VCR built in and another freestanding beside it, electric typewriter, cassette-based answering machines, boom box, the whole nine.

I didn't have much of an answer, figured I'd been programmed queerly, early on, or else had given up, never much went in for free upgrades and the lot. 'Don't even give my phone number at the gas station even though I know the Club savings are in my best interest.'

'You work for a living, eh?' he quipped, chucking my shoulder as I lit a cigarette and took in the surroundings, gaped at the tumble-down façade of the building. 'I've never had to do that …' he supposed '… though such stays a well-guarded secret. Never like to come off as though I'd been suckled by a silver spoon and swaddled in slave cotton, so to speak.'

I took this opportunity to point out how unexpected the grounds we stood on were. 'You play the part of the lowly proletariat well—the Peter Falk auto, the mess in your motel. Hey—did you even eat all that pizza, drink all that junk?'

He winked while snapping flame to his cigarette. 'When I get to play tourist, I tend to go whole hog.'

'How well-guarded a secret?' I decided to keep the interview going.

'You mean were Nathan or Benjamin aware? Never, at least so far as I know. I've reason to believe it would've stirred ill-blood amongst us. Money breeds distrust on all sides.'

I could tell there was a specific narrative kept out of this summary, a formative event reduced to an offhand flit of his wrist—something I didn't probe any deeper as he changed gears to telling me the history of the vehicle we'd arrived in, how long it'd taken him to track down and acquire the exact lemon he'd been after. I had a feeling he thought we'd bond over this—that he reckoned my own relics were objects hunter-gathered and prized rather than flotsam and whatever I hadn't lost during the countless asinine moves I'd made in my young life, so much being jettisoned each time.

Tilt of his head, I fell into step and, after some to-do involving four keys working the same antique latch, we passed through a front door which'd been painted a garish shade of orange, not recently but at least years after the last time any inch else of the building's outside had been so much as touched—the interior of the place had a feeling I could only associate with black-and-white cinema or Technicolor mausoleum sets from certain horror cheapies from the nineteen-seventies ... I wanted to say it smacked of *Hammer Studios* or *Amicus*, but the layout sorely lacked the aesthetic organization to inspire atmospheric awe ... for the most part, it seemed abandoned, a haunted house from a carnival servicing *New Haven, population now twenty-eight*, except for an area or two I could glimpse which seemed frequently traveled and decently upkept ... after locking several bolts more of the main entrance than he'd unlocked, as well as three on the anteroom's door, the wall-switch he flapped only lit four miniscule lamps, sore-thumb modern, box-store essential variety, arranged to suggest a ground floor path off to the left which he seemed in no hurry to venture down.

I confirmed it was okay to continue smoking, this drawing a chuckle. 'I know it seems like a mansion built of kindling, but there's no risk we'll go up like flash-paper.' He pointed to sprinklers while I explained I'd been more concerned about the scent staining the walls—a guffaw this time and the fingers of his free hand wriggling to indicate I should lend him a ciggie, too, the folder with the manuscript tucked under his opposite arm, cassette a clear bulge in the hip pocket of his slightly overlength linen coat. He smoked slow enough I was able to finish mine and another before he casually motioned me to follow him, moving in the opposite direction of the lit lamps—first through a narrow gate locked behind us, down a corridor with peeling wallpaper and what seemed pages from defunct magazines littering the floor, then through another gate at the end of said hall, which he locked, also, before proceeding steeply down a staircase, door at its bottom opened, closed, locked, into an area wide as a cinema lobby, furnished with coat rack, sofa, and beyond which lazed a lived-in, upkept, modern parlor, halls leading to rooms down that way and that.

I kept questions to myself, followed quietly, obedient though having received no direction to behave any particular way, and soon he pushed through the heavy, leather-adorned entry to a private study, reaching into the sack-cloth darkness until he found the lights—the room revealed, I'd have called it stately except the better descriptor was generic, absolutely sterile in a way, almost nondescript despite I could've spent an hour listing off details and nuance to the furniture and its arrangement, cataloguing the mix of colors speckling nooks and crannies stuffed with what seemed spiral notebooks and paperbacks, globes from different periods, and no shortage of near *Barnum and Bailey* curio, a room so jam-packed it, in effect, became nullified to a matte painting, a suggestion not to be examined, a tone more than a physical space. A key retrieved from his desk drawer freed up the mechanism of a combination dial on the entrance to a room on the parlor's far side, said dial manipulated in a manner which seemed like a kid playing at safecracker, opening what I'd term a repurposed walk-in closet, but only relative to the vastness of the building I now felt the immensity of above me and all around—this new space, after all, sat four times larger than the one in which I dwelt.

A temple to *They Might Be Giants*, straight away I could tell we'd entered the Holiest of Holies: posters, most of them autographed, patchworked the wall in bold primary colors, surrounding them black-and-white, red or green framed broadsides, worse-for-wear gig announcements, Dial-a-Song adverts, and all manner of visual bric-a-brac from points spanning the band's career, early days to contemporary—news clippings, headshots, what seemed to be fan art all arranged atop a collaged background, lacquered to the wall, built from local listings for episodes of Letterman or Conan O'Brien plucked out of *TV Guides* which were blown up to Andy Warhol proportions. A single bit of shelving, curved to a half-circle and suspended by what appeared to be rusted brown wires, spanned the square of the space, and upon it lay records, cassettes, CDs, flexi-discs—at the room center stood a stale, government issue work desk, its perch a disused barber chair which seemed salvaged from the dumpsters behind some shop, on which were arranged a record player, a radio with cassette and compact-disc capability, a pocket Dictaphone for microcassette, plus four rather cheap portable speakers, set at the corners.

Sullivan allowed me to drink everything in, as though I was a devotee who'd be properly stunned by the avarice of his collectible bent—then, after several minutes silence during which I idly poked around, he intoned 'It's taken me a lifetime to amass this, Marc ...' gestured a hand to the music alone '... these are the rarest editions, the choicest pressings of everything.' He explained, at length, how '... even the Dial-a-Song offerings are originals, as much as can be, procured from fans who'd made them by holding recorders to their telephone receivers or allowing the tunes to play out on speaker, captured by their radios' in genuine grit and real time. I'd paid top dollar to have the artifacts people'd kept personal possession of for decades, allowing the owners to make reproductions if such was their desire. This is as close to everything as there can be without raiding the private archives of Flansburg and Linnell.'

He pointed to an arrangement of CDs and cassettes given individual sheepskin packaging, explaining it represented the most in-depth assortment of bootlegged Live Shows available, in one place, anywhere in the world—a set it would take forever to fathom and which contained entirely impromptu alterations to lyrics of perennial favorites as well as in-the-moment, off-the-cuff one-offs, songs concocted blindly on the spot, never to be repeated. 'But such material must not be considered—such has been confirmed to me by this manuscript of Benjamin's and his vocal addendums. Signal and noise, Marc, signal and noise ...' he said as he placed both printed document and cassette upon the desk, caressing the newsprint as he turned to address me directly. For some time, he expounded on the subject of how much blood he, Benjamin 'and even Nathan' had sweated over the years, trying to philosophically, mathematically, and spiritually sort what differentiated ranks, laying emphasis to how he, personally, had always felt a 'further mechanism, a centrifuge, of sorts' must be included in the task, a means by which to conclusively distinguish particulate from ephemera—believed he understood now, more deeply than he ever had, how every angle, argument, dissolution, and falling out between the three minds had been essential '... not merely fuel to the engine, but the very centrifugal energy I'd intuited.' All of this was expressed as though I were right with him, a fellow traveler, context understood without exposition or elaboration—old chums, Marc and Sullivan, it seemed, enough it leaned me uneasy ... felt I was totem, a stand-in for his dead brothers, that he'd be distressed to realize it was only my ears the passions he was speaking out were reaching, preferring the ghosts of comrades I sensed him growing convinced he'd had hand in destroying.

'Have you seen *Indiana Jones and the Last Crusade*?' he abruptly asked me flat, a non-sequitur I paused at, finally shrugging 'Who hasn't?'

'While you'd be surprised, Marc, I think you see what I'm alluding to: there was one *honest* grail amongst a crafty selection of topazes meant to confute even those who'd seem pure enough to be worthy for having deciphered the clues, undertaken the journey, traversed the precautions, and found themselves stood before the Knight Templar.'

I conceded I understood where he was coming from very well, though my own thoughts were turning to films concerning devil worship, cult murder, virgin sacrifice, and all the colors of giallo—to stave off the terminal creeps, I redirected us, quite pat in my asking 'And what is it I'm going to be witnessing, precisely? You're going to ... listen to Benjamin's list?' He nodded. 'What's the deal? From lowest ranked to highest?'

'Oh yes—except only a portion of it ... the Sequence contained within the Total ... the Absolute which could only be distilled once the Perfection had been discerned.'

'Dandy ...' I nodded '... yeah, that's real horrorshow ... but, if it isn't in bad form to inquire ... how long is this going to take?'

The music itself, now that he possessed deepest understanding of what to include and what to cast off, ought take no more than twelve or thirteen uninterrupted hours. 'Of course, I'll need to be certain, before I begin—spend more time with the cassette, the manuscript. All must be in order, as the slightest mispronunciation might suborn disaster.'

'*Mispronunciation*?' I asked but don't think he noted, continuing his monologue unabated, moving into digressions concerning how several of his own long-held theories were already kaput.

'No more than three days, I don't think. I'll sleep tonight, if I can—for I feel as though a child on Christmas Eve, you must understand—and spend the full of tomorrow in study, rest again overnight, begin preparation upon waking. Afterward, I shall begin the incantation, itself.'

'*Incantation*?' I asked, but again he paid the question no mind, wondering instead whether I'd anyplace in particular to be.

'Is it your career in hospitality worrying you, Marc? On the cusp of being audience to something wholly singular, an occasion incomprehensible to human experience, is it matters of your pocketbook on your mind?'

Wanting to keep matters jocular, I told him how my hopes, at present, were entirely centered on not winding up hog-tied and bled dry in some sort of Norwegian forest ritual—but as I'd have to trot along home, eventually 'Yes, Earthly concerns still have a place in my heart.'

'Home?'

'I do have a family ...' I said almost meekly '... a son ...' but went no further than that.

He regarded me with an expression strikingly empathetic, nodded after what felt a full minute, approached me slowly, laying a hand paternally to my shoulder, and told me I mustn't worry, he'd arrange for my child, if doing so would put me more at ease.

'Arrange for Viggo ..?' I squinted as he withdrew his hand but did not take even one step to distance himself.

'You can name your price, Marc. Which isn't charity or bribe— Heavens no! Nor am I teasing, simply to guarantee you won't slink off while I'm secluded in my chamber, attentions consumed. You aren't a fan, as I understand it ...' he winked in a fatuous way '... so I've no intention of asking you to listen with me—indeed, I'll tell you, in no uncertain terms, how such shall not be permitted. I intend to secure myself, here in this sepulcher ...' he spread his arms to indicate the shrine where we currently stood '... and I, alone, am going to experience this miracle. You are to be witness, only—you shall report your account to the world and such duty is something I have no hesitancy in compensating you for.'

Though what I'd without blush term a 'mad gleam in his eyes' likely mooted the veracity of any response, I couldn't help asking 'You'll pay me?'

'Of course.'

'Then ...' I decided to inquire, feeling as though I was taking my life in my hands '... why hadn't that been your opening gambit?'

He seemed perplexed, but soon enough his eyes widened to what I was asking. 'To buy the original off you—offer you money when I'd believed you in possession of it?'

'Yes,' I said because there was nothing else to and no reason not.

'I thought I'd explained that, quite well ... demonstrated ... or that you'd come to understand, by now ...' he shrugged, seemed a touch disappointed.

Anxious to keep the air from going bad between us, I pivoted to inquiring what I'd be giving account of. 'Or is that something which'll be left to my personal interpretation?'

At this quip, a relaxed grin settled to the thin of his lips which a rather pale tongue moistened slowly, he then admitting to not knowing *precisely* what would transpire. 'I am, Marc, going to experience, with open heart, a legitimate Truth. The Truth. Which did not, until this music, until Benjamin, until myself, at all exist—which could not have, despite how strange and incomprehensible most minds would find such proposition. A metamorphosis, is my hope—but in what terms, I think it best I not allow myself the arrogance of expectation or preference. Certain words summon Kandarian demons, as you no doubt know from those late-night double-feature picture-shows you so cherish, while others are only rumored to've been uttered, leaving nothing but folklore and dime fiction as speculative legacy of, both making claim that there are matters incomprehensible adrift in our realm which hair will turn white at mere peripheral brushes with.'

'Might make it tough to do a write up about …' I swallowed, doing my best not to tick eyes toward the exit lane.

He blinked, seeming only then to recognize the pickle his words were presenting me. 'All the more reason I should've been the one to offer compensation, up front—in whichever form secures your loyal attempt.'

A bit harder to do so now, I rolled my eyes in half-jest, got a cigarette to my lip, lit it, and suggested 'Cash on the barrelhead does little good if tentacles taking a shine to me or my torso being tugged inside-out via the anus aren't entirely off the table, eh?'

I could make fun, yes—and he could understand my irresoluteness '… yet here you stand: The man with the least reason to be present and with more reason than anyone to be anywhere else—you're a little proof, in and of yourself, Marc, even you must be thinking as much.'

'I'm blushing, stop,' I managed as no doubt I drained pale.

'You mentioned a child—*Virgo*?'

'*Viggo* …' I slowly pronounced, fingertips brushing my wet palms in tickles.

'What amount of currency, tendered in the name of Viggo, would secure your presence during my sojourn? You've no need to persist in nervousness …' he stepped away from me, pacing off toward the desk at room center '… I've no intention of chaining you to the radiator or even securing you by duct tape to the very comfortable leather sofa you may've admired in the parlor. You are free to go, if you so choose—I would take that as a definitive item: *the man with no reason to stay verifying he'd no desire to and could not be coerced* or else *the man with no reason to remain, yet willing to for a price*. In my way of viewing the world, it'd be most elegant if you, being the symbol I believe you to be, deigned to remain for the sheer exultation of experience … but money makes the mare to go—even this music would not exist as it does, without commerce.' He claimed he'd gladly bequeath me his every material estate, except felt doing so would be showing himself too presumptuous in the face of what was about to occur. 'Whatever it is, Marc—I admit, being pilgrim, I do not know the face it will take.'

Here was a development I'd have never expected and which I didn't trust as far as I could throw ... but still was more than intrigued by, was hungry for. There were fringe benefits to befriending a lunatic, it seemed, so I did my best to not appear flummoxed while my eyes darted with the calculations I made ... I was in serious trouble, after all ... my life on the scrapheap, but good ... the very least I could do was think of others, for once ... of Viggo, at least. 'No money if I scamper, I suppose.'

'Leave if you wish—the compensation is conditional, however.'

'I can leave *unthreatened*?'

'What could I threaten you with?'

No ... something was rotten. 'All these precautions erected, but you'd be willing to take your eyes off me, knowing full well I might pop out and return with Detective Hellpop after laying on him any crazy tall-tale I figured'd bait the lure?'

He wagged a finger at me as though I was being a rascal, told me I really needed to stop being so paranoid, all the time. 'You legitimately are free to depart, Marc—all risks in your doing so are understood and appreciated. You turning out to be turncoat, while disappointing, would have no bearing on anything.'

'Let's call it a year's wages, then,' I shrugged, ready to pivot this to a joke if he balked or became angry, revealed the offer had been a test which I'd failed.

'Very well—how much is that?'

I blinked, realizing the screwball was dead serious and I'd just lowballed my legacy—Jesus, simply the room I stood in proved the existence of zeros after dollar signs. 'Well ... let's make it a round figure: one hundred thousand.'

He told me he'd step to the parlor in order to contact his bank.

'Contact your bank ... about *what*?'

'Your son's money—I'll arrange the fee be made payable directly to him and no party else.'

'How—he's only just turned seventeen …'

'An instrument created in his name, accessible only to the young man, and irrevocable, my personal attorney retained for such purpose.'

'*Irrevocable?*'

'I want your mind at ease …' he all but lullabied, after which he spoke nothing further about the matter to me directly—I simply watched and listened numbly as he conducted business over the telephone, filling in a few details he required of me for reasons of legalese, a surreal act of possible theater which was over and done inside an hour, the long and short of which was: lawyers were duty bound to contact Viggo, at present via his mother, informing him the account, freshly funded, would be accessible to him upon his coming of age.

Considering the matter duly settled, Sullivan moved on with explaining I had full run of the lower portion of the house—all amenities, could choose whichever room I preferred for my repose—but was not to leave. 'In the event anyone shows up, attempts to enter, you are, under no circumstances, to allow it.'

I was visibly startled at this sudden proviso. 'How am I supposed to …'

'I'm not calling on you to physically prevent such a thing, Marc. Other than this …' he motioned to the one he'd just used '… there are no telephones—the front gate, the front door, all locked fast, as you saw. The upper estate windows are shuttered, as are those on this level. My sanctum, itself, will be impregnable even to you, once I enter—and if there does come a time you so much as fear someone may've swum the moat and attempted to raise the portcullis, you're more than welcome to close yourself in here …' he made wide gestures of the study, drawing my attention to the extra locks only I would possess interior key for, and the three metal bars which could be lowered to keep the place from being battered '… not that you have anything or anyone to worry about.'

Knowing it unwise, I nonetheless pressed him as to who it was he reckoned might show up. 'Whoever offed Benjamin and Nathan—if it honestly hadn't been you?'

He simply sighed at the query and, in a blasé tone, explained how, hook or crook, anything I or anyone else did couldn't touch him, now—whether I wanted to go on as who I'd always been or as a man reinvented was up to me, but it was time we settled our transaction, once and for all.

I rolled my eyes like yeah yeah yeah, held up my hands, pushing my luck just a step or two further because, frankly, I had it in mind to split, regardless, and he probably already knew it, everything from bear traps to poison darts fashionably hidden to stop me. 'If I stay, when you emerge ...' I waved my hands ghostly and put on a spooky voice '... *if you emerge* ...' dropped arms to my side, palms flopping against my thighs '... I expect another fifty thousand—check made payable to Cash.'

'When I emerge, Marc, I truly believe there will be something of far less corporeal value you'll desire ...' motioned for a cigarette, winked slow as he leaked a seemingly too long amount of ash-blue out his nose, his mouth, both, then told me '... but, yes—you scratch my record and I'll scratch your back, you may rest assured we have a deal.'

[*clap our hands and wait for the sound*]

It was the best living I'd lived in, frankly, decades, not even the years before my divorce and sinking into the sludge of *Laampray* had ever come close to the poshness of the cave I felt locked up in, a bug in my snug little rug—another basement room, to be sure, but one more like a bourgeoise survival pod lodged firm down a mine shaft while Cthulhu tromped riotously the expanse of *terra firma*, above. I saw neither hide nor hair of Sullivan, didn't register so much as a peep even with my ear to his 'sanctum' door—amused myself with the thought that, once his liturgy was complete, he'd slap a big red button, incinerating *The Giants* materials he'd gathered together, safeguarding against any soul else being able to walk his footprints and thus horn in on his posterity.

By the middle of the second day, after a sound sleep in a bed which made me appreciate why most people owned one, my every noia and fear seemed frivolous—only a silly sausage, indeed, would waste a moment fretting they'd been left all alone, abandoned while Sullivan snuck out a secret passage to summon John Law down, or that they'd simply been entombed in high style, crimes pinned on, body never to surface, authorities left to assume them gone into hiding. In the peace and quiet, I couldn't fathom why I'd entertained such fancies for even a moment—this was the rarified luxury of being nobody on somebody else's tab.

Nothing in the study was off limits to me, no drawer locked or curio case secure against tactile curiosity—even the ledger from which my reward check was to be cut lay in plain view, flopped open, naked for inspection, and I spent a good deal of time leafing through it, attempting to gauge the scope of Sullivan's fortune, though understood little of the information handwritten on most of the stubs beyond the underlined sums, some of which might as well've been hieroglyphs, so far as I was concerned, the amounts far beyond my personal or cultural experience, a few I only comprehended the dim way I might images composited from the data collected by deep space telescopes. I expended some focus on relatively paltry amounts—anything fifty grand or less seeming quite the outlier—briefly obsessing over certain checks cut on dates which might be termed 'on or around' when Hotel Detective snuffed it or Benjamin, Terrance, Nathan had moved on to greener pastures ... I wanted to be able to consider whichever payment to Cash or numbered account 'near enough in time' to be suspicious ... was more disquieted than I'd bargained for when the date of Nils Dolphy trashing Cabin Eight of *The Calico* loosely corresponded to a payout in the amount of seven-thousand ... though there were other minor payments connected to no date I was privy to intrigue occurring on or around ... and considering fifty-thousand clams were being baked my way just for loitering and that certain *They Might Be Giants* paraphernalia had been procured for amounts ten-thousand plus, it was difficult to believe larceny or murder-for-hire got transacted at bargain-basement rates.

I found it odd how nothing in the study bore any relation to the band, despite everything clearly being rare—even the scent off various books or curio probably ought to've come with a price-tag! If I'd stuffed a duffle bag so much as a quarter-way with random bric-a-brac, no doubt it'd fetch more than the payment I was set to receive ... not that I'd know how to fence anything ... and doubted very much I'd get on with whoever might be in the market for a senator's signature on some milquetoast legislation or what I knew from a plaque was a genuine Stegosaurus bone but which really seemed to me was only half-a-Stegosaurus bone, at best.

I ate very modestly, as such was the only way I knew how, didn't trust my inner workings to know they weren't being poisoned if I introduced them to foodstuffs most wouldn't think to add the *stuffs* to—peanut butter sandwiches, mostly, though I did indulge in an overly rich frozen pizza, suffering wicked pangs of cramp for the transgression. There was no shortage of alcohol, but I didn't overindulge, sipped from bottles worth more than my Golden Years while I watched movies I'd already seen before, too overwhelmed by the expansiveness of Sullivan's DVD collection to branch out—the man owned a complete-series bootleg of *Step-Bot*, which about blew my mind!—and didn't even bother trying to suss how to operate the projector, load in one of the original 35mm prints of grindhouse curiosities he had arranged, as though haphazard overstock, in the Entertainment Room corner.

The second day bled into the third with a slightly more fitful night's slumber, up every hour or so, drinks downed, but only modest ones, enough to drift me back off only long enough I wasn't sure if they had or if I'd laid on the verge, thinking they were about to before having another—it was a cavity of time which seemed to span months but also felt akin to a stay in some dentist's Waiting Room ... too long, never long enough ... just enough time to settle in before it was time to leave ... except it wasn't time to leave so I'd start to settle in, again ... just long enough it felt I had before it felt time to leave, once more ... a loop which wasn't long enough to round, a dot that was also a tangle, when magnified.

On the morning of the final day, I exited the shower, trying to take stock of myself in the steamed reflection—it seemed about right, how I looked, though less and less as I cracked the door, the humidity allowed to vent, my nudity revealed. I flexed awhile, but not only did musculature not pronounce over my skeleton, my skin couldn't be bothered with going tighter when stretched—I toyed with the idea of streaking some pomade through my shampooed locks, but only got so far as smearing my palms before chickening out, it taking so much effort to rid the greasy feeling of peppermint scented paste from my fingers I felt dirty like from a jog. Donned a towel, plodded the corridor to the room I'd been using as home-base, and wondered was anyone searching for me—Detective Hellpop, my family—but also wondered why would they or, at least, why would they yet, give it time. Wondered had Benjamin wondered the same things, minus probably the cops, when he'd done what he'd done, was curious how intensely it'd hung on him when he'd given it all up—had he believed he'd return home ... had he ever intended to? For all I knew, there'd been a murder pact, paid in full, arranged by the man himself to start some crazy ball rolling—the premonition Sullivan fancied his friend had experienced no more than a misdirect meant to ease me into this further intrigue. My head was so full of the unreal, again and all of a sudden, I felt ill belonging in the unexercised skin I sported, every visible splotch like a truth melting through a cheap coat of sealant ... or rather I couldn't shake the impression that my appearance suggested mold growing bread.

I was brewing coffee when I thought I heard stirrings from across in the study, strained to eavesdrop while tabulating some sums—figured it must be all over, whatever it was, so took a steadying breath, bolstered myself, hopped up and down, prepping for my day in Claims Court, ready to argue, to really lay out a case to be given what I'd been guaranteed. Over my dead body was Sullivan reneging on the money he'd already arranged for Viggo and though I knew expecting another fifty was a pipe dream, I'd not accept as much without a touch of pique. Oh he'd tell me he'd only been joking and I oughtn't be greedy—would be correct, come to think of it, because what'd I been thinking, nobody'd put me out anything and these events I'd got caught up in were only because I'd literally shoehorned myself into them. The funds for Viggo, though—I'd demand evidence all had gone as promised. As a matter of fact, I'd command Sullivan to travel with me to his bank, have the previous instrument annulled, if possible, and get cash money tendered directly to me which I'd personally transform into a check made out in my son's name—the son-of-a-bitch had more money than sense, obviously, I was wearing one of dozens of silk robes with soft faux-fur insides, for God's sake ... or maybe actual fur, how was I supposed to know ... point being any three articles of his loungewear likely equaled my next month's rent, gas, and food. When I definitely heard movement in the study, I yet allowed myself to finish the sandwich I'd constructed, having decided to throw caution to the wind, eat like a human for once—devoured bread so rich it might as well've been steak, cheese and chicken so delicious it got imbibed more than chewed and made me understand, finally, how foodies understood the term 'perky,' then took my time with an extra cup of coffee, a cigarette, plus one more.

Dressed back in my own clothes, key in hand, I made my leisurely way to the parlor door, hoping I hadn't been meant to wait until summoned—if he'd experienced the toe-curling of whichever epiphany, maybe letting him linger in its afterglow went without saying ... and if the literal nothing which most certainly'd transpired had rattled him, decorum might suggest doling him an entire day to psych himself out of disappointment, at least a few hours to concoct some cockamamie spin to put on matters so his vanity wouldn't be scathed.

I wanted out, though, and the sooner the better—would endure whichever speech he'd prepared, put on a swell show of gee-golly or whatever he required of me, but wanted to make it quick, as everything could still bend weird in a metric ton of ways, no way our morning was gonna consist of a casual *How'd it go? Great! Hey, that's terrific, well I suppose I'll mosey on down the trail, then.* Sullivan would no doubt dictate explicitly what I was to report to the world I had 'witnessed,' along with detailing to whom such Gospel be addressed and when—before he'd temporarily entombed himself, it'd seemed he'd felt I'd know, a giddy apostle, ready to be crucified inverted, filled with arrows, all that jazz ... but now that there was gonna be nothing to report, his ego'd require kid gloves and sharpened scalpel.

After I'd knocked, unsure the sound would penetrate, I turned the latch and pressed the door inward a sliver, a sound of it groaning as though begrudging me. 'Sullivan?' Waited, ventured the door open a tiny tap more. 'Sullivan?'

Figuring he'd perhaps returned to his cell, I shrugged into shouldering the study open, full—immediately and involuntarily, every cell of me clamped down, jolting me violently backward, the side of my head striking the door, impact drifting me dizzy in a redirected lurch sidewise, nose meeting blunt the flat of a set of shelves several items plummeted from, one shattering in a tremendous to-do made louder by the fritz of my vision burning bright, blurring dull, settling on something like having been too long unggogled in warm water thick with chlorine, until, doubled over, I hiccoughed rather painfully, each percussive glug from my throat causing my ears to ring a different rung of the xylophone.

Sullivan Shallcross was hanging by the neck from a sturdy rafter on the chair-side of the hand carved desk at room center: dead—oh he was most certainly dead, there was nothing for it, not a twitch to him, though still a little bit of sway, the motion as silent as the oblong shadows accompanying it, not even the creak from the cord he'd utilized for the deed most motion pictures had conditioned me to expect, the puddle of urine a lot of even the most macabre flicks leave out in evidence on the carpet below him, splashes and splashes and drip-drip-drip speckling the overturned chair, a fecal odor mingling with the cigarette I must've lit without even thinking to or the one I saw half-burnt on the carpet, perhaps having fallen from his mouth as the noose went taut, presently leaking the last of its scribble-smoke as though yet sketching the horror above.

My first conscious reaction was nothing, my second was to do the first even better, my third to shut the door and turn all four locks—third-and-a-half to consider lowering the metal bars but also to think the better of it—fourth and fifth was to think what the fuck had I just been thinking I'd been thinking better than—*crash boom bang* they fastened to place—and sixth was to confirm that I was actually seeing, paper-weighted to the desk blotter, a check ... made out to me, not to Cash ... in the amount of fifty-thousand dollars ... handwritten note informing me the funds could be drawn from Sullivan's bank, address provided, and that I'd be expected, would encounter no question ... memorandum in the ledger beside the payout reading: *I have become who I am.*

Describing the next patch of time is nearly impossible, even with tossing far-from-accuracy to the winds and the rain: thinking didn't much happen or happened so much it paralyzed, I didn't touch the body, only twice caught glimpses of the nightmare bloat of its bulged purple face, tongue appeared almost raisin textured and twined into a braid, one eye closed, the other so thin-red and mixed with stabs of putrid vermillion it seemed a stillborn egg-yolk or that three overlapping pupils were present, smoked through my pack, went through the desk drawers as though there'd be others, settled for a stubby cigar from the humidor I discovered on a bookshelf, twice made the gagging mistake of accidentally inhaling but refused to give the implement up, something to manually occupy myself with absolutely mandatory.

I remember a thought finally striking me, bringing with it the colors of reality and focus: *I cannot stay here, cannot be here, need to leave, to say nothing to anybody about any of this—this must never have happened* ... but knew that was the one thing it couldn't do. An idiotic whirlwind of concerns about fingerprints and DNA telltales throttled me—but what was I suggesting, that I give a thorough scrub to every last place I might've so much as stood? Spent five minutes thinking how dreadful it was that seminal evidence might be discovered in the shower drain, residuals on one of the bath towels, and next moment considered burning the place down—really and truly spent fifteen solid minutes in an effort to sort out how one goes about orchestrating arson on a grand scale, what all was logistically involved in making certain a building was reduced utterly to cinders ... perhaps the upstairs had a fireproof floor ... if I torched the shuttered-up lower level, really did a number on it, maybe no sign would creep to the outside world ... like in that submarine movie starring Bruce Greenwood I so enjoyed ... behind the airtight latch, the entire crew had exploded ... a lightbulb flicker and radio silence the only indication ... when the latch opened, nothing but stale, hydrogen-rich air and charred corpses ...

Turning to cult B-movies in time of crisis wasn't a good sign—it was a real world The End closing in on me and I knew it. Even if I dynamited the joint, my name'd pop up during any investigation— if I zapped the entire manor into another goddamned dimension, nothing left but a rose garden I'd conjured to replace it with, there'd still be questions put to me, ones I'd better be ready to answer or else!

Snatched up the new check, as though there were a chance someone in authority would arrive before I could pocket it or that Sullivan might yet possess life enough to rescind it ... money ... I had money ... enough to run a long way away with ... except I couldn't run free ... running brought me closer to being run down, run aground ... when detectives discover a person-of-interest in multiple murder investigations dangling from rawhide, another person-of-interest in the exact same crimes suddenly able to spend like MacHeath, it's gonna get a poke ... not to mention the hundred large earmarked for Viggo was gonna seem proper convenient! *Where'd this dough come from? Your old man? First of all, bullshit, he's not worth the ink it takes to type 'dime' and, second ... tough titty, kiddo, you can't have it, that's evidence now.*

Wheeled around, wanting to spit on Sullivan, but wheeled back at the blurry sight of him—was any of the money now nothing, could I not leave, cash my check, pronto, have tangible, cold hard currency I could hold onto for Viggo as a just-in-case, eventually hitting on some way to ferry it to him ... but when ... after years ... would I have to disappear, first, let him know me a fugitive from justice or else consider me dead ... did that matter ... did anything? What in the name of God had happened—how had this fork been come to, in the last five motherfucking minutes!?

I couldn't focus or see clear to how I'd ever be able to emerge into any kind of society, again ... but perhaps was overreacting ... in shock, simply not enough of it to dream money from a dead man could have a blind eye turned to it ... Sullivan didn't exist in a vacuum ... if I cashed out, that left a trail, he'd be missed, he'd be found, I'd be missing, I'd be found—oh for Christ's love, it crashed bricks down on me how over and done with I was! 'For what!?' I demanded of the empty air. 'For what, goddamnit!!??' Flapped and sawed my arms around. 'I don't even like the band!' I bellowed, laughed, had an honest to God bit of a stark raving breakdown, assailed by all the outlandishly unfathomable ways this scenario might be painted, zero with me coming out with even a spit shine. 'They're going to have to make this make sense ...' I found myself sitting in the leather chair, facing the hanged man, calmly explaining '... all of it. Nobody will let there not be a cohesive narrative ... but the more I try to explain, the more I'll be assured a posh spot at the lowliest asylum they can find to stash me away in ... I'll never come back from this ... and all for what?'

I pondered the query as I stood, suddenly possessed that an answer might be discovered in the room Sullivan had locked himself in for his listening ritual—there seemed no signs of distress, the music was stacked primly on the center table beside the various playback devices, the decorations all lovingly in place, even the ashtray had been emptied, the trash-bags spent provisions had been chucked into all tied up as though waiting for the maid to whisk out of sight. So ... he'd listened to the list, experienced *They Might Be Giants* in Benjamin's magical order, then been met with the same ol' banal air he'd breathed every minute of his measly life previous—thus off he'd trotted to end it all?

I spun around, for a moment certain this was murder rather than suicide, one like Hotel Detective or Terrance ... except what was the check doing on the desk, then? Had The Doc Cunningham Killer waited for it to be written, then left it behind—why, when it wasn't even made out to Cash? Did someone desire it to appear I'd finagled money out of Sullivan, trussed him up myself, gone on the lamb ... it was all too unreal, was completely impossible ... I felt dead and buried ... but also felt calm.

In the blink of the lighter getting my cigar puffing again, everything switched to: 'Well hold your horses, Marc—what actually had happened?' A relaxing, reasonable thing to ask, it seemed. 'Something had. Other things hadn't. I know about those—but I'm the one who hadn't done them. Who had didn't matter if it could be proven they weren't me.' Paced around, giving patient-toned, reasonable explanations. 'I haven't done anything wrong, after all, and justice—actual justice—could and would prove out as much.' Sullivan dead didn't mean the world was allowed to make up the reason why, on a whim—to the contrary, now there was a definitive thing to address and any opinion on the matter, even mine, was removed from the equation. This this this this and this had happened in this this this this and this order and that was all there was too it—even the money had been tendered in a perfectly legal way, by a living man, all of his own free will. 'People'll be jealous, if anything! What an adventure! I'll make a fortune off the film rights, alone! Or the tale'll at least get me interviewed somewhere, a Human Interest feature in the local Gazette! People love to obsess about mind-boggling mystery and I'll be—as I was destined to've been—the one and only witness. The Arbiter!' Before, I'd been nothing more than deadbeat dad dying in East Bumblefuck, Noplace—had I worked myself into the grave I'd never've been able to provide for my son what this quirk of chance had afforded me opportunity to … and once the official leg of the aftermath wound down, whatever I said was what'd go, seeing as who was in any position to do anything but spin fan-fiction yarns or nurse pet theories, otherwise. 'Yes … yes … yes, yes …' I muttered, an engine trying not to flood '… this was all a very good thing, a lucky break!'

I re-entered Sullivan's sacred chamber to verify absolutely the original manuscript remained on hand, discovered it alongside the cassette in its case, next to both found the pages with the listed music, in order, set in their own stack—many items struck out with red pen in accordance, I supposed, with Benjamin's verbal instructions and whatever other assortment of clues Sullivan had discerned from the manuscript text or scholarship unknown … then a handwritten list in Sullivan's penmanship … only the tracks the nonessential had been culled from … noise trimmed from signal. I apprehended how these were the most valuable items available to me—not for any hurdy-gurdy associated with this trio of lunatics, but on account of the lot of them now being posthumous. In a peculiar epiphany—one which felt as though knowledge wedged into me, absolute—I understood there was nothing for me to be fearful of. The only thing which shook clear to sense was that Sullivan, in ways I had no call to even attempt sleuthing out to any third party's satisfaction, had been the one who'd scooped up all copies of the manuscript—perhaps committing murders in the process, perhaps not. Seeing no evidence of copies, I had to assume the man dangling from his basement ceiling had destroyed them—having set the stage for whatever he'd expected was going to transpire, he couldn't have risked my report alerting others to the existence of free-roaming replicas of the precious source material. He'd said so, himself—no one but he, the only actual Believer, was to experience The Truth, because he'd concocted what it was to believe in and what it meant to believe. If I told the world his Good News, they'd either dismiss it or treat it as folklore, urban legend—any attempt to duplicate what he'd experienced impossible.

He'd left this original for me—to *truly* witness—and I owed it to the man to do exactly that, did I not? If I were to suggest so to anyone, all they'd hear was me willfully confessing I'd lost my ever-loving mind ... but hadn't I ... hadn't I from the start ... from before that ... hadn't I always?

[fork! snail! garçon! cocktail!]

In a kind of car-crash, medicine-head slow-motion which nonetheless felt hasty like silent-film era footage, images in a series at once zany, eerie, and unremarked, I gathered up the recordings, used one trash-bag for what seemed to be the 'final set' Sullivan had sorted from his vast kit-n-caboodle based on which songs from Benjamin's Master List were deemed proper, so far as playback, then spilled everything else over the desk lip into another, no point running the risk I'd come up short in the clutch—to further keep on the safe side, decided I'd lug record player, CD-cassette capable boombox, and micro-recorder out to the car, closed snug in the trunk, protected against jostles by an assortment of randomly snatched up towels and bedclothes. I secured the manuscript, cassette, and Nathan's letter, still unopened, in a very fine, felt-lined mahogany box, yoinked from off one of the parlor shelves, emptied of its antique revolver and seven embroidered slugs—and after locking tight Sullivan's sanctum, such that I'd not be able to gain entry again if I wanted, I turned every latch of the parlor door locked, resolving to ditch the keys in a waterward fling once enough driven miles had been put between my fleeing self and the manor.

It crossed my mind to cut Sullivan down—but what purpose could something like that possibly serve? Not only was such display how the man had chosen to go out—far be it from me to muck up a fella's final statement—but any molesting of the grim tableau would only lead to pointed queries when the crime scene was eventually uncovered ... if it ever was ... the more of the passage and stairway doors I secured behind me, the more it settled in my mind how Sullivan's corpse might truly remain down there months, years, longer ... if I'd shut him inside *The Giants* shrine, the space would've served as his official mausoleum ... and once the vestibule and front door were tended to, along with the gate onto the property proper, I had to imagine it'd be one Helluva time for anyone to get in, other than whoever may or may not be in possession of duplicates to the very one-of-a-kind feeling twists of metal I'd be disposing of ... police would likely have to jump through red-tape hoops to prove reasonable cause for search, if it came to that ... and since it wasn't as though I was gonna ring them up to drop a dime concerning the suicide, a solid few days were probably mine to burn before the first sniff of anyone's prying.

It felt peculiar, contemplating departure—adrenaline no longer a blitzkrieg all up and down me, minutia took odd contour. The junked-up car, for example: it didn't belong to me and was quite conspicuous—were an all-points-bulletin to be issued, blending in was well off the table. Nodded somberly to remind myself I'd be twenty-four hours and hundreds of miles distant in a direction nobody knew before anyone knew they didn't know—plus the car wouldn't be considered missing so much as assumed parked behind the locked gate, a mile down treelined driveway, and that only if anyone in Sullivan's life was cognizant of its existence.

But such matters of crime and punishment weren't what had me antsy—a deeper disquiet began taking hold, concerning the face of what I'd become embroiled in. 'Sullivan couldn't possibly have had it in mind to kill himself, from the start—right?' I asked like I was somebody I could get an answer from. 'Why not?' I retorted but didn't let myself get the upper hand, volleying back a third-grade 'Well—*why*?' 'Because he'd murdered his friends and possibly their offspring, as well as perhaps some total strangers, and knew deep down in his private-most pit he was off his chump' seemed feasible, but I interrogated such notion with a sarcastic 'Just all of a sudden, you reckon he went on an obstruse killing spree—had been waiting for just such an occasion to break giallo and top the trick off with a touch of Andrew Telfer cosplay?' Trying a less discount paperback application of human psychology on for size, I floated another possibility: the death of Benjamin, the thwarted love of Sullivan's life, snapped the poor dude's mind like a celery stalk—when he'd learned the manuscript had gone missing, and on the heels heard vague chatter of it prestidigitating in duplicate, being offered around by a mysterious figure, Nathan meanwhile sniffing here there and everywhere, he'd decided the savviest strategy'd be to play out the communal fantasy of 'forbidden knowledge having been uncovered' to its very last dreg.

'Why does this matter?' I batted my hands as though clearing gnats, entirely fed up—but I was who'd asked, I reminded myself '... my point had been ...' I retorted '... will the money really be waiting, is the car clean?' Did I think I was going to come up with an answer—would even 'Fuck no, Marc—your goose is cooked, numbskull!' keep me from leaving, walking into the bank, doing whatever it was I had in mind, after? Decidedly not, but I couldn't be faulted for being the meticulous sort who wanted some schoolyard rationale for some part of something at the ready, just in case. Settled on: 'After various negotiations, I'd been compensated for delivery of the original manuscript, Sullivan requesting I stay on while he'd performed what he'd only described to me as *a ceremony*, the financial arrangements through his lawyer for Viggo, the check cut for me, all of it was business, nothing more—sure, Sullivan had struck me all manner of loony, yes it was bonkers to receive the payday I had, but I couldn't help it if I'd gotten lucky.' It'd make perfect sense to insist how, from my perspective, all had seemed copacetic when he'd made good our transaction, after which I'd left, promptly—there'd be no sign of foul play or third-party involvement in the hanging because he'd done it himself, a reality forensically provable.

'And the business about Nathan also wanting the manuscript ... being dead ... so on ..?' Show me a single way that could have anything to do with me and I'd show you how there was none! 'I'd given Nathan his own copy of the manuscript and that much has already been verified ...' I acted out as though a sitcom shrug was all it'd take to shoo Hellpop '… same as I had the author's kid. There'd been nothing transactional to those interactions—just furnished interested parties some Xeroxes, you know? But when Sullivan not only was willing to pay for the genuine article, but had insisted on it, how was I supposed to turn my nose up?'

Nodded, nodded, smoked, nodded, nodded, smoked in the parked car, nodded, smoked as I drove, as I parked, and a little more after I'd pulled into a service station to ask directions to the bank, which twenty minutes after another three cigs I entered the limeade scent and air-conditioned hush of, approached by a spic-and-span employee before I could even regret not having dressed in some one of Sullivan's fancy suits—explained I'd been sent by Mister Shallcross when quizzed 'May I help you?' and was right away referred to as 'You must be Mister Limoncello.'

Didn't know about *must be* '… but yes, Marc Limoncello. I was given a check …'

When an unbidden dubiousness warbled across my eyes, the agent smiled, holding up hands like 'Don't shoot' while chuckling how I absolutely mustn't worry. 'Mister Shallcross informed us to expect you—with a sum such as this, we've prepared it for discreet transport and, if you'd prefer, can have someone walk with you to your vehicle.'

As apparently all this was actually happening, I decided I might as well wave the kindness off with a cavalier 'I don't think that'll be necessary.'

'Very well, sir.' But the agent insisted I accompany him to an office inside of another office, where two staff members, in addition to the chap who'd greeted me, confirmed the count and then had me confirm the count, all of us signing a very heavy, carbon paper, triplicate form, after which I was escorted to a side door and given a nod indicative of how an eye would be kept on me until I'd left the property—probably some kind of liability on their end, based on the chance I was a huckster who'd pull a fake stick 'em up, 'cause can't never be too careful, these days.

And that, it seemed, was that—half-hour later, I was half-hour down a road I'd selected at random, was still for a stretch longer, the activity thoughtless ... by choice, I was driving, unattached, free. But as hours passed and my level of fatigue increased, the shape of my mood contorted, tightened to vice-grip, and any will to corral my thoughts slipped from my grasp—I was a pinball, was paddles batting me, a mechanism but one not built to exert total control over anything. I'd now absolutely committed a crime—a whole honking series of them—and there was no wresting out of it ... said crimes constituted direct involvement in a string of others I'd had no part in, making my innocence in them null and void. There was a bag of fifty-thousand cash dollars on the floor of the for-all-intents-and-purposes stolen automobile I'd driven from the scene of an unreported suicide after the victim had instructed his attorneys to do up an ironclad financial trust for my underage child—so much as my drifting thoughts keeping me from noticing a Stop sign, clunking too fast over a speed bump, changing lanes without signaling, or getting rear-ended might call for a license and registration to be produced and from that moment it was hop-skip to 'Step out of the vehicle, please' to some officer having a look to 'Would you care to explain ..?' to 'Just as soon as Mister Shallcross vouches for you, you're free to go.' Meanwhile: 'Can you tell me anything about why you'd been flagged in the system by a Detective Hellpop from outside some town called *Laampray*?'

Come nightfall, any illusion I'd been maintaining about 'life goes on' crumpled—I'd no strength left, mind figgy pudding, car slowing in an involuntary lean to the side of the road where it stopped and I wept, ugly, bulbous, cacophonous, cursed and screamed and bashed the steering wheel, the dash, flung my head around, punched my thighs, slapped my face, carrying on entirely unhinged until I passed out ... woke to discover slight drizzle had coated my car, the freckles of it cast out long before me in the headlights turned bright against the night fallen proper, my view nothing but oily smears of taillights and scattershot versions of headlights approaching first distant, upon me, then gone.

Told myself I'd take a room at the next motel I came to, would that very night listen to everything, do it, have it behind me, and once it was, I'd learn at the same time as everyone else what I'd do next—but before any of that, I needed to speak to my son.

The rain fell, kettle drum, kick drum, tuba, pots-and-pans in gatling until I spotted a public telephone, unlit and standoffish—lulling the car to a halt, I waited through four cigarettes' worth of talk radio in a language which might as well've been ancient Sumerian the static turned it so Greek to me, then pushed through the accordion door, shuddering it shut behind me. Windows streaked wet on the inside and drips to the floor through the ceiling, the racket from outside seeming inside and three times as belligerent, the booth was like standing in a discarded ticket stub—the dark of it pleased me, however, no need to spotlight my final scene. Fished coins from my pocket, set them in the return slot *clink clink* while I sparked a cigarette humming, worked my fingers in to retrieve them and *plunk plunk* one-by-one they gulped down the slot's gullet, a dial tone burping with each—let out a drag I could taste the stale textures of as the air around me hotboxed and gave the keypad my best *beep bop boop*, bracing myself.

Viggo's non-sequitur message, indicating he was presently unavailable, filled my ears—his imitation of a favorite line from *Space Ghost: Coast to Coast,* 'Hey Donny, Donny, Donny hey hey hey hey hey Donny ... where do we go when we die?'—and I thanked God for cellular, as there'd be no way he could abruptly jump on the line, interrupting me halfway through my last words.

Was coughing when it got my turn to speak, said a few sorrys as I got myself centered, said one more, then began: 'Hey Vigs, it's your dad. Sorry about the clatter and—shit, I hope this receiver even works—I know you don't wanna hear from me, but I kind of hope you know you actually do, because I hope you actually do ... or that you'll grow to be glad you did, anyway ... fuck ... Lookit: there's no way to explain anything, kiddo. I've no idea what you've been going through because I've no idea what you've been told or by who, by now—and though I've no doubt it's kinda some of it partway true, there's so much more to it ... but so much more to it than what I could never begin to explain, anyway ... so I don't know where to begin ... so can't fucking fathom how anyone else'd be able ... so I won't try—that's not why I'm calling. Viggy: I know I skunked it all up—I flushed everything out and did it so long ago, but I never meant you to be part of it. Listen: I want you to know you'll be taken care of, okay? There's gonna be some lawyers about some money and it's no gag, it's no scam, nothing can be done about it, that money is yours, man, only yours—they're gonna tell you that and when they do it's the truth. I'm promising you how the money was come across is all clean and good, and no matter if anyone tells you there's something up about it there isn't, okay? You'll always be taken care of ... but I don't mean the money ... your mom will take care of you, Viggo, she always has and—hey!—maybe someday down the road something I've said or done will be of help, too ... but I can't say, that'll be up to you. I want you to hear me, okay? I'll never forget you—and I never have forgotten you—I'm a louse, an earwig, there's no way to explain myself or how I've failed you and keep on doing, but I never had anything except you down my heart, wherever that is, whatever that is. I know you won't understand one goddamn word of whatever I'm saying right now and you'll think what you think and, regardless of anything I say, you're gonna do what you do—maybe you'll do the opposite of what I say, to spite me or because you just would, but I'm so greedy I need to say all this to you and think to myself that, even if you don't listen, it'll be somehow something you do because of me. There has to be some connection—you understand? Whatever you do, however I enter in—even if not at all—I want to tell myself you'll know I love you, no matter what you do me, love or kerplunk. This is going to sound insane, but please listen to what I'm about to say. Viggo: Don't listen to that fucking band—don't ever listen to *They Might Be Giants*. It couldn't hurt you, I know that—I understand none of what's happened can happen again or is anything to do with you and that the music can't touch you—but please just stay far far away from it. Do that one thing for me, I'm literally begging. Destroy anything of them you have—forget it, it isn't real, it never happened,

alright? I know I'm the one who told you about it, but pretend I didn't—or pretend you did get it from me and that's precisely why you'll cast it away and be done! Shit ... son ... I promise you, I know exactly how insane I sound, right now—better than you ever could, man, okay? I've no idea what you'll come to learn after I hang up, here ... but the only thing that matters to me is that you know I would've given anything on this shit-hole of a planet—anything!—to've gone to that fucking Film Fest with you, you idiot! I wanted to share that—to share everything, share myself, wanted us to breathe each other's whole goddamned lives ... but I fouled it rotten, all the way from the jump. Listen to me, Viggo: Just be you, be brave, be beautiful, be a face staring out of a hole—I don't care! Oh God, Viggo—your face, kid ... your face ... it's a beautiful architecture, okay? That's the only way to say it, so just know what that means, can you—know it's impossible to say what I think of you, but that you being possible is the finest, truest thing I've ever stumbled on. I know this might be scary, everything I'm saying ... you might've stopped listening ... I know other people might be listening, too ... but you're the only one I'm speaking to, man. I love you, Viggo. I'm sorry. You'll always be okay, Vigs, I promise—you'll always be ...'
But I couldn't keep it up—my voice went dull then breathing then silent. I hung up, depleted, deeply ashamed I'd ended things exactly as he'd expect me to, which was by not—I was a man who didn't even know how to vanish.

I tightened and shivered in a palsy of tears, lit up, automatic, and tried to smoke through the salt of my mucus—slammed myself left and right, full weight into my shoulders, but the booth didn't budge it just grew annoyed, so I stepped out awkwardly, allowing it the privilege of feeling it'd spat me, hocked up a furball, a flabby coin of phlegm. In the rain, attempted to finish my smoke and then to light another when I couldn't—shielded my crumby Bic and *Lucky Strike* with my hand, my coat, wasted two, three, four ... one last even when trotting back to the car I could easily have stepped inside for protection.

The night shrank to an enormous size, but less than the enormity of any other—all the world condensed around the car I cowered in. Talk radio picked back up right where it'd left off, as far as I knew, crackle-voices prattling while I let the cabin grow overwarm and allowed smoke to seep out the cracked window—I spent awhile trying to focus on clouds in the dark, doing my damnedest to sound profound as I insisted how if there was always this much dark, we'd never have known there were clouds, and if there were always this many clouds, we'd never have learned the sea wasn't blue just never would've thought it was ... circumstances ruined so much. Recollected I'd once told Viggo about how, when I was his age—he'd been quite small, at the time—it'd never disappointed me to learn the moon wasn't really following me, but had infuriated me to discover I couldn't follow it—that no matter how firmly or stealthily I moved, I was never behind it, never in front, it had no face, no back, and all I did toward it was away and all I did away from it was neither. 'What if that was all he remembered me by?' I asked as, without much meaning to, I started the engine, pulling onto the road. 'I'd really quite like that,' I smiled ... but knew it was something he already didn't remember and wondered if I liked that, even more.

Then was on the road long enough to know I couldn't yet drive, posed legitimate danger to the innocent, my head far too adrift for activity, but also knew I couldn't risk falling asleep, so pulled over slowly, terrified of Highway Patrol or of good Samaritans—if any human being so much as offered me a hearty Hello, I'd either shatter to pieces or lash out, leave them a pile of useless limbs leaking an odor, one more thing to regret, another moment I'd be unable to explain. It was uncanny to feel as though I understood everything while unable to articulate even where it was I thought myself going, felt certain there'd be a next day and then a next—another another another and other others after those ... was more uncertain than ever, in fact, that there'd ever come a The End, succumbed to a terrifying sense of surety that nothing would ever be over for me or had ever once had the slightest intention of being. What I was was strange, raveled, and absolute—I was something happening which'd even stop-going-on forever.

It was a hundred miles before I had to pull over again, this time to vomit out the driver's door, still seat-belted, onto pavement wet with a rain which seemed Hell-bent on imping me no matter which direction I scurried—dry heaved into the sink at a Rest Stop toilet, next, nearly half-an-hour of cackling up fetid air, cheeks tasting sour, fists slamming every flat surface I knew in my heart was sturdy enough not to break but flimsy enough that my striking it wouldn't hurt too badly.

The entire time I ventured the random way to my final motel, I continued to mumble words out to Viggo—even if I was just thinking the phrase-work it was a mumble, a mutter which not even I could decipher. The sensation in those moments was like dissolving in stale cola while make-believing other moments in which I'd have another chance to correct myself, opportunity to add one more detail to my Past—two, three, fifteen, as many as I wished I'd never need to. There was no honest reason I couldn't say more and I knew it—it was a simple matter to call my son from wherever I'd stop, or else to drive home ... drive to Viggo ... plain as day, there existed a life in which I might speak to him ... but the life I was driving in already wasn't it. Turning off the road I was on would feel pretend, a betrayal—the least I could do was hold true to my word, not backpedal from the honesty I'd dumped on him, undeserving ... what a fiend I'd be to make him experience that only to follow-up with a 'Hey, just kidding, pal—I get that way sometimes.'

Made a deal, finally, that I'd fill up the tank only a quarter-way at whichever service station I crossed paths with and then drive those few dollars to fumes—knew I'd find where it was I needed to be, exactly as I could go no further, knew exactly how many hours I'd require, behind closed doors, and wondered, in terror, how many I'd get, after those.

'There's no reason for anything but there's a reason for that—couldn't be, yet there is—while, at the same time, nothing dissected or post-mortemed changes how there's a reason for everything but no reason for that, just the same ... whatever we say, we're saying the same thing ...' is what I mumbled for Viggo—what I should've mumbled to him, said to him, sung to him, what maybe I had, once, when he was too young to know anything I was saying and I too young to've meant what I did, now—and even if I had, now still wished I had better.

[*a duck and stryker was a turtle*]

No reason for it, but I paid up front to keep the room a solid week and, for a jape, decided I'd sign with the name *Rasputin Evangeline*—my plan, so far as I had one, was to hit the road as soon as I'd listened to the music, gotten myself rested up, though which road and where to were details left murky, half-baked, irrelevant. Did my affable best to explain away the shabby state of me to the woman who'd no interest in hearing any such thing but was chained to the desk with the bad luck of having to—improvised a detailed recounting of the entirely fictitious saga how I'd, two hundred miles ago, gotten ash-canned from my job then been kicked to the curb by my live-in girlfriend, on top, so'd hopped in my trusty automobile to make a clean break of mid-life. It only later occurred to me how, despite my pusillanimous prattle, the poor creature might've thought I'd been making a pass at her or had it in mind to see how low she'd stoop for an honest day's wage—considering the cash I'd insisted on flaunting, lettuce crisp bills so snappy they seemed hot off the press, not to mention how belabored a point I'd made of requiring 'a room in back and as far away from anyone else as possible, because I might get a tad bit noisy—I'll sure as heck pay more if guaranteed isolation' there were only so many conclusions available for the lady to draw.

Spent far longer than necessary fiddling with the blinds, as though on the brink of a science which could make *shut* into its own brand of gravity, then activated the coffee pot and indulged in a vigorous brush of my teeth despite knowing the cigarette already waiting on the countertop was straight away going to ruin any improvement I managed—got the room nice and smokey, in short order, the only thing missing some bourbon ... which thankfully I learned I'd possessed the good sense to've swiped off Sullivan in my clattering mad dash of beating feet, a bottle of libations named after someone I'd never heard of, the priciness of which stood apparent from the mere thickness of the glass, bundled amongst the bedsheets protecting the playback devices. These I set up on one of the two twin beds at my disposal, spending a concentrated while sorting out the various cassettes, records, discs, wishing I'd brought along Post-It notes, as there was gonna be a whole bunch of back-and-forth between one format and another as the albums did an endless do-si-do—found a memo pad next to the room phone, so decided I'd use it to keep myself methodical ... though oddly didn't have much fear I'd need any worksheet ... I'd intuit all when the time came ... the lusciousness of a first snootful of my purloined hootch reminded me how unlikely any of this coming off correctly was, to begin with ... whatever 'correctly' was even supposed to be, by this point.

Sullivan's handwritten list contained only five-hundred-thirteen selections out of the well-more-than-one-thousand on Benjamin's Master—so what was even the deal? All this trouble of insisting on painstaking, definitive order only to do things *a la carte*, in the clutch, based on—what?—an interpretation of his old pal's dithering into a Dictaphone? 'Not to mention ...' another *glug-glug-glug* of bottleneck at forty-five degrees had to add '... that nothing tangible was ever going to've happened.' I nodded how correct this insight was—spooky as using the favorite playthings of the freshly dead felt, to me they meant nothing and thus represented no danger. It wasn't my business why Sullivan'd topped himself, but it sure wasn't on account of putting together a sub-par mixtape—plus, even if it was, I'd no horse in the race, thus stood impervious to whichever virus had diseased the sad bastard's wit.

The more time I spent in banal preparation of the correct versions of the correct songs in the correct order, the more ludicrous the enterprise revealed itself to be, even for cryptic mumbo jumbo—why was there no accounting for how much time must elapse between each, where were the occult specifications of day of the year, type of the moon, how were the vague terms *in-a-row* or *back-to-back* enough to proceed under the jurisdiction of? Not that I knew why I was arguing with myself about such falderal— I was strictly monkey-doing what monkey'd seen and going even that far on account of the flimsiest just-in-case I'd ever heard of.

The letter addressed to Nathan I'd placed atop the television, wax seal snapped off, but no immediate molestation further ... because I did have a case of the creeps and had to fess up to as much ... more than that, still felt compelled not to read, not yet, not until the music was going ... though I'd not only no idea how come but felt actively resistant to the condition even as I acquiesced. Furthermore, I discovered myself entirely unable to stall, an uncannily intense draw toward getting started tugged me, as though even the effect of the alcohol in my blood had been overridden, my focus not adrift, rather single-minded to a degree which didn't seem possible considering I was pickled to the tune of a third-of-a-bottle—I do recall explaining to myself how such attentiveness was almost certainly an illusion, brought on precisely because I was soused near incoherent, the sort of headspace which wouldn't be recalled, come morning, and one I figured I'd experienced many times before, my lack of memory on the matter an Augustinian Proof of as much.

Sure enough, after a minute or two spent adjusting the volume dial on the heels of setting the first tune spinning, any resistance to reading the letter drained from me—I strode across the room, snatched it up, almost a laugh, a sneer, like one part of myself was goading another. 'Go ahead, it's not like it'll do you any good now,' I may even've said aloud ... maybe curled my lip or pouted it in response to so distinct a sensation a nose had been thumbed my direction. The communique was a single sheet, no more than two-thirds of a front page, not-quite-half of a reverse, typed, unsigned, and speckled stiff as though a cough had been coughed by a head turning away, not quite in time, after a bad sip of coffee— I sat to the bed lip, placed it beside me, attention turned to setting the next selection going, this time from a cassette I half-wondered how I'd known would be queued up properly, curious why I'd taken it as a matter of course that Sullivan'd set it back to proper start position ... another odd sensation, the first of many similar ... an un-earned certainty coupled with an unsought understanding that there'd be another selection off the same cassette, later on, which I'd take the time to get in place while vinyl spun or compact-disc whirled ... as though an entire schematic of sequence had been stamped on my brain, cajoling motions automatic, my will soft like gelatin, no weight of exertion to any labor I undertook.

Only while the music played, in the helpings of moments wherein I knew several coming tunes were set in fine order, did I seem to, all in a blink, turn full attention to reading—then, in a blink twice as rapid, I'd set the missive down, mid-sentence, mid-consideration, as though a scribbled bloop had appeared in the corner of a projection screen to prompt me it was time to spool the next reel.

> Nathan, I am sorry. If you're reading this, know that. Sullivan, if you're reading this, know that I know you'll never share it with our friend, and know this is a betrayal I forgive. Nathan, if you're reading, know that if Sullivan had kept my words from you, it would have been just as well. These words are for you though, Nathan. Sullivan, if you've found them, know that whatever you do with them will not matter, that I begrudge you nothing, understand you, always have, and accept what is to come as I accepted what came before.

I'd no idea the context or deeper meaning behind anything I read and don't know how reading it made me feel, too down my own head to truly claim I comprehended anything anymore—every crumb of the world, language to flesh, by then too far out in leftfield to be taken in rationally. What seemed suddenly of vital importance was: Why hadn't I read this, before, opened the envelope, back at the very start—why had I resisted doing so at any occasion it would've seemed appropriate, kept it secret from Nathan, from Sullivan, waited until this room, music surrounding me, closing me in its maw? I'd experienced hesitation on the matter before pressing Play for the first time, but this present wave was far graver—an internal lashing began, as though some component of myself was contained in a glass box inside me, conjoined yet peculiarly apart from ... I felt divided, made sectional, each portion alive, total, and of its own mind, yet only one piece in command at a given time, all others following along or else waiting in dull patience for their turn ... until it felt only one section held primacy ... that I was it, but wasn't ... had reduced to no more than a sentient fragment, being permitted the tension of thought under strict parental supervision ... no longer seemed I was the one with thoughts, despite more than ever being aware it'd been my thoughts, before whichever fracture had taken place, which'd brought me where I was ... as though my previous thoughts had been a requirement but were no longer, still present but ignored, understanding they weren't in any danger, merely of no contemporary utility ... awaiting some remaining purpose, only perhaps yet to come ...

> Nathan: none of this is what you'd dreamed. You know, for myself, I never dreamed it anything, have been merely governed by the compulsion of whichever notion infected me, or else am the infection to whichever notion I've corrupted the natural order of. It's impossible to know who coupled with what, what with whom. Linnell had a lyric for everything, so we always asserted, and I find it almost quaint how the one most fitting to me is the one which is most everyone's first very favorite. Yes, Nathan: I am underwater, but don't know if I'm wet and can tell the water has no idea if it's me.

I felt I was where I belonged ... where I was *necessary* ... except it remained undeniable that had I never entered the narrative, discovered the manuscript, cassette, letter, if all parties concerned had come into possession of what Benjamin'd intended them to, for whatever reason he had, nothing would've transpired differently than how I'd witnessed it, all involved bound to've proceeded exactly as they had—I was a part ... but not of anything.

> I never told you I'd taken in one more live show, after our last together, which I'd so somberly promised you was The Last. It was during this performance I'd attended alone that my marching orders became set. Somehow, though I'd heard tell it happened often enough, it was the first time I'd heard those lyrics sung, the ones written in the liner notes but which we'd believed left out of the performance, on purpose, as though hearing them was not meant to have connection to commerce, as though they could not be contained, recorded, caged. But the pulsing words must have required personal interface, inducing Flansburg to seed them out to vital audience, at times, dispersing them like dandelion spoors. I was soil, it seemed, which could accept them. You know the ones, know them well: *You said you were the King of Liars / and I believed you and called you sire / but I realize now that I have been deceived.*

Nathan would've taken the manuscript and, with it, continued to plod fruitlessly at his theorems, remained zealous, obsessed with capturing a power or codifying some connective proof of everything—had he read the words Benjamin'd left, would've twisted what seemed their earnest entreaty to stand down into a mandate he do anything but, convinced himself Benny, The Conduit, had only been capable of carrying matters so far, and how it was fear for his friends which'd caused him to flinch, lurching off the path at the worst possible moment. To a mind like his, the true meaning of his lost friend's missive would've been interpreted as unconscious communication, born of a languageless understanding that both he and Sullivan needed to make up their own minds about the materials Benjamin'd bequeathed—after all: if the directive were 'Do Not Proceed,' he might as well have destroyed the tools which'd allow it.

Likewise, Sullivan would've construed the remarks as Benjamin's method of proving, once and for all, that Nathan was incorrect while he, himself, always had been and remained in the right—whatever the manuscript would accomplish was too personal, individual, and absolute to be treated as a limp data set, a carcass to dissect postulates from—he'd have taken in his dead fellow's pleas but never heeded them, warped their intent to suit whatever he'd desired to accomplish, treated them as instructions to eliminate from the board anyone who might possess the merest hint of what the document made possible ... Nathan, therefore, the most vital to dispense with.

> You may discover what it was you wanted, Nathan, but you will find nothing in it. Or perhaps you shall land on exactly what it is you've sought all this time, unearth more of it than you'd dared hoped would be in evidence. I've no idea, and frankly, never concerned myself with such trivia. No matter if you find what your heart desired, what is in these pages, truly, is not anything you, I, nor anyone could ever have conceived even the most peripheral notion of.

But all my understanding, vague to the point of pudding, struck me as of increasingly little relevance, as meanwhile the music swirled as though sweating through the motel room around me, tune after tune I felt unable to halt myself queuing up, disc, cassette, record, a *drip drip drip* of melodies and lyrics chewing their way into my unlistening ears while nicotine coursed down me, bourbon kept me passively lubricated, while pressure yet built behind my eyes to explain myself ... why ... hadn't ... I ... read ... the ... letter ..? Countless times I could've opened it, at least, photocopied it the same as I had everything else I'd scrutinized—what had possessed me to insist on retaining the originals but to keep myself from auditing the one sheet of content a flimsy sealed envelope contained until, all of a sudden, I found myself compelled, at a point I'd not be able to stop myself even as I felt myself desperate to?

> If you've found them, Nathan, please tender these pages to Sullivan, too. Sullivan, if you have them in hand, I know you'll never share them with our friend, so shall not implore you, rather will

admit how, in a way, I truly am thankful for your greed. But I warn you—please Nathan, if you have found this, share my warning with Sullivan, duly—that while everything he had always spoken of he most certainly will find, I can only beg him, with all the love we once shared, to walk away. Sullivan, what you are and what you will become is here, my once dearest, but only one of those things ought be held precious. Who you were, Sullivan, and who yet you are—there's no need to become what you sought to. Better to have never been than to become that, as I know, no doubt, you shall see. Perhaps, reading this, you will call yourself uncaring of your fate, perhaps call yourself accepting. Regardless, you will see.

It was as though I was, for the first time, realizing how nothing I'd experienced in the previous weeks made any sense to me while, at the same time, knowing I knew damned well I'd experienced nothing but that exact realization since the starting gun—there *was* sense to be made, however, and I entrenched myself in such stance, infantile in my insistence that sense also always *could've been*. While dwindling to delirium, I understood: Benjamin had written the words on the sheets I held, addressed them to Nathan yet knowing Sullivan might discover them first and choose never to pass them along, sealed everything meant for the both, all together, in the vent of a motel, seemingly in a bout of fatalism and exhaustion, drained to the point he'd felt out-of-body, out-of-mind—the Rational and Irrational had collided for him, as it seemed they were for me, and the only method to reconcile the two was by plugging myself into the equation, believing me crucial to some process, a checkpoint on a life-cycle, a stage-of-development or a predatory entity circling a larval one, something to do with all, and all to do with me, since the beginning ... I was the thing Benjamin had warned his friends there mustn't be, acting exactly as it must.

In the broken quiet of a ramshackle fifty-bucks-per night rental bedroom, mind epileptic with music it seemed to be attempting to dislodge, as though heads of ticks nuzzling ever deeper subcutaneous, I couldn't get shut of needing to know, experience, understand how what I'd become involved in wasn't over, couldn't be, until I made it so—since it *hadn't* been without me, it *never could've*.

> I am already ended, for I have already composed and already listened. It was a pleasure to do and my thoughts were only of us three. What is to come is what I am, even now, causing through writing these words, which I both resist and insist on. Yes, please know I am resisting, even as I struggle to address you, to ward you off, that I know the same words which might achieve their purpose will instead achieve its opposite and yet must be written for their intended aim in spite of their understood and unavoidable end. I watch my hands type sentences even as I fruitlessly will them to cease, or to allow only some and not others, to trick what cannot be halted, and as I do so, I embrace the impotence of both acts. I see before me all that will come to pass after I am gone the same as I see how I shall come to pass and know I will walk myself to it. These words you read are moments already after me, yet I move through them as though a grave-mouth awaiting its ghost. It is my fault. I am doing this to you because I have already done it. I am doing it to myself because I could have done nothing else. It is no different for either of you who found me, as innocent of knowing who or what I was as I was myself. You were always what you are, which is what you will be, were what you'd become before becoming it. I no longer fancy I could have existed in this only myself, dragging no others down alongside me. I found this music and shared it after it had found me and colonized. You simply found me and there can be no fault in that. It is my fault, but I understand fault is a word which simply describes some of us, while faultless is the word which defines all. We are, all of us, born of ourselves only to birth somebody's Armageddon—but it is all I can do to, at least, not have you tromp toward yours still blind to its face.

Whatever would happen to me when the music stopped, it'd been killed for—even were it nothing, the ether had blood soaking its hands. For whatever reason, the prospect of Sullivan having taken his own life after experiencing whatever he had didn't frighten me, nor did it unnerve my spirit that I'd grown absolutely convinced he'd taken other lives to make certain what I was now experiencing would be experienced by him alone ... or had he done what he had so that I might be the one to experience ... unwittingly paved my path forward ... though I'd no path I knew of, even as I trod my way, partway automaton ... had he done the same, a mechanism of his own outlook, assured of himself to the point he shrugged off choice, accepted instruction in place of it, feeling blessed that the automation foist on him exactly resembled his heart's content? He hadn't destroyed the materials, either, had left them behind, exactly as Benjamin, knowing full well I possessed means to scoop them up, might replicate each and every particle of what he'd achieved—had done so despite every other action I presumed of the man demanded him incapable of that very thing.

> These materials must be destroyed, dismembered, never combined, Nathan. Sullivan, I beg you to heed this, as well. While even still I compose this and sense I will leave things to exactly the opposite of that fate, I find I am allowed to, compelled to give this warning. Take what you want of what I have written and then present it to Sullivan, keeping only this letter for yourself, speaking from it to our friend only my plea that he halt. Sullivan, explore all to your soul's content even after reading these words, but keep them from Nathan, I beg you. Please know the safest I could make the world was to leave parts assundered, no one person with any understanding of how they combine. At best, you each shall toil in the same playful games of comparison as we once so joyfully did. At worst, so much worse.

I made earnest attempt after earnest attempt to narrate the tale to someone, as though a crust of ancient history rendered into a cogent chain of events, ticking from Nathan, Sullivan, and Benjamin meeting, to their various views developing, to the manuscript's composition, to my discovering it, to the moment I spun there, reading Benjamin's letter aloud in mocking tones of yakkity-yak while swaying a ramshackle boogie to whichever song leaked from cheap speakers, filling the room slowly to drown me—but it didn't seem possible, the story always one of those concentric circles of conspiracy within conspiracy proving no conspiracy at all, simply the windmills of our minds, the imperious need to sort meaning of chaos, chaos of meaning, unwilling to settle for or to let go of either.

> Nathan, Sullivan, whichever of you holds this letter, I beg you to understand it is the only item which must be destroyed. There are no words in it but for you, regardless, and I've no inkling what might happen if, by horrible error, some hapless person were to put use to what is in my work without any understanding of what you hold dear, can make even less a stab in the dark at what they'd do with no understanding of anything. For the love of all that is holy, let there be nothing left behind, Nathan. Sullivan, I beg you, let, at least, Nathan be.

The only way any manner of narrative worked out was if I'd always, specifically been meant to discover exactly what I had, as I had, when I had—for everything which'd transpired to've led me to the moment I was experiencing, such moment always having been designed to lead me to accepting my part in all which preceded it: to understand I'd never had a choice, but choice didn't matter, because I'd have chosen everything exactly as had been dictated, regardless ... I was an aberrant, a free-will whose lack-off free-will didn't raise revolt in itself but rather confirmed the tranquility of its sublimation.

To finish anything out, I'd needed to listen to the music, exactly as I was—only the appropriate tracks, chosen through methods as random and without meaning to me as those which'd led to their composition, all played in the designated order distilled from the absolute, in full possession of all information Benjamin had imparted. I was the only person actually capable of doing what Benjamin had intended while being precisely the one he'd insisted should never—none who'd come to this point before me, or even possibly might've, had been privy to the full spate of requisite elements: manuscript, cassette, and warning contained in the letter ... no one but me, The Unbeliever ... and Benjamin, beset with regret.

Oh, it was easy-breezy to soothe myself with how everything

may've been for this reason or for that, was fair enough to posit how even were I to listen to the music in the order prescribed, exactly as I was, it'd turn out harmless because I didn't believe anything would, or even possibly could, happen—yet there I was, the music playing into the void of me even as I refused to give it attention back. I wondered what I was afraid of, how I'd explain myself if asked 'Did you listen?' and answered 'No'—what would be revealed of me were I to've walked away, right at the end, when the only other end awaiting me was one I wanted no part of ... how would I be looked at if my last words on the matter were 'It hadn't seemed worth it—I wasn't interested, wasn't curious'?

> This never should have been. I am sorry, for I know I am nearly done writing. Would that I could go on forever. But now, none of us can go on, even much longer, at all.

Well I was as curious as venom ... lugged the radio into the bed with me and there inserted the disc which contained the final necessary track, laid down, pressed Play. As the guitar, the drum, the vocals began, I felt unmoored, both perversely and correctly myself, more actual than I'd ever been, and smiled as though I could sing along to words I'd never heard but felt I knew better than the voice crooning them—about the crane they'd need to take the house I'd built for her apart and how, baby, wait, I'd never meant to say 'nightmare' ... giggling in self-referential pleasure as I stared at—

[*every four is waltz again*]

—the room ceiling ... except ... no ... my eyes were closed, so could stare at no ceiling ... and yet my eyes were staring ... *my* eyes were closed, staring ... *the* eyes were closed ... *eyes* were ... I couldn't quite put my finger on it ... *the* finger on it ... *a* finger ... experienced a deep swell of confusion, word choice, orientation all out-of-whack. It wasn't dark, for example, the world was simply on the other side of eyelids I could've sworn'd been open ... except I knew, also, how if I opened my eyes it *would* be dark on the outside of them ... knew not just in the way closed eyes could somewhat make out which degree of illumination they'd open to, but because they'd been staring into dark, at a ceiling, before I'd closed them ... a jockeying for control, for supremacy went on in my thoughts, *the* thoughts, *thoughts* ... and when it struck me there was no music—how it didn't seem there had been any and also that there had, music which I'd heard but hadn't listened to, was inventing, not remembering—whichever eyes the eyes were opened.

It *was* dark, turned out, and a ceiling *was* there and music wasn't ... I was ... but didn't quite feel I was ... while feeling I was, less-and-less ... didn't quite feel I wasn't ... while feeling I was, more-and-more. The room was dark, not twilit, artificial dark caused by artificial light removed, dimmed, or blocked by the not-quite-closedness of a door a bright world was leaned against the opposite side of—dark in that way you can see perfectly well until you actually attempt to look at something, see it, focus. I knew this, despite I wasn't looking around, just up at the ceiling ... at *a* ceiling ... thought to myself how the room was dark in the way rooms are when depicted as dark on television ... images of such rooms filled my head ... strategically lit, presented to suggest pitch black while remembering an audience needed to see, blue tints diffused, smeared hints of orange, sort of soot-brown mingled in, shades of colors all the world had settled on for nighttime when nighttime was built on a soundstage for a big screen or a television set when up too late and listening for footsteps more than to whoever is hiding from whatever they might be in the dark which isn't, in the scene which isn't real, and which glows the room around you not-at-all-bright and all-the-darker-for-it ... couldn't tell was *I* thinking this ... or was *I* ... or what the difference was ... merely that there was one ... and that, either way, whatever either *I* was thinking was being *thought*.

It took what seemed a long while and also didn't seem any time to settle my mind on what was so peculiar about the ceiling: it was how I *did* recognize it, not that I *didn't*, and not a *general* recognition, either, far from it—to pass the time, to drift myself asleep, I'd specifically designed a little game of connecting certain darker dots in the speckled pattern of a ceiling tile and had decided a spot of discoloration mixed with a bit of shadow looked, from one vantage, like a hand stuck halfway down a can, from another, like a stout submarine, adrift, bobbing, at peace, and from yet another, like a scruffy goat with its tongue out, coughing, not braying, those dots on that further panel representing the expectorate spritzing away like the gasp of cola commercial carbonation. The sounds around me were familiar, too, but in a *barely* way—in fact, seemed less familiar for my listening, as I seemed to've already gotten used to them enough to not listen or individuate any, heard them long enough to just know them ... yet hadn't and, in fact, didn't know what they were at least as much as I did ... they weren't familiar like from television, no, rather from having been proximate to them, awhile, the sort of background collage which'll be acutely missed when first moved away from then never really recalled or ever thought about again with any specificity ... I was accustomed to them, yes, but didn't know what each was ... never had, either ... or rather, I could guess, but in a manner which felt *too precise* ... as though I could guess, now, better than I'd been able to, moments ago ... more-context poured in to drown less-context out ... I seemed to understand the outline the voices in the corridor would have if I could make them out fully, certain ones over a speaker, muffled from where I lay, the sound of wheels on tile, of telephones, papers shuffled, footfalls, beeps of varying variety, elevator dings ... I knew them all from quite recently but also things like them from for-a-long-time ... a long long time longer than I could exactly say was possible, other than like how time functions in a dream or when telling a lie.

Sitting up was difficult—I knew why and didn't, mouth cotton, lips pasted shut, almost painful to part, dehydration, but not exactly ... reached to a cup I knew had recently contained juice, was prepared for the flavor, the lukewarm thinness from ice a few hours melted, drank it down too quickly with a mouth too small and coughed so feebly I wanted to cough, again ... except when I coughed even as hard as I could manage it felt incorrect ... not only for the amount of effort required, but for failing to be as large as a far weaker cough should've been ... I felt light, small, *puny* ... a headache convinced me, for a moment, this was because of a fever or medication coursing me, but my hands argued otherwise ... hands the sight of which didn't alarm me, though it feels peculiar to say so: hands I recognized immediately as my own, immediately as not-my-own, the conflicting impressions neutralizing each other ... turned them over and over and over ... girlish hands, childish, the wrist barely a full doodled circle around ... opened and closed the hands, watched myself do it, watched it done ... and understood myself to be twelve years old ...

All of my memories contradicted this—recollections which felt hot of tears and stale from music half-listened to and fearful of and for names I knew I most definitely knew—Sullivan, Nathan, Benjamin ... *Viggo* ... these names, Viggo most of all, weren't as though lingering impressions from a dream ... in fact, *other* memories I possessed were more akin to those, especially the memories of the dream I'd been having what felt like only hours ago, before I'd opened my eyes after thinking they already should've been ... memories of the room I lay in, how I'd come there, the circumstances under which, even the games with the ceiling tiles, grew increasingly unreal ... real but *diminishing* ... *fading* as though a dreamt joke remembered upon waking, one you feel you'd laughed hard enough at there'd be no need to write down and only later understand you'd never laughed at, only dreamed you did ... if I didn't jot down the impressions which seemed to be ticking themselves out of belonging to me, they'd be gone forever, while meanwhile the impressions growing stronger in me, which I knew weren't impressions but recollections of all that I was, couldn't be scrubbed clear for trying ... even if I did write the losing impressions out, in detail, I'd never truly recollect them, would simply have words to read over, disembodied language, perusing a document would be the only way it'd feel I was recalling and even then, with each successive review, I'd know all I remembered was having read the words a previous time ... which felt *strange* ... I wanted to understand it better, to express it more pristinely to myself before I knew I'd not only never be able to but would never again harbor any desire to or know I ever had ... but I couldn't reckon how to make that happen ... how to make the Self I was *forgetting* be the Self I *was* ... how to make any part of myself *unforgotten* ... or any one of my *selves* ...

I was exactly like something I'd always said, except knew I'd never said it, as well—was akin to a song I'd heard the way you hear a song before writing it or even thinking it up, for real. I recalled telling Viggo how it'd be impossible to prove you hadn't only this very instant sprung into existence—that whichever moment you found yourself cognizant of might as well have been your first, ever, and that despite an ability to speak of the Past, what'd already happened might as well not've and other people who'd claim they remembered it the same as you did really would *remember it the same as you did,* suddenly, completely, contradictory, and not at all. I'd told him that the knowledge of the Past is all *there* and all *false*, beginning its existence only in the first moment of yours, told him the Past is just language, the same for everyone who'd only started in the same moment you had, language enough for all to remember but never verbatim, to think of exactly as differently enough to convince ourselves there was a moment before our first. 'In the past twelve minutes ...' I'd one time said '... you could've died and come back forty-three times over—might've lived a whole life as someone else and, precisely when that somebody perished, immediately started being who you are now, even though somebody else was them before and will now never know they're not ... or maybe nobody else was before, period—what *you're* thinking *is* thinking for the first time, the last time, and again, all at once.' Why I'd told Viggo such things, I didn't know ... but knew I had ... and when I had ... when he'd been too young to know what I'd meant or that I was making up what I meant as I went ... and when I hadn't been too young for him to be so young ... when I'd never believed what I'd said could truly be true, might happen, had instead known it didn't and couldn't ... all it'd been was something to say ... like so many things ... like everything, then.

It felt suffocating to recollect myself, the previous days of hanged men and bags-of-cash and driving and telephone calls and driving more exhausted me to know about, and the days leading up to them, the months before, the years alone, the decades with others stretching behind me made me weary ... to be able to think all the way back to when I would've been the age I was now but when I would've been myself being it ... except ... I *was* myself being it ... and soon would be ... soon *only* would be ... it felt pummeling, as though *me* was something being mashed through the mesh of a drain ... knowing there existed *nothing* beneath the drain ... existed literally *nowhere* for what was mashed to go and so it'd *become* the nothing it was being mashed into ... a nothing with no parts ... an *everything* if only it were anything enough to call itself that ...

I lay back down, closed my eyes, told myself to sleep or to stare at the ceiling until I thought about it how I'd thought about it before, but could no longer recall having played the game of dots—didn't see the shapes I'd seen, even though there were only so many places they could be hidden and though if I'd ever seen them at all I oughta be able to see them, again ... especially already knowing what they were ... only so many dots ... so many stains ... only so many patterns to recognize or claim to ... even if someone else told me 'When I look there, I see an elephant on fire—can you?' I'd be able to make it out or to make something up in order to convince myself I did ... but I couldn't see what I'd seen, any longer ... only remembered what it'd been *called*, not how it'd *looked* ... only remembered being confused by how I'd know I'd know what it was called ... only remembered not knowing, yet knowing the name of what wasn't known.

  'Do we all see the Man-in-the-Moon, or do we all see something else that we call Him, so think we agree?' I remembered a friend asking me that ... not a friend ... no ... I remembered being asked that by Viggo ... remembered Viggo asking 'What would thinking be like without any language?' ... then telling me he'd decided there could be no thought ... remembered how I'd argued that even animals think, so there must, in fact, always be language ... and how he'd argued how things don't need to think to be, don't even need to react to exist ... 'If randomness truly is random, it oughta never seem that way, right?' ... who'd told me that, asked me that ... I asked myself, but also already knew who had ... it was simply that the me which was now just part-of-me and which shortly wouldn't be and would then be forgotten-by-me-entirely didn't know and was screaming in anguish against my ability to answer things it couldn't, my certainty a ghoulish affront, the proof of my absoluteness attained at the expense of its anything.

  I vaguely felt there was supposed to be someone else in the room with me ... vaguer still was the feeling of who ... I saw evidence of their now absent presence as I scooted myself from the bed ... a coat, a paperback, the scraps of a finished meal, tray set on the floor, blanket, pillow ...

My bare feet to the tile felt appropriate but shocking, a touch more the latter, the full weight of my body peculiar to the point of discombobulation—made me feel I ought be capable of bounding through the ceiling, while at the same time the fatigue to the limbs was entirely appropriate. Tottered toward what I knew was the restroom, a toilet I'd sat on before, not often enough it was familiar, and also not ever—a light sliced active in an outrage of mint orange, settled to brown, tan, teeth-tartar-white once my eyes unwound from their recoil at the stab. Experienced no jolt at the sight of my face, despite I knew I was deeply unsettled how there wasn't a jolt and how the face wasn't mine ... it wasn't *mine*, it was *me* ... though no touch to my pre-adolescent torso seemed incorrect, no wave of my arms, as I took poses, made faces ... I wasn't *mine*, I was *me*.

Before long, I felt faint from exertion ... anxious also, like I'd not want to explain myself having left the bed ... didn't want to cause any worry in ... *someone* ... fretted at having to field questions I felt in no shape to offer sensitive reply to ... tightened into a tremor of terror at the prospect of having to speak ... another at recalling a book titled *The Tremor of Forgery* which I'd read many times but also hadn't ever heard of ... discomfited by the word *forgery* ... felt I was being *forged* ... felt I was being *forged* ... the two words the same, the two meanings not ... some would supply only one to both, think the other mere repetition, and were one to replace the other, for most such replacement would slip by unnoticed, a word existing authentically in the way only a *doppelganger* does.

I began shivering as I climbed back into the bed, settled in as snuggly as I could manage beneath the at once too thin and too heavy covers, fiercely aware that all the things I should know I soon wouldn't and how, without them, I'd be unable to explain myself—couldn't keep from tensing over how much trouble there'd be when anything I'd be able to explain would mean nothing to anyone it'd be told to, that my life would be taken as frightening invention, coming from a child, the things I remembered deemed no more than imagination, now ... which, in a sense, felt appropriate ... The Past was, more-or less, imagination ... My Past, now, just definitively was ... The Past and My Past—those things seemed the same but were far different, as the Past which part of me still felt I should have shrank and shrank and the one I knew I possessed became cemented in its displacement.

  I believe I passed out at some point and the first dream I had was of nothing—not *no dream*, rather I dreamt *Nothing*, knew it, knew *Nothing*, tried to conjure up terms to describe it in, the ways it felt: nothing with all manner of somethings clinging to it like lint, settling as the brown-black of car exhaust does to slushing snow, the saliva you know covers a spotless clean cat, the hair which falls invisibly from another yet never seems less, doesn't grow or go away, just *is* despite having a process ... the dream amused me, though I couldn't say why or even what it was ... the thoughts building atop it or else just in reference to what it might've been, might've not even been, what truly entertained.

  Then came another dream, in which, it struck me, I was myself but the size of a spec, so miniscule that to call me the smallest thing wouldn't be overstatement, but also not small, comparative to me, perhaps larger than ten-times what *me* actually was—and what was moving toward me in the dream was immense, so large that no matter what size I was I might as well view myself as a single crystal of salt, sugar, something more alive than a grain of sand, but only just barely. This object of unfathomable majesty loomed my direction—I'd have said it was rolling, except it was so much a behemoth it moved through a void there'd be no rolling in, so vast even the planet I lay alone on, the firm ground beneath me, would hardly register to it as any larger than myself. In one way, the object seemed so colossal that even were it to press into or crush down against my planet-backrest it shouldn't be able to touch me—it so mammoth, me so miniature—but I knew, from the angle it was tracking, that, as it passed, turning but not rolling—itself inside a space which boasted absolutely no direction, me sprawled in and subject to a gravity which'd in no way affect it—the Gargantua would touch against me with the very smallest portion of itself, all its weight behind that precise point, pressing directly down on me ... I'd be crushed, knew it, tried to scream, but my throat was only the crumb of sugar or salt that I was, too dry to shriek, too solid to have a hollow for voice ... I was suffocated by myself ... and the sensation was peculiarly lovely.

When next I awakened, there was daylight through curtains, the room a white I knew meant *hospital*, scents a semi-false I knew meant the same—I was far more alarmed than before at the feel of myself, at the glimpses I caught, at my memories present at the expense of what still felt my memories, too. The blanket belonging to whoever it was had been with me and still would be was folded, the pillow, the coat, the tray from the floor gone, the paperback absent—I barely knew who'd been there and, even knowing, did not. My lower lip began to tremble, tears welled in my eyes, the fact I could have so much sadness and anger over forgetting someone I already didn't remember only making matters worse—but there was something profound in the comfort of knowing I *should* know precisely who those belongings belonged to even while having no idea, should know who was theirs and whose they were, know it as well as I knew myself, better than I knew myself—or had known myself—even yet knew myself, if only as the part of me angry for not knowing and growing slimmer and slimmer, still.

There was a churn of bitterness and lament, also, for what I did know becoming clearer, more actual, the memories of all that'd happened to me taking on scalpel sharp clarity—those memories were who I was, what I'd done, how I'd gotten here ... except they weren't, not any longer ... or it didn't matter that they were ... didn't matter how they weren't ... because they no longer existed, except that I said so—and all I could say was that they *once had* but in a time which *hadn't yet* ... I told myself so, because I'd never be able to tell anyone else.

When I heard a flush, I understood I'd next hear water, then some indistinct noise, then a nose blown, a pause, the door would open, a woman would walk through it, move gently toward me … but also knew I shouldn't know … and soon wouldn't … not how I still did, just then, but only from how I'd acclimate … how I'd have to … didn't want to … did.

The face was a familiar warmth but a cipher, the voice likewise, no more than an object, an arrangement, a color, a tone, the woman a world of paper which other paper could be placed upon, nothing I might pin to it real, each thing less so for how all could be interchanged, even the love which I sensed radiant from her and for her a doll to pretend upon—I was terrified at how I was terrified and I was terrified at how I wasn't, wanted something to break, definitive, in either direction, and knew all too well exactly what would and which … experienced the first certainty of what was draining from me and what would remain, an inside-outing of the ethereal parts of myself, a straightening-to-proper those same parts but different, tangible, the sensation both appropriate and perverse.

I turned my head down from the offered smile, reached for where the juice cup had been, the memory of its presence only the recent one, my own—stopped my hand short at the growing unfamiliarness of its limb as my eyes met a pile of cards on the bedside table, each oversized to my reaching fingers, gigantic cardboard, though perhaps perfectly appropriate, myself what was misfit. The first I lifted was coolly generic, the embossed words GET WELL, a textured illustration of flowers, so ordinary and applicable to anyone it hurt to imagine a single hand actually having drawn it, and when I parted it open some sentiment—other cards similar enough to be the same, garbled handwritten address in all sizes, in inks this or that color, block-letters or attempted cursive, one-size-fits-all well-wishes, some remarks long and illegible, no doubt heartfelt.

My eyes blurred as I refused to focus, a voice I could only call 'now unfamiliar,' despite it also being the first time I'd heard it, explaining to me the objects I lay inspecting had been dropped off by my teacher—words of this-or-that cadence about 'everyone misses you' and how people'd been told I'd return to class soon, 'Hopefully home today, maybe school come Monday, no rush.' I understood everything the unknown woman was saying but knew none of it, then heard her promise she'd be right back, a sound of shuffling flats over tile, a burst of noisier corridor, hush of a drifted closed door, the inside of my head, pulsing—I was sidewalk chalk no longer able to resist garden hose or rainfall.

    Lifted a new card which, in a sharp pang, I gripped my fingers to claws around, partway crumpling the thing, hands tightened as though I was hanging onto the last ember of me, unaware my own grip was what'd starve it of oxygen, cupped palms spreading to reveal only themselves ... but when I opened my eyes from a shut which sounded like the cracking cut to a garlic clove, I knew there was yet some final residual of this other voice hanging on, some terminal part of the me I no longer considered me which hadn't entirely extinguished, still considered itself *itself*, considered itself *me* even though it knew that *me* wasn't me and I wasn't it. It was those eyes along with my eyes which scanned blurry over the card's interior, then came to rest—and the last I remember of some part of who was no longer me remembering itself was it, with a bemused grin, regarding the words: *Hello John Linnell. I don't know you. John F.*

AUTHOR'S NOTE

In addition to the direct lifts of *They Might Be Giants* and *Monopuff* lyrics, various allusions to their songs, and direct, in-text references made to certain other music, novels, works of theatre, films, and television programs, the following are very consciously referenced/quoted within the novel's text, though are not explicitly named:

The Club Dumas (novel by Arturo Perez-Reverte) as well as *The Ninth Gate* (film adaptation of said novel, directed by Roman Polanski, screenplay by Roman Polanski, John Brownjohn, and Enrique Urbizu)

Broadcast Signal Intrusion (film directed by Jacob Gentry, screenplay by Phil Drinkwater and Tim Woodall)

Pi (film directed by Darren Aronofsky, screenplay by Darren Aronofsky and Sean Gullette)

Gigantic (A Tale of Two Johns) (documentary film by AJ Schnack)

www.ingramcontent.com/pod-product-compliance
Lightning Source LLC
LaVergne TN
LVHW031608060526
838201LV00065B/4778